Not every match is made at the marriage mart . . .

After a disastrous, short-lived engagement and years of caring for her ailing grandmother, Phoebe Hallsmith is resigned to spinsterhood. But if she must be unmarried, far better to be of use than languishing at home, disappointing her parents. As an employee of the Everton Domestic Society of London, Phoebe accepts a position at the country home of an old friend and discovers an estate—and a lord of the manor—in a state of complete chaos.

Losing himself in the bottle has done nothing to ease Markus Flammel's grief over losing his wife. Not even his toddler daughter can bring him back from the brink. Now this fiery, strong-minded redhead has taken over his home, firing and hiring servants at will and arousing unexpected desire. As not one, but two suitors suddenly vie for Phoebe's hand, can Markus move past loss and fight for a future with the woman who has transformed his world?

Visit us at www.kensingtonbooks.com

Books by A.S. Fenichel

The Demon Hunter Series
Ascension
Deception
Betrayal

Forever Brides
Tainted Bride
Foolish Bride
Desperate Bride

The Everton Domestic Society
A Lady's Honor

Published by Kensington Publishing Corporation

A Lady's Honor

The Everton Domestic Society

A.S. Fenichel

LYRICAL PRESS
Kensington Publishing Corp.
www.kensingtonbooks.com

First Electronic Edition: April 2018
eISBN-13: 978-1-5161-0584-7
eISBN-10: 1-5161-0584-2

First Print Edition: April 2018
ISBN-13: 978-1-5161-0587-8
ISBN-10: 1-5161-0587-7

Printed in the United States of America

A long time ago, I knew I had to write this book. To heal myself and to let people know that there is room inside each of us for more than one love of our life.
It took almost fifteen years to find the courage.
For Jimmy who taught me how precious love is while he was in this world and after he left it.
For Dave, you expanded my heart and renewed my world.

Acknowledgments

No book is written without a community of people who keep me going.

Thanks to the KickAss Chicks: Sabine Priestley, Sarah Hegger, Kyra Jacobs, Kristi Rose, Juliette Cross and Gemma Brocato. You all give me a safe place to fall and a smart place to ask questions.

Thanks to the Early Bird Writers for pushing me even when I just want to sleep. You ladies are an inspiration every day. Heidi, Stephanie, Kristi, Corinne and Janna, love you all.

Special thanks to Martin Biro for saying no and making me think. If not for your push, the Everton Domestic Society would not exist.

And thanks to Penny Barber for hours of brainstorming and troubleshooting to make this series work. You always ask all the right questions.

Prologue

Phoebe breathed in the warm, cherry pipe tobacco that scented the Everton Domestic Society's offices. Lord Rupert Everton only smoked in his private lounge, but the homey smell wafted through the building. From the moment she'd set foot in the aging townhouse, she'd been more at home than in any of her family's estates. Fresh flowers filled the vases on the entry table and at the bottom of the handrail.

Tired from a long assignment, she took care to silence her practical shoes on the scarred wooden floors. A Persian carpet ran the length of the steps. If she could get there unheard, she would be sure to make it to the solitude of her private room above-stairs. Waking dreams of flopping down on her own bed had kept her awake these last few weeks. Not that she ever slept well, but lately it had grown worse.

Dark wood adorned the walls with little to mask any sound. The door to her right opened and Phoebe gasped. Lady Jane's voice drifted out. "You have nothing to worry about, Lady Castlereagh. I will send someone to Rosefield in a few days."

"I have no doubt," replied Margaret Flammel, in a stern voice. The Countess of Castlereagh stepped into the front hall. Petite but formidable, she patted her dark blond hair into place and turned toward the front door. She locked gazes with Phoebe and stopped.

With an inward sigh, Phoebe dropped into a curtsy. "How do you do, Countess?"

"Lady Phoebe Hallsmith? I had heard you had embarrassed your mother and gone into service. I did not realize it was here at Everton's. Not quite as bad as becoming some nanny, but not exactly what your family would have expected from you. I heard that brother of yours disowned you." Her green eyes flashed with accusation.

For a year, she had managed to avoid people who would say directly what all of the ton was thinking. It was a miracle she had managed it so long. Phoebe forced a smile. "I go by Miss Hallsmith now. It is nice to see you, my lady. I hope your daughter, Dorothea, is well."

"Married, as I'm sure you know. Not well married, but happily, for whatever that is worth." Lady Castlereagh pulled a handkerchief out of her waistband and dabbed her cheek.

"I imagine it is worth quite a lot to Dorothea."

Lady Jane Everton cleared her throat and stepped next to Lady Castlereagh. Jane towered over the countess. Her dark hair pulled back in a severe bun, she always brought calm to every situation. Her gray skirt and light blue blouse were pressed to perfection and gave her a severe, staid appearance. "Miss Hallsmith has just returned from her second assignment this year. Both were very successful. You may have heard, she assisted with the Mayfield girl for her debut season."

With a nod, Lady Castlereagh said, "Velvet Mayfield is a shy wallflower. I imagine you had your work cut out for you, Miss Hallsmith."

The typical labeling done by society stoked Phoebe's ire. Velvet was a wallflower. Phoebe was a spinster. Where would it end? It wouldn't. People like the countess would always pin labels on people of whom they disapproved. "You will be happy to hear that Miss Mayfield is soon to be Mrs. Harrington Wormfield."

Though Lady Castlereagh's shocked expression only lasted a moment, it was more gratifying than Phoebe could have imagined.

Lady Castlreagh said, "You must be very good at your job if you got that one married off."

She restrained the joy bubbling inside her over Velvet's impending marriage. There was no response that would be kind to Velvet. Phoebe turned to Lady Jane. "I am happy to be back, my lady. I will be ready for my next assignment in a day or two."

Looking her up and down, Lady Castlereagh circled Phoebe like a cat about to devour a mouse. "Lady Jane, I think Miss Hallsmith might do very nicely for my contract with Everton's. She has breeding, even if she has wasted it. I have always known her to be a resourceful girl, even though her temper is legendary. She knows my son and was friends with his deceased wife. She would not need to be educated about the situation. She grew up near Rosefield and probably has heard all the rumors already. It would keep the situation close rather than exposing our family to a stranger."

All of England knew the rumors. There was little need to be coy. Markus Flammel had taken to the bottle after his beloved wife, Emma, died in childbirth. It was two years since her death. Phoebe had hoped Markus would come to his senses, but if his mother was seeking help from the Everton Domestic Society, things must be quite bad.

Lady Jane frowned. "We do not usually let our ladies assist friends as it can be a conflict of interest, Countess."

"I hope I will not have to insist." Lady Castlereagh lifted her chin, tucked her handkerchief back in her waistband and stepped toward the door. "I expect to hear from you in the next day or two with details of Miss Hallsmith's arrival at Rosefield."

The butler, Gray, opened the front door, his wisps of white hair catching the breeze. Once the door closed behind Lady Castlereagh, Gray bowed to Lady Jane and left the front hall.

Jane shook her head. "Are you up to a chat about this assignment, Miss Hallsmith, or do you need a rest?"

Phoebe said, "It is probably best for us to speak first. I will never rest with this on my mind."

Gesturing toward the office doorway, Jane invited Phoebe inside. The place of business was softer than the entry hall. A muted blue rug and matching drapery warmed the cold wood. Cream and sky-blue upholstery made the overstuffed furniture comfortable. Every table held a vase with fresh-cut flowers. The scent mingled with masculine cherry tobacco. Sunlight streamed through the tall windows and the wind sang against the side of the house. Once they were seated, Jane folded her hands atop of the desk and sighed. "What do you know about Markus Flammel?"

Her heart hurt thinking about him. She crossed her ankles and put her hands in her lap where she looked down at them. "Quite a lot. The countess is right about that. I was good friends with his wife, Emma. She was a wonderful girl and they were very much in love. I was still in Scotland when Emma died. She had written to me every week up until then telling me how happy they were about the coming birth of their first child. A few weeks later my mother wrote telling me that Emma had died and the child, Elizabeth, had lived. Mother wrote quite often after that with gossip about Markus and his drinking. I understand from my brother Miles that Markus has not maintained his home."

Jane leaned back in her chair and let out another sigh. "That is more or less what the countess said. It would also seem that Lord Castlereagh's antics have finally caught up to him. The family could be in trouble if

Markus does not come to his senses. For now, his sister's husband, Thomas Wheel, is holding things together."

"That is kind of him." Phoebe didn't want to say more about the relationship between Lord Castlereagh and his son-in-law, Thomas. Talking about Markus was part of the business but anything more about the family constituted gossiping. Thomas had many reasons to harm the earl and if he was helping him, it was for the sake of his wife and his old friend Markus. Miles had written to Phoebe just before she returned from Scotland with an account of a duel between the two men where Thomas was nearly killed.

"Yes," Jane said. "It would seem Mr. Wheel is an extraordinary man. Mrs. Wheel is a lucky woman despite what her mother might think."

"I am sure if Mr. Wheel were titled, Lady Castlereagh would have another opinion. However, my brother was very close with both Markus Flammel and Thomas Wheel at Eton. They are both fine men. If Markus has fallen this far, he needs help and the fact that his mother came to you must mean she is quite desperate."

"Agreed. Will you take the assignment, Miss Hallsmith? I know you were counting on some time off, but it would be difficult to sway the countess from her demands." Jane pulled a pen and paper from the drawer to her left. "This is the contract Lady Castlereagh signed. If you agree, I will put your name on it."

Phoebe hoped she didn't look as weary as she felt. "I will require a few days to rest, but I feel I must help Markus and Elizabeth for Emma's sake. She was a good friend to me. I called on Markus a year ago, after my grandmother passed. I had just returned to England. Markus was not at home and the housekeeper did not know when he would return. I will need a chaperon."

"Yes. I think Lady Honoria Chervil is the only Everton dowager available at the moment." Jane frowned, but there was amusement in her gray eyes.

"I know some ladies complain about her eccentricities, but she makes me laugh." Even the thought of Lady Chervil gave Phoebe a chuckle. She was irreverent, flamboyant, and energetic. Maybe just the thing Markus Flammel, the viscount of Devonrose and his estate, Rosefield, needed.

Jane nodded. "I will put you both down for the Flammel assignment and order a carriage for Friday. Will that give you enough time to recover?"

Four days with nothing to do but rest. It sounded like heaven. "Perfect. I will be ready to go. If you would not mind, I think it would be best if I brought Arwen with me again. It is best to have a lady's maid when living with the ton."

"Of course. Lady Chervil will no doubt bring Margery with her. Just make sure you keep to the rules of the companion. None of the Everton Ladies or their staff are to be a burden to the clients."

"I will stick to the companion's rules." She patted the side of her bag where the booklet resided.

"By letting you go I am already breaking from the rules. It will be difficult for you not to become personally involved with the client when you already know him and are sympathetic to his situation." Jane shook her head and jotted Phoebe's name on the contract.

It was personal. There was no getting around it. Still, Phoebe was determined to be the best Everton lady to hold a companion and keep to the rules. "Rule twenty may be bent, but it is not broken, Lady Jane. I will remain unaffected and do what is necessary to resolve the situation."

"I have complete faith in you, Miss Hallsmith."

Chapter 1

No. 6
*Upon arrival, an Everton lady will seek the head of
household and announce her presence and purpose.*
—The Everton Companion
Rules of Conduct

Years in Scotland caring for Grand had kept Phoebe from Rosefield
and her best friend, Emma. Along the front of the grand estate, Emma's
beloved rose bushes were overgrown and the facade loomed with sorrow
and loss. Hesitating on the first step, she brushed aside her imaginings
about the stones mourning Emma's death.

There were no words that could comfort Markus Flammel.
What would she say?

A wayward branch from the rose bush lay in her path.

Rubbing the chill of October from her arms, she took a breath, clasped
her bag with her Everton lady's companion inside and pulled her shoulders
back. She had faced her grandmother's recovery and eventually her death;
she could face this too.

She climbed the ten steps to the door and pushed aside her anxiety.

"This place is a bit unkempt, Phoebe." Honoria Chervil pranced up
the steps beside her.

"Yes. That's part of why we are here, my lady." Phoebe grabbed the
brass ring and knocked.

"We are arriving very early for paying a call. Perhaps we should have waited for the carriage to be repaired and come later with our belongings."

The hired hack rumbled back up the drive away from Rosefield. There would be no speedy escape.

Drawing a long breath, Phoebe pulled her shoulders back and her chin up. She was ready for whatever might come. "No. This is not a social call, Honoria. I did not wish to get a late start and it will take hours to have the wheel fixed at the inn. This will be better and the rest will follow this afternoon."

Glass shattered inside. Yelling and screaming and wood crashing sounded through the door.

"What on earth?" There was nothing worse than standing on the steps while screams and crashes filtered out. Phoebe pushed the door open.

As if her presence froze the scene, five pair of eyes stared at her in the threshold.

Two maids were on their knees surrounded by glass, faded flowers, and water. The round table lay in pieces behind them.

Mrs. Donnelly's bonnet was askew, her hair stuck out in all directions, and her chubby cheeks were as red as the overgrown roses in front of the house. The housekeeper scooped up a screaming toddler who was inches from getting into the dangerous glass.

Watson, the butler, stood like a statue staring at her with his hands in the air.

"What in the name of heaven is going on in here?" Phoebe never imagined her arrival would look anything like this.

Watson lowered his hands, smoothed his graying hair and approached. "I'm afraid you've caught us at an inopportune moment, my lady. The master has just arrived and we are preparing."

A maid sniffed as tears ran down her face and she used a rag to pull shards into a pile.

"Preparing for what?" Honoria asked.

"What on earth could be prepared by what I am witnessing?" Phoebe might have been out of line in questioning the staff of Rosefield before she'd even made her purpose known to Markus, but something was terribly wrong here.

Phoebe's mother had written about Emma's daughter, Elizabeth, being raised mostly by servants, but this was ridiculous. Elizabeth continued to wail as if being beaten with a stick and Mrs. Donnelly shushed her to no avail. Elizabeth grabbed a handful of Mrs. Donnelly's hair and they both shrieked until Phoebe's ears hurt.

"You might try back at another time, Miss Hallsmith." Sweat dripped down the side of Watson's long face.

Phoebe had a hundred questions, but would get no answers with the servants. What started as worry grew into annoyance, and she had to swallow down her emotions to remain calm. She turned to Mrs. Donnelly. "Madam, give me that child before she does you real harm."

Never had a woman of such girth moved with such speed. She foisted Elizabeth into Phoebe's arms. "It's not Little Elizabeth's fault, Miss. She misses her father and he—"

"That will do, Mrs. Donnelly." Watson's scolding tone stopped any further explanation and started the maid crying again.

Phoebe propped Elizabeth on her hip. "You are far too small to be causing so much chaos. I cannot imagine what your sweet momma is thinking looking down on you. Now I expect you to act like a little lady."

Just like her father, Elizabeth had large green eyes, and they were wide open staring at Phoebe. A black smudge marred her left cheek and some kind of jelly stuck all around her rosy lips and pert little nose.

"She doesn't speak, my lady, though we try to teach her," Mrs. Donnelly said.

At two years old, Elizabeth should have some vocabulary. Phoebe's heart clenched. She should have come sooner. Of course, that hadn't been an option, but it did not soothe her guilt. "Well, we need no words for the moment. I'm sure when Miss Elizabeth has something important to say, she will do so. I do not go by a title any longer. Miss Hallsmith will do."

Elizabeth relaxed and her little body conformed to Phoebe's side as if they were two parts of a whole.

"You know, your mother and I were very good friends, Elizabeth. I think that you and I will be as well, but you must behave with more manners. Shall we go see your father?"

A wide smile showed off several teeth and brought a lovely pink to her sweet cheeks.

Watson stepped forward but kept enough distance as to not fall into Elizabeth's reach. "That's what started all of this, Miss. I'm afraid his lordship does not wish to see...anyone."

A low growl issued from deep in Elizabeth's chest.

Taking another step back, Watson paled.

"Ladies do not growl, Elizabeth. Where is his lordship?" Phoebe had spent years reining in her temper and learning to act like a lady even when she wanted to tear someone's hair out. It was becoming obvious that she would need to use all she had learned to get through the next few moments.

"In the study, but as I said, Miss Hallsmith, he does not wish to be disturbed." Watson held out his arms blocking her way.

Lifting Elizabeth higher on her hip, Phoebe turned toward the study. "I could not possibly care less about what his lordship wants. Lady Chervil, will you please wait here and explain our purpose?"

Honoria's chest puffed out as she lifted her shoulders and double chin. "I will be happy to, Miss Hallsmith."

Phoebe strode past Watson to the door and pushed through.

The enormous desk that Emma had purchased as a wedding gift for Markus took up most of the room. Phoebe's heart broke at the memory of how proud her friend had been of the custom-made gift. She had thought the sun rose with her husband, and the two had been the perfect couple. Wood, though dusty, paneled three walls while one boasted three large bookcases separated by two benches. A musty odor, from disuse and lack of cleaning, tickled Phoebe's nose.

Markus faced the cloudy window overlooking the side garden. "I do not wish to be disturbed. Go away."

The petulance of his tone only raised Phoebe's ire. Behavior of that sort should be disregarded, even if on the inside she seethed. Placing Elizabeth on the floor, Phoebe said, "That is too bad, my lord, as you have company who will not be turned aside. I am here on business."

His chair scraped across the wood floor as he stood and turned. He narrowed green eyes, shadowed with dark rings and sunken into pale skin, and he swayed. The strong, handsome man Emma had loved and married was no longer present in Markus Flammel.

Elizabeth froze.

Phoebe propped her fists on her hips and met his gaze.

"Phoebe Hallsmith?"

She dropped her hands and fell into a polite curtsy. "My lord."

"What are you doing here? Emma is gone."

His raised voice brought a whimper from poor Elizabeth who shrunk back and hid her face in Phoebe's skirt.

Turning, Phoebe called out the study door. "Mrs. Donnelly?"

Still frazzled and tattered, the housekeeper poked her head in the door. "Miss?"

"Please take Miss Elizabeth to the kitchen and see if Cook has a nice biscuit for her. Then see that her hands and face are washed before you bring her back here to visit with her father."

Mrs. Donnelly's face went white and she stiffened. "Little Elizabeth does not care for face washing."

"Do not tell me you are afraid of that child, Madam. I will not hear of it. Miss Elizabeth will be happy for the cookie and act the proper lady when it is time to wash. Isn't that right?" She gave Elizabeth a pointed look.

Red-faced, Elizabeth stared at Phoebe with her mouth open. Never taking her gaze away, she toddled over to Mrs. Donnelly and took her hand.

Once they left, Markus ran his fingers through his overlong hair. "How did you do that?"

Phoebe wanted to feel sympathy for him but she couldn't keep her annoyance in check. "What on earth is wrong with you? How can you talk about Emma that way in front of your daughter? I am well aware of the loss of my dear friend, so your attempt to hurt me was wasted. Why is your house in chaos? Why are Emma's roses along the front entrance overgrown? Why is your staff terrified of a small child? Where have you been that they are shocked at your arrival? I demand answers."

"You demand? Who are you to demand anything? Where were you when Emma lay in her coffin and they covered her up with dirt? You have no rights here." He collapsed into his chair.

Guilt swelled inside Phoebe, and she sat across from him. "I was in Scotland with my grandmother. She was ill and I could not leave her. I received a letter from my mother about Emma's passing, and you may believe me when I tell you I was quite devastated. However, there was nothing I could do for her as she was and is in God's hands." Pulling herself together, she added, "I have been sent here by the Everton Domestic Society at the behest of your mother."

"I do not care why you are here. Get out of my house. You only serve as a reminder of her."

Where was the Markus of old? The man who Emma had gushed over. Markus would stop in and enjoy tea and conversation with the ladies. "Answer my questions. Then maybe I will leave you in peace."

He lifted a bottle of liquor out of his desk drawer, banged it onto the surface, removed the top, and took a long pull.

Phoebe had never seen this side of Markus. Running might have been the smart thing to do, but she held her place and swallowed her fear. He had always been calm and polite. Everything admirable had gone with her friend and the child suffered for it. Something had to be done. "Have you taken to the bottle as well as neglected your responsibilities, my lord? I always imagined you were smarter than your father."

Markus's face colored a horrible shade of purple, and he hurled the bottle across the room. It shattered against the wall in a starburst of glimmering shards. Brandy ran down the wall in rivulets and the stench of alcohol swamped the room.

If she left now, she could escape whatever wrath she had unleashed inside of him, but where would that leave poor Elizabeth? "Are you quite through or are there other objects you'd like to destroy? Maybe you will hack up that desk Emma bought you next?"

The air went out of him and he slumped onto his folded arms atop the desk. His shoulders rose and fell several times before he sat up. "I have not been home because everything here reminds me of her and I am not strong enough. As to your other questions…" He shrugged. "I fired the gardener and the child has put a strain on the household. Did you say my mother sent you?"

Many things she should have said, but his eyes shone from too much brandy and practical matters needed addressing first. "I work for Everton Domestic Society. Your mother contracted for someone to help you with Rosefield."

"Help me? How can you help me? No one can help." He put his forehead on his arms.

Nothing was ever easy. She needed a dozen questions answered, but one or two would have to do while he was in this state. "Why is there no nanny?"

"I may have fired one or two." He leaned his head back against the leather and closed his eyes.

"What about your mother? Has she not come to help with the staff?"

The green of his eyes was as intense as his daughter's. He scoffed. "I tossed her from the house the last time I was home. I think she said something about never darkening my door again. Just as well."

The situation was coming into view, and the remedy would not be an easy one. "I see. Lady Chervil and I each have a lady's maid. We will need rooms made up. I expect your staff can handle that small task. Our carriage needed repairs so we hired a hack this morning. The Everton Domestic Society's carriage with our bags and maids will arrive later today. They will need to be brought in. I will explain to your staff my needs and expectations."

He stood, and pressing his knuckles to the wood, leaned forward. If the desk had not been so big, his looming might have been threatening, but as it was, he was too far away to leave her awed.

"You cannot live here. I am an unmarried man," he said, voice cracking.

It wrenched her heart. "Everton's is aware of your situation. That is why Lady Chervil is here as my chaperon. She is speaking with Watson now."

Raising his voice, he pointed at Phoebe. "I do not want her or you here. I do not need you here."

"Your rage does not scare me, my lord, so you might as well save it for someone else. You could tell me you will hire a reputable nanny and allow her to sort out your house. You might tell me you have met a fine woman and plan to remarry. You could step up and be the man Emma married and take care of your own house. If you can look me in the eye and guarantee me these things will happen, I will walk out that door and report to my superiors that all is well here and leave you in peace."

He sank back into his chair. "I will not be responsible for you or Lady Chervil."

"No. I imagine you are not even responsible for yourself these days. One more thing, my lord. When Mrs. Donnelly arrives back here in a few moments with your daughter in tow, you are to put aside whatever sorrows you have and pay her the attention she deserves. Do I make myself clear?" If she was overstepping her boundaries, she didn't care. He had suffered, but so had Elizabeth and at his hand. There was no time like the present to start a change.

"She looks too much like Emma." Pain etched lines around his eyes and mouth.

Sympathy shared the space with her disgust. He was in pain but his behavior could not be ignored. "And quite a lot like you too, Markus. She is a smart child and she needs you."

Tugging at his badly tied cravat, he pulled it loose. "You have been here not twenty minutes. How do you know she's smart?"

Phoebe sat on the edge of the monstrous desk. "Your daughter is two years old and has not spoken, yet she clearly understands what is said to her."

He sat up. "Has not spoken?"

It took a force of will not to rail at him for being so self-absorbed he didn't know his child was mute. "According to your staff, Elizabeth does not speak. I think that is a sign of her intelligence."

"How so?"

"To be so filled with sorrow at her age that she chooses not to speak to anyone means she understands a great deal of what is happening in her world. Perhaps she has nothing to say in a world that left her without a mother and a father."

Staring down at his hands in his lap he nodded.

One scratch at the door and it opened. Elizabeth ran several steps into the room, stopped and stared at her father.

Softening his expression, Markus looked up. "Come here, Elizabeth."

Elizabeth looked from him to Phoebe. She spotted the broken glass on the far side of the room and took a step back.

Phoebe smiled. "It's all right. Go to your father."

Going to one knee, Markus opened his arms.

Blinking, Elizabeth cocked her head before running into his embrace.

It was all Phoebe could do to keep from breaking down into sobs at the sight of father and daughter hugging. What had she gotten herself into? She must be mad. If Emma had not been her closest friend, she would have left Markus Flammel and his problems to someone else at Everton. Though, now that she'd seen Elizabeth, she wanted to see her happy.

Mrs. Donnelly watched from the doorway. She dabbed her eyes with her apron and sniffed back her tears.

Lifting Elizabeth, Markus sat in his chair and propped her in his lap. "I am sorry I have not been at home, Elizabeth. I promise to try to do better."

Elizabeth put her palm on his cheek and father and daughter stared into each other's eyes.

It was a start. Phoebe shooed Mrs. Donnelly from the study, followed her, and closed the door, giving them some privacy. "I will need two rooms made up for Lady Chervil and myself. Once they are ready, I expect you to begin the process of getting this house cleaned. It is a crime how far Rosefield has fallen in two years. It is clear Elizabeth needs a proper nanny and Rosefield needs a gardener. I will put those things at the top of my list."

A wide smile spread across Mrs. Donnelly's face. "Will you be the new mistress here then, Miss Hallsmith?"

"Do not be ridiculous. I am an Everton lady. I shall help get his lordship back on his feet, if that is possible, and I will see that the house and child are in order. Once that is done, I will leave them to their life." Fear and sorrow spread through Phoebe's chest. Was she doing the right thing? Would Emma approve?

Her gut twisted as it always did when she imagined the end of an assignment. The client went on their happy way and Phoebe moved on to the next client's life. She never moved on with her own. Going to Scotland at the age of eighteen meant that she had missed several key seasons where she might have found someone to love. At twenty-four, Phoebe's time to find a husband and have a family was at an end. Everton's had been a boon for her. If not for Lady Jane, she would be listening to her mother and eldest brother natter on about how disappointing she was.

Phoebe sighed. "Watson, we arrived in a hired carriage as ours had a wheel that required fixing at the inn this morning. I expect it will arrive in a few hours with our maids and trucks."

Watson straightened his coat and smoothed his hair back. "I understand, Miss."

At least he was acting like a butler again. That was a small piece of progress. Phoebe would take some comfort in that. "Mrs. Donnelly, please knock on the study door in twenty minutes and take Elizabeth to the nursery. I am sure this will be very tiring for her."

"And for his lordship as well," Mrs. Donnelly said.

It was true, but Elizabeth was Phoebe's first worry. "I am less concerned with his lordship's condition. That child has suffered a lifetime. Well, her lifetime anyway."

"Miss, am I to understand that you will be taking over as housekeeper?"

Phoebe squeezed Mrs. Donnelly's hand. "I am not taking your position. I will leave when the house is in order. The viscount needs assistance and I need you to continue as the housekeeper Rosefield deserves. I would like to know: How have things gotten this bad, Mrs. Donnelly? Why have you not managed the house at least?" It was harsher than Phoebe had intended, but Rosefield was a mess. It was clear two years of neglect were at fault.

Mrs. Donnelly turned red and fussed with the keys at her waist. "I do not wish to speak against his lordship, Miss. He has been a good master for many years despite all the restrictions his father put on him. After my lady perished bringing the babe into the world, he was not the same man. More like the earl every day, he was. Drinking and disappearing for weeks on end. When he would come home, he'd fire half the staff. Some folks who had been in his service for years lost their posts for no good reason except his grief. It isn't possible to keep up a house of this size. We have only four of us left and the child to care for."

Horror smacked Phoebe in the face. "Four? You and Watson, the cook and one maid?"

"Cook was fired last year. The upstairs maid has been acting as cook. She's a fair one too."

"But it means there is only one maid for this entire estate." Drawing in a full breath, Phoebe made a mental list of all that would need her attention. "Things are far worse than I expected. It's a good thing I am here."

"Yes, Miss."

Honoria bustled in from down the hallway beside the stairs. "Do you know there is no staff in this house, Phoebe?"

Phoebe liked Honoria's directness, but sometimes wished she would save it for when they were alone. "I have just been informed, my lady. When the other carriage arrives, the driver and footman will have to bring our bags upstairs before they return to London. I will help get the rooms ready."

"Of course, my dear. I fear you have your work cut out for you." Sighing, Honoria ambled out the front door.

That much was certain. Wishing she had her grandmother's council, Phoebe climbed the stairs to find two guest rooms.

Emma's house was not the loving place it had once been, and perhaps being estranged from her own family did not make Phoebe the perfect choice to correct things. Still, she was determined to create a safe place for little Elizabeth even if that meant removing the child. As she entered the first guest room, she prayed that would not be necessary. Emma would not want Markus to be left all alone. She shook off the dismal notion.

Chapter 2

No. 18
*An Everton lady will see to the welfare of any child
before anything else.*
—The Everton Companion
Rules of Conduct

Certain his heart was breaking all over again, Markus knew he should keep holding Elizabeth, but he couldn't bear it. He turned her toward the desk.

She slapped her chubby little hands on the sturdy oak.

"Your momma bought me this desk as a wedding gift."

A moment passed, and then she turned and looked up at him before examining the desk again.

The knot in his chest tightened. His gut twisted. The day his sweet Emma had the monstrous piece delivered flooded back to him. She'd been so proud of the gift and cried when she realized it was too big for the room. Markus had assured her that he loved it and it was the perfect size. She had known he lied, but it didn't matter. He'd cherished the eyesore from the first day. Now it only served as a reminder of all he'd lost. Each week his secretary stacked papers on it, and on his rare visits Markus ignored the mess.

Phoebe Hallsmith was right, damn her. Emma would be ashamed of him.

Elizabeth patted his cheek and her green eyes glistened.

"I know. It is far too big, but she loved me and it was a gift." Her tiny fingers, soft in his hand, ripped his soul out. It was too much.

A knock at the door startled them both.

Mrs. Donnelly peeked in. "I thought the little miss might need to take a nap, my lord?"

Watching Elizabeth rub her face, he nodded. "I suppose we have had a trying morning."

Elizabeth toddled across the room, only looking back once, took Mrs. Donnelly's hand, and left.

It would be normal to feel loss, but Markus flooded with relief as the pain in his chest eased. Opening his drawer to drown his feelings with brandy only reminded him of the mess he'd made. He took out a piece of foolscap. He didn't need help and would write to Miles Hallsmith telling him to keep his sister at home where she belonged. That girl should be married and running her own house by now. Slamming the drawer closed, he rose.

First to find another bottle. Sure he had some in the cellar, he left his study, determined to complete his mission.

* * * *

Afternoon sun poured into his study and glared off the desk. The last Markus remembered he'd cursed Phoebe Hallsmith after downing half a bottle of brandy. Most of the day was lost to that bottle, but at least he'd not thought of his poor Emma in that time.

The house must have been on fire to cause the commotion clanging down the halls. Markus held the side of his head to keep his skull from splitting. The grandfather clock on the west wall read two o'clock. He must have drunk more than he thought to sleep so long.

Elizabeth's high-pitched shriek forced him upright and sent the room spinning. He sighed and pulled the cord for Watson.

The butler entered with a ridiculous grin spread across his normally dour face. "You called, my lord?"

"What on earth has gotten into you, Watson?"

Straightening, Watson wiped all expression from his face. "Nothing, my lord. It is only that Miss Hallsmith and Lady Chervil are in the foyer and it has been rather lively. The carriage with their luggage has arrived. They each have a maid, of course, and Everton's sent a footman and driver, who are assisting the transition. It is almost like old times. Of course, the footman and carriage will leave when the ladies are properly settled."

"Why would she bring her own footman?"

"I assume for protection on the roads, my lord. However, since you fired all of ours, it's a lucky circumstance."

Head aching, stomach churning, he had no patience for more of Phoebe Hallsmith's antics. "I did not ask your opinion, Watson."

"Did you need something, my lord?"

Markus grabbed a stack of papers from the desk and threw them at Watson. They rained down all over the room but none hit the butler, who watched without remark or expression. "I need silence."

Watson raised an eyebrow. "Miss Hallsmith wishes an immediate meeting with you, my lord."

Why couldn't everyone leave him in peace? "A cup of coffee and some toast would be nice, Watson."

"Yes, my lord." Watson stepped out of the room and closed the door.

Shouting and the clunking of trunks resounded through the walls. Elizabeth's laughter mingled with the cacophony. He jotted a quick note to Miles about his brutish sister and getting her taken away. Standing, he resolved to tell her to leave. This was still his house, and his mother had no right to send that woman to upset things. The foyer loomed chaotic. Two men in unfamiliar gray livery carried bags and trunks up the steps at the constant order of a plump, gray-haired woman in a floral day dress and white cap. Standing on the third step brought her to the shoulders of the footmen before they started the climb.

Phoebe waved her straw bonnet about and scolded him from across the marble floor. "This lack of staff on your part is very inconvenient, my lord. I cannot keep Everton's footman or driver. We have brought our ladies' maids, but more than that was impossible beyond the initial move."

"This is my house, Miss Hallsmith. You were not invited and might consider that when criticizing." There, he had set her straight. He was in charge here and no one would usurp his authority.

"You did not invite us?" The woman on the steps trudged down and crossed to him.

He'd have been exaggerating if he said she was five feet tall. "No, I did not."

"Phoebe, what is the meaning of this?" A wiry gray hair escaped her loose bun, and she flicked it off her cheek several times, all without success. She propped her fists on her hips and a deep frown creased her etched face.

Phoebe scurried over. "The Countess of Castlereagh entered into the contract to assist here at Rosefield."

She looked from Phoebe to him. "You said he needed help. I assumed that meant he *wanted* our help. This is very out of the ordinary. I much prefer to be welcomed on my assignments."

Waving the comment off, Phoebe sighed. "I only said that, as a close friend of his lordship's wife, it was my responsibility to help. His mother indicated he was at the end of his wits and would fall into an even graver situation if no one helped. No one implied that he was in favor of the prospect."

Elbows jutting out at her sides, Lady Chervil squinted at Phoebe while shaking her head. "Once again, you have manipulated the facts, Phoebe."

"No more than you would have, if you found yourself in such a position." Phoebe's smile was at once wicked and sweet.

Markus's heart skipped a beat or two, followed by a flood of guilt. He fisted his hands and pushed aside the stupidity.

A childish giggle tumbled from Honoria. "So true, so true. Well you had better do the honors, sweet girl."

All the silliness fled Phoebe's expression as she folded her hands in front of her. As demure in appearance as any debutante, she nodded once. "My lord, may I introduce Lady Honoria Chervil. She is a dowager who gives her time to the Everton Domestic Society in instances where it would be inappropriate for one of the ladies to go alone. Honoria, Markus Flammel, Viscount of Devonrose."

Honoria dipped into a pretty curtsy, leaving Markus no choice but to bow. "I apologize that you have come all this way at such great inconvenience, but as I told Miss Hallsmith, I need no help here at Rosefield."

Her fists returned to her hips and she narrowed her eyes at him. "Why have you no servants?"

Becca, Katy, Mrs. Donnelly, and Watson all stared at him. He pointed to them. "I have servants."

Rolling her eyes, Phoebe said, "Four. You have four servants for this entire estate."

He tried to think beyond the fog of past inebriation, but only hazy moments filtered through. Some of the staff had been at Rosefield since before he had inherited the estate. He wouldn't have let them go. "That cannot be right."

Watson said, "I guess it is five if you include Duck."

A new bout of annoyance flashed through him but his aching head took precedence. He'd kill for a cup of coffee. Trying to rub the pain away, he remembered the argument he had with the overbearing stable-master. "Becca, go and get me a cup of coffee."

She appeared as harried as he felt. Her dark brown hair stuck out in wild curls around her face. Wide-eyed, she scurried off toward the kitchens.

Elizabeth peeked out from behind Mrs. Donnelly's skirts. Fear etched in her tiny features, the laughter he'd heard from his study a distant memory. Tears dampened her cheeks. She sniffed and wiped her nose on the voluminous skirts before retreating behind their safety.

Somehow, he had become his father.

The entire household feared him. Worse than that, his own daughter shied from him, afraid he might fly off at her. Maybe the meddlesome girl was right. He hated that notion. Brushing aside what he didn't know, he focused on what he did. "I know I fired Duck. Why is he still here?"

"He refused to leave the animals with no one to tend them." Watson raised an eyebrow, but said no more.

"At least someone around here as some sense," Phoebe said.

"Are you saying that codger has been on my property, tending my livestock, without pay?" It wasn't possible. Why would anyone do such a thing?

Watson nodded. "For the past six months, my lord."

His valet would know the answers and dispel all this nonsense. "Where is Blakely? He will set this all right."

"I believe he is now valet to Mr. Tolsbury in Shropshire, my lord."

Hopeful, he asked, "He quit me?"

Eyebrow still raised, Watson said, "If memory serves, you told him he was a nefarious cheat and a black-hearted thief before you physically tossed him from the house."

A hazy memory of the scene prodded into Markus's mind. He rubbed his temple and clenched his shaking hand. A drink would steady that shake. The bottle he'd found in the cellar still had a few swallows left. All he had to do was step back into his study and shut the door, and he could make all of this go away. Closing his eyes did not change anything. Not his aching head, not the chaos that took over his home, and not the fact that Emma was dead. Continuing to drink himself sick wouldn't change the last, either. "Ladies, please join me in the study." He backed away and let Honoria and Phoebe precede him inside.

They stood amongst the scattered documents on the rug and waited for him to round his desk.

"Please forgive the mess. Be seated. I suppose I have put my estate in danger and should be thankful you have come." The words stung like hot lead in his gut.

Honoria sashayed into a chair by the window. She smiled and hummed as she stared into the garden.

Smoothing her pale green skirts, Phoebe sat in the chair across his desk. A warm smile tugged at her full lips. "I do not want or need your gratitude, my lord. I only want to do my job, my friend's home to be restored to a respectable state, and to be assured her child is cared for in the best way."

What could he say? He had failed and now he needed help to pick up the pieces of the mess he'd made. Sitting, he rubbed the back of his head. "What do you need from me?"

Clearing her throat, she fidgeted. "I hate to be blunt, my lord."

Honoria chuckled.

He wasn't immune to the irony either. "Please, do your worst, Miss Hallsmith."

"Your finances, my lord. Do they permit the hire of a proper household staff?"

The papers peppering the floor stood as a looming reminder of the loss of at least a year's revenue. Still, his failing wasn't permanent. "I shall make good the salaries of a proper staff."

She clapped. "I will begin the hiring process tomorrow."

Had her skin glowed like that when she was Emma's friend who visited from time to time? Tiny freckles dotted her cheeks and nose, warming her face. He'd never regarded her as pretty before, but she had grown into her looks and a lovely woman sat before him. "Is that all?"

"No. Two more things."

His stomach churned with hunger. "Only two?" Leaning back, he closed his eyes.

"You will spend time with Elizabeth every day."

It sounded like such a small task, but the idea shot pain to his heart. Little Elizabeth brought the night of Emma's death back as if it were yesterday. Bringing her into the world had killed his beautiful wife. Emma would not approve of his behavior and she would have gladly offered her life for Elizabeth's. "If the child wishes to see me, I will not object."

She sighed. "Not exactly gushing with adoration, but it is a start."

"And the other?"

She stood, forcing him to rise. "No more drinking, my lord. You will have to deal with your life."

The nerve of the woman. No one had the right to speak to him in such a way in his own home. He pounded the desk.

From the doorway, Becca shrieked and upended the tray. Coffee and toast crashed to the floor in a mess of porcelain and the lovely smelling brew.

He was doomed to do without coffee and it was his own fault. "Dammit! Who do you think you are?"

Becca began picking up the mess.

"Becca, please leave that for now," Phoebe said. "Lady Chervil, can you give me a moment with his lordship?"

Becca ran from the room.

Standing, Honoria narrowed her gaze on Markus. "My wrath can be quite daunting, my lord."

"Of this I am certain, Madam."

With a nod, she left and closed the door behind her.

"You have put your home and family in jeopardy with your wasteful drinking, Markus. Emma loved you and that is the only reason I am willing to help you. If it was not for her faith in you, I would have let someone else come here to sort you out. They likely would have taken one look at the scene this morning and taken Elizabeth from this house. Then what? Do you want your mother raising your daughter? I suppose we could write to your sister and see if she will take her. Is that what you want?"

Dory would take the child and she and Thomas Wheel would raise her as their own. His chest contracted until he couldn't breathe. "I do not wish to send Elizabeth away. Emma would not like it."

"Good." She drew a deep breath. "I do not care if you waste away or drink yourself to death, but Emma would and so would Elizabeth. It disgusts me what you have done to yourself, but I will help you under the condition that you stop drinking and make efforts to put your life back together. Everton's has very strict rules and I have broken several of them with my directness, but I think it important that you and I have an understanding. No more drink."

Everything inside him tightened and seared with unspeakable pain. He sat in the chair next to her. "You ask the impossible. You cannot know what I suffered, what I still suffer."

"No. I cannot." She shook her head and met his gaze. "You have lost more than I can imagine, but it is not an excuse to ruin yourself."

"I cannot just get over her and move on. Emma was my life." He'd taken drink enough to fill the Thames, but loss still gouged at his soul. His heart had contracted to a stone and the damned world kept spinning. The sun kept rising. Night loomed long and painful. People went about their days as if nothing was wrong. But something was wrong. Everything was wrong, and still life went on.

Placing her soft fingers over his, she said, "No one is asking you to. That would be absurd."

He looked into the most expressive golden eyes surrounded by long russet lashes. His heart stopped and he had to force breath back into his lungs. "Then what are you asking?"

"That you learn to go on without her. To live and raise your daughter to remember her mother as the good and kind woman she was. Nothing will ever be the same. I do not think it is supposed to be the same. I cannot compare my grandmother's death to losing a spouse, but still, there is a hole where she once was. Yet, we must go on and be happy, or would you prefer to leave your daughter with neither mother nor father to raise her?"

Tears he'd not shed since the funeral rolled down his cheeks and he was at a loss for how to stop them. A long pull on the bottle in his desk would chase away his pain for a few hours. "I do not know if I can do what you ask."

"I know, but if you only take one moment at a time, Markus, I know you can do it. For Elizabeth's sake, you have to do it."

Tugging his hands away from hers, he breathed until his emotions were in check. Fingers fisted, he yearned for the contents of that bottle and the oblivion it would bring him.

The door creaked open and Elizabeth poked her cherubic face through the crack. Eyes like lonely lakes, she stared across the room, looking for something in him he could not find himself. Her chubby fingers clutched the doorjamb. So much worry in such a little person and all because he was weak. Her mother was gone and her father a monster who showed up only to tear the house down. It was impossible to recognize himself in the shell he'd become.

"Come in, Elizabeth. Everything is all right." His voice was rougher and less assured than he'd ever heard it before.

On sturdy legs, she toddled along the edge of the rug taking the long way around the disheveled room to his desk. At his knee, she stared up, blinking.

Markus lifted her to his lap and Elizabeth settled against his chest. Her thumb popped into her mouth and her eyes closed. The scent of porridge and clean linen softened his heart as he brushed curls from her rosy cheeks. "Hire the help we need, Miss Hallsmith," he whispered.

"When Lady Chervil and I are settled in, I will need to discuss with you a schedule for Miss Elizabeth at least until I can find her a proper nanny."

"As you wish."

Elizabeth's soft hair tickled the underside of his chin and her breath came slow and even.

Phoebe walked to the door but stopped at the threshold. "Shall I send Mrs. Donnelly in to take Miss Elizabeth to the nursery?"

It didn't matter to his daughter if he was a monster. She wanted him anyway. Emma had wanted him despite his shortcomings.

Elizabeth rubbed her nose and scrunched her sweet face before resuming sucking her thumb.

If his heart burst from his chest he wouldn't be the least bit surprised. It pressed against his ribs and threatened him with the emotions he'd been running from for two years. "I will take her up in a few minutes, thank you."

Chapter 3

No. 14
*An Everton lady must be in control of her
emotions at all times.*
—The Everton Companion
Rules of Conduct

Overstepping boundaries was a condition Phoebe was all too familiar
with. People had been telling her all her life that she'd gone too far. Perhaps
this time she had. Tugging the next dress out of her trunk, she could have
kicked herself for being so harsh with Markus. She should have been
gentler, but his neglect was so blatant.

"Why are you frowning so?" Arwen, her maid, asked, in a thick
Scottish accent.

It reminded Phoebe of how much she missed the countryside of her
mother's people.

Arwen took the dress from her, shook it out, and hung it in the wardrobe.

Phoebe had helped the under-maid, Katy, dust the room and ready it
for guests. Honoria and her maid, Margery, banged around in a similar
room next door.

"I think I was too unkind to his lordship. He's suffered so much."

"Ach! Someone had to tell him true." Arwen continued to pull dresses
from the trunk, shake them, inspect them, and put them away.

Sitting on the bed, Phoebe traced the lace pattern in the coverlet. "I know, but if you could have seen his eyes and the pain in them, you could not have gone on as I did. Maybe I am as heartless as they say."

As much friend as servant, Arwen dropped a pale blue gown back into the trunk and sat next to her. She took Phoebe's hand in both of hers. "You are here because you have the kindest heart I know. You mustn't let what a foolish group of men said ruin you for the rest. Gavin Durnst is no one and he's hundreds of miles behind you now."

Gavin and his friends in Scotland had spread rumors saying Phoebe was cold as Loch Ness and not half as interesting. He had been brutal, and those terrible words echoed inside her head as she shivered with regret over her treatment of Markus.

"He said I was only marrying him to keep order and peace. Maybe it is that warped sense of right and wrong that drives me to put Rosefield back together. Maybe it is why I joined the Everton Domestic Society and disappointed my family." The set down flooded back to her as if her engagement had ended yesterday rather than a year earlier.

"A fool is what he was and you are much better off not married to a fool. In time, you would have come to know it and by then it might have been too late." Arwen shook her head, stood and brushed out her skirts. "Now, you go get something to eat. You never eat enough and are far too skinny for good health. I'm sure there's a bit of bread in the kitchen. Margery would thank you if you took her ladyship with you."

"You are right as usual, Arwen. Thank you for being so good to me." Having a friend through the last five years had been more blessing than Phoebe deserved.

Arwen dismissed the thanks while shooing her out the door.

Phoebe knocked on Honoria's door.

"Enter," Honoria called from within.

Pushing the door open revealed Honoria wearing three hats and at least forty pieces of jewelry. She had wrapped herself in three capes, which she favored as part of her evening ensembles. Grinning, Honoria pranced around the room as if playing to an audience.

"What on earth are you doing?" It was impossible for Phoebe to hide her amusement.

"I am enjoying the fruits of my labor."

Sweat plastered Margery's graying curls to her forehead and neck as she rolled her eyes.

"What labor is that?" Phoebe closed the door and plucked one hat from Honoria's head.

Stopping her parade of one, Honoria stood, arms akimbo. "I married three useless but wealthy men so that I might have all of these lovely things. Why should I not enjoy them?"

"I thought you said you loved William Wharton."

A weepy smile came over Honoria's face at the mention of her first husband. "William was handsome, charming and of a good family. I love him still." She sighed. "He also left me quite a lot of money, which I live very well from. The other two were kind enough to leave this earth before me and supplement my finances. I even managed to gain a title from the last one, making it possible for me to do as I please."

"You sound quite mercenary. Why do you work if you have the fruits of your labor, as you call it?" Stomach rumbling, Phoebe plopped down in a chair by the empty hearth.

Honoria chuckled. "Do I? I like the sound of me being mercenary. I work for Lady Jane because I like to keep busy. There is no fun sitting home alone, waiting for invitations. When you are old, no one is interested in having you at their ball or house party. With Everton's I get to travel with lovely young women who all have interesting stories and assignments." She flung a hat across the room and it landed on the bedpost. Delight lit her face. She tried the same with the last feathered confection. This one missed flying out the window by an inch before landing on the floor.

"Madam," Margery scolded. "Miss, please take her for a walk or something."

Laughing, Phoebe stood. "I came to see if you wanted to go with me to the kitchen to beg a bit of bread before dinner. I am half-starved."

"Oh yes, you are skin and bones. Let's get you fed." Honoria pulled off the capes, dropped them on a chair and removed several rings and bracelets. It took a few minutes, but she pared it down to just a matching sapphire set.

"That is still too much for a kitchen raid, I think."

Crinkling her nose, Honoria frowned. "I suppose so. When we get this house in order, you and I will go to London, where we shall attend every ball and party and wear every piece of my jewelry."

"A fine idea." When the last of Honoria's trinkets lay on the writing desk, they left Margery to her work and took the main stairs down.

Downstairs, on the main floor, they walked through the empty dining room. The windows stood seven feet tall and muted sun shone through the dust and grime. The gardens were more wilderness than most English estates could bear, a reminder that the gardener had been sacked as well. She made a mental note to add it to her list.

"Phoebe, I think I will explore the garden. I could do with some air and I am not very hungry." Already headed to the French doors at the far end of the room, she drifted out of sight.

Through the archway at the other end of the room, Phoebe entered a butler's pantry and discovered the steps leading down to the servant level, hidden behind a door made to blend with the woodwork. She admired the clever construct. The warm aroma of coffee drifted up from the kitchen and Phoebe followed it. Large and clean, the kitchen was a huge contrast to the rest of the unkempt house. A loaf of fresh bread cooled on the counter near the oven. Yeasty and familiar, it made her stomach growl.

"If you are willing to risk Becca's wrath, I will take a piece as well," Markus said.

Phoebe spun toward his voice.

Markus sat alone at the long farm table. Coffee cup cradled between both his hands, he watched her. "Sorry. I did not mean to startle you."

"What are you doing here?" The question snapped out more from her initial surprise than anger. Still, she cringed at how peevish she sounded.

"I live here. Why are you angry with me, or are you always so quick to annoyance, Miss Hallsmith?"

The fight went out of her. It was a flaw in her character. Father had said her red hair made her fiery. Mother blamed Father's indulgence. Phoebe had only herself to blame. A lady should be in control at all times. "I suppose that is one of my failings, my lord. I am short tempered, though I am working to improve myself."

There was no joy in his laugh, but it was better than no laugh at all. "Emma was always even tempered, but I often could get her riled up. It was one of my great joys." His eyes widened and he took his hands away from the cup. "I think that is the first happy thought I have had since…"

There was no need to tell her when his last happy moment had been. Phoebe sat across from him. "I hope you will remember many more to overshadow the one horrible memory."

This time his smile brightened his eyes. "There are a thousand wonderful ones."

"Perhaps you might focus on those and be thankful you had someone who gave you such joy, even if it was only for a short time."

He stared into his coffee before he took a sip. "Some things are easier said than done, Miss Hallsmith. I am sorry to hear about your grandmother. Emma thought you a saint for going and taking care of her."

Emma might have been the only one with that sentiment. Her mother had made her disappointment clear, saying Scotland was a waste of time and demanding Phoebe go to London and find a husband before it was too late. "No one else in the family was equipped to nurse, and I was the only unmarried female of an age. I loved my Grand very much. It was an honor to make her last years comfortable."

He cocked his head. "How old were you?"

"Eighteen." She blurted it out before she realized it was an impertinent question. The solitude of the kitchens made their conversation more intimate. She should leave.

"You gave up a lot then. I'm surprised your family allowed you to go and stay for so long." He sipped his coffee and his chest rose and fell in a deep breath.

A change of subject was in order. "Did Becca brew you that coffee?"

"Yes. Then she ran off complaining about all the work she had yet to do today."

"Do you know if the larder is kept locked?" She breathed in the warm bread scent and her mouth watered.

The light returned to his face. "I do not believe so."

"If you will find us some butter, I will take my chances and cut that scrumptious smelling bread before Becca can stop me."

He was up and moving down a narrow hall before she'd finished spelling out the plan.

Her stomach made another complaint about the lack of food she'd consumed that day. She rubbed away the grumbling and had to admit her clothes were ill fitted since Grand's death and joining Everton's a year earlier. Placing two plates on the table, she pushed aside her sorrow, cut two thick slices and placed them on plates. The soft center was still warm enough to steam, and Phoebe placed one in front of Markus and sat behind the other.

He offered a butter knife to her.

"Are you being a gentleman or are you afraid of your own servant?" She scooped out a good amount of the sweet churned cream and smeared it from end to end of her bread before handing the knife back.

With a wipe of his index finger he tasted the butter before spreading it on his own bread. "Both."

The bread was crisp on the outside and warm and soft on the inside. Yeast, flour, butter in perfect proportions until Phoebe's toes curled with delight. "It will be worth a scolding. This is scrumptious."

Nodding, he took another bite. "I know we are in need of a proper cook, but perhaps keeping Becca in the kitchen would be advantageous."

"Mmm." Phoebe tasted the warm richness of honey in the mix. Her senses overflowed with each bite.

"I hope the two of you are enjoying that bread, as you'll have none with your dinner now." Becca narrowed her gaze from the doorway.

Before the maid-turned-cook could give them a scolding, Phoebe spoke around a mouthful. "We were just discussing whether or not you might prefer to stay in the kitchen after I hire on more help, Becca."

She uncrossed her arms and took a step toward the table. Her cheeks pinked and she stared, wide-eyed. "You mean become a proper cook and not clean and wash?"

"If that would interest you. I have only had this wondrous bread, but I hear you have been doing a fine job in the kitchen. Is that something you might like to do permanently?" Phoebe popped the last crumb in her mouth.

"Is that possible, my lord?" Becca's voice filled with wonder and she bounced in place.

He, too, ate every last crumb on his plate. "You have a knack for cooking. If you would like the promotion I see no reason to hold you back, unless you have other aspirations."

"I'm just an under-maid." Her voice shook.

Phoebe loved how excited Becca was. "Now you are the cook to a viscount, Becca. I will find a few more maids tomorrow. After you have completed your duties for today, you may consider this your last day as an under-maid. See me tomorrow and we will speak of the increase in your wages."

Markus got up and held his hand out toward Becca.

She took it and they shook on the matter.

"I wish you good luck, Becca. Well done." He left and his heavy footsteps sounded on the stairs until the upper door closed.

"I don't know how to thank you, Miss," Becca said.

Getting up, Phoebe felt better than she had in years. At least she'd made a difference in one person's life. She stacked her plate on top of Markus's. "No need to thank me. You have weathered the worst of the storm and earned your promotion. If the bread is any indication, this household is in for a treat with you as cook."

Becca took the plates and knife from Phoebe. "I'll take care of this, Miss. You should rest awhile. You look a bit pale."

Touching her cheek, she stalled a wave of weariness. "It has been a busy week with leaving one assignment and starting another. I think I will lie down for a while. Thank you, Becca."

* * * *

Her second day at Rosefield was filled with cleaning, polishing, and making lists of what needed to be done. She'd barely spent a moment where she didn't see something out of order or misused. It would take time to put it all back together.

At dinner Phoebe had difficulty working up an appetite for the lovely fish Becca had prepared. If Honoria's *oohs* and *aahs* were to be believed, it was all exceptional.

Unable to sleep, Phoebe threw off her covers and opened the window. Cool night air relieved the stifling heat from the fire in the hearth. She would ask the maid to refrain from making such a large fire for her. She hated sleeping in a hot room.

It had been foolish to come here and try to fix Emma's husband and daughter. Perhaps the policy Lady Jane had about not sending ladies who were familiar with the family was a good one. The state of Rosefield and the family broke her heart. She saw how familiarity could be distracting from the task at hand.

Toads croaked out their song in the distance and crickets sang their last refrains before the night grew cold and all would be quiet. England seemed tamer than Scotland. The wilderness of her grandmother's lands and farm were twice as loud in the night. Sighing, she pulled her wrap from the chair and stepped into her slippers. Perhaps some warm milk would help her sleep.

Rosefield creaked and groaned as she padded down the steps and through dark halls. Her nerves were on edge, and all the unexplained noises didn't help. Expecting a ghost to jump out at her, she clutched her wrap and rushed down the servants' stairs.

A lit candle in the kitchen flooded her with relief.

Markus turned toward her from the other end of the kitchen.

Shock and interest gripped her middle. "What are you doing here?"

"I live here, Miss Hallsmith." He made a courtly bow. "And I have it on good authority there are chocolate biscuits in this room."

The words *chocolate* and *biscuits* were enough to stop her heart. "Becca puts chocolate in the biscuits?"

"Watson told me it was an experiment that went very well." He opened a jar and closed it again, frowning.

Lining the back counter were a dozen jars of various sizes and colors. The faded blue with an oversized round handle said sweets to Phoebe. She pointed, excitement making her mouth water. "Try that one."

He lifted the lid and held his candlestick over the top. A wide grin spread across his face. Jar in one hand and candle in the other, he turned and put both in the middle of the table. "How did you know?" He went to the hamper, kept at the bottom of the pantry, and retrieved a bottle of milk. Brushing sawdust from the outside of the bottle, Markus brought the milk to the table.

Pulling two glasses from the shelf, Phoebe said, "It looks exactly like the jar in my grand's kitchen. I could always find a biscuit or two in that jar when I could not sleep."

He poured them each a glass of cool milk and waited for her to sit.

It wasn't ladylike to rush into sticking her hand in the jar, but the idea of a chocolate confection exceeded any embarrassment. Chocolate and butter, along with the dark brown richness…She couldn't wait an instant. The combination of sweet and bitter melted in her mouth. Perfection. She closed her eyes and let the flavors envelop her. Her senses came alive with the new and wonderful discovery.

"I think I could spend a good deal of time watching you eat, Miss Hallsmith."

Dear God, she'd forgotten he was there. "It is quite good, my lord."

"I hardly want to taste it myself for fear it cannot live up to the expression on your face." He sniffed the cookie.

A bout of giggles welled up from her center. The chocolate might have been spirits for how silly she felt. "You should see for yourself. It is delicious."

He took a bite. "Mmm." Closing his eyes, he chewed and smiled. "You were right. This is delicious. Perhaps these could replace my drinking habit."

"Then you would grow fat, my lord."

Raising a brow, he sighed and ate the rest. "Perhaps, but I would be sober."

She took a drink of milk. "I am pleased that you have not had a drink tonight. It cannot be easy."

"I could not sleep."

"Nor I, but with not so good a reason." She pulled another biscuit from the jar and ate.

Rounding the table, he took his handkerchief from his pocket. "You have as much reason as anyone."

"Have I?" she asked.

His eyes glimmered like a deep lake in the candlelight. The spark of something lit them in a way she had not noticed earlier in the day. He closed the gap between them.

Her heart pounded against her chest.

Leaning down, he said, "You have milk on your lip, Miss Hallsmith." Hesitating with his handkerchief raised, he handed it to her.

She dabbed away the mustache and wondered at how close he'd come to doing it himself. Embarrassment and the energy of his closeness merged until she didn't know which was more acute. "If you like, you may call me Phoebe."

He eased back and met her gaze looking at her as if he was seeing her for the first time and seeing more than the girl who'd come to visit Emma. "Indeed?"

"We will be living in the same house for a few weeks, perhaps months. It seems silly to continue with so much formality." She was making a fool of herself, not to mention breaking another companion rule, though she forgot which one. He would think she had no manners or sense of propriety. "In Scotland, it was less formal. I suppose I preferred that to how it is here in England. I apologize if I have offended you, my lord." She stood, grabbed a third sweet and backed toward the door.

"You are running away." He sat.

"I am just going to bed. We should have warmed the milk. It would have helped our sleep."

Staring at his handkerchief, he shook his head. "I would be honored to call you Phoebe in private if you will call me Markus."

A boulder settled in her throat. She was losing her mind. This was Emma's husband, and she was the disowned daughter of the viscount of Thornbury and had three brothers to boot. She was no one and would never be anyone but the disappointing old maid and daughter of a wealthy gentleman. Whatever admiration she had seen in his eyes was only a trick of candlelight. Her heart beating like a hell-bound carriage was due to the late hour and lack of food and sleep. Chocolate was like coffee. It had been a mistake to eat it so late. She drew a long breath. "We have made progress, my lord."

He cocked his head.

"Markus. I apologize. We are on speaking terms. It will be no time at all that your house and daughter are taken care of and you will be rid of me."

Sorrow eased back into his eyes. "Good night, Phoebe."

She ran up the steps, down the hall, and into her bedroom as fast as her feet could take her. The biscuit crumbled in her fist by the time she pressed her back to the inside of the door. Tossing it in the trash bin, she lamented the waste of such a treat, but she'd gone downstairs to ease her insomnia and found only things that would keep her awake.

Maybe she should have stayed in London.

Chapter 4

No. 22
*The purpose of the agency is not to find a spouse. Everton
Ladies will refrain from flirting.*
—*The Everton Companion*
Rules of Conduct

Waking without an aching head and blurry vision was something Markus
had only a vague memory of, but the sensation was not at all unpleasant.
The sun crested the horizon in pink, orange, purple, and gray, inviting a
promising day. He penned a note to Mr. Blunt, his secretary, and had to
stop twice due to the shaking in his hands.

A bleary-eyed Watson took it for delivery.

Damned inconvenient having no footmen. It would take over an hour
for Watson to ride to the village of Benton, deliver the letter, and ride back.
He was getting up in age, and the task should have fallen to a younger man.
Watson was also charged with announcing the news of Rosefield hiring
maids and footmen. Hopefully, Markus had not chased off all prospects
with his behavior.

He penned another note to his sister, Dory. He had much to say, but
settled for telling her he was feeling better and hoped she and Thomas
were well. He'd post it later or in a few days. No need to overtax Watson
by sending him running again the moment he returned.

A high-pitched shriek rent the early morning quiet.

Markus followed the sound to the breakfast room. Mrs. Donnelly was attempting to spoon porridge into Elizabeth's mouth while Elizabeth screamed with delight over a wooden horse clutched in her hand.

Banging the horse on the tray sent the spoon to the carpet.

With the hint of a smile tugging at her full lips, Phoebe put the newspaper down, reached over, and took the horse away. "Perhaps you might break your fast first, Elizabeth. Then play with your new toy."

Elizabeth narrowed her eyes on the horse, standing on the table too far away for her to reach.

"That toy is far from new." Markus strode through the doorway and picked up the toy. "I spent long hours riding this horse across the African desert and even spanned the wilds of India."

Whatever protest Elizabeth was going to make vanished as she gaped at him.

Mrs. Donnelly shoveled a spoonful of porridge in before Elizabeth could close her mouth.

Markus held back his laughter. It had been so long since he'd had the urge to laugh, he almost let it out. "If you eat all your breakfast, I shall take you to the library and show you the routes I took on my journeys. Would you like that, Elizabeth?"

Clapping, Elizabeth opened her mouth for more food.

Becca delivered a steaming cup of coffee, its bitter aroma swirling around the breakfast room. Toast, butter, and jam already waited at his place setting.

His stomach grumbled in favor of the fare. "Thank you, Becca."

Beaming, Becca scurried back to the kitchen.

"Impressive," Phoebe said, nodding at Elizabeth, who now ate without complaint.

"I loved that horse as a child. Where did you find it?"

She blushed the most stunning peach color. "I stole into your attics last night and found a box of old toys. I thought it might be nice to bring one down for Elizabeth. I would have brought the entire box, but it is too heavy for me to carry. I'm going to ask Watson to get it later today."

"I will bring it down. Watson has enough to do." Markus didn't want Watson injured doing the job of a footman or kitchen boy. Another wave of guilt washed over him. How much danger had he already put his household in? These people were under his care and he had let them down, let himself down. Worst of all, he had let Emma down. The pain lurking in his chest tightened.

Mrs. Donnelly lifted Elizabeth from her chair. "Come now, Miss. We'll get you cleaned up so you can have a nice visit with his lordship."

When they had left the room, Phoebe covered his hand with hers. "Whatever you are thinking, you must not punish yourself too severely, Markus. Everything is going to be all right."

Staring at her tapered fingers and creamy skin where she touched his sun-darkened hand stirred more than his doubts. "Will it?"

Her eyes lit up as the smile spread. "Of course."

If his heartbeat sounded against the large window overlooking the courtyard, it would not have surprised him. Shaking away his reaction, he pulled his hand away. "I had thought the entire situation hopeless."

"There is always hope."

Bells tinkled in the hall. Honoria breezed into the breakfast room, a chain of tiny bells on each wrist. Stopping, she lifted her arms and gave them a good shake in case anyone hadn't heard her approach. "Don't you just love the sound of bells?"

"Good morning, Lady Chervil. Did you sleep well?" Phoebe folded the newspaper and handed it to Markus.

Honoria flounced to the table, her frilly morning dress billowing around her. "Like a dream. Oh, that reminds me. I had such a wonderful dream about fields of flowers crushed under the massive feet of elephants."

There was something perfect about Honoria's timing and even her ridiculous dialog that made Markus wonder if she had been standing outside the room listening. Had she burst in on the scene to rescue them from the malaise of the conversation or did she possess a gift for arriving at just the right moment? Either way, he was glad for the distraction. "Have you seen an elephant, Lady Chervil?"

"Oh, no. Now you have done it." Phoebe muffled the words with her napkin.

"I heard that, Phoebe Hallsmith." Honoria gave Phoebe a stern look, which lasted half a second before she brightened and turned her attention back to Markus. "I traveled to India with my second husband, Whittaker Moorewhistle. He was an emissary to the crown. The first time I saw one of the lumbering beasts it was sent to carry us from the border to our home in India. I thought, surely this animal will kill me. But Kesavan was a sweet girl and would not hurt anyone. Not true of all elephants, my lord. Some are quite dangerous. Whittaker screamed down all of India on the journey. Not much of a man, if you must know. Terrified of everything. However, I loved the ride and made similar trips with my servants to shop and see the country." She nattered on about India, elephants, Bengal tigers, and rhinoceros until distracted by the arrival of a plate of food.

The sausage on her plate made his toast seem a paltry fare. His stomach grumbled at the rich spicy steam wafting from her plate of meat and coddled eggs. "Becca, is there more of that in your kitchen?"

A wide smile spread across Becca's face. "You always ask for coffee and toast, my lord."

Normally he would be nursing a headache and his stomach would be in knots. "I find I am hungry this morning."

"I'll bring you a plate, my lord." Becca bounced out of the room.

Markus opened the paper, but only for a moment before Phoebe's staring drew his attention. "Miss Hallsmith, you are staring. May I help you with something?"

"I am just happy to see that your appetite has returned." She sipped her coffee.

Honoria gazed up from her plate. "Perhaps yours will return as well."

Taking a bite of her toast, Phoebe narrowed her eyes on Honoria. "I eat plenty."

With a grumbled word, Honoria returned her attention to the food.

Intrigued by the information and relationship between the ladies, Markus decided it better to change the subject. "I heard you sent word to the village for footmen and maids?"

Checking a gold watch hanging from a chain around her neck, she practically jumped from her chair. "Yes. I have a lot to do before they start arriving. I must find Mrs. Donnelly."

"Will you find a nanny in Benton as well, Miss Hallsmith?" Markus didn't know why the notion turned his stomach.

Shaking her head, Phoebe stacked her dirty plate and silver, folded her napkin and looked as if she might clear the table too. She touched the edge of the plate, took a breath, and left the mess for Becca to clear. "Probably not, my lord. I will have to advertise for a reputable nanny with references. It will not be as easy as replacing a scullery maid."

"I see." Though he didn't. How hard could it be to find a woman to care for Elizabeth?

She brushed out her skirts. "What are your plans for the day, my lord?"

"I plan to meet with my secretary. He should return with Watson this morning."

With a nod and a curtsy, she dashed off in search of Mrs. Donnelly.

Honoria popped the last of her coddled eggs in her mouth and watched him.

"Miss Hallsmith is quite tenacious, my lady." Taking the newspaper, he opened it to a headline of the goings on among the ton in London.

"She is an angel disguised as a hoyden, my lord. You would do well to remember that." Honoria patted her lips with her napkin and pressed the cloth next to her plate.

"I do not have the slightest idea what you mean. She is a bit bossy, but hardly a hoyden. I have not been in her company long enough to determine if she is an angel."

Eyes narrowed, Honoria sat forward and propped one finger on the table between them. "I am going to tell you about her, not because you deserve to know, but because she will never tell you herself."

Part of him wanted to run from the intensity of Honoria's gaze, but curiosity kept him rooted to his chair.

"Phoebe gave up her best chances of finding a husband by going to Scotland to care for her grandmother, Lady Gower. No one expected the old woman to live more than a few months after her apoplexy. Phoebe would not hear of it. She worked like a dog to teach her grandmother how to walk and talk again. Nothing can stop Phoebe Hallsmith once she sets her mind to a thing. All the doctors said her ladyship was a lost cause. I know Phoebe's mother quite well. She indulged Phoebe because she thought her mother would die in a few months and she would have many years to marry her daughter off to some rich Englishman. Despite the predictions of several doctors, and through Phoebe's determination and Lady Gower's will, she recovered almost entirely before her heart gave out. Lucretia should have been thrilled to gain five additional years with her mother, but she only complained about an unmarried daughter. It might have all turned out right, if she married in Scotland. She was engaged, you know?"

Stomach knotted, Markus shook his head.

"That idiot Durnst broke her heart with the things he said and still she stayed in Scotland and ignored all the rumors."

"What rumors?" He shouldn't have asked, but he was so engrossed in her description of Phoebe, he longed to know more.

Snapped out of the moment, Honoria sat back and blinked. "That is Phoebe's story to tell. I am no gossip. I only tell you about what she did for Lady Gower because you should know joining Everton Domestic Society, and therefore helping you, she gives up a lot."

"What are you talking about?"

Rolling her eyes, she drew closer. "At her age, her time to find a husband was wasted on a scoundrel in Scotland and her kindness to her grandmother. Lucretia was determined to take her directly to London and pray for a nice man to fall in love with her before she is put on the shelf for life." She wiped a tear from her papery cheek. "Phoebe could not take the constant badgering from her mother and eldest brother, Ford. She left the country home and joined Everton against her families wishes. They have not spoken to her since. It's a shame really. Phoebe deserves to be worshiped and adored."

"I did not ask her to come here."

Honoria chuckled. "No. Of course you did not. Your mother insisted that she was the best person for the job. And for Phoebe's part, she saw a need and will do whatever she can to fix this mess you are in. There is no stopping her now that she's set her mind to it. I learned long ago, to adore this drive in her. I wish Lucretia was as understanding. She threw a fit when Phoebe said she was moving to London to take employment. Any other woman would have cowered under the wrath of Lucretia Hallsmith, but Phoebe smiled and continued to pack her things as if her mother were singing a lullaby rather than screaming down the house."

"I should send her away. My problems are my own. It was never my intention to cause trouble in the Hallsmith home. I have known the family all my life. Miles and I attended school together." Even as he said the words, he knew he didn't want her to leave. The house wasn't so hard to be in, with her there. He had to get his finances in order and if he let his mind linger on Emma's death, he would have to leave again or drink her away. Phoebe and Honoria took his mind off his grief. It was selfish, but he wanted her to stay.

Standing, Honoria fluffed her skirts. "Just do as she says and stay the course, my lord. It would take an act of God to pull her away from this house until she sees her mission through."

Despite his worry over Phoebe's fate when she left Rosefield, he nodded his agreement rather than voice his concerns.

Becca arrived with a scrumptious plate of food.

Honoria patted her stomach. "I am going to walk in your wild gardens. It will be a shame when Phoebe hires a gardener. I love how natural they are with no one tending them." She flounced out of the room.

* * * *

Markus's secretary, Jared Blunt, examined the office as if he'd stepped through the gates of hell. It was the first time in weeks Markus had not stormed out of the room and told the poor man to go to blazes. The papers, picked up by the maid and stacked haphazardly, had Blunt huffing and restacking. "I do not understand how this could have happened, my lord. I had everything in perfect order for you to go through. These piles were perfect."

He'd repeated the same thing a dozen times already and Markus was getting quite sick of hearing it.

Markus longed for a just a sip of brandy to take away his care over Blunt's insidious complaining. "I'll show you exactly how it happened, Blunt. Someone annoyed me as you are doing now, I picked up a pile and..." Markus rained papers down over his desk and Blunt.

"My lord, have you lost your mind?"

Rubbing his forehead, Markus thought the same thing. "Perhaps. I apologize for that." It was all he could do to keep from laughing over the distraught expression on Blunt's face. At least he hadn't punched him in that long, pointed nose or blackened his eyes. Some paper on the floor was easily fixed.

"Maybe you should go regain your composure outside the office, my lord. I will put this all back in order and we can reconvene in an hour to go over the accounts."

"I will help you sort this mess out. I made it after all." Markus grabbed a page of a land deed.

Blunt snatched it from his hand. "No! That is not necessary, my lord. It will be easier if I put it to rights."

"As you wish." Markus rounded the desk and left his office.

In the foyer, a steady stream of people from the village filed through. Watson sent them into the ballroom.

"Watson, what is going on? How many servants are we hiring?" Markus avoided bumping into a man with a cane and a patch on one eye. What on earth he was applying for, Markus couldn't guess.

"We seem to have quite a few applicants, my lord. I'm sending them to the ballroom and Mrs. Donnelly is sorting them before Miss. Hallsmith conducts the interviews." Watson was as stoic a butler as you'd find in any home in England, but when he mentioned Phoebe, his eyes glimmered like a young man talking about a lass he fancied.

If it hadn't been so comical, Markus might have told him to remember his place. After all, Phoebe was the daughter of a viscount. Even if her idiot brother had disowned her. He couldn't have his servants falling all over themselves about her.

Markus admired the production and visited the ballroom where several dozen people waited in groups. Mrs. Donnelly had organized them by the position they applied for: maids, scullery, grooms, footmen, gardeners, etcetera. It all served as a reminder that he needed his valet back. He would send a note to Shropshire and see if he could beg forgiveness and get Blakely to return. Crow was not his favorite meal, but the notion of training a new valet was even worse. Blakely knew all his likes and dislikes. There was no harm in asking.

Unable to return to his own office, he stomped around the garden before going to his room and using the small writing desk there. Without any fanfare or flowery words, he penned a note apologizing for his behavior and requesting Blakely return to his post at Rosefield. Once the letter was tucked into an envelope, addressed, and sealed, Markus placed it on the tray with the message to his sister to be posted.

Determined not to be thrust out again by Blunt, he returned to his office. A feminine chuckle trickled through the open door. Markus pushed the door wide.

Phoebe's smile lit her eyes and her cheeks pinked.

Standing entirely too close to her, Blunt spoke in tones too low for Markus to hear.

Every muscle in Markus's body clenched so tight he physically ached from head to toe. What nonsense. He had no claims on Phoebe. For all the fuss, she was only his temporary nanny. Perhaps that was harsh, but he certainly had no interest beyond her helping to put his home in order and care for Elizabeth until a proper nanny could be hired. She was an Everton lady and would go on to some other assignment as soon as she was done with him.

Still, seeing her so close to Blunt and blushing made Markus's blood catch fire.

She backed up a step and turned toward the open door. "My lord, I was looking for you."

Blunt stared at her as if she were the moon.

Biting the inside of his cheek, Markus focused on Phoebe. "I am here." Sounding like a jealous lover, his tone was less disinterested than he would have liked.

Phoebe cocked her head and stepped away from the desk where Blunt still ogled her. "There are so many candidates for the various positions. I wonder if once I weed out the bad eggs, we might sit down and go over my notes before I hire on the new staff?"

Blunt closed the gap she had put between them. "I would be happy to help."

Holding his position near the door, Markus would not be drawn into a triangle. He had no interest in Phoebe Hallsmith. Still. "I see no reason why you would extend your duties beyond this office and my holdings, Mr. Blunt."

"I only wish to help Miss Hallsm—um—you, my lord. I only wish to help you get Rosefield back in order." Blunt tugged on the bottom of his frockcoat and pulled his shoulders back.

"Very admirable, but you may best do that by focusing on my financial situation."

"Yes, my lord. I am ready to discuss those items at your convenience." Blunt stepped back until the desk stopped his retreat.

"Miss Hallsmith, when you are satisfied with the list of applicants, we can go through them. I would appreciate if you gave priority to any returning staff. I am sure I have put some of them into difficult situations. I would like to remedy that as soon as possible."

A wide smile spread across her face and illuminated her eyes far brighter than the flirting with Blunt had. "Wonderful, my lord. I shall find you later today with the list."

The idea of her seeking him out, no matter the reason, lit something inside him. Something he had not felt in a long time. Joy, happiness, a sense of purpose? No. He shook the notion away and bowed. "Until then, Miss Hallsmith."

She rushed from the room.

It took a force of will not to watch her go. Blunt, on the other hand, stared after her like a lost puppy. Markus wanted to punch him in his too perfect nose. "Are you ready to get to work, Mr. Blunt?"

* * * *

Neck and back aching, Markus pored over hundreds of neglected documents. His annoyance over Blunt's obvious infatuation with Phoebe faded with the realization that without Blunt keeping his accounts, he would likely be homeless by now. Sitting back, he rubbed his eyes. How could he have let things get so bad? Blunt had made several decisions in Markus's name just to keep the bill collectors at bay. It would take weeks to put it all back in order, but he was thankful to have the wherewithal to make it right again. A few more months at the bottom of a bottle and he might be begging Father for help. He cringed and dispelled the notion.

Besides, if what Jared Blunt said was true, Father was in a worse situation than Markus. With no one to keep him in line, the Earl of Castlereagh was in trouble. Once Markus got things at Rosefield under control, he would deal with Father's mess.

The parcel of land at the far east of his property was the most productive on paper. George Harper worked that land if his memory served. Picking up the accounting of the different farms, he went in search of Blunt, though he had a pretty good idea where he'd find the secretary.

Taking a detour through the ballroom, Markus found only one young man left waiting and a very tired Mrs. Donnelly slumped in a chair. "Are you all right, Mrs. Donnelly?"

She jumped up, but her eyes smudged blue underneath and the slump of her shoulders told a different story. "Just tired, my lord. It's been a long day."

A young man stepped in. "The lady will see the next person now." He waved and left.

With a sigh, Mrs. Donnelly said, "You're the last, Ed. Go on in and be smart about it."

Ed ran his fingers through his light brown hair while clutching a cap in his other hand. Jacket frayed at the wrists and pulling tight across his back, he walked out of the ballroom.

"That's the last of them for today, my lord. I'm happy to have this over and have a regular staff on hand again. I'll just run and check on Becca and little Elizabeth."

Strange that he'd spent months avoiding his daughter, and all she reminded him of, and now he'd missed her after one day at his desk. He handed Mrs. Donnelly the paper in his hand. "If you will take this back to my office, Mrs. Donnelly, I will go and fetch Elizabeth from the kitchen."

It took her a moment to close her mouth. "That would be a help, my lord. Thank you."

The Harper farm could wait until tomorrow. Markus went to find his daughter and the idea was not repugnant. In fact, he was excited to see her.

Squeals echoed up the steps from the kitchen. What he found was the most delightful mess he'd ever seen. Bowls and pans spread across the table with flour and other ingredients strewn and slopped from one end of the room to the other. Elizabeth sat on the table, wearing more of the batter than she stirred and screaming with delight.

"Are you planning to bake my daughter or some confection, Becca?"

Eyes wide, Becca made a quick curtsy. "My lord, we were just making some of your favorite biscuits."

Stepping forward, he forced a frown to hide his bubbling amusement.

Elizabeth watched him warily, waiting for him to fly into a fit. Her hands stilled on the bowl and spoon, and through the layer of sticky batter, her little knuckles turned white.

Markus stuck his finger in the bowl, scooped out a taste, and stuck it in his mouth. Sweet and buttery, just as a good biscuit should be. Very few would make it to the ovens, but those that did would be wonderful. He let his smile break free of the farce he played. "These will be the best biscuits I have ever had. May I help?"

Screeching with a wide smile, Elizabeth lifted both hands and the one with the spoon splattered batter in every direction. One rather large dollop landed on Markus's lapel.

Both Elizabeth and Becca froze, horror etched on their faces.

Using his index finger, he wiped the sweet from his clothes and ate it. "You are right, of course. I should take this off. That is if the cook does not mind another helper in her kitchen."

Through liquid eyes and a bright smile, Becca said, "I would be glad for the help, my lord."

Markus draped his soiled jacket on the back of a chair, rolled up his sleeves, and waited for instructions.

"You can add two cups of flour to that clean bowl at the end of the table, my lord. From the looks of things, we may need a second batch if you're to have a snack tonight."

So, his late-night snacking was known by the servants. Did it matter? Did they also know he no longer snacked alone? He found the only clean bowl in a sea of messy, dirty crockery and put the flour in as instructed.

Becca walked him through the dry ingredients then the wet before telling him to add the first to the second and stir.

Abandoning her own batch, Elizabeth scooted across the table to sit with him.

Carefully and without the mess and splatter, they stirred the batter until it came together. Elizabeth's chubby hand under his on the spoon was so right, it spurred an ache deep in his chest.

As they finished the batter, Becca cleaned the disaster on the table and countertops. Laughing and giving instructions the entire time while scrubbing her kitchen clean. By the time the biscuits were on a pan and in the oven only the floor was still flour and sugar splattered. Several eggs had been lost down there as well. "You two have been excellent helpers."

Markus had never cooked anything in his life, though he enjoyed the fruits of other people's labors. There was something satisfying about turning a few ingredients into something else. "Shall we help you get this mess off the floor?"

A loud laugh burst free and Becca covered her mouth with her hand. "No, thank you, my lord. I will take care of that. You and the little miss should go and get some fresh air. It's a beautiful day and we may not have many of them left before winter brings cold and snow. I'll bring you a warm biscuit when they're done. For sure they'll be ready by tea time."

"What do you think, Elizabeth? Shall we go to the gardens?"

Becca wiped a wet cloth across Elizabeth's face as she nodded. After a quick wiping down, Elizabeth held her hands out to Markus.

Heart lodged in his throat, he lifted her. Emotion pressed behind his eyes.

A sniffle from Becca proved he was not the only one moved by the rapport building between them.

He gave Becca a nod as she wiped her watery eyes, and he and Elizabeth left the kitchen in search of some fresh air.

Chapter 5

No. 13
Everton Ladies are to remain aloof and never get personal with a client.
—The Everton Companion
Rules of Conduct

The last of the day's applicants left the small parlor at the back of the house. Phoebe hadn't known what she was getting into, but it had been a good day and she had assembled quite a few excellent candidates for positions at Rosefield.

Jared Blunt had come to help her. Markus must not have believed her capable of handling things herself. Initially annoyed, she had to admit he had been excellent at organizing her notes about each applicant.

"Is there anything else I can do for you, Miss Hallsmith?" Jared placed the last of the notes on the pile. His smile revealed crooked teeth with a small gap between the front two. His brown eyes sparkled like a child who had discovered some bit of candy. Tall and lean, he was not bad looking, though perhaps too eager to please.

The smart thing to do would be to encourage a well-employed young man with obvious interests in her with some light flirting. How she hated all the regular things about courting. "No. Thank you for your assistance, Mr. Blunt. I can manage things from here. You have been a great help to me."

If it was possible, his smile brightened and he stood straighter. "It was my pleasure, Miss Hallsmith. I would be happy to come back tomorrow and assist you."

"I would think you have much work to do with his lordship. I can manage this with Watson and Mrs. Donnelly."

His grin dimmed and he shuffled his feet. "Yes. There is much to do in the office."

Relief flooded her.

"Perhaps I might impose on you after work for a walk in the gardens, Miss Hallsmith?" He stared and clasped his hands.

There was her dread again. "We shall just see how things go tomorrow, Mr. Blunt. One never knows how a long work day will end up."

He took her hand and bowed over it. "I understand your hesitance. You do not know me at all. I shall endeavor to remedy that. Until tomorrow, Miss Hallsmith."

Honoria breezed into the room, humming a happy tune.

Jared bowed to her before leaving.

"He is quite handsome," Honoria said.

"I suppose he is." Phoebe gathered her papers, tucked them in a leather satchel, and sat.

Taking the seat the applicants had used, Honoria studied Phoebe. "You do not like him?"

"He is very nice." It was true. He had come and helped her without treating her like an imbecile. Most men did not think women capable of rational thought or organization. He was meticulous and kind. Still.

"He has good employment and comes from a respectable family."

Phoebe narrowed her eyes on Honoria.

Shrugging, Honoria said, "I asked Watson about him."

There was nothing surprising in that admission. Honoria might be forward thinking in many ways, but she was still part of English society and, just like her mother, very keen on marrying any young woman off to the highest bidder. "I am sure Mr. Blunt is a fine catch for a woman of my station."

"There is no need to say it like that, Phoebe. If you do not like him, then forget I mentioned it. It is only that he looks at you as if you are the sun and the moon. I believe with very little encouragement he would court you and perhaps make you an offer. Is it not beneficial for you to explore the idea? Watson tells me Mr. Blunt has a very nice home just outside of Benton. He even has a carriage. Of course, he has no title and therefore is beneath you. Still, you have been disowned, so that is of little consequence."

The idea of crawling under the small Queen Ann desk appealed to Phoebe. Jared Blunt was nice, had a good living, and probably liked her, but to spend every day for the rest of her life with him... "I will give the matter some thought."

Honoria clapped. "Excellent. Now go and get some air. Your cheeks are white as alabaster. It is not healthy to sit in one room all day long and get no air. I am sure there will be tea in thirty minutes, but you have time to catch a breath before then."

Thinking of courting and social status made her wish she had her Grand to talk to. Grand had a way of putting everything in perspective. Choking down her sorrow, she said, "I will go immediately. Would you join me?"

"No. I need to rest. I have been touring the grounds with Mr. Duck for over an hour." Honoria touched the back of her hand to her cheek.

"Mr. Duck?"

"The groundskeeper, my dear. He is a fine fellow with copious knowledge of Rosefield. The viscount is lucky he did not leave." Honoria stood, fluffed her pale-yellow skirts, and smiled.

Phoebe would have to investigate this Duck fellow. Leaving Honoria to find her rest, Phoebe went to the garden.

Overgrown and wild, there was barely a path left to follow, but Phoebe wandered along what remained and let the sun warm her face. Leaves floated down in gold, orange, and brown, further hiding the stone and grass.

"Jack climbed the beanstalk way up into the clouds." Markus's voice cut through the breeze. With Elizabeth curled in his lap, he sat in the grass in his shirtsleeves and told the story.

Elizabeth had her thumb in her mouth and twirled her hair around a finger of her other hand.

"He climbed and climbed until he reached a new land and saw a castle in the distance. The closer he got to the castle, the bigger it loomed. Far larger than anything Jack had ever seen before."

Seeing her first, Elizabeth untangled her finger and pointed at Phoebe.

Markus made to rise, but Phoebe stopped him. "Do not get up. I only meant to take a walk, not to disturb the story."

"Will you join us, Miss Hallsmith?"

She should go away and keep to her own business. Only there to help them get back on their feet, she need not become attached. "Thank you." She sat. The cool grass and warm sun were a perfect contrast in the little wilderness. "It is lovely here."

"It needs a good pruning back, but I have always been fond of this garden. Have all the applicants gone for the day?" He brushed the hair out of Elizabeth's face.

The sight was as heartwarming as it was devastating. Poor Emma never lived to see such a sight. She would have been so happy. "Yes, I have quite a lot to go over with you after tea."

"Has Mr. Blunt gone as well?"

Elizabeth looked from one to the other as they spoke.

"Yes. I believe he will return tomorrow."

Darkness shadowed his eyes. "I am certain we will see a lot of Mr. Blunt."

"He is your secretary."

"I do not think that is why we will see him often at Rosefield, Miss Hallsmith." One hand caressed the side of his daughter's face while the other fisted in the grass.

"If it bothers you that Mr. Blunt is giving me attention, why did you send him to assist me?"

"It does not and I did not. If Mr. Blunt assisted you, he did so of his own accord." He adjusted Elizabeth on his lap and fussed with a smudge of something on her dress.

A blanket of relief flooded over Phoebe. Markus had not doubted her abilities. It shouldn't matter, yet she could not deny her pleasure at the new information. "I assumed you had sent him. In any event, he was very helpful."

Markus's regard was direct. His gaze never left her face. "How old are you, Miss Hallsmith?"

Unexpected and impertinent, she closed her teeth down on a cutting retort. "I cannot see how that is any of your business."

He smiled but it didn't reach his eyes. Those green depths remained sad and distant. "It is absolutely not my business. You may disregard the question if you like."

Oh, how she hated society's rules. "I am four and twenty."

"I see."

"What do you see? That I am too old to make a good match and had no choice but to join the Everton Society? That I have wasted my best years? That I should be married and raising a family by now? That I am an old maid put on the shelf to be pitied and despised by the women of the ton?" Her entire body had clenched into a frustrated knot. It became hard to breathe and even harder to keep from raging at him. It was a miracle that she had spoken without raising her voice. If Elizabeth hadn't been watching them, she might have delivered a setdown that even her mother would be proud of.

He raised his eyebrows. "Who was that just now, Phoebe? Your mother? Your brother Ford?"

Breathing too hard to respond, she took several long breaths to calm herself. "I apologize, my lord. I have failed to control my emotions again. As I told you before, it is something I am working on."

A spark of something lit his eyes. "I do not think you an old maid. I am certain that Jared Blunt does not think so either. He looked like he might devour you when I walked in on the conversation in my office."

Cheeks flaming, she clamped down on her emotions. "I was looking for you. Mr. Blunt was there."

"You need not explain yourself to me. I am not your warden nor your father."

A short unladylike laugh escaped. "No. You are certainly not."

"I only meant to say that you are not on any shelf. You could marry if that is your wish. Blunt is only one man and I'm sure there are many who would wish to wed an attractive, intelligent woman like yourself. As to why you joined the Everton's, I would not presume to know. Perhaps one day you will share those details with me."

His cool tone set her nerves on edge. Clearly both Markus Flammel and Honoria found Mr. Blunt a perfect match for her. Perhaps they were right. So, why did the idea make her nauseous? "Perhaps it would be best if you went back to your telling the tale of Jack the Giant Slayer, my lord. I believe he had just reached the giant castle."

A happy squeal from Elizabeth indicated she too had enough "adult" talk for one afternoon.

Markus returned to the telling without so much as a knowing look, for which Phoebe was grateful. The problem of her marital status could wait for another day and certainly was not a subject to discuss with Markus. She closed her eyes and let the warm, rounded tone of his voice lull her as it did Elizabeth. Phoebe had nearly dozed when Mrs. Donnelly came to fetch them for tea.

Markus stood with Elizabeth in his arms, stopped, and offered Phoebe a hand up.

In her haste to get out of the house, she'd forgotten to don gloves. She didn't care for the silly things and often conveniently forgot. Though when her fingers met Markus's, she wished for a barrier between them. His skin was warm and rough and the contact sent a pleasant chill down her arm to the pit of her stomach and lower. Rising, she tugged away and met his gaze.

The surprise in his eyes mirrored her own shock at the effects of the simple touch.

A touch from Markus Flammel was more unsettling than the few kisses she had shared with her fiancé. Gavin had not sent chills down her spine or given her goose flesh. "Pleasant" was how she once described it to Arwen, when asked. Just touching Markus's hand was far more than pleasant.

Emma's face flashed in her mind. Intense guilt shot through her, nearly buckling her knees.

Markus caught her with one arm around her waist. "Are you ill, Miss Hallsmith?"

She pushed away. "No. I am fine. I just rose too quickly is all. Perhaps I had better go and lie down."

Grunting, Elizabeth smacked Markus's chest.

"I believe Elizabeth would like you to taste the biscuits we baked earlier. They will be served at tea."

Staring at her was the sweetest face in all of England. There was no way she could refuse. If she were honest, she didn't want to be away from either of them. Wanting the wrong things was another one of her flaws, and she must correct that as well. With a sigh, she preceded Markus and Elizabeth into the great parlor.

Becca brought the tea in as they arrived in the freshly dusted room. Katy must have worked like the devil to clean the tall widows. Every inch of wood was polished to a high shine. It still held the musty odor that came from a room being closed for a long time, but the frills and lace reminded Phoebe of Emma and made her happy with memories.

As soon as they took their seats near the coffee table, Elizabeth grabbed a biscuit and ran out of the room.

"Elizabeth." Phoebe stood.

Becca laughed. "I'll keep an eye on her, Miss. You enjoy your tea."

"Thank you. She should be ready for a nap too." Phoebe poured the tea.

Watson cleared his throat from the doorway. "Mr. Hallsmith is here to see you both."

Heart in her throat, Phoebe cringed. "Ford is here?"

"Do not panic, Phoebs, it is only me." Miles Hallsmith crossed the threshold and stepped around Watson. His smile warmed the room immediately and his good nature warmed her heart.

She ran over and hugged him. "Oh, Miles, it is good to see you. I was very disappointed that you were in London when I arrived home and I have not a moment since to see you."

"Nice to see you, Hallsmith." Markus approached and shook Miles's hand.

"You are looking better, Markus." His gaze went from Phoebe back to Markus.

"Yes, well, your sister has forbidden me from drinking my brandy."

Mrs. Donnelly brought another teacup, they all sat and Phoebe poured her brother a cup. "Did you ride over just to see me, Miles?"

He sipped his tea and wolfed down a biscuit. "It had been over a year since I have seen you, Phoebs. I was very disappointed when I got home and found you gone already. Mother went on for hours about your decision to become employed."

"I am certain she did." Phoebe could practically hear her mother's voice screeching down the walls of her family home.

Smile never dimming, Miles continued, "Also, there was a note from his lordship telling me to get my sister out of his house."

A rock clogged her throat. Markus had sent a note to have her removed. That was why Miles was there. Markus wanted her gone. She swallowed down the stone and pulled her shoulders back. "I will leave when the situation here is in hand."

Honoria floated in. "We have company. How wonderful."

Phoebe rose with the men. "Lady Honoria Chervil, may I introduce my brother, Miles Hallsmith."

Miles's grin widened and he bowed low to Honoria. "It is a pleasure to meet you, my lady. Are you here as chaperon to my sister?"

"Your sister is my favorite Everton lady. It is my pleasure to work with her."

Markus remained standing until Honoria sat, but he didn't meet Phoebe's gaze.

Once again unwanted. It was to be expected, since she foisted herself on people who were perfectly happy being miserable. She should learn to mind her own business or at least not care so much about the outcome.

Markus cleared his throat. "How are things at your brother's estate, Hallsmith?"

"All is well, running smoothly. Ford hasn't the slightest clue where his money comes from or where it goes, but we all live comfortably." Miles grinned around another biscuit.

"What will he do if you ever strike out on your own?" Markus asked.

Shrugging, Miles brushed crumbs from his trousers. "I have no plan to do so, but any good secretary could take over. I keep good records in case anything were to happen to me."

Unable to keep the horror of losing Miles silent, Phoebe gasped. Her teacup rattled in the saucer and she put them down before she made a mess. "You should not say such things, Miles."

Miles reach over and squeezed Phoebe's hand. "Nothing is going to happen, Pheobs. I am fine. I only meant that I take precautions to keep my family from suffering in my absence. You know Ford has no interest in the finances and only what they buy him. He only cares about gambling and drink. It's all I can do to keep him from wasting it all. The family is lucky he has some skill at the card table or things might get dire."

Ordering her pulse to slow and her breathing to steady did little good. "I know you are too good to him."

"I enjoy the work, and you, Mother, and Aaron are my main priority."

Phoebe hmphed. "One day you might like to marry and have a family of your own, Miles. You cannot run our brother's life forever. You need not worry about me. I can take care of myself."

Elizabeth's high-pitched squeals pealed through the parlor as she ran in. Spying Miles, both she and the noise stopped.

"Hello," Miles said. "This must be the one running the house these days."

Cocking her head, Elizabeth studied him.

Phoebe said, "Miss Elizabeth Flammel, may I introduce my brother Miles Hallsmith."

Miles knelt in front of Elizabeth who gazed from her father back to the newcomer. He held out his hand and she backed up a step.

The most distinctive expressions crossed Elizabeth's face. Fear, wariness, surprise when he knelt then acceptance as she offered her own little hand in friendship.

Bowing over her hand, Miles said, "It is an honor to make your acquaintance, Miss Elizabeth."

Showing all her teeth, she grinned at him before snatching a biscuit and running back into the hallway.

Miles laughed and sat in the chair. "She seems like quite a handful."

"She is full of life and spirit," Honoria said. "Just as a little girl should be. How long are you staying, Mr. Hallsmith? Have you just come for tea?"

Phoebe felt his gaze on her but she couldn't meet it. Staring into her teacup, she did something she hated more than anything. She let men decide her fate.

"I brought the large carriage in case you ladies needed transport."

"Goodness, no. There is much to be done here. His lordship needs a staff, and Phoebe is still amid interviews. The child needs a nanny and the advertisement was only posted to London this morning. We shall not leave for several weeks at least."

Avoiding looking at her brother did not make the conversation hurt any less. She lifted her head to meet Miles's gaze, but he turned and addressed Markus.

"Can I count on you to see to their safety, Markus?" A rare and serious frown settled on Miles's face.

"My note to you was premature. I apologize. Miss Hallsmith and Lady Chervil are my guests and can stay as long as they like, or leave with you if that is their preference." He spoke through a clenched jaw.

* * * *

Once Miles went home, Phoebe spent the rest of the day avoiding Markus. Cordial at dinner, she poked at her food, eating little. She had no right to feel betrayed. He'd never pretended to want her at Rosefield. Still, approaching him with her notes could wait until her ridiculous wounds healed.

What did she expect after she had thrust herself into his life without giving him the option to decline? She twisted and turned in her sheets for hours until she couldn't bear it anymore. Her stomach grumbled loudly. It was late enough. Markus would have come and gone from the kitchens by then.

She padded down the stairs but when she reached the servants' level the glow of candlelight filtered out of the kitchen. Frozen on the bottom step, she decided to rush back to her room. She turned. The stair creaked. Closing her eyes, she waited, praying that he hadn't heard.

"Please do not run away, Phoebe."

Turning back toward the kitchen meant swallowing down fistfuls of emotion. He could not see how much he'd hurt her. Donning a mask of indifference, which she'd learned long ago from her mother, she faced him.

Even in the shadows of the candlelight, he shone with energy that drew her in. The glowing light came through his loose blouse and detailed his torso.

Mouth dry, she trudged past him to find a snack. "I expected you would have gone back to bed by now, my lord."

He followed and sat at the table. "There was little point. I will not sleep anyway."

A mulberry pie sat untouched on the counter. "How did this survive your raid?"

"I suppose I lacked the appetite." He traced a circle in the grain of the wood. "I wrote that note the day you arrived. I was still drunk from the night before."

"A drunk man's words are a sober man's thoughts." Betrayed by her own growling stomach, she cut two pieces of the pie and sat across from him. She pushed one plate and fork over.

After a bite of pie, he closed his eyes. His lips mesmerized her, and her own tingled with the idea of touching him. He stared at his plate and used the fork to track a pattern in the berry juice. "That may be true, but allow me to have changed my mind, Phoebe."

"I suppose I should be thankful you wrote to Miles and not Ford or my mother. They would have dragged me away by the hair and happily so. I would be in London attending balls by now. Then I would have to start again by leaving for Everton's and listen to my mother's disappointment all over again." The pie rolled in her gut.

"Most women enjoy balls. Do you not find them distracting?"

Better to stop talking and eat the pie. These late-night meetings in the kitchen were dangerous and foolish. Still, his eyes danced in the candlelight and his tone soothed away years of disappointment. "I do not like to be paraded around like a trophy to be snatched up by the winner of the race."

He laughed and finished his pie. "You would be a wonderful wife and mother, Phoebe. Do you not wish to have a family of your own?"

Everything inside her chest and stomach clenched. All her wants and desires jumbled up in opposing forces. "Of course, I wanted a family. It is only that I did not want it as much as I wanted my grandmother's last years to be good ones. And I do not care for the process devised by the ton."

"It is rather mercenary. Do you not care for the pie?"

She pushed the plate across to him. "It is delicious, but I have lost my appetite."

He wolfed down her pie too, put his fork on the plate, and locked his gaze with hers. "It would seem you have lost your appetite for many things."

"I beg your pardon, my lord?" The truth stung more keenly than he might have intended.

"Markus. You may be angry with me, but that is no reason to spew titles at me." It was a gentle scolding. "You barely eat and you do not wish to dance and enjoy your youth."

"I am hardly young anymore. My years to find a husband have likely passed anyway. I would only be going to satisfy my mother." It did no good to command herself to stop talking. Somehow the intimacy of the kitchen late at night dragged information from her soul and placed in on the table for him to sneer at.

Only he didn't sneer. Markus smiled in a sad way, unique to him. "I think Jared Blunt would beg to differ with you. He is smitten. It would take little encouragement from you to secure a marriage proposal."

"And you think I should do that?"

Markus traced the pattern in the wood, pushed his plate to the center of the table, and tugged at the ties at the throat of his blouse before looking at her again. "It does not matter what I think. Mr. Blunt is a good man. If you like him, he would make a fine husband."

"For a girl like me."

"What?"

Markus was no different than the rest. Marrying her off to the first man who shows interest and getting rid of her in the process. "That is the end of the thought, is it not? Mr. Blunt would make a fine husband for a girl like me."

Something flashed in his eyes before they narrowed. "What kind of girl is that?"

Standing, she stayed her emotions. Once she had pushed her chair back under the table, she met his gaze. "The kind of girl who has been disowned, without dowry or family to recommend her. The kind of girl who is past her prime and should be happy to have any man show her attention. It would be foolish of me not to simper at Mr. Blunt. He will likely be the last man to show interest."

Every word she spoke tore more of her soul out. There was nothing wrong with Jared Blunt and yet the idea of him sickened her. There was very little wrong with Gavin, but she withheld affection until he ran from her. Running for the door, she couldn't get away from him fast enough.

At the threshold, Markus wrapped his fingers around her arm and held her there. "You have value, Phoebe. I do not know why you cannot see it, but you do yourself a disservice by believing you must settle."

She swallowed the lump in her throat. His warmth spread through her along with the warm, masculine scent that muddled her mind. "I am a woman past her time to marry well, with little to recommend her. I know my worth, Markus, but I am realistic and know my limitations. Joining the Everton Domestic Society at least gives me some power over my own life."

His grip tightened and he drew her forward until his body pressed hers. "You are a smart and beautiful woman, tenacious and witty. Anyone who does not see that is a fool."

Unable to move, she stared up at his lips. He spoke words no one had ever said to her, yet from him she almost believed them. Dear God, he was going to kiss her and she was paralyzed to stop him. Didn't want to stop him. His breath mingled with hers. "Markus, this is wrong."

He froze and his eyes regained their focus. Releasing her, he took a step back. "I am sorry."

Heart lodged in her throat, Phoebe ran out of the kitchen and up the stairs. She didn't stop running until she was behind the closed and locked door of her bedroom. She knew Markus wouldn't follow, but she locked it just the same. Perhaps more to keep herself in than him out. "Oh, Emma, I am the worst friend in the world. What is wrong with me?"

Chapter 6

No. 20
An Everton lady will not think of the client romantically.
—The Everton Companion
Rules of Conduct

Markus had managed only a few moments' sleep all night. Awash with guilt over nearly kissing Phoebe in the kitchen, he found no peace. After hours of tossing and turning, he wrote several letters and made a plan to get away from Rosefield, before the situation drove him back into the bottle. Since Emma's death he'd believed a clear mind would be his undoing, but he found the opposite to be true. Dealing with his loss was easier without the brandy. If he'd been inebriated in the kitchens, he might have done something he would truly regret, and worse, Phoebe would regret it even more. If he'd been drunk, he might have ruined a good woman who was trying to help him. He prayed he was not that far gone, but couldn't be sure. Self-loathing engulfed him and his fingers shook while he fumbled through tying his cravat.

He pulled on his long coat and handed his letters over to Watson. "I am riding out to the Harper farm then intend to visit Marlton. Tell our guests I will return in a few days."

"What shall I tell Miss Elizabeth?" Watson tucked the envelopes into his pocket.

Fear screamed inside his head, "Run!" but his conscience cried out another message. "I will go up and tell her myself."

"Very well, my lord."

Taking the steps two at a time he rushed into the nursery. His heart stopped. Every surface screamed Emma. Pink damask walls and creamy lace all done in the last month she was with child. Hours of decorating managed for the joyous event of their daughter's birth. Emma was so certain it would be a girl, she sewed a dozen pinafores in pink, yellow, and every other pastel color. Grabbing a dresser to keep his feet, he forced breath back into his lungs and stared at all the beauty his sweet Emma had created for their daughter.

Wide-eyed Elizabeth stood in her crib, watching him.

Markus swallowed and dashed the tears from his eyes. "Good morning, Elizabeth. I had forgotten how pretty your momma made this room for you."

She cocked her head then raised her arms for him to lift her.

Cradling her, he sat in the large rocking chair. "She loved you very much, you know. I am so sorry you never got to meet her and see how wonderful she was."

The room didn't make him sad the way he'd predicted. Avoiding the room hadn't made him happy, either. Seeing all the things Emma had done made him miss her but it also reminded him of the wonderful last month of her life.

Elizabeth popped her thumb into her mouth and sank against his chest.

"I have to go away for a few days."

She stopped sucking and gawked up at him.

"Only for a few days, Elizabeth. I promise I will not stay away long. When I return, you and I shall go on a picnic. Your momma loved to picnic even when it was too cold."

There was nothing as perfect as Elizabeth's sweet face. Intelligence sharp in her eyes as she watched him. She touched his cheek and wiped away an escaped tear.

"I will be back soon. I only wanted to tell you goodbye before I left." Lifting her, he put her back in her crib. "You and I are going to survive, little one. I do not know how, but we will manage it."

He watched her until she curled into a ball and closed her eyes. As long as Elizabeth loved him, with really no reason to, there was hope for the future. With luck, she would sleep until Mrs. Donnelly or Phoebe came for her. He had not kept a promise in two years; he prayed he could keep the ones he made now.

* * * *

Riding like the devil was on his heels cleared the fog from his sleep-deprived mind. He slowed as he approached the Harper farm. Growing potatoes and other vegetables, the fields were already harvested. The rich, dark soil beckoned Markus down from his horse. Even after a long growing season, the earth was good. Taking a handful, he breathed in the musky, fresh scent he'd loved since childhood.

"I wasn't expecting you, my lord. Didn't even know noblemen woke this early." George Harper towered over Markus by at least five inches. He was a giant of a man with enormous shoulders and scruffy blond curls.

"Some do when we are curious as to how one farm outgrows the rest." Markus dropped the dirt and clapped the remainder from his hands before offering one to Harper for shaking.

Harper's hand swallowed Markus's when he shook it. "You want all my secrets?"

"If you are willing to share a few, I would be grateful."

A wide smile spread across his face. "My wife is just making breakfast. Why don't you join us and we'll chat about why my potatoes are the best in the county? On the way, I'll take you to see my broad beans. They'll be ready for harvest next week."

The beans were the biggest Markus had ever seen. Not even in Italy, where they called them fava beans, had they grown as plump and long.

George Harper and his wife, Pearl, lived in a neat cottage, which Markus provided. It was clean and well maintained. A small fire burned in the hearth and bread baked in the oven cut into the brick above and tea steeped on the table. Pearl served coddled eggs and toast with a bean mash more flavorful than any gruel.

"I wonder if you would share this recipe with my new cook, Mrs. Harper?"

Blond hair falling lose from her cap, Pearl blushed. She was of average height, and beside her husband looked a tiny frail thing. "I'm pleased you like it. I will give the recipe to Becca when I see her at church on Sunday."

"I did not realize the promotion was common knowledge already." Markus finished his food and put down his fork. Gossip was like a disease, and he hated to think about how much of his life was fodder for the mill.

Pouring more tea, Pearl said, "Becca's mother is our neighbor. She was so proud of her daughter she came by to boast a bit. Becca is a good girl. We're all happy for her promotion."

Markus relaxed. "She is a wonderful cook and baker. I am happy for her as well."

Smiling, George drank his tea down in one gulp. "Come with me, my lord. We can look over some repairs that need doing while I tell you all about manure."

Two hours later, Markus rode toward Marlton with a short list of things the Harpers needed fixed and a head full of farming techniques that produced the best vegetables in the county.

There were precious few pretty days left before the English countryside would fall to winter snow, rain, and cold. It was just after noon when Markus rode up to the looming facade where his close friend Daniel Fallon lived. The family sat in the grass not far to the left of the yard.

Daniel stood as Markus approached. "This is a surprise."

Dismounting, Markus said, "A welcome one, I hope."

"You are always welcome at our home, Markus." Sophia brushed her long black hair off her shoulder and smiled up at him from the blanket where three-year-old Charles ate with enthusiasm. "You look well."

"You mean I look sober and you are too polite to say so."

Sophia laughed. "I'm American, Markus, I always say what I think."

Markus bowed. "One of the many reasons we all adore you, Sophia. Young Charles has grown a foot since last I saw him."

"You have not been here in a long time." Daniel shook his hand then slapped him on the back.

"I hope I have not done anything in the past few years to harm our friendship." The worst part of being sober was not remembering what he had ruined while soused.

"Not possible. We have been friends too long. If you came all this way to make some kind of apology, you could have saved yourself the ride. Thomas, Michael and I will always be at your service, Markus."

It was a relief to know his oldest and dearest friends were still behind him. He had not seen much of them, but he did remember an embarrassing visit to Thomas Wheel's London home where he drank the man's brandy and had to be put to bed. Since then Thomas had married Markus's sister, Dory. He had many reparations to make.

The reason he had come gnawed at him. "I could use a talk if you have the time, Dan?"

Daniel gazed at his wife.

Sophia waved a hand. "You two go inside and chat. Charlie and I have some running and playing to do after he's laid waste to that chicken leg."

Still focused on his meal, Charles gave a laugh and smeared some bits of food across his cheek.

Laughing, Daniel put his arm on Markus's shoulder. "Come in the house. Would you like some tea?"

"I would love a brandy, but the tea will do." Markus flopped onto the couch near the window in Daniel's study.

Once he'd rang for tea, Daniel sat adjacent to him. "You have given up drink?"

"My mother has employed the Everton Domestic Society on my behalf. Miss Hallsmith has taken over my home and demands I not drink. To be honest, I needed to stop. Being drunk all the time is tiring and has put my holdings at risk. Also, as Miss Hallsmith pointed out, it's very much like my father." He cringed at the admission.

"Is that Miles's sister, Phoebe? I have not seen her since she was in braids."

The tea arrived and the housekeeper poured for them.

"She is no longer in braids." His heart expanded with memories of her red hair and the smattering of freckles on her cheeks, but his head pounded with too many worries over right and wrong.

Daniel raised an eyebrow. "Oh, she has grown up well then? She went away if I recall. Scotland, was it?"

"Her grandmother suffered an apoplexy and Phoebe went to take care of her. From what I understand, she nursed her grandmother back to health and stayed five years caring for her until her death."

"Wasted her entire courting years." Daniel sat forward with his elbows on his knees.

The tea was strong and eased the tension building inside Markus. "She is still young enough to marry."

"I assumed you came here to discuss Emma, but it seems you came for other reasons. Do you have feelings for Miss Hallsmith?" Daniel put his tea on the table and pushed it away. A pointed stare accompanied the question.

It wasn't possible to have feelings for Phoebe. He barely knew her. Whatever happened in the kitchen was due to the intimacy of the moment and his loneliness. There was no other explanation.

"No. Maybe. I do not know. My secretary is smitten with her. Part of me finds her curious and smart. She is as efficient as any man and more determined than most. I have never met a woman like her. The rest of me is appalled by the idea that I might like her. I came here today because I could not stand to be there and I knew I could keep my promise to not drink at Marlton. Also, I would never discuss this particular subject with anyone else and I knew you would listen." He sounded like an idiot. Grown men didn't behave like schoolboys because a bit of skirt appealed to them.

"How is Elizabeth?"

The light hiding in Markus's heart returned to full brightness. "She is an angel. After all I have put her through, she loves me. I do not know how or why, but I am grateful for it. I was a fool to stay away from her for so long, and she has suffered. So much so that she has not uttered her first word."

"Sophia and I visited a few months ago. You were not at home. We had thoughts of bringing Elizabeth here until you were feeling better, but the staff was adamant that they had been charged with her care and would not relent. Elizabeth went into a rage, so we did not push the issue further. Sophia wrote to your sister about the matter."

Crushing guilt battered him from the inside out. "Since Phoebe's arrival, the tantrums have stopped. We will be patient with her finding words for a while longer. I will take her to London for medical care if necessary."

"What does Miss Hallsmith think of that?" Daniel asked.

"I have not discussed the matter with her." Though he knew she would not be keen on the idea of subjecting Elizabeth to scads of doctors and tests. Phoebe was certain that when Elizabeth had something to say, she would do so.

"Exactly what is Miss Hallsmith doing at Rosefield?"

The nights in the kitchen when they talked and got to know each other flew through his mind. "She is hiring staff, seeing to the household needs, and caring for Elizabeth."

"A lady, doing all of that? How strange. And is it just the two of you in the house?"

"Of course not! Everton provides a chaperon. Lady Honoria Chervil is also in residence. I would not have let her come without a chaperon. Hell, I did not want her to come at all."

"But she did come and she has taken control of your home and now you are here to discuss her. How long has she been with you?" Daniel sipped his tea and sat back, watching.

"Three days, or maybe it's four." It was impossible that it was only a few days. She had turned his miserable life upside down in such a short time. "I should toss her from the house."

Choking on a sip of tea, Daniel sputtered. "You should hold on to her as tightly as you can."

"What? She is disruptive and bossy." He would go home today and send Phoebe and Honoria back where they belong.

Daniel drank the last of his tea and returned the cup and saucer to the tray. "You and I have been friends a long time, Markus. We were in short pants when we met and I could not break you out of your depression or stop you from drinking yourself ill. Thomas and Michael also tried to help you get back on your feet. Your mother and sister came to your home and you threw them out. The women in your family are not easily battled, and yet you forced both out. In four days, Phoebe Hallsmith has returned order to your home, made you see your daughter as an angel, and convinced you to stop drinking. In my opinion, you had better hold on to that girl with both hands. She has done in less than a week what the people who love you could not accomplish in two years."

Heart pounding and hands wet with perspiration, Markus hated to admit any of what Daniel said was true. "But, Dan, she is too close. I do not think her being in my house is a good idea."

"You mean because you are attracted to her?" Daniel shrugged. "I do not think Emma would want you to be alone forever. She loved you and would want you to be happy. If Miss Hallsmith makes you happy, I see no reason to avoid her."

The idea of dishonoring Phoebe shook him and he forced his fists to relax. "I do not need or want a mistress."

Shoulders stiff, Daniel stood and walked to his desk. He moved a glass paperweight but then returned it to its original position. "Sometimes I see no resemblance in you to the man I grew up with. Miss Hallsmith is a lady, not the kind of woman who one makes a mistress."

"I will never marry again. Emma was my wife—is my wife. That will never change."

Daniel ran his fingers through his blond hair, loosing part of it from its queue. "Then let her hire your staff, find a nanny for your daughter, and go back to London where she will help the next family in need. Or perhaps she will benefit from a match with your secretary."

"Yes." It was as if someone were gripping his heart and squeezing the life out of it.

"I would be very happy to see you find someone to love again, Markus. With Miss Hallsmith or someone else, it would be good for you to find love again." Daniel leaned against his desk.

"No one can fill my heart the way Emma did. I have no room for another. Nothing could ever be like my marriage with Emma. She was the other half of me." The voice tightened and he struggled to draw breath.

"It would not be the same, that is true. Before I met Sophia, I believed myself in love with Jocelyn. Maybe I was in love with her, but the love, the feelings, the relationship was not the same as what I have with Sophia."

"Jocelyn had an affair before you were even married. She was not the right woman for you. You cannot compare the two." Markus couldn't keep from scoffing.

Crossing his arms over his chest, Daniel straightened away from the desk. "My point exactly. Regardless of Jocelyn's feelings, mine were clear. I cared for her enough to want to marry her. I was smitten and wanted to spend every second with her, which led me to finding her with her lover. However, when she was no longer in my life, I was certain I could never love again, never find a woman who made me feel that way. And I was right."

"I do not understand."

"The feelings I have for Sophia are completely different from those I had for Jocelyn. In my heart, Jocelyn is dead. At least, the woman I thought she was is long buried. My heart was so full with her that when she destroyed our love, I hardened myself against any woman taking her place. It was just as well, because no woman could or should. Sophia did not take Jocelyn's place. She made her own place in my heart, which has room for more love than I had ever imagined."

As the vice around his heart eased, it allowed guilt to push in. "It is not the same. Jocelyn is still in the world."

Daniel spread his arms with his palms out then shrugged. "I know my situation is not the same as yours. You love Emma still. I hold only the memory of my youthful belief in Jocelyn in my heart. The reality was much different. But I believe your heart has more than enough room for a different love. Not a love to replace Emma. No one can do that, and it would be unfair to the woman to compare her. A love that inspires the man you are today."

"I do not think I can do that, Dan."

Daniel nodded, crossed the room and sat. "You don't have to make any decisions now, Markus. Nothing has to change beyond you staying sober and taking care of your home and family. I only suggest you release yourself of all this extra guilt."

"I should feel guilty. I am guilty. I put everything I own at risk and now I behave like a boy in short pants." Markus should be flogged; at least that would make him feel better.

Slapping his back, Daniel smiled. "Go home, Markus. No one is forcing you into a relationship with Miss Hallsmith or anyone else. I am saying you need not feel guilty over your feelings and to keep an open mind on the subject of loving again."

He had planned to spend the night at Marlton, but heading to London might be a better idea. He could find a pub along the way and forget all of this. Golden eyes and russet hair would fade at the bottom of a fine brandy. His own weakness disgusted him. He had already broken too many promises. He would honor his agreement with Phoebe and his duty to Elizabeth. "I will return home. Thank you for the talk."

"I am sorry I could not be of more help."

Markus rose. "You have given me a lot to think about, Dan. Forgive me for interrupting your picnic."

Waving off the apology, Daniel said, "Feel free to visit anytime. Bring Elizabeth next time and she and Charlie can play together."

"Thank you." They walked out of the office and to the front door.

In the yard, a maid cleaned up the picnic while Sophia chased after Charles in the field beyond.

"Please tell Sophia I said goodbye. I will be in touch soon." Markus shook Daniel's hand, mounted his horse, and rode away from Marlton.

* * * *

When Markus reached Rosefield, he walked his horse to the barn. It was dark, but he managed to light a lantern, and since there were no grooms, he watered, unsaddled, and brushed out the stallion. There was something healing in taking care of the beast. It was real and laborious and had nothing to do with him. His selfishness mirrored his father's and he couldn't bear it.

Surprised at how eager he was to go inside, he forced his breathing to slow. It was late and the house would be asleep.

Watson did not open the door, since Markus said he would not be home for a few days. Knowing the front would be bolted, Markus stole in through the servant's entrance near the kitchen. It was dark as pitch, but he managed to find his way down the hall and up the steps. There was a squeeze of disappointment without Phoebe stealing a snack in the kitchen, but he let it pass.

Instead of going directly to bed, he passed his room and opened the nursery door. Elizabeth might have played and laughed all day long, but he found her as he left her, curled up in a ball with her thumb in her mouth. He ran his finger along her soft cheek before sitting in the rocking chair. How long he watched her sleep, he didn't know.

"You are home?" Phoebe whispered from the doorway.

Her hair flowed around her shoulders loose and wild and her feet poked out from under her nightgown. Whenever she came to the kitchen she wore slippers and a robe, but she stood in Elizabeth's room barefoot and in only her shift. "I decided not to go to London."

"Where did you go?" She stepped inside the room and crossed her arms over her chest. "Forgive me. It is none of my business."

Rising, he ran his fingers through his hair. "Are your feet cold?"

She crossed her arms over her chest and stepped onto the wool rug curling her toes into the pile. "I heard a noise and when I opened my door the nursery door was open. I was concerned."

"I went to speak to a farmer then rode out to Marlton to see the earl." Mesmerized by her bare toes, he couldn't take his eyes from them.

"I see. Watson said you would be gone several days."

"Yes. I told him as much, but changed my mind." Their whispered conversation didn't disturb the gentle breath of Elizabeth's sleep.

Stepping closer, Phoebe peered into the crib. Her arm was close enough to his that her warmth infused him. "Why did you change your mind?"

"You ask a lot of questions, Phoebe."

"I'm sorry. Always poking my nose in where it doesn't belong. It gets me in a lot of trouble. Another thing to add to my long list of flaws." Moving to the edge of the carpet, she put space between them.

He closed the gap and tucked her cerise hair behind her ear, a tiny gasp his reward. "You always forget all the wonderful qualities you possess, which counterbalance those tiny flaws. No one is perfect, Phoebe. You may continue to ask your questions, but must accept that sometimes I will decline to answer."

"Fair enough." So close, her breath mingled with his.

If he leaned down a fraction, he could take her mouth and ravage it until they were both breathless.

She dropped her arms, leaving her pert, round breasts outlined by the moon shining through the window. Only a thin piece of cotton separated her from his touch. It was all he longed to do, and the one thing he could never do. Betrayed by his body, which strained to be with her, near her, inside her. Good lord, he was going mad. He kissed the tip of her nose and stepped back. "You should return to your room before you catch a chill."

Crossing her arms again, hiding her attributes.

He was grateful for the added barrier. How much could one man take?

"Elizabeth will be glad you are home. She missed you today." Eyes wide, she backed away until her shoulder bumped the doorframe.

"I missed her too. Good night, Phoebe. I look forward to hearing all about the candidates for Rosefield staff in the morning. Shall we meet after we break our fast?"

With a nod, she ran from the room. Her feet padded away down the hall and her door closed with a nick and the sound of her throwing the bolt.

Good. He needed her to lock her door.

Chapter 7

No. 11
Everton Ladies are inconspicuous.
—The Everton Companion
Rules of Conduct

How could one person become so familiar and necessary in such a short time? Phoebe ran back to her room and bolted the door. Ordering her heart to slow down did no good. Her skin tingled with the possibilities. He had only kissed her nose. An innocent peck, but there had been more in his eyes, and she wanted all that was within those green depths. Desire of that magnitude was new and terrifying.

No amount of denial would change the way she yearned for Markus. If he had taken her in his arms in the nursery, she would have let him kiss her and maybe more. Goodness, she had lost her mind. It wasn't as if she'd never been kissed. Gavin had kissed her many times. It had been pleasant, but nothing to warrant so much attention.

Somehow, even though Markus had not taken advantage of her, she knew his kisses would be different. Pressing her fisted hands between her breasts, she scolded, "Enough."

Trudging across the room, Phoebe berated herself for being such a fool. He only needed her to get his house back in order. Markus Flammel was a viscount and one day would be an earl. His sons would be titled. He would never have any interest in Miss Phoebe Hallsmith. She was disowned and disinherited, not to mention how disliked her brother Ford was amongst any good society. Nothing would change that, and it was just as well. He was Emma's husband, and anything more than friendship was not acceptable. She threw back the covers and climbed into bed.

When she'd seen him watching Elizabeth sleep, joy flooded her as it never had before. Trying to push the memory away, she closed her eyes, but it only made the image more vivid. Even wrinkled and dusty from travel, the sight of him relieved her. Gavin had been out of her life for over a year, and she never missed him as she had missed Markus after one day. And she had nearly married Gavin.

A lifetime of Gavin ordering her around and reminding her how thankful she should be to have married him. A girl in her position should have been thrilled with a wealthy gentleman's attention. He had said those things more than once, but the day he ended their engagement he drove his point home by adding that she did not appreciate him. He rescinded his offer of marriage and added that she was incapable of any deep feelings. "A cold fish" had been his final insult.

Lucky for her, he had no honor, or she might be married to him and miserable the rest of her life. Though a lifetime of spinsterhood did not make her heart sing, either. At least if she had married Gavin, she would be cared for and could have children to dote on. After a time, he would have found a mistress and left her and the babies in peace. It might have been all right.

Phoebe pounded her fist into her pillow and turned over in search of a comfortable position.

At dawn she gave up, washed her face, and dressed.

A walk in the cool morning air was what she needed. Leaves tumbled around her, blowing in the breeze and falling to the long grass. She pitied the new gardener's job of cleaning all of this up. It would be sad to lose the little wilderness, but a fine English garden would take its place. She walked the path while the sun warmed the Earth. The uncertainty of the night before eased and normalcy returned to Phoebe. She had a job to do at Rosefield. That was all. Once she had completed the task, she would leave and probably never see Markus again. Worrying about his feelings for her was idiotic. He could never care for her, and rightfully so.

She stopped at the clearing, closed her eyes, and turned her face to the sun.

"Am I disturbing you?" Jared cut into her peace.

She startled, but recovered. "Not at all, Mr. Blunt. You are here early. We have not even broken our fast yet. Do you have an early appointment with his lordship?"

Kicking the dirt from the path, he stepped closer. "I desired to see you before I get started with his lordship's business."

Dread rooted in the pit of her stomach. "Oh, what did you need to see me about?"

He offered his arm, and with no polite way to decline, she took it. Markus had spent months ruining his health and he still felt sturdier than Jared. Threading her hand through his elbow revealed the thin softness of a man who spent all day behind a desk. His pasty skin another sign he rarely took to the outdoors, she wondered at his hardship in searching her out.

While Markus filled her senses with spices and masculinity, Jared reeked of ink and the hair tonic he used to slick back his brown locks. "I wanted to tell you how much I enjoyed working with you the last two days. You and I make a good team."

"Thank you. I appreciate your help. You are very organized." It was the best she could come up with in way of a compliment.

Puffing up like a pigeon, Jared's grin spread wide. "I had the very same thought about you, Miss Hallsmith. You are meticulous and organized, rare virtues in a woman. Most women are so frivolous, but not you. You have purpose and determination."

For Jared, these compliments were likened to another man saying her eyes were like the moon and her skin like silk. They did not have the same effect. "Thank you, Mr. Blunt. I cannot remember anyone ever saying such things to me."

Leading her back toward the house, he cleared his throat, then stopped. "I would like to ask permission to court you, Miss Hallsmith. Whom should I query?"

Processing the question took more than a comfortable silence. "One would think you would ask me."

Laughter, more like grinding teeth, tumbled from him. "Of course, but I meant should I seek permission from your father?"

"My father is dead. You could petition my brother Ford, the viscount of Thornbury. I wish you luck with that. You see, I am disowned." Telling him not to bother sat at the tip of her tongue, but the prospect of a lifetime without marriage or children replaced a curt reply with the facts.

"Disowned? Well, that might change in time. Yes, Ford Hallsmith. I met his lordship once at a town meeting. Fine fellow. I will make time to see him as soon as my duties allow." Another strike against Jared if he'd met Ford and enjoyed any part of the experience.

At least she was reprieved from more courting for the moment. "You will let me know how that meeting goes?"

Jared cocked his head and stopped. "You will know by the fact that I have started courting you. Was I not clear in my desire?"

"Very clear."

Smile returned, he escorted her into the house. "I have work to do. You can manage from here?"

"I believe I can get myself to the breakfast room. Thank you, Mr. Blunt." Nothing about him was appealing as he straightened his bony shoulders, tugged his ill-fitted jacket, and strode away toward the office.

Markus sat next to Elizabeth, when Phoebe arrived and took a plate from the sideboard. Food had been laid out and the savory spice of sausage filled the air. "Good morning."

Elizabeth lifted a piece of sausage in the air and laughed before accepting a spoon of porridge from Mrs. Donnelly.

Phoebe's stomach rebelled at anything heavy. Taking some toast from the array of choices, she lamented the coddled eggs. She sat at the other end of the table and spread jam on her bread.

"You should eat more, Miss Hallsmith," Markus said.

"I am not hungry." Tearing a morsel of bread free, even that didn't appeal.

Frowning much like Honoria did when she refused to eat, he stared down the table. "Regardless, you should eat more. Have some eggs and sausage or I will have Becca bring you some porridge."

The servant's door opened and Becca brought a cup of coffee. "I'll run down and get you some now, Miss."

"I am really not hungry."

Becca pulled a stern look. "We do not let the little one leave the table until she's eaten something. You want to set a good example, don't you?"

"That is playing dirty. Bring the porridge." Phoebe laughed and accepted the newspaper from Markus.

With a clap, Becca charged out of the breakfast room and down the servants' stairs.

"And look how happy you have made Becca. You should be pleased." Markus drank his coffee to hide his grin.

There was something very familiar and nice about their breaking their fast together. Almost as if they were the family she yearned for. Too bad none of it was real, which reminded her... "Mr. Blunt met me in the garden. He is already waiting for you in your office."

"Why was he in the garden?" All humor drained from Markus's face.

Elizabeth whimpered at his sharp tone.

He patted her knee. "I am not cross, Elizabeth. Eat."

Looking from Markus to Phoebe, she took a breath and went back to her food when Mrs. Donnelly prodded her with a spoonful.

Phoebe longed to tell him it was none of his business. "He was looking for me. I took a walk this morning."

"You should not be alone in the garden with Jared Blunt."

It was hard to argue with that. "As I said, he sought me out. He intends to meet with my brother to ask permission to court me."

The spoon clattered in the bowl. With an apologetic look, Mrs. Donnelly picked it up. "He is a fine catch, Miss Hallsmith."

The color of Markus's face was somewhere between the roses out front and the burgundy carpet in the front parlor. "I see. You told him you would court him. I am happy for you both."

"Actually, he never asked me. I suppose he assumed I would want to court him. I'm sure he thinks himself a fine catch, just as Mrs. Donnelly said."

He put down his cup with a snick in the saucer. "The rest of your life with a person who brings no joy is a long time, Miss Hallsmith." Placing his napkin on the table, he stood, then bowed and left the room.

* * * *

Phoebe accepted that Markus was avoiding her. He had postponed several appointments to go over the staffing options. After a full week, all she had managed was to bring back the few servants fired by Markus and willing to come back. At least they had a footman, under-gardener, stable boy, and a scullery maid. Those only because they had family close and were unwilling to leave the area for employment.

A letter from London promised that a nanny would arrive soon. Phoebe knocked on the office door but pushed through before anyone could tell her to go away. "I need some of your time, my lord."

Sitting behind his desk with Jared hovering over his left shoulder, he looked up. "Can it wait?"

"It has waited a week. I have a life I would like to get back to. If you would?" She sounded more like herself and the sound was enough to make it real. Skulking and jumping any time she thought Markus might be present was not like her, and she didn't like it. Doing what she came for and getting back to London was her plan, and she would see it through.

"Mr. Blunt, can you excuse us?" Voice even, Markus stared her in the eyes.

Deep creases formed around Jared's mouth as he nodded, stared at Phoebe, and left the room.

"If I was too forceful, I apologize, but you have been putting me off for several days." She kept her shoulders back and looked him in the eyes. "Yes, and you have a life to get back to. So you said. Mr. Blunt will be quite happy to be a large part of that life as well. Will you court here in the country or go to London and see how he stacks up to the other available men of the season?" Markus patted a stack of papers into a neat pile, eased them to the side of the desk, and leaned back without taking his gaze from hers.

Phoebe resorted to the Everton company line. "Markus, I am here to do a job and that is all. Whatever Mr. Blunt intends is of little interest and none of your business. I want to do what I said I would then get out of your house. You said yourself that you wanted me gone. You wrote to my brother and demanded he take me away. Why is it such a shock to you that I have plans to leave? I work for Everton Domestic Society. I take an assignment, complete it, and move on. It is what I do."

Jaw ticking, he closed his eyes. When he opened them the fire was gone. "What would you like to go over?"

She had crushed the nanny's letter in her fist and smoothed it out. It was a good thing the rest of her notes were protected in a leather portfolio or everything would be a mess. "I have had a letter from a reputable nanny. She sent her credentials. Perhaps we can check her references and offer her the position."

Taking the letter from her, he offered her a seat. His eyes darted across the page before he rose, rounded the desk and sat in the chair next to her. "This Mrs. Horst sounds qualified. What are your concerns?"

The letter expounded upon Mrs. Horst's many achievements as a nanny in four well-to-do homes. "Why does she have no reference letters included? Why did she work in four homes?"

He read the letter again. "Perhaps she neglected to ask for a reference letter. Nannies change homes when the child grows, and in the case of boys, they go off to school."

"True. Perhaps I am being too picky." The wording of the letter and tone still didn't sit well with Phoebe. She couldn't put her finger on what the problem was.

"In my opinion Mrs. Horst will suit." He passed the letter back.

Taking it, she sighed. Once she'd put it at the bottom of her papers, she said. "I will write to her immediately."

"If it will make you feel better, write to Lady Wortripple. That was Mrs. Horst's last post. Perhaps that will ease your concerns."

Phoebe made a note to write both letters and post them immediately. "I have hired back a few of the staff, but most have found other positions." "I would expect so." Looking at the short list, he frowned. Wishing she could give him good news that would make him smile, she pressed on. "Here is the list of potential servants. Watson and Mrs. Donnelly gave me the posts and the numbers, but if you want to change anything, please let me know."

"No. They know best." He was all business. None of the intimacy they had shared remained while they spoke of staffing the house.

Becca brought tea and lemon cake, and they talked through the meal, discussing each candidate at length. By week's end, they would have most of the positions filled.

"Shall I hire you a valet or would you prefer to do that?" It would have been difficult for Phoebe to manage without Arwen. Perhaps it was different for men, but her brothers had employed valets for as long as she could remember.

"I hope Blakely will return. I have written a letter to that effect." Markus ran his hand through his hair.

Urged to fix the part he left sticking up, she fisted her hands to keep them in her lap. "That must have been difficult."

"The mistakes I have made require amends." He shrugged. "It is not pleasant to apologize, but it is necessary."

"On that same subject, there is the matter of Duck." She cringed. The last time the groundskeeper's name came up, Markus went into a rage.

Fire flashed in his eyes, but vanished a moment later. "What about him?"

"I went to the stables to see him yesterday, and he is quite vexed with you. He refuses to take his salary and wishes to be replaced."

"And you do not think we should replace him?" Resignation rang in his voice and he held his head in both hands, elbows on his knees.

Even though he had done this to himself, she ached to ease his discomfort. She touched his hand, the silky hair poking through his warm fingers. Goose bumps ran up her arm and continued until every inch of her skin was sensitized. "It would be even more disruptive to lose him. I am told, despite his rather caustic demeanor, he is very good at his job."

Markus turned his hand and took hold of hers. Looking up, his eyes filled with emotion, which she refused to put a label on. If someone would look at her that way for the rest of her life, she could be content, maybe even happy. Time stood still and the only existing world was in that office wrapped around the two of them. Her heart pounded out the rhythm of the universe.

A knock on the door broke the spell.

Pulling his hand away, he said, "I will speak to him."

It took a force of will to get her pulse to slow and her breath to return to normal. She swallowed down desire. "Thank you, Markus."

Another knock, this one less forceful.

"Come in."

Honoria popped her head around the door, smiled, and floated into the room followed by Jared Blunt. She contemplated the tea tray, then Phoebe, and frowned. "I see you have had your tea. Phoebe, you look about to drop. Should you not go and rest until dinner?"

Markus sat up straight and stared at her. "Are you unwell?"

"I did not sleep last night. I am fine."

A grunt sounded from Jared. "You should take a draft if you are not sleeping."

"I do not care for the way they make me feel." This was not a conversation she wished to have with Jared. "I will go up and rest for a while, if we are finished here, my lord."

He stood with her and took her hand before bowing over it. "We are. Thank you, Miss Hallsmith."

Determined to continue, Jared said, "Feel? They make you sleep."

Phoebe turned to Honoria. "Will you accompany me upstairs?"

Giving Jared a stern look, Honoria nodded. "Of course."

"My lord, you should insist she take a sleeping draft."

Phoebe bit the inside of her cheek to keep from responding. Who did Jared Blunt think he was? He had no right to force his will on her.

"Miss Hallsmith is a grown woman. She need not take advice from you or me, Mr. Blunt." Markus's firm, even voice followed her out the door.

His words rang in her head long after she lay in bed, staring at the ceiling. If she were smart, she would pack her things and leave Rosefield immediately. She'd come to help Markus and Elizabeth. Developing feelings for him had not been part of the plan. No. She was stronger than that. It had been a long time since she had been courted, and she'd lost her head. That was all. It was ridiculous to consider loving Markus Flammel. He was Emma's husband, and Emma was her best friend.

A small, distant voice called back, *Emma is gone.*

Sitting up, she shooed away the unpleasant voice. Dead or alive, she loved Emma, and more importantly, Markus loved Emma. She was not worthy of him anyway, so the point was moot. All she had to do was finish her task and go home. Once the staff was back and working and a nanny was hired, she would have no reason to stay at Rosefield and she would never see Markus again. In a week or two this would all be a distant memory.

Chapter 8

No. 19
A child shall never be scolded in anger. While a need for discipline exists, if one finds herself losing a grip on her state of total calm, she should take a few moments and recover before continuing.
And should someone else break this important rule, the Everton lady must and will take action.
—The Everton Companion
Rules of Conduct

Whenever Markus made progress away from his sorrow, life reminded him nothing would ever be the same. His attraction to Phoebe might not be wrong in the strictest sense of propriety, but it wasn't right, either. Emma's friends surely were off limits. But there was something about Phoebe that was not there before when she visited Emma. Perhaps all of this was just because they had both suffered a recent loss.

After all, Phoebe's grandmother had died only a year before. She had suffered a long battle with her health. She was lucky to have had someone to care for her.

Emma was gone only…He had to think. How long had it been since he lost his sweet wife? There had been snow on the ground. His stupidity at thinking he could drink away his sorrow had robbed him of so much.

Markus walked out the door into the chill of the garden. There would be snow soon. Could it be two years since Emma's death? Of course, it was. Elizabeth would be two in a few weeks. His loss was not so recent, yet it hurt as if it were yesterday.

Gripping his coat to his chest, he walked the path to the stables.

He'd only ridden out of need recently. Once he'd gotten a lot of pleasure from his horses.

A tall black named Warrior strode to the fence, pranced, and puffed clouds from his nostrils.

Markus petted his soft nose. "Good to see you too, boy. I hear your old friend Duck is still caring for you. You are in good hands in my absence."

"As if you cared." The gruff voice of Duck growled from the corner of the barn.

With one last pat for Warrior, Markus turned. "I have been neglectful."

"You look about to drop. Are you ill?" While the question sounded concerned, the tone was more bark.

Drink and lies had brought his life to a standstill. It was time for honesty. "I was thinking of my wife."

Duck's sharp brown eyes shifted to the ground. His hands were swollen at the knuckles as he rubbed the leather harness he held. "She was a good woman, your lady."

Markus walked forward until he stood in front of Duck. The man's knuckles were swollen and he winced as he put the harness on a hook near the door. He'd been caring for all these animals with little or no help for months without pay. Shame staggered Markus. Pulling his shoulders back, he stared Duck in the eyes. "I lost myself in my grief, Duck. It is not an excuse, but it is a fact. I found solace in the bottle. I am not proud of these things, but I mean to make amends for the wrong I have done."

"That baby of yours needs your amends more than old Duck does." Duck sat on the bench next to the barn and patted the place beside him.

It was only a small gesture of kindness, but Markus swallowed down tears threatening. "Elizabeth has suffered the most from my neglect. It is beyond me how I will fix that. Though I intend to spend my lifetime trying."

"She is like her mother and will have already put it in the past."

Emma had forgiven him anything without even the need of an apology. He had often scolded her for letting him and everyone else get away with any manner of transgression. The servants adored her but often took advantage. Even when he scolded her, he admired her capacity for forgiveness. "Emma was a much better person than I am, Duck."

"You'll forgive her one day, my lord." The sharp edge was back in his eyes.

"Forgive who?"

"Lady Emma."

"She is dead, or have you forgotten? I have nothing to forgive her for. She is dead." His heart tightened painfully and he gripped his chest. Unchecked fury surged to the forefront, squashing his dreaded anguish. Duck nodded. "She left you. She died and left you all alone, tore the love out of your life and left you in tatters. It's a hard thing to forgive."

Markus dashed away a rebellious tear. "What do you know, old man?"

"It took me three years to forgive my boy for going to heaven when he was only nine years old. I was better prepared for when my sweet Gail was called home. Still, I was angry as you are now, my lord. It may be too soon, but one day you'll have to forgive her."

Forgive Emma? Markus pounded his fist on the bench, sending a shock of pain to his shoulder. She forgave his stupidity, drinking, antics, tantrums, and his horrible parents when they visited. All he had to forgive her for was dying.

Duck struggled to his feet and faced Markus. "Now, what was it you came all the way to the stable to say to me?"

Standing, Markus fisted his hands at his sides. The fury threatened to overwhelm his purpose. "I came to offer my apologies for my behavior. I would like for you to stay on here and allow me to pay you for your time spent. I will hire you as much help as you need and hope you will train your successor when you are ready to be pensioned."

"I accept your apology, my lord." Duck stuck out his gnarled hand for shaking.

Surprised by the strength of the shake, Markus still swallowed down the desire to punch the old man in the face. "Good."

"It's a start, son."

Emma's eyes flashed behind Markus's closed eyes. He shook his head to clear it. "I will saddle a horse and go for a ride."

Handing Markus the bridle from the hook, Duck nodded. "Take Warrior. He'll take care of you."

Warrior stomped and tossed his head, his black mane swooshing through the air, in favor of the suggestion.

Markus saddled the stallion while Duck ambled away. Never would he have imagined a conversation with Duck of all people would bring out such overwhelming emotion, but he had to wipe tears from his eyes to secure the girth. Once in the saddle, he rode south until he and Warrior were both exhausted. Tears streaked down his face, freezing in the cold wind.

Standing in one of his fields at the far edge of his property, he felt nothing was real anymore. His life a distant memory and the life he once had gone forever. Choices had to be made: a lifetime of misery and self-loathing, or possible happiness. Rage burned in his belly like the fires of hell. He'd been punishing himself for two years to avoid the truth. His fury at the person he loved most had sent him over the edge of reason and left him for dead. If he could have died with Emma, he would have been perfectly content. Many times, he wondered if death was not preferable to the purgatory he was living. His heart beat on, no matter how much he prayed it would stop.

Warrior stomped the frozen ground.

Markus walked a few feet away leaving the horse to munch on the stubs of harvested crops poking up from the soil. Walking to the edge of the forest that bordered his land, he turned and gazed back. Hope died with the sight of nothing but rolling fields of a spent growing season. Clouds grayed the sky, blocking the sun and bringing gloom to his already dead soul.

Emma did not stand waiting for him to arrive home after a long journey. Never again would she smile and tell him to calm himself. There would be no gentle touch when he drank too much at a house party to remind him of his duty to not become like his father. She had left him, not of her own free will, but she had left him alone in the world. For years, he poured all his love into her, matching her goodness with as much heart as he could spare. An empty shell remained and he didn't know how to fill it.

Elizabeth's sweet smile and infectious laughter brought some sense back.

Tears freely rolling down his face, he knelt. The cold seeped into his bones. "Emma, what am I to do?"

The wind howled from the north.

"You were the only thing keeping me from madness. I have become my father without you."

Warrior blew a frustrated puff from his nose and kicked out both back legs.

"How do I go on? Father would drink until he forgot or did not care, but Elizabeth has suffered enough. I want to be the man you loved, but without you, I do not know how."

The temperature dropped a few more degrees with the whip of another wind.

"I have not had a drink in over a week, but I long for one daily. Phoebe has come to help get the house in order. She and Elizabeth are fast friends. She cares for Elizabeth as if she were her own babe. I wish you could see."

Warrior clomped closer and nudged Markus's shoulder.

Markus petted Warrior's silken nose and sat on the cold ground. "What do I do? I have not had a drink. Rosefield is coming back together. I see my daughter, my sweet Elizabeth, and have fallen in love with her. But, Emma, I cannot forgive you. I want to, but I cannot. You left me with nothing."

Shivering in the dropping temperatures, Markus leaned his head against Warrior's lowered nose. He cried until his bones ached and his tears spent. "I must go home before I freeze to death, Emma. Tomorrow I will try to forgive you."

He stood and ran his hand down Warrior's neck. It was comforting to have the horse with him, nudging him back into the saddle. Climbing up, he took a breath and headed for home. His tears abated, replaced by a sense of calm he'd not had in a long time. The time for mourning was passed, and indulging in self-pity had to stop. Becoming a man like Father left him empty and beaten. He wouldn't have it.

Having ridden Warrior hard to reach the edge of his land, he did not exceed a trot on the way back. Killing the horse was not in his plans. At the stables, he took the saddle and bridle off Warrior and brushed the horse down. Extra feed and water in his stall, Markus gave him one last pet along his sinewy neck before walking to the house.

In the few hours he'd been gone, several staff members had arrived to take their posts. Those he remembered from before he'd started drinking he asked to see in his study, where they each received an apology and a bonus check. It was not enough, but it was a start.

Anna, an under-maid, blushed and thanked him as she rushed to leave the study with her bank notes in hand.

"You may leave the door open, Anna."

"Yes, my lord." She curtsied and ran out.

Markus leaned back in his chair and closed his eyes.

"You are a willful and stupid child. I see I have my work cut out for me. Let to run like a wild animal. You are too stupid to even speak. What on earth am I to do with a mute imbecile to govern?" The unfamiliar female voice cut through his moment of peace.

His chest tightened and he stormed toward the hallway.

"Who do you think you are speaking to in that manner, Mrs. Horst?" Phoebe's voice was sharp and as scolding as the new nanny's.

Markus halted in the shadows of the door. Phoebe was too far to the left for him to see, but he had a good view of the hawk-nosed Mrs. Horst and her crisp navy dress with bright white cuffs. Not a single hair escaped her cap, and she narrowed her eyes in Phoebe's direction.

"It is my job to educate this child. I will thank you not to interfere, Miss Hallsmith. After all, you are no one in this house." Mrs. Horst smoothed the front of her dress with a deliberate stroke.

"Elizabeth, come here." Phoebe said.

Elizabeth scurried down the hall.

"In this house, we treat each other with respect. I do not pretend to know what lesson you believe you are teaching by demeaning this child, but it will not happen while I am in charge. Since my time here at Rosefield is short, Mrs. Horst, you may consider your duty here completed."

Markus's heart leaped and he wanted to cheer.

Mrs. Horst's face twisted in ugly rage. "You have no right to sack me."

"I hired you, Madam, and I can fire you just as quickly. In fact, I just did."

"You have no right. I will go to his lordship." She stomped her booted foot.

Phoebe marched into view fists on her hips and Elizabeth clinging to her skirts. "You may do as you please, but you will never speak another word to this child. Lady Elizabeth deserves a nanny who will encourage and cherish her, not a bitter, angry banshee. Do what you like, Mrs. Horst, but do it elsewhere."

"I will see his lordship. You will be the one leaving."

Had anyone ever defended him like that? He hoped his little Elizabeth would always have an advocate like Phoebe to stand at her back. Swallowing down a wave of emotion, Markus stepped into the hall.

Both woman stared, wide-eyed.

Elizabeth smiled, showing all her shiny new teeth.

Having been raised by bullying parents, he knew what it was like to be called stupid. Finding good friends and having a kind nanny was the only thing that had saved him, if he was saved. "You have seen me, Madam. Now you can repack your things and get out of my home. You should count yourself lucky I do not have you flogged for speaking to my child like that. Further, you are fortunate Miss Hallsmith got to you first. I might have physically tossed you from the house had I not had the time to calm my fury."

Stammering, Mrs. Horst made to argue.

Markus pointed toward the stairs. "Go and pack, or I will have you removed with just the clothes on your back."

She ran up the steps, mumbling about pantywaists and madmen.

Lifting Elizabeth into her arms, Phoebe said, "I suppose I must start again to find a proper nanny. I apologize for hiring that woman. On paper, she is quite qualified."

"No apology necessary. I should have listened to your caution and demanded references. One never truly knows from a letter or resume." He took Elizabeth from her arms. "She really was lucky you got to her first just now."

Phoebe's lips quirked into half a smile, making him long to kiss her. "I am certain she knows that now. You were quite intimidating, my lord."

"I used the same tactic when you first arrived and it had no effect." He kissed Elizabeth's forehead.

"I am not easily cowed. Perhaps it is because I have always had to deal with my brothers."

Elizabeth popped her thumb in her mouth and rested her head on his shoulder.

"She's tired. Shall I put her to bed, my lord?"

"My name is Markus and I will take her up, Phoebe. You should get some rest. You look a bit worn out yourself."

"I might say the same about you, Markus." She walked to the servants' door to the kitchens.

"I too had a trying morning."

"Is there anything I can help with?" Her eyes rocked him with her concern shining within.

He swallowed. His arms and legs ached from the hard ride on Warrior and his head pounded from spent emotion. "Perhaps, but not just now. I will put this bundle to bed, then find my own for an hour. Rest is just what I need. Suddenly, I feel about to drop."

"I will just let Mrs. Donnelly and Watson know that Mrs. Horst will be leaving us."

"I'll see you at dinner, Phoebe."

She cocked her head, hand resting on the door. A blush rose in her cheeks and traveled down to where her breasts rose above the cut of her dress. "Yes, dinner. I will see you then, Markus."

He shook off the distraction and longed to know why she blushed. It might have been easier to ask her rather than wondering, but there was something delicious in pondering her emotions.

Elizabeth's fingers curled in the back of his hair, and he kissed her nose. "You and I could both benefit from some rest, my darling."

He put her in her crib and tucked the blanket around her. Already sleeping, she continued sucking her finger and sighed.

Having missed her entire life thus far, regret flooded Markus as he brushed her curls away from her cheek.

In the hallway, Mrs. Donnelly rushed toward him. "My lord, I was just coming to help you."

"With what?"

She searched around him. "With little Elizabeth."

"She is asleep. I go to rest awhile as well. Did you need anything before I retire?"

Mrs. Donnelly fidgeted with a handkerchief. She worried the material to a twisted mess. "I will assign one of the new maids to check on her every few minutes."

"That will be fine, if there is one you trust with the task." He didn't like the idea of a stranger too close to his daughter.

"Faith has returned, my lord. She was here when little Elizabeth was born. I will have her take charge until Miss Hallsmith finds a suitable nanny." She fisted her hands, standing rigid.

"You think it was a mistake to let Mrs. Horst go?" His housekeeper's opinion shouldn't matter, yet she had stayed with him. She loved Elizabeth, and it was strange for her to show temper. If it was directed at him, he wanted to know.

Her expression softened. "I didn't like that one from the moment she set foot in the house. Too haughty by half if you asked me."

"Indeed. She was not appropriate for Elizabeth. I am sure Miss Hallsmith will rectify the situation soon." Yes. Phoebe would fix everything. It was what she did if he was any judge of people.

"Have a good rest, Sir. You look ready to fall out."

He drew in a long breath. "It has been a trying few days."

Pity edged the wrinkled skin around Mrs. Donnelly's eyes. She turned and went into the nursery.

The hallway stretched longer than ever before as his legs struggled to carry him to his own bed. Once there, he flopped on the mattress fully clothed and stared up at the ceiling. Sleep would not come despite his exhaustion. Duck's words spiraled through his mind and refused to cease. There was a catharsis in apologizing to Duck and the other returning staff. Markus's heart was lighter with the understanding that he needed to forgive sweet Emma.

He dragged himself from the bed and crossed to his writing desk in the corner. Dark clouds rolled in as he pulled paper and pen from the drawer. He wrote to his sister, Dorothea, first. His first letter had been all about himself. It was starting to be clear how selfish he truly was. He had neglected her, not been to her concert at the Royal Music Hall. She had done something no woman had done before, and he had been too self-absorbed to attend. He would always regret missing her moment in the sun. He ended the note with an invitation to visit and a suggestion to bring Mother along.

Sighing, he let the dread of that apology shake him. It had to be done and he deserved whatever censure Mother would deliver. He did not extend the invitation to his father. If the blackguard joined the party, he would deal with him. It was an unlikely problem, as Dory and her husband, Tom did not associate with Father any more than Markus.

Once the message was addressed, he rang for Watson and asked it to be posted immediately.

Another layer of dread lifted from Markus as he handed the missive off for delivery. He removed his clothes and climbed into bed.

Chapter 9

No. 8
*An Everton lady will go to bed at a reasonable hour
and rise by dawn.*
—The Everton Companion
Rules of Conduct

It took nearly two weeks for the London agency to send another nanny candidate. Save a valet for his lordship, the rest of the house and grounds were completely staffed. All was in order. Still, Phoebe hesitated to leave Rosefield. She padded down to the kitchen after midnight, knowing the familiar sight of Markus would give her peace.

He smiled when he saw her. "I have pilfered spice biscuits from the pantry. I think Becca was hiding them from us, but she did not do a good job of it. She put them in the empty flour jar, but I know all her tricks by now."

"You're in a good mood." She sat and accepted a biscuit along with the milk he'd poured for them both.

Cocking his head, his expression turned thoughtful. "I am feeling more myself, though even that makes me feel guilty."

"Why would you feel guilty?" Phoebe longed to smooth the crease between his brows.

She had warned herself not to grow attached to a man she could not have. Jared Blunt would be a much more realistic choice, yet her heart did not respond to Jared as it did to Markus. Jared had no interest in her opinions while Markus always listened and gave his thoughts on any matter on her mind. Truthfully, the idea of a lifetime with Jared made her skin crawl, but the next twenty or thirty years alone was a terrifying prospect. She shook off both notions.

"I miss Emma every day, but not with the misery that ruled my life a month ago." He plucked a few crumbs from the plate and ate them.

"And you think this is a bad thing?" She handed him another biscuit.

He sighed and bit off half the biscuit. "I realize how ridiculous I sound. It should be a good thing to have stopped wallowing in my own misery. Yet, this new contentment has brought a new set of problems. I could be happy, but how without Emma? It is wrong to be happy when she is gone."

"Emma would not expect or want you to be unhappy, Markus. No one will ever doubt your love for her." A lump clogged her throat and she forced the last words out.

"A few weeks ago, when you sent me to talk to Duck, he said something that has continued to haunt me."

They had met in the kitchen almost every night, yet he had never mentioned any problems with Duck. "Why did you not say anything? I could have spoken to him about keeping his place."

He shook his head and reached across the table to take her hand. "No. In his way, Duck is wiser than you might think."

It was an innocent touch, but her breath caught and her pulse throbbed in her ears. "What did he say?"

Staring at where their hands touched, he rubbed her fingers before pulling back. His breath shuddered. "He said that I would have to forgive Emma at some point."

"Forgive her for what?"

"For dying."

Mortified, Phoebe prepared to storm out to the cabin where Duck lived and give him a piece of her mind. "He had no right to say such a thing. I am sorry for bullying you into apologizing. I will have a talk with him in the morning."

"Do not do that. He was right, Phoebe. I am angry with her. My rage at the person I loved most in the world is eating me alive. It poisons my heart and soul." He left the remaining bit of biscuit on the plate and stared at the table.

"Why did you not say something to me before, Markus? I would have tried to help." She shook from the tears she held back. His pain flooded her. What he suffered should not be born.

"I was ashamed of these feelings."

"Why are you telling me now?"

He stood and walked to the end of the table. With his back to her, he said, "In the past few weeks I think we have become friends, Phoebe. I need someone to talk to. I need a friend to understand."

Rising, she rounded the table and stopped in front of him. Aching for him in a way she had only ever ached for herself. She empathized with Grand and wanted to ease her pain, but this agony she shared with Markus was different, stronger and all encompassing. "You may always tell me anything, Markus. I wish there was more that I could do for you. I would ease your suffering if I could."

He brushed her hair back from her shoulder and ran the back of his fingers along her jaw. "You listen. That is quite a lot."

Everywhere he touched her set her skin on fire. Here he was telling her his innermost feelings about poor Emma, and she longed for his touch more than she longed to draw breath. She stepped back. "It is nothing."

"Do not pull away from me. Why do you do that each time we get close?" He closed the gap and cupped her cheek. In the light from one candle on the table the green of his eyes glowed, piercing her soul.

To get the words out, she had to swallow down a stone of emotion. "I am not a good person, Markus. What I want is so wrong I pray daily for strength. You will be all right now. It might be best if I take my leave of Rosefield."

Leaning until his lips were only a breath from hers, he said. "You are the best person I have ever met. Nothing you might want could ever be wrong."

Her head told her to pull away, but she lifted onto her toes to reach his lips. Soft and strong they pulled desire from her.

His arms encompassed her.

This was what she wanted. To be in his arms, in his bed, in his life. He devoured her lips and she opened for him, clutching his jacket with both hands.

Phoebe couldn't breathe, didn't want to breathe. She melded to his body like a wanton, drawing his lips and tongue into her mouth and savoring his taste. The voice in her head screamed, *This is wrong.* She shoved against his chest and stumbled until her back hit the counter. "I am sorry, Markus. I cannot do this. I loved Emma, and what we are doing is a mistake. The nanny is hired. I will pack my things and Honoria and I will be out of your house tomorrow."

He called after her as she sprinted from the kitchen.

His footsteps followed her all the way back to her room where she bolted the door and leaned against the cool wood and closed her eyes.

From the hallway, his voice filtered through the door. "I know you can hear me, Phoebe. These feelings I have for you may be wrong, but I cannot deny them. I assume by your distress that you share the same feelings, but if all of this is too difficult, I will keep my place and not pursue you. Please do not leave yet. Elizabeth and Rosefield still need you. I need you." The light clomp of his footsteps moved further away until they faded. She opened her eyes to the moonlit room and stared into the eyes of Honoria. Her heart jumped into her throat and she stifled the scream. "Good Lord, Honoria, you scared me to death."

"Clearly not." Honoria stood from the chair near the dwindling hearth.

"What are you doing in my room?" Phoebe added a piece of wood to the fire and waited for it to catch. Winter was nearly upon them and the drafty house grew cold.

"I heard a noise but when I got here you were not in your bed. I know of your habit of snacking in the wee hours, so I waited to make sure you were all right." She cocked her head. "Are you all right?"

Flopping into the other chair, she puffed out the breath she'd been holding. "I hardly know."

"Has his lordship fallen in love with you?" Honoria sat with her hands in her lap. Her gaze piercing, she held back the quirk of a smile.

"No. He is fond of me, perhaps, but love...No. Still, I think it best if we leave tomorrow morning." Resolved to do the sensible thing, she tugged her wrapper tighter and made a mental list of things she would do in the morning to make sure Rosefield was in order.

Honoria stood and rounded the chair. She put her hands on the high back and watched Phoebe. "If you think that is best, my dear. From where I stand, it seems you might like to stay here awhile. After all, two men vying for your attention at one location is cause to stay rather than flee."

"I know at my age I should be begging one of them to marry me, but..."

"Do you love one of them? Maybe both of them." A full smile burst onto Honoria's face and she made no attempt to hide her glee, clapping and letting her eyes go dreamy.

"I most certainly do not love them. Love is for fools."

"Your friend Emma was no fool and she clearly loved his lordship. Why should you think loving him would be foolish?"

Flustered, Phoebe added more wood to the fire. "I am not in love with anyone, so the point is moot."

"Fine, no need to burn the house down, Phoebe. If you wish to leave, we will leave."

It took a force of will to push the next words out. "I do wish to leave."

In truth, she wished for a great many things, none of which included leaving Markus and none of which were possible. Leaving was the only option. The nanny, Miss Walker, had arrived and appeared kind, if not very bright. She would be fine. Phoebe had wished for someone sharper, but Miss Walker was the best the agency could offer for the moment.

"I will have Margery pack my things after we break our fast. Good night, my dear." Honoria walked to the door. "I am sure Mr. Blunt will continue his interest in London. He hardly seems the type to let distance stand in his way."

"Good night, Honoria."

When the door closed, Phoebe opened the window to let some cool air in. The roaring fire had turned the bedroom into an oven. She rolled her eyes and wished Grand was there to give her advice.

* * * *

The servants whispered at the bottom of the stairs when Phoebe came down to break her fast. "What is going on?"

Mrs. Donnelly broke from the cluster and shooed the maids back to work. "It has been an interesting morning, Miss."

"Has it?" Phoebe reached the bottom step and waited for more information. Interesting could be good or bad. Arwen was in her room, packing her things. Whatever it was, it would make no difference in a few hours. She would go back to Everton and await her next assignment.

"Oh yes. Mr. Blakely, his lordship's valet, has returned and the two have been closeted in the study for nearly an hour."

There, all was well. She could leave in good conscience knowing Markus was fine. "That is good news."

"There is more. His lordship fired Miss Walker within moments of waking this morning. It seems he gave her a month's pay and put her in his carriage back to London."

Phoebe's stomach clenched. "Why on earth would he do that? I know she wasn't perfect, but she was all that was available."

Mrs. Donnelly shrugged. "His lordship did not explain his actions to me. Why would he? He just said she would be leaving and sent the new driver, Dobson, to take her all the way back to London. Fine style to travel for a girl of her status."

"It took two weeks to get that nanny. Lord only knows how long it will take me to find another with whatever qualifications his lordship wants." Phoebe sat on the bottom step and put her head in her hands. What was she to do now? She couldn't leave Elizabeth to be raised by maids and cooks, no matter how kind they were.

The door to Markus's study opened and a thin-faced man in his mid-thirties exited. He nodded to Mrs. Donnelly and took the steps two at a time.

Phoebe walked to the threshold of the open study door.

Markus sat behind his desk penning a note.

"What have you done?" she asked.

He looked at her then back at his note. "I am writing to my brother, Adam, at Eton. I have a note from my sister that they will visit and wanted to see if my brother might join us as well."

"That is all well and good, but why did you fire Miss Walker?"

He put his writing aside. "She was unsuitable to the job."

"How so?" Remaining in the door meant that when Honoria descended the stairs, she walked directly into the conversation.

"You fired the nanny already?" Honoria walked past Phoebe and sat in the chair near the desk.

"I did, my lady. I found the girl to be inept."

Honoria fussed with the lace at her sleeve. "In what way?"

"I just asked that." Phoebe gave in and sat in the other chair.

"This morning when I came down, she was sitting on the stool in the alcove sewing a piece of scrap. I was sure Elizabeth was awake by that time so I asked her what she was doing. She said she never went to get a child before eight bells. I thought that a strange rule, but perhaps not so terrible. It might teach Elizabeth patience if she had to wait. So, I asked Miss Walker what she intended to teach Elizabeth today and she said they would learn some geography. Intrigued, I asked how she would teach a child of two such a topic, and she said she would show Elizabeth shapes. At that point, I explained her services would not be needed, paid her for one month, and sent for the carriage."

Honoria bubbled with laughter.

"You could have given her more time." Phoebe's declaration lacked conviction, even to herself.

His smile was warm and stunning and Phoebe wanted to cry. "Time to learn the difference between geography and geometry? I think she might have learned that long before she was meant to teach my daughter. But to be fair, I did inquire about her command of language and it turned out she only spoke English. No French or German as her references indicated."

"We were leaving today."

Markus stood. "If you must go, I understand. You are welcome to stay, of course. My family will arrive at the end of the week, and it would be nice if someone was here to care for Elizabeth properly. However, I can manage on my own for a month or so until a proper nanny can be hired."

Imagining him fumbling around with Elizabeth's care and perhaps becoming overwhelmed and taking to drink again rocked Phoebe's resolve to leave. "I will go and tell our maids to stop packing. You really must stop firing the staff, my lord."

Laughing still, Honoria followed her out but went to the breakfast room when Phoebe climbed the stairs.

When she returned to break her fast, she was ravenous and filled her plate from the delights on the sideboard. He had manipulated her into staying. Why?

Becca brought her chocolate.

Jared arrived and sat next to her. "You look lovely this morning, Miss Hallsmith."

Men and their useless compliments. She was tired and hungry and had not bothered to smooth her curls. Nothing about her was lovely, yet he issued the compliment anyway. "I thank you, Mr. Blunt. You are here early."

"Yes. His lordship and I have a busy day."

"I'm sure you do." She stuffed a piece of sausage in her mouth, hoping it would deter further conversation.

"I finally got an audience with your brother yesterday."

The notion of her brother Ford was enough to make the food in her stomach churn. "How nice for you."

"It was a good meeting." There was something smarmy about his smile.

She hadn't noticed it before, but her skin crawled. Determined not to ask, she bit into some coddled eggs.

Clearing his throat, he leaned forward so she was forced to look at him. "I have not gained his approval to court you, though he did not outright deny my petition. He mentioned something about another offer being imminent. Is this true?"

Tension forced her back straight. Ford was up to something and that was never good. "Mr. Blunt, I cannot imagine what he is talking about. As I told you, I am estranged from my family."

His frown deepened and a nasty little grunt pushed up from his chest. "You really should make amends. It is unfortunate for a woman to be without friends."

"Mr. Blunt, I believe you have just overstepped your bounds. Please refrain from any further advice with regard to my life and how I live it."

He huffed. "I only meant…"

Elizabeth giggled and Mrs. Donnelly used the opportunity to push a spoonful of porridge into her mouth. Making bubbles with the gruel made the most disgusting mess roll down her sweet face.

Jared gagged. "Is it necessary for that child to be at the table with adults? Shouldn't she be fed in the kitchen or nursery?"

Phoebe took longer than necessary to chew and swallow her sausage. A lifetime of simple things disgusting Jared flashed through her mind. She supposed he would not look upon his own children until they were of school age for fear of vomiting at the least bit of mess. "His lordship likes to have Lady Elizabeth close at hand during meals. He was here a moment ago. Perhaps you would like to discuss his daughter's care before your important business?"

Mrs. Donnelly smothered a laugh and scooped the food from Elizabeth's chin and back into her mouth.

Another gag from Jared. He might become sick from watching a baby eat. "It is not my place to discuss such things, but I was not allowed to eat with my parents until I was out of school."

Phoebe's appetite fled. "No. It is not your place. You should go to the study."

Just noting her annoyance, he stood. "I will be here for several hours. Perhaps you and I could walk in the garden later today when the sun warms the ground a little."

"I am very busy today." It was too bad Ford's lack of approval hadn't dissuaded Jared's attempt at courting.

"Doing what?" His sharp tone set her teeth grinding.

The feeding had stopped in light of the argument building between Phoebe and Jared. Mrs. Donnelly and Elizabeth both watched with wide eyes and open mouths. "I need not report to you, Mr. Blunt. When a lady tells you she is too busy to walk in the garden, you should be polite and say you will see her another time. Just as when a child of a viscount is fed in the breakfast room, you might say nothing and mind your own business. I wonder that this need to correct the behavior of others is not a flaw in your own character. If you will excuse me." She stood, dropped her napkin on her chair and turned toward the door.

Honoria stood in the threshold grinning like she was watching a stage play.

"Must you be at the center of everything all the time?" Phoebe rushed past and up the steps.

"Time to go to work, Mr. Blunt. It seems you have done quite enough here." Honoria's voice lilted after Phoebe.

She reached her room, and thankfully Arwen had finished her duties. The room was blissfully empty. Opening the window, Phoebe let the cold blast ease her annoyance. Men always wanted to change things to suit themselves. Some wanted to change women too, but Phoebe could not and would not change. That had become clear in Scotland. She would never make that mistake again.

A knock startled her and the cold sank in. "Come in."

Markus opened the door and stepped inside. He left the door standing open. "I heard yelling, then stomping. Are you all right?"

"I am fine. Can no one leave me in peace?"

He took a step back. "You are angry with me?"

"No. I am tired of men who think they know better." Returning her gaze to the garden, she watched Duck shooing some goats from the path toward the gate.

"I am not at all certain what you are talking about, but I can assure you I do not know better about anything. I hope that makes you feel more content."

"Oh, but you think you do, Markus. You thought it would be better to fire the nanny before we found a new one."

He stepped close until he stood just behind her. "Is that what you are upset about? Perhaps I should have consulted you, but at the time I felt the girl was completely unsuitable and would do more harm than good."

"It does not matter." She turned, but his closeness was too much, and she skirted him and stood near the hearth. "Your family is coming to visit and I should not be here. Honoria and I will leave as soon as I can arrange for another nanny. Even if it takes a little while for her to arrive, I see no need for me to stay. Elizabeth is safe and in better spirits since you are taking time with her. I will only need a few days to communicate with the agency and make the arrangements."

Fisting his hands, he stood straight as a tree. "If you are so keen to go, then you should go now. I can certainly pen a letter to the agency. Though I do not see what you are in such a rush to get back to."

It took her several full breaths to be sure her voice would be steady. "My life, you arrogant man. I have a life. I missed all my best years taking care of my ailing grandmother. I should be married with children by now but instead I am taking care of you and your family."

"Then you will go off and help someone else. What life is it that you have? I find this self-pitying side of you unpleasant, Phoebe. You went to take care of your grandmother because it was the right thing to do. You have spent the last month here, because you knew we needed you. If you want to go, then go, but do not blame me. You made your choices, and if I recall, I did not want you to come here to begin with."

He was right, of course. Slumping into the chair, she sighed and put her head in her hands. "I never regretted my decision to care for Grand. I had five wonderful years with her and nearly married in Scotland. It would have been nice to have had a season in London where I could have enjoyed myself with youthful enthusiasm and not worried that I was too old. My life this last year has been tolerable, and I have people to take care of with each Everton assignment."

His expression softened and he sat next to her. "I do not want to fight, Phoebe. I only wanted to make certain that Blunt had not upset you. Now I see that whatever has upset you goes beyond Blunt or even me. You may tell me anything. I am your friend, and will listen to whatever worries you have."

Impossible. He was the last person she could ever talk to about her problems. "I thank you for your kindness, Markus, but I am fine. My only problem stems from a lack of sleep for far too many nights."

"This is something I can understand. Maybe we are going about it the wrong way. Eating each night does not seem to get us anywhere, but it has added to my waistline." He laughed and the sound tingled along her skin.

"What do you suggest?"

"Meet me in my study tonight instead of the kitchen. Perhaps a little reading would be better medicine than pie and biscuits."

A clandestine meeting was a big mistake, yet she didn't have the strength or desire to say no to him. Only a fool would meet a man who she could never have in his study in the middle of the night. "If I cannot sleep tonight, I will come to the study."

Chapter 10

No. 15
*An Everton lady will never bring her personal issues to
the client's attention.*
—*The Everton Companion*
Rules of Conduct

Having the impossible had been Markus's goal for as long as he could remember. He'd wanted parents who were loving and kind. Of course, that wish was out of his control. He had wanted Emma and had done everything in his power to win her. No man could have wooed a lady more devoutly.

Wanting Phoebe was out of the question and yet he stood in his study looking through tomes of poetry and verse in search of the perfect remedy to insomnia. A few weeks ago, a nice brandy or ten would have been the thing he reached for, and though he wanted one badly, he refrained and searched the shelves.

She cleared her throat, producing the most delicate sound.

Turning, his heart leapt in his chest. She appeared iridescent in her white nightclothes with a pale blue blanket wrapped around her. In the lantern-lit study, her state of undress was more intimate than it had been in the kitchen. "You came."

"Foolish, I know, but I could not sleep." She tugged her blanket tighter around her shoulders and stepped inside.

"I trust you had no more issues with Mr. Blunt today?" His hand rested on the binding of a book and he pulled it down.

Phoebe flounced down onto the couch at the far end of the study and pulled her feet under the blanket. "Mr. Blunt said Ford did not give him permission to court me and he avoided me today. Perhaps that will be the end of his courting."

"I am sorry."

"Why?"

"I thought you liked Mr. Blunt." He sat next to her, placing the book on the cushion between them.

She shrugged. "He is a man from a good family and has a steady income. I suppose he would suit, and my mother would be happy to see me married to anyone at this point."

"What does Honoria have to say on the matter?" Suddenly, his secretary was the most abhorrent man he'd ever known.

"I do not think she is very fond of Mr. Blunt. Though I cannot say why."

The way she scrunched her nose when she was thinking warmed him like nothing else. "You did not say if you are upset by the idea of the loss of his affection."

"Did I not?" Plucking at the edge of the blanket, she let the cloth relax, revealing the swell of her breasts above the neckline of her nightgown.

Markus swallowed the lump in his throat. "No. You only told me how everyone else might feel."

She shrugged. "I suppose that is because I have little feeling on the subject. That is probably not a good way to think of a prospective suitor."

"Probably not," he agreed, but joy swamped him from head to toe.

"Have you found something boring enough to put us to sleep?" She nodded toward the book.

Holding it up he read the title. "*Shakespeare's Sonnets.* Not really for sleeping but it's better than eating every sweet in the kitchen."

She leaned in closer when he opened the book. "Will you read aloud to me, Markus?"

"Sit closer, so if you get tired you might rest your head on my shoulder." A silly ploy, but it worked and soon the heat of her body pressed against his side. It was a tiny bit of heaven to have her close with the warm clean scent of her filling him. He read:

Let me not to the marriage of true minds
Admit impediments. Love is not love
Which alters when it alteration finds,
Or bends with the remover to remove.

O no! it is an ever-fixed mark
That looks on tempests and is never shaken;
It is the star to every wand'ring bark,
Whose worth's unknown, although his height be taken.
Love's not Time's fool, though rosy lips and cheeks
Within his bending sickle's compass come;
Love alters not with his brief hours and weeks,
But bears it out even to the edge of doom.
If this be error and upon me prov'd,
I never writ, nor no man ever lov'd.

Never in his life had he read a poem and had the words rivet him so directly. He'd chosen randomly when he opened the book, yet Sonnet 116 fell from his lips as if it had been written just for them.

Her breath was quick and shallow and she turned up her chin to meet his gaze. "That was not boring."

No man could resist such temptation. "Not boring. I know you think this is wrong, but I would like to kiss you now, Phoebe."

"I would like for you to kiss me, Markus."

Pushing the book aside, he captured her lips with his. Soft breath escaped her mouth as she gasped. When she breathed out, he breathed in as if they were one entity. He found the edge of the blanket and slipped his hands beneath where the soft cotton gown was the only separation between his fingers and her sweet flesh. "Phoebe."

She clutched his shirt, pulling him closer, then wrapped her arm around his neck while the other caressed his back.

Everything he wanted pulsed in his arms but was still out of reach. "I want you, Phoebe."

Gasping, she pushed away. "Markus, this is not right. Emma was my closest friend."

Easing his hold, he did not relinquish her completely. "I know that, but my feelings are what they are."

"I am not worthy of you. I am disowned by my family. Even with all your troubles you must know that attaching yourself to me would be scandalous. Nothing about this is appropriate. All we can ever be is friends." She toyed with the tie at the top of his blouse and her breath tickled his neck.

"You are so far superior to me, it does not bare mentioning. Let society be dammed, I need you."

When she drew in a long breath her breasts pressed tight to his chest. Delicious desire curled in his groin, but he made no move to take what he wanted most in the world. Their future had to be Phoebe's decision. Any other way would always leave doubts between them.

She pressed her forehead to his shoulder. "Must we talk of this, Markus? My mind is so jumbled with a million things and confused by lack of sleep. Would it be too much to ask that we just rest here?"

Holding her in his arms for a few hours was much more than he'd hoped for when he asked her to meet him. A few minutes of her time was all he had expected. The kiss still left its wondrous impression on his heart and her heat still warmed his soul. "I would be honored to hold you while you sleep."

Her lids fluttered closed and her muscles eased against him.

Leaning back, he let her body form to his and brushed the hair away from her cheek before he closed his eyes and leaned his head back.

* * * *

"I have no idea what to say," Honoria said.

It ripped him from sleep. Sun shone through the windows, blinding him for several beats.

She turned and shut the study door.

"Honoria, I can explain." Phoebe pushed against his chest to disengage herself from his embrace.

The loss was keen but unavoidable. "Perhaps I should explain, my lady."

"We were only sleeping. Nothing happened." Panic laced Phoebe's words.

Honoria crossed her arms over her chest. "Only sleeping? Nothing happened? This is not how you were raised, Phoebe Hallsmith. Women of good standing do not 'sleep' with men. What were you thinking?"

Rising, Phoebe hung her head. "That I would do anything for a good night's sleep."

Looking from one to the other, Honoria shook her head. Her gaze settled on Markus "I have clearly failed in my duties as a chaperon, but what do you intend to do about it, my lord?"

He rubbed his eyes. Had nothing happened? For him, quite a lot had changed in the last eight hours. Falling asleep with Phoebe in his arms had been one of the most wonderful moments in his life, but for her it had only meant a restful sleep. "I am prepared to make an offer if Miss Hallsmith wishes it."

Phoebe spun, eyes wide and arms clutching her blue blanket. "Offer. You would marry me because we were caught asleep in the study?"

"It is the right thing to do. Despite what you might think of me, I am a gentleman." It wasn't exactly the romantic proposal a woman wishes for. In fact, it was even disappointing from his perspective. Still, the idea of waking to Phoebe in his arms every day for the rest of his life filled him with more joy than he should ever expect. Guilt hovered over him.

Phoebe threw her hands up. "The right thing to do? This is not a reason to marry a person, and I will not be bullied into a marriage because I had not slept in weeks and dozed off in the study."

After Phoebe had fled the room, Honoria once again closed the door. "Do you love Miss Hallsmith?"

It was rude to sit in the presence of a standing woman, but Markus sat on the couch and put his head in his hands. "I do not know. She makes me feel, and I did not think that would ever be possible again."

Skirts flouncing about her legs, Honoria paced the study with one hand on her chin. "If you want her, you will have to win her, my lord. I will not pressure her about this incident. As long as the details remain a secret between the three of us, you will not be forced to marry her. It is not my intention to make either of you unhappy." She sat across from him on a wooden bench between the bookcases.

"Marrying Phoebe would not make me unhappy, but as you saw, she is not as keen on the idea." Between the guilt over his feelings for Phoebe and her rejection, Markus longed for a large draft of brandy.

"She is confused. Her time in Scotland taught her that men, even men who profess love, cannot be trusted."

"Phoebe honored me with some of what happened between her and Mr. Durnst."

Covering her mouth with one hand, Honoria said, "Did she?"

"It seems we both have trouble sleeping and have a habit of stealing off to the kitchen for a late-night snack. She trusted me with a few details of her engagement to that imbecile."

Honoria stood. "You should marry her, my lord. I cannot make her see that. Phoebe has the kindest heart in all the world, but she rarely affects her kindness on herself. She is stubborn and suspicious of anything that might bring her happiness. I will do what I can, but it will be up to you to win her."

Heart pounding, he rose. "Forgive me, Lady Chervil, but I am surprised by your approval. I am not exactly what most women would want in a husband. Not even the marriage mart mommas would advocate my bid for one of their daughters."

She laughed, actually gave a hearty guffaw. "You are a man with many flaws and a sad past." She shrugged and sighed. "Still, Phoebe must love you or she would not have slept here or trusted you with her secrets. Even if she does not yet know her own feelings, I have known her long enough to see that she is not given to emotional disclosure."

Love him? It was impossible. How could anyone love the man he'd become? No, not become, but revealed. His father had been lurking inside him for his entire life and losing Emma freed the bastard. "I am sure you are mistaken, my lady. Phoebe is far too smart to ever harbor deep feelings for a man like me."

"One would think." She chortled as she left the room.

He needed a bath and a long think.

Blakely waited, standing like a statue, in the master's chambers as if he had never been away. His long pale face was a welcome sight. "My lord, you look refreshed."

"I finally got a good night's sleep. Would you arrange a bath and keep anyone who might need me away for an hour or so, Blakely?"

"Of course, my lord. Watson tells me Mr. Blunt has already been asking for you this morning. He tried to enter the study but was sent away."

The magnitude of the disaster that had been averted sent a shiver up Markus's spine. He adored the idea of Phoebe being his, but not like that. Not forced to marry because an idiot couldn't keep his mouth shut. Markus was sure Blunt was such an idiot. It might be time to find a new secretary. "It is good to have you back."

"Thank you, my lord."

* * * *

Despite a thorough search of all the rooms in the house where he usually found Phoebe, he did not find her. In the nursery, Arwen played patty-cake with Elizabeth and both smiled up at him when he poked his head in.

The game stopped and Elizabeth ran toward him with her arms up for lifting.

"Good morning. Did you sleep well?"

She patted his cheek and grinned at him.

"I did too. Perhaps we can have a ride in the country this afternoon. The weather is growing cold, and we will not get many more days to ride."

Clapping, she planted a wet kiss on his cheek.

Arwen crossed to them. "Your father has to work this morning, Miss. Come, we'll get you into something warm and go for a walk in the garden."

He relinquished Elizabeth into Arwen's care. "Where is Miss Hallsmith? "She has a visitor." Arwen frowned.

"Is it Lord Thornbury?" What bad timing if Phoebe's eldest brother had arrived. Tugging on his jacket, he was ready to go do battle at Phoebe's side.

"No, my lord. Mr. Gavin Durnst has come all the way from Scotland, and it seems when he did not find the miss at her family home last night, he came here first thing this morning."

The news shook Markus in his boots. Forcing himself to use a reasonable voice, he asked, "Where are they?"

"In the back parlor, my lord."

It took all his will to calmly bid Elizabeth and Arwen goodbye before he rushed downstairs to the back parlor. Standing outside the door, he breathed in and let it out slowly. His jealousy would not go over well. Yes, it was jealousy, which he had no right to. Despite their friendship and night in the study, Phoebe did not belong to him. She had made it clear that she would leave when her assignment was finished, and after that, it was unlikely their paths would cross again. It had only been his manipulation and the terribly inept governess that kept her at Rosefield.

Pulling the door open, he stifled the urge to act the jealous lover.

Phoebe stared at him with wide eyes while her visitor narrowed his. Gavin Durnst was better looking than Markus had hoped. Blond curls fell to his shoulders, and Markus longed to blacken both of his sharp blue eyes.

"Miss Hallsmith, I heard you had company. I hope I am not intruding." Markus forced a smile and stepped inside.

Light shone in the tall windows from the garden. Phoebe's pale blue dress matched the winter sky. She stood, as did Durnst. "My lord, this is Mr. Gavin Durnst, an acquaintance from Scotland."

Durnst bowed before stepping closer and offering his hand. "More than an acquaintance. Miss Hallsmith and I were betrothed."

The short, brisk shake was more than Markus cared for. "Yet the lady described you as such and I shall take her at her word. Besides, if you were betrothed, would you not still be?"

The question took Durnst back a step. "I—we…had a misunderstanding, which I hope to rectify. It is the reason I have come all this way. I stopped at the Hallsmith estate and was horrified to hear that my dear Phoebe had taken a position of service."

"Horrified, really." Bashing Durnst over the head with the fireplace poker flashed through Markus's mind.

Phoebe sat. "I was explaining to Mr. Durnst that I am not forced to work for the Everton Domestic Society. It was my choice to go and I have no intention of quitting the post."

The band strangling Markus's heart eased an inch. "I see."

Crossing his arms, Durnst shot Phoebe a scathing look before settling his gaze on Markus. "I have, of course, ordered Miss Hallsmith back to her family's home until such time as I can have a contract drawn up for our renewed engagement."

Markus strode to the settee and sat next to Phoebe. He stretched his legs out and forced his expression to be mild. "Let me see if I understand you correctly, Mr. Durnst. You broke off an engagement with Miss Hallsmith, she has moved on with her life, and now you find you cannot live without her?"

"That is correct, my lord. I realize I made a grave mistake." Durnst sat in the wingback chair, his back straight as a pole.

"What was the catalyst for this realization?" Markus had seen the type before. Pretty, dim, and ruthless. He would have hated Gavin Durnst even if his jealousy had not forced the disgust.

"I do not know what you mean. I am here because my feelings for Miss Hallsmith have not altered in her absence and I mean to have her as my wife."

Markus leaned forward and put his elbows on his knees. "Miss Hallsmith, is that what you wish as well?"

"Of course not. I have no intention of marrying him."

Durnst stood and took two steps forward so that he towered over Phoebe. "I have the wishes of your family on my side, Phoebe. You will do as your brother and mother wish or you will come to no good."

Phoebe leaned back. Her eyebrow lifted. "What else have you been promised by my brother Ford? Was a dowry offered? Land? Why am I suddenly the object of your affection again when you thought me a cold fish when you ended our arrangement in Scotland?"

Neck on fire, it was becoming impossible for Markus to hold his temper. "I leave it to the lady, but in my mind, you should leave this house, Mr. Durnst. It seems your attentions are not wanted."

Cool demeanor slipping, Durnst's face turned nearly purple. "You have no choice but to marry me. Ford is the head of your family and so what if he sweetened the pot with a few things? You did not dispute the inclusion of your dowry when you agreed to marry me before."

Phoebe opened her mouth.

The door burst open and Jared Blunt stumbled through. "Stop. Miss Hallsmith is going to marry me."

"No, I most certainly am not." Phoebe stood.

The entire scene was becoming comical, though Phoebe did not look amused. Gavin and Jared stood nose-to-nose arguing over which of them would marry Phoebe, and her face was bright red. Her hands fisted, and it was possible she would punch one or both of them.

Markus closed his eyes and pushed down his jealousy. "Enough!" Rising to his feet, Markus had to bite his tongue for a full beat. "If you gentlemen wish to fight over a woman who just said she will not marry either of you, you can do so elsewhere. Miss Hallsmith works for me and is therefore under my protection until such time as she decides to leave Rosefield. Until that time, Mr. Durnst, you will refrain from visiting, and Mr. Blunt, you will limit your time at Rosefield to working with me. If Miss Hallsmith wishes to see you, she will alert you and advise me of her decision. Have I made myself clear?"

"Perfectly clear, my lord." Blunt hung his head and spoke to the carpet.

Durnst met Markus's gaze. "I understand, my lord. I intend to seek satisfaction with Lord Thornbury, and we shall see what he says."

"You may do as you please, Sir. As long as you do it elsewhere."

A growl issued from Phoebe. It was the most unladylike sound and she stomped her foot. "I have had enough of all of you telling me what I will or won't do. All three of you are on my last nerve. I joined the Everton Domestic Society because of men like you trying to push me around and decide my life for me."

Markus couldn't fathom why she lumped him in with the other two. He only sent them away. Before he could ask, she hurried out of the parlor.

"I hadn't realized Miss Hallsmith had such a temper," Blunt said.

"I've seen worse. It's the red hair." Durnst shook his head and took up his hat and gloves from the table.

Knuckles white from holding back, Markus narrowed his gaze on the two idiots. "You should both leave now. I do not care for the way you spoke to or about Miss Hallsmith."

Blunt stepped toward the door, but Durnst came closer. "What is your interest in the lady, my lord? You seem far too involved for her to just be someone in your employ."

"I do not care for your tone, Durnst."

"I do not care for my fiancée living under the same roof with another man." The purple had returned to his face and he stepped closer.

Markus longed to break his perfect nose, but Durnst had more claim to Phoebe than Markus had. It was maddening and his own fault. "I do not decide where the lady works. She has an employer and a chaperon.

However, as long as she is in this house, I will not have her harassed by either of you. Get out before I have you tossed out."

The rise in his voice did the trick and both men took their leave.

Chapter 11

No. 21
An Everton lady will discourage any client from romantic thoughts or actions.
—*The Everton Companion*
Rules of Conduct

Men were the most infuriating creatures. Phoebe stalked along the path. Several under-gardeners were pruning back the plants allowed to grow wild for months. As she passed, they backed away, giving her room. Winter was bringing cold, but there was still time to put some order to the chaos. If only Phoebe's problems could be solved with a few snips and shears.

Between her stupid brother Ford and the three inside Rosefield, she was ready to declare she would never speak to another man for as long as she lived. If only that were possible. Still, she would not be bullied into marriage by anyone.

Phoebe pushed through the gate and out toward the open fields surrounding the property.

The cold seeped through her dress, as she did not stop to take a wrap or coat. Stopping, it was obvious she couldn't get far without the proper outerwear.

"Miss Hallsmith?" Honoria spoke from behind her.

Ready to tell Honoria everything, Phoebe turned. Open-mouthed, she was stopped by the presence of Duck walking next to Honoria. "Mr. Duck. How do you do?"

"Fine, Miss. I'll just be letting you ladies talk. I have work to get back to. Thank you for the walk, my lady." He nodded and ambled toward the barn. Honoria stepped closer. "Why are you out here without a wrap? You'll catch your death."

"I needed to escape a pack of men who I would have preferred to bash over their thick skulls." Phoebe rubbed her arm doing little to relieve her freezing state.

"Let's get you inside and you can tell me all about it over a nice hot cup of tea." Honoria pulled Phoebe close and shared her wool wrap with her as they walked to the house.

Once closed in a small parlor upstairs, Honoria called for tea while one of the new maids built a fire.

"Is there something I should know about you and Mr. Duck, Honoria?" With a sigh, Honoria sat back. "He is a nice man and a widower. We have much to talk about and it's nice to speak with a man of my own age. However, he is not for me if that is what you mean. If I ever decide to marry a fourth husband, it will be because he has money and position. I can remain friends with Mr. Duck without having to become Mrs. Duck." She giggled at the idea. "But that is not why you were storming around the garden in nothing but your day dress. Something sent you out without a care for your health. What was it, Phoebe?"

"Gavin Durnst made a financial arrangement with Ford to marry me. Mr. Blunt thinks he has some claim on me though I have given him no encouragement. And Lord Devonrose thinks he can order everyone about." She wished she could take the last back. It was weak even to her own ear.

"He is the viscount and this is his home. Did he renew his wish to marry you?" Honoria sat forward.

Phoebe's heart ached. "No. He only told the others that they should go, as I was not interested in their attentions."

"So, he was protecting you?"

"Yes. No. I do not know. He doesn't want me, so why should he protect me?" The dull ache in her chest spread until she longed to go to her bed, roll into a ball, and weep for a few days.

"He said he would marry you. Do you find his lordship to be a dishonest man?" The door opened and Honoria held up her hand, stopping anything Phoebe might have said.

Katy brought the tea, set it on the table, curtsied, and left the room.

When the door was closed, Honoria asked, "Do you?"

The truth was torturous. "He only said what he said because he is a gentleman and you caught us alone together."

"Sleeping. It is not common to sleep with a man whom you are not romantically attached to, Phoebe. And I doubt his lordship would have said he would marry you if it was not something he wanted."

"He is the husband of my dear friend. He still loves Emma. I am beneath him since Ford has disowned me. Even though Ford seems to have forgotten his decree, it would be a scandalous match. Perhaps when Papa was still alive, but certainly not now. Nothing will change any of those things. Most of all, I cannot love Emma's husband. The idea of it rips me in two." Phoebe dropped her head into her hands and prayed the entire situation would disappear. She could go pack her things and return to London. Maybe Lady Jane would let her hide in her room for a few weeks until it all blew over.

Honoria sat next to her and took her hand, forcing Phoebe to sit up and look at her. "First, Markus Flammel is not anyone's husband. He is a widower and has been for two years."

Phoebe opened her mouth to push the second point forward, but Honoria shushed her.

"Second, he does love Emma and he always will. That fact will not change and should not. It does not mean that he has no room in his heart for another. He clearly is attracted to you, and you like him. Neither one of you can sleep but you managed to look quite comfortable on the couch together. There must be some level of friendship and trust to have found rest together. As to your third, it is not relevant. You are the daughter of a viscount and a gentleman and he is a viscount and a gentleman. There is nothing keeping you or him from acting on your desires. As to your feelings, you must work that out for yourself. He is an eligible man and you might be happy together. Life does not give us that many opportunities for happiness, my dear. Keep that in mind when you toss one away."

"I had no idea you made speeches, Honoria." Phoebe pulled her hand away and poured the tea.

"I am not finished." Honoria took the offered tea and sipped. "All of that being said, you do not have to marry anyone. You are an Everton lady. You can refuse all three offers of marriage and stay with the Everton Domestic Society. You can one day take on the role of an Everton Dowager and travel with younger women as they do their jobs. It is not a bad life. I quite enjoy it."

"But you do not have to do it, Honoria, dear friend. You have the means and an estate where you could go if you wished." Phoebe sipped her tea.

"True, and you do not have to, either. You could apologize to you mother and brother and go home, or you could accept one of your proposals and become Mrs. Someone. It is entirely up to you. How wonderful for a young lady to have so many choices."

Phoebe was torn between her desire to stay with Markus, her duty as an Everton lady, and her loyalty to Emma. "I think we should find a nanny for Elizabeth, then return to London."

Sadness shone in Honoria's eyes. "Then that is what we will do."

* * * *

Phoebe kissed Elizabeth goodnight and went down to dinner.

Markus stood at the bottom of the stairs waiting. "You look lovely, Phoebe."

The dark blue satin had been a whim. If she was to take control of her own life, she would do it looking her best. At least that was what she told herself when looking at the daring neckline in the glass. "Thank you. Why are you waiting here? Is something wrong?"

"Must my attentions to you always indicate a problem?" He frowned and offered his arm.

"It is not so much that they must, as that they always have." Taking his arm, she thrilled at the warmth that light touch brought.

"Perhaps a change is in order. I used to be quite self-sufficient, you know. I managed my lands and my father's for many years before things fell apart." He led her into the study where Honoria, dressed in lavender and white lace, waited already with a drink in hand.

"I am aware of that, my lord." She dropped her hand away from his arm. "Honoria, what are you drinking?"

"Champagne, my dear. I recommend you have a glass. It is very fine."

A new footman, whose name Phoebe couldn't remember, poured her a flute of the bubbly liquid. "Thank you."

"Nothing for me, Peter," Markus said. "I have some news, ladies."

A surge of pride swelled in Phoebe. Here was an opportunity for him to break his promise without guilt, but he didn't. She put the champagne back on the tray. "What news?"

Turning, he leaned on the desk. "A letter arrived from my sister an hour ago. It seems she, my brother-in-law, and my mother will be arriving tomorrow. They are anxious to see me, and Tom was able to wrap up some business earlier than expected."

"How nice. You will be happy to see them, and Elizabeth will get to know them better."

"I will be happy for them to get to know you ladies as well." He included Honoria, but his gaze never left Phoebe.

Lord, what was she doing? "It might be best if we returned to London and gave you time with your family, Markus."

"I see no reason why you cannot continue in your capacity as my assistant while my family is here. There is still the matter of finding a suitable nanny for Elizabeth." Where he gripped the desk, his knuckles turned white.

She searched for some reason to leave other than she was unsuitable for him to court. Since they weren't courting, she couldn't use that. She was assisting him at his mother's request. She would continue as any Everton lady would. "As you wish, my lord."

Honoria smiled and finished her champagne. "What a lovely idea the champagne was, my lord. I thank you very much."

"Feel free to have as much as you like, my lady." His smile was devastating. Phoebe felt its effects down to her toes.

"Oh no. One glass is enough."

"Dinner is served," Watson said from the door.

Markus offered Honoria his arm. "Oh that I could stop at one, my lady. It would be nice to have that control."

She patted his hand. "What is important, my lord, is that you recognize that you cannot and have taken the necessary steps to regain your life."

"That is kind of you to say." He led her to her chair and held it for her until she was seated.

Watson held Phoebe's chair, and she sat across from Honoria.

The table setting was very fine compared to the weeks prior. Phoebe ran her finger along the delicate flowers painted around the edge of the plate. "Is this a special meal? I have not seen this china before."

Sitting, Markus grinned. "It seems the staff, including our new cook, have decided they need a proper run-through of a formal meal if they are to serve my mother tomorrow."

"That is a fine idea." Phoebe was glad the staff she'd helped hire was thoughtful and caring. It wouldn't do to have them misstep with her ladyship under the roof.

"Or they might be concerned that I will take one look at Mother and begin drinking again. It is hard to say."

Honoria tutted through her teeth. "I doubt that is the case, my lord. Has Miss Elizabeth gone to bed?"

Frowning, he sighed. "Yes. It seems having her at the table is not done. However, I won the battle to keep her at breakfast and luncheon. Supper is to be an adult affair. When I checked on her earlier, she was laughing and eating without concern for my absence."

"The situation is improving daily," Phoebe said. Her heart broke and she had to give herself an internal shake. This was what she wanted. It was her job to get Markus and his household back to a happy place where Elizabeth might have a good life. Then why did the fact that she had nearly accomplished her goals make her so sad?

The first course arrived. By the time the trifle arrived, Phoebe was completely stuffed. "I do not remember the last time I ate quite so much. Do you think your mother will be impressed, Markus?"

He wiped his mouth and placed his napkin next to his plate. "I have never seen my mother impressed by anything. Perhaps she will appreciate the quality of Becca's cooking. I am certain Dorothea and Thomas will be delighted."

"I understand your valet has resumed his post, my lord." Honoria ate a spoonful of creamy trifle and closed her eyes savoring the delight.

"Blakely was kind enough to forgive my transgressions. I am relieved to have him back."

Honoria removed her napkin from her lap and allowed the footman to remove her plate. "Then all that is left for us to do is make sure you have a proper nanny and Phoebe and I can return to Everton's. I must say, I will miss it here. I like this house and the countryside very much. Perhaps I will buy a small estate here."

"You already have two homes, Honoria. Why would you buy another?" Phoebe's heart was in her throat. She longed to depart, yet losing Markus's friendship would leave her desolate. Even if he did say he would marry her, she could not risk that kind of attachment again. She had not loved Gavin, yet his abandonment had hurt. When Markus abandoned her, she would not recover in her lifetime. What a situation. The best thing would be to get as far away from Markus as her feet could take her.

They got up from the table. "Would you ladies care to join me in the library? I would be happy to read for you, or perhaps Phoebe would play the pianoforte for us?"

Wanting to cry, Phoebe cringed at the idea of more time pretending her feelings for Markus didn't exist. "I think I will go to bed, but thank you for the invitation."

"Are you unwell, Phoebe?" Markus asked.

"I am quite well. Just tired. I will see you both tomorrow." Running up the steps, she didn't give Honoria or Markus time to ask her anything more. She needed to get away from him and find a way to stifle her feelings. Falling in love with Emma's husband was not an option.

The moment she was in her room with the door shut tight, she slumped against the wall. "Oh, Emma, what you must think of me."

The log in the fireplace popped.

Phoebe's heart jumped, and she had to catch her breath.

Arwen tapped at the door, forcing Phoebe to move away and stand near the fire.

"Miss, do you want me to help you out of the gown?"

"Yes, please."

Setting about untying the back of the gown, Arwen hummed.

"I think we will return to London in a few days." Phoebe rested a hand on the bedpost.

"Huh, I thought perhaps we would stay at Rosefield." The last lace undone, the gown fell to the floor.

Soon her knuckles ached from gripping the wood too tightly. Phoebe stepped out of the puddle of blue fabric. "No. We do not belong here. This is not our home, only an assignment."

"It's a funny thing about where one calls home. It can be almost anywhere." She untied the corset and removed Phoebe's stockings before helping her into her nightgown.

Anywhere but here. Phoebe dashed a tear and watched Arwen gather the clothes and leave the room. Being alone with her own desires did not help her situation. Her room was warm, so she opened the window, allowing the cool air to distract her for the moment. The garden was lit by a full moon. Most of the wilderness of the unkempt garden had been trimmed away and put in order.

Things were looking more and more like when Emma was alive. The roses out front had been cut down so they could grow again in the spring. Markus's family would arrive tomorrow, and his mother would see that Phoebe's work here was nearly done. The signs were all around her.

She closed the window and climbed into bed, but sleep would not come. Without Markus's strong arm around her, all she could do was stare up at the ceiling and think of the life she would never have.

It would be so much easier if she could like Jared Blunt. He was smart and had good employment. He did not live as a gentleman, but why should that matter? He could support her, and Miles would force Ford to supply a dowry despite his claims to have disinherited her. That would give them a good start. If they had children, they would be kept quiet and out of sight of their intolerant father. Phoebe could live with that.

Gavin Durnst had broken her heart. No. That wasn't true. He had said things that had hurt her feelings, but she had never loved Gavin. He was a wealthy gentleman who had asked to marry her and she had said yes because she was afraid of becoming an old maid. He was only in England now because Ford had promised him a prize for marrying her. Maybe Ford wanted to wipe away the embarrassment of having a sister in service or maybe he had other reasons. Ford rarely did anything where his own gain was not the goal.

Markus. She sighed. The clock in the hallway chimed two o'clock. Pushing the covers away, she slipped into her shoes, grabbed her wrap, and headed for the kitchen. After the huge supper, she couldn't imagine eating anything else, but she went anyway.

One candle illuminated the long table. Markus sat at the far end and lifted his gaze to hers. "Hello, Phoebe. Are you all right?"

"How long have you been here?" She stood across the table from him.

"Awhile. I wanted to make sure you were well."

"I am fine as I told you before."

"You seem distracted." He pulled a biscuit out of the jar and offered it to her.

Taking it, she sat and ate it. "I have a lot on my mind. The last few days have been hectic, and I must plan for my return to London. I am sure I will have news about a nanny any day."

"Why did you not send Durnst away the moment he arrived?"

"What do you mean?"

"You were engaged to him and he ended that agreement. He is no gentleman. He hurt you. Yet you did not toss him from the house the moment he arrived. I wonder why that is. Are you in love with him?"

"No," She said. "I was never in love with him."

"He hurt you, though."

"He injured me, but I do not see how that is any business of yours."

Markus stood and walked to the window overlooking the kitchen garden. "It is not my business. What did he say that hurt you? Why did he end your engagement?"

Her brain screamed at her to say nothing and walk out of the room, run up the stairs, and have Arwen pack their bags for a quick departure in the morning. To do that, she'd have to ask Markus to loan them his carriage. She would write to Lady Jane and ask her to send a carriage as was expected.

He faced her. "You will not answer?"

"I do not see why you want to know."

He marched over, forcing her to stand. With only an inch separating them, he stopped. "I wish to understand why any man who had been lucky enough to secure your hand in marriage would be foolish enough to betray that agreement. And more than that, I long to understand why you would consider rekindling any relationship with that cad."

Heart pounding like thunder, she stared into the green depths of his eyes. Captured by him, she couldn't look away. "He did not feel that I was marrying him for the right reasons. He thought my heart was cold and incapable of love or tenderness, and my only reason for agreeing to the marriage was to keep order and please my mother. At least, that is what he said. Thinking back on it now, it was quite out of character for him to give emotions so much value."

A slow smile spread across Markus's face.

"You think it is funny?"

"No. I think Gavin Durnst is an ass. Why didn't you toss him from Rosefield, Phoebe?"

"I suppose some part of me is still afraid of breaking the rules of society. It would not be terrible to make my mother happy in some small way after all the disappointment I have caused her." Saying it out loud was sickening. She would never marry Gavin and live with his disdain every day.

Markus sighed, lifted her hand to his lips, and brushed a kiss across her knuckles. "You may have agreed to the marriage to please your mother and you just said you did not love him, but to say that you are incapable of love is ridiculous."

"Why do you say that?"

He brushed her hair away from her cheek and his fingers left a trail of heat in their wake. "Look at how good you are to Lady Chervil or how you have cared for my daughter."

"It is my job to care for Elizabeth."

"Not in the loving way you have. It is your job to keep her safe and see that she has all that she needs. Do you love Elizabeth?"

"Of course I do, but that has nothing to do with having tender feelings toward a man." He was too close, and she stepped back from him. "Gavin claimed I had no passion in me and he was right. I am not like other women, and it makes perfect sense that I have ended an old maid." So why did saying it aloud leave her aching to throw herself into Markus's arms and weep until the pain went away?

Markus closed the distance again and ran his finger along her jaw. "You have passion. No one with your temper can be passionless. Do not let Durnst ruin you for love, Phoebe."

"My chance to find love is long past, Markus. I have accepted my place in the world."

"You could marry Blunt. He is quite keen on you." Leaning down, he brushed his lips over hers.

Her breath caught. Flames ignited in her belly and traveled down between her legs. "I have no intention of marrying Jared Blunt."

Markus pressed his lips to hers, probed with his tongue, and devoured her mouth.

There was only that moment. Her arguments faded to nothing as his arms wrapped around her and his lips danced with hers, sipping and tasting while driving her mad with need.

Kissing her cheek, then her ear before tickling the flesh behind her ear, he whispered, "I want you, Phoebe. The last thing you are is cold or indifferent. You have made me believe in happiness again. I thought that was impossible."

She pushed back. "We cannot do this. You are only grateful to me for doing my job. An Everton lady never gets involved with her client. Markus, your family will be here in less than a day. What about Emma? I cannot do this to her."

"My mother hired you, not me. She is your client. I have come to think that Emma might not disapprove. She might want me to be happy. Certainly, she would want you to be happy. This thing between us is more real than anything else. I am grateful, but it has nothing to do with my feelings for you." He ran his hands down her back and pulled her into a hug. His lips pressed to the top of her head.

Markus's scent was spice and desire and she wanted him too, but there were rules and she could not lose her place at Everton's. Where would that leave her, back at her brother's house? No. She pushed away.

His wounded eyes seared her.

She gripped her wrap tighter. "I think it best if I write for a carriage. My work here is about done. It will take a few days, perhaps a week, for Everton's to send the transport. I am sure we will have a suitable nanny by then. I am sorry if my being here has caused you any undue pain, Markus. My intentions were honorable."

"Pain? Phoebe, why are you running away?" He reached for her, but she backed away another step.

The world was coming apart around her. One thing that Gavin was right about: she liked order and could not tolerate chaos. The longer she was in Markus Flammel's presence, the more out of control she felt. "I most certainly am not running away. This was my assignment and it is drawing to a close. You have been very kind and I am happy to have your friendship, Markus. I think we both know it can never be more than that. You are a viscount and will someday be an earl. My place is at Everton's with other ladies of my station and situation."

He stepped back and scowled at her. "I do not like how meanly you think of yourself. Your brother is an ass to have disowned you, but that does not change your station. Which, I might add, is exactly the same as mine. I will not stop you from leaving if that is what you want, but you go of your own accord. I would much prefer you stay."

More than anything in the world, she wanted to be wrapped in Markus's arms and forget their circumstances. "It is not mean, but realistic. I am what I am and this life is good enough for me."

His Adam's apple bobbed several times while his fists clenched. "I must disagree, but you may have your way. I will see you tomorrow. My family arrives for luncheon and I hope you will join us for the meal."

"Of course, my lord. I would not miss it."

Sorrow that nearly undid her pooled in his eyes. "Please, Phoebe, not that. Do not take us back to formality. You said we are friends. Cannot friends call each other by their Christian names?"

She didn't know if she was strong enough to be friends with a man she was falling in love with and could never have. But she couldn't be cruel either. "We are friends, Markus. I will see you tomorrow."

Emotions spinning out of control, she could not get to the main level fast enough. She nearly slipped several times before sprinting up the main stairs to her own room.

Out of breath, she leaned against the bedpost and imagined Markus carrying her up the steps to his bed. Would he have made love to her if she'd allowed it? She might be in his bed and wrapped in his arms being showered with a thousand kisses that made her burn as she never had before.

Sitting on the nightstand was her Everton Companion. She let the book fall open.

No. 20

*Everton Ladies are to remain aloof and never get personal
during their assignments.*

Oh dear, she had certainly gotten personal and attached to this man and this family. Her heart would break when she left, but she had no choice. She would rather be an old maid than marry a man who was only doing his duty as a gentleman. Besides, Markus would have come to resent her, and her love for him would wither and die in time. All things did.

Chapter 12

No. 7
An Everton lady is never to lose her temper or raise her voice.
—*The Everton Companion*
Rules of Conduct

An hour before luncheon two carriages arrived with Markus's family. At least, part of it. The youngest, Adam, was still at school and would remain there. Father's whereabouts was unknown, and as long as he was nowhere near Rosefield, that suited Markus.

Watson lined the staff up on both sides of the steps leading to the house, and Markus stood at the top with Phoebe and Honoria until a footman opened the carriage doors and his mother stepped out.

Markus trotted down the steps. "Hello, Mother. It is good to see you." She narrowed her eyes on him. "You are looking better."

"Thank you." Markus didn't expect a lot of affection. If Margaret ever made a display of emotion, he would have no idea how to react.

His sister, Dorothea, and her husband, Thomas, rushed over from the other carriage. Dory smiled, and her red hair blew in the breeze. "Markus, you look wonderful. Really. I am so happy you are doing well." She wrapped him in a hug and kissed both his cheeks.

"It is good to see you too, Dory. I am sorry to have missed your performance for the prince. I shall never forgive myself." Markus's heart contracted and guilt swamped him. He should have been there, meant to be, but had gotten drunk and forgotten all about it.

"I suppose if you must batter yourself about it, you can, but I have already forgiven you." Dory gazed at the house just as Arwen walked outside with Elizabeth in her arms. Her face lit up and she rushed up the steps. "Oh goodness, how she's grown."

Thomas shook his hand. "Markus, you all right?"

Thomas had been Markus's friend since their school days. The two of them, Michael Collins, and Daniel Fallon had been inseparable since the first day at Eton. Markus had been too drunk to care when Dory and Tom had eloped to Scotland. His list of regrets from the last two years continued to grow.

"Better than I have been in a long time, Tom." It was true. Even with the looming truth that Phoebe would not accept his offer of marriage and she would leave Rosefield for a life of toil in London, he still felt stronger than he had in years.

"I am happy to hear that. I have a lot to discuss with you this week. Your father has been unable or unwilling to handle his affairs, and things became perilous for a time."

It wasn't a surprise, but Markus still shuddered at the notion of more finances to sort out. "Let's talk after luncheon, Tom. I am certain you have very little good news and a full stomach might soften the blow."

Tom laughed and slapped Markus on the back. "It is good to see the gardening is being looked after again. Last time we were here things were looking bleak."

"It was a disaster," Mother said.

"Well, much has changed in the past few weeks. Miss Hallsmith has hired a staff and put order back in Rosefield. I suppose I should thank you for sending her, Mother."

Already climbing the steps, Margaret ignored his gratitude and walked to Dory, who held Elizabeth. Both stopped talking at Margaret's approach. "Do you remember me, Elizabeth? I am your grandmother."

Elizabeth narrowed her eyes at Mother but then leaned forward and patted her cheek.

It was not exactly a smile, but Mother's expression softened and she took Elizabeth's little hand for a moment before sweeping inside the house.

Dory laughed. "Perhaps I should try that approach to softening Mother."

Taking Elizabeth from Dory's arms, Markus shook his head. "I am not certain that particular technique works for anyone but Elizabeth. She has used it on me several times and it was equally effective." He kissed Elizabeth's soft cheek and was rewarded with a wet kiss of the same type.

Markus turned to Phoebe. "Dory, do you know Miss Hallsmith?"

A wide grin spread across Dory's face. "Of course, Phoebe and I have been friends for many years."

They curtsied and hugged.

Markus finished introducing Tom and Honoria, and they all went inside to find Mother already seated in the parlor with a cup of tea and Watson assuring her ladyship that luncheon would be served promptly at one. "Mrs. Donnelly thought you might like a few moments to relax after your ride before sitting for a meal."

Mother stared him down for several beats before nodding. "Very thoughtful."

Watson bowed and left the room.

Sipping her tea, Mother's gaze fell on Phoebe. "You have done wonders here, Miss Hallsmith."

"Thank you, my lady." Phoebe poured tea and sat in a small wooden chair off to the side.

"I had my doubts anyone could fix the mess Markus had made of his life, but things seem much under control. I am pleased." In contrast to her words, she frowned, leaving deep crevices on her face.

Phoebe's neck pinked. "Most of the issues could be handled by hiring staff and some organization. All the rest was entirely fixable."

"I hope you are not leaving any time soon, Miss Hallsmith. You have done wonders and I am anxious to renew our friendship." Dory took a biscuit from the tray.

"We are waiting on a new nanny for Elizabeth, then Lady Chervil and I will be on our way. I had a letter this morning from the agency. Miss Winnifred Cavot will be arriving in two days. The letter came with very sound references. I am certain she will be more than suitable."

Markus's chest tightened and he had to force his hand down to his side so as not to clutch at something. He wanted to grab Phoebe and beg her not to go. "You did not mention the letter."

"It came only a few moments before the carriages pulled down the lane. I hoped to discuss Miss Cavot and her qualifications with you this afternoon." She would not make eye contact with him.

"I see."

A heavy silence shrouded the room.

"Assuming it all works out, which I'm sure it will, we will be leaving directly after she settles in." Phoebe sipped her tea as if all was as it should be.

Markus was dying inside, but held his tongue.

* * * *

"Tell me about Miss Hallsmith." Sitting across from Markus's desk, Thomas stretched his long legs out in front of him.

"What do you want to know?" Markus scanned through his father's accounts. His gut twisted at the damage to the family finances, but Thomas had kept them from debtor's prison, and it was all recoverable.

"She is Miles Hallsmith's sister?" Tom crossed his feet.

"Yes."

"And she's part of the Everton Domestic Society because she's no longer of marriageable age?"

A fire kindled in Markus's gut. "She is four and twenty, for goodness' sake. Why does everyone act as if she is twice that age? And, I'll have you know, she has had several offers of marriage just this week."

Sitting up, Tom stared Markus down. "Have you offered for her?"

"No. Not exactly."

Tom narrowed his eyes. "Who *exactly* has offered for Miss Hallsmith?"

"Jared Blunt made her an offer."

"Your man of business? That seems an unlikely match. She is a viscount's daughter. I cannot imagine Hallsmith would be too keen on his sister marrying a man in service."

"I think Ford Hallsmith paid off Phoebe's former fiancé to renew his offer, though I'm not exactly sure why. A Scottish *gentleman* by the name of Gavin Durnst arrived a few days ago. It shows how low Ford will stoop. It is unlikely he is thinking of his sister's happiness. Perhaps he just wants to save face by keeping her out of the gossip." A good bottle of brandy would make him forget all the notions running through his head. At least for a little while, but then the regret would follow. He shook it off. He wasn't good enough for her, and she knew it. Hell, he knew it.

"I never did like Ford. Miles is the best of men, but his brother always rubbed me the wrong way. Ford loses at the card table and Miles finds ways to improve the family earnings. He has been bailing his older brother out for years. This story is not changing my mind about Ford. What do you think he's getting from Durnst?" Tom shook his head and crossed his arms.

"He is an ass, and you're right, he must have a reason."

"I cannot imagine he would pay a man to marry his sister just to save face. It would need to be a lofty sum too." Tom cringed. "Sorry, I mean no insult to Miss Hallsmith. She's a lovely girl but steeped in scandal this last year."

Markus wanted to throttle Ford and Thomas, but he held his temper. "Scandal caused by Ford's public denouncement."

"And her going into service," Tom said.

Holding on by a thread, he gripped the edge of his chair. "Everton's is a respectable establishment. It's not as if she's selling her body on the street."

Thomas waved him off. "Of course not. Still, society can be cruel. But never mind all that. Tell me what you meant when you said you did not exactly offer for Miss Hallsmith."

Markus put the accounting book aside. "She and I share the same difficulty sleeping. We have met by coincidence several nights in the kitchen and enjoyed conversation and whatever sweets Cook left for us. The other night we met in the library. I thought reading might help with our rest. I was right, and Lady Chervil found us asleep on the couch."

Thomas raised his eyebrows. "Did her ladyship demand you marry Miss Hallsmith?"

"No, but I said I would if Phoebe wished it. However, she doesn't want me. She should find a man who will make her happy. I am too broken for a girl like her." Saying the words aloud made them more real. Markus forced breath into his lungs.

Thomas's scowl said it all before he spoke. "Most women like romance in a proposal, Markus. If you want this woman, you will have to do better than saying you would be obliged to marry her if she wants. She needs to know it is what you want."

"I am in no position to take care of a wife, Tom." More truth he hated to say.

"It seems to me Miss Hallsmith can take care of herself. But let's put that aside for a moment. You look sober. Am I correct?" Thomas was always direct. "Last time we came you were several drinks in and the house was in shambles. Your staff was down to only a few servants and they were frantically trying to care for Elizabeth. Dory and I offered to take the child with us, but you went into a rage and the staff would not give us Elizabeth. Your sister left here in tears. Do you remember any of that?"

Closing his eyes, Markus tried to remember. "Only vaguely."

"Yes, well, that is not surprising. Are you still drinking?"

"Not since Phoebe made me promise not to. However, I have had little sleep and more clarity than I care for."

Thomas laughed. "I imagine the revival of Rosefield has been exhausting and trying, but if you could stay sober during all of that, surely you can continue. How is Elizabeth?"

All the heaviness lifted from his heart and was instantly replaced by the image of Elizabeth's sweet face. "She appears happy, but still does not speak. Phoebe believes she can and chooses not to. I cannot blame her. Nothing in her life has been as it should have. Emma died, then I left or was a drunken madman. There is much to make up for."

"I have no doubt you will do right by Elizabeth, Markus."

"How can you be sure? I have done nothing but ruin her life so far."

Thomas leaned forward and put his elbows on his knees. "Because it is my old friend Markus I see before me. The man I met here last time I visited was unrecognizable. You are a good man and will make this all right."

Was he a good man? He had not felt like one in a long time. "Thank you, Tom."

"There is one other matter we must discuss." All the joy washed from Thomas's face.

"Is it about my father?" Dread and shame warred inside Markus.

"I wish I could say it is not, but he has been missing for almost a month. I went to see James Hardwig over on Bow Street and even sent out runners to find him. No one has heard from or seen his lordship."

Standing, Markus drew a deep breath. He hated talk of his father and hated even more how like him he'd become. "I know of a few women whose houses he frequents. Perhaps he is with one of them."

Thomas shrugged. "It is worth inquiring, but if we do not find him soon…"

He let the sentence hang, but Markus cringed at what wasn't spoken. His father was a lecherous ne'er-do-well, but declaring him dead left an emptiness inside him. How would he face his mother? People would think he was after the man's title. Not to mention the fact that the family would be required to mourn, and what if he showed up in a month or two? "I shall wait some time before I go to drastic measures. My father has his flaws, but I have no great desire to become the Earl of Castlereagh any time soon. I'd just as soon wait for him to show up in London, preferably alive."

"And what of his estates and holdings?"

"I will hire a second man of business to handle those and manage it all. I have done so on the periphery for years. I will have to take a stronger role, but those holdings will be mine one day. I cannot thank you enough for managing it all in my absence, Tom. You are a good friend and a fine brother-in-law."

"It was nothing. Even if I were not married to your sister, I would have assisted you in your time of need. I know you would do the same for me." Thomas rose and crossed to the door. "Speaking of Dorothea, I should tell you, she is with child."

Joy and terror crashed together. He could lose Dory the way he had lost Emma. Getting up, he stuffed his fears and crossed to Thomas with his hand outstretched. "I am very happy for you both, Tom."

"I am certain this news comes as a shock to you. All I ask is that you try to act happy in front of Dory. She so wants you to be happy for her." Thomas held Markus's hand a bit longer and made eye contact.

"My fears will not cloud the fact that this is joyous news." Even though he meant what he said, when Thomas stepped outside his office, Markus had to sit with his hands over his face for a long while. When he finally got his mind around the idea of Dory having a baby, he went and congratulated her before returning to his room to dress for supper.

* * * *

In the blue parlor, Markus had a fine pianoforte, which was rarely used. When dinner concluded, he invited everyone to the parlor for cake. "Dory, will you play? It has been ages since I have heard you."

Dory's smile lit the room. "For you, I will play, Markus. Tom and I just finished writing a piece for four hands. Perhaps he would join me."

Nodding, Thomas took her hand and escorted her to the instrument. They sat and she leaned into him for an instant. It was a private moment between husband and wife and perhaps not meant for anyone to notice.

Thinking of the kiss he and Phoebe had shared, he wondered if he would ever have tiny moments like that again with another. Of course, he and Emma had hundreds of such intimacies. That was what he missed most, the little daily expressions of love.

Dory and Thomas played together as if they had been doing so all their lives. Where one phrase stopped, the next picked up in a seamless melody deepened with a soulful harmony. When they rested their fingers on the keys as if in one motion and the music stopped, Markus had to remind himself to breathe.

Shaking off the deep musing, he burst into applause, as did Phoebe and Honoria. Mother lightly patted her gloved hands.

"That was wonderful. You two play together like nothing I have ever seen." Markus stood when Dory did.

Mother turned. "Do you play, Miss Hallsmith?"

Wide-eyed, Phoebe gaped. "I...I would be embarrassed to play after such an impressive performance. My skills are for a schoolroom, while Mr. and Mrs. Wheel are true musicians. Perhaps if I had played first, my lady."

To her credit, Mother didn't push the issue. Phoebe had said just the right thing so as not to offend yet also get out of what might have been an embarrassing moment. Few people played as well as his sister. Even Thomas's skills paled in comparison.

Dory blushed when Thomas leaned over and kissed her cheek. "Play another, my dear. Perhaps the final original piece you played for the prince."

With a nod, she settled onto the bench alone. She put her fingers on the keys, but held her breath before turning and looking Markus in the eye. "I titled this 'Emma.' "

Not one note had been played, but Markus's pulse stuttered.

When her fingers tapped out the sad melody of the first phrase, he could hardly breathe. The music highlighted the laughter and delight that Emma brought to everyone she touched. The sonata ended with pain that Markus thought only he knew. Somehow it helped hearing the piece. His sweet sister knew his suffering and had put it into the most beautiful music he had ever heard.

At the close, he wrapped Dory in his arms and pushed down his tears. "Thank you. That was the most beautiful thing I have ever heard. Emma would have loved it."

"I was terrified to play it for you. I thought you might be angry." Dory wiped her tears away.

With a kiss on her cheek, he stepped back.

Phoebe ran from the room.

Markus swallowed down his desire to call after her and turned to Dory. "I think it was a good thing that you waited to play it for me. I might not have been strong enough to hear it before now. I shall always cherish this gift, Dory. You are a wonder."

"I am so happy to have been here to hear that." Honoria ambled over and took Dory's hand. "You are a stunning musician. I had read in the paper that you played for the prince, but I had no idea you were so gifted. I hope you will play a few more."

Dory thanked her and after cake was served, she played several more pieces. She kept the rest of the music light and happy and by the time they said goodnight, Markus's only worry was about Phoebe and why she had run out of the parlor and never returned.

Waiting downstairs until the rest of the house was secured in their rooms, Markus finally made his way upstairs. He stopped outside Phoebe's door. He should continue to his own room, but he couldn't. She might be ill. He knocked.

The rustle of cloth filtered through the door before it opened a few inches. Phoebe's eyes were ringed red, and she sniffed. "Markus, what are you doing?" Her voice was tight.

"I was worried about you. Are you ill?" Afraid she might slam the door, he put his foot on the threshold.

"No. I am fine. I was just emotional and did not wish to make a scene." A tear leaked, and she brushed it away.

"You are still crying. Because of the music?"

"No. Yes. The music and other things." Sighing, she stepped back but did not try to close the door.

Markus stepped inside. He told himself to leave it and go to his own bed, but his heart ached for Phoebe. He longed to know what other things had been so upsetting she'd been crying for hours. She stood near the open window in only her shift and a white wrap. It was no different from what he'd seen her in dozens of times when they snacked in the kitchen together, yet he yearned to touch her. He stroked the soft skin where her shoulder and neck met. "Tell me."

"I have made enough of a fool of myself for one evening, Markus. Please leave me be." Her shoulders shook.

Pulling her back against his chest, he wrapped his arms around her. "Do not cry, Phoebe. You can tell me anything. No one even knew you were upset. You might have left for any reason tonight."

"Then why are you here?"

"I know you better than they do and I was worried. Tell me what upset you about Emma's sonata?" He kissed the top of her head and his reward was wildflowers on a spring day. Phoebe was sunshine in his arms.

She let her head fall back against his chest. "At first it was just the sweetness of the music, but then I began to think about how tender the gesture was. How your sister had created something so perfect and emotional for Emma and for you. I couldn't bear it. No one has ever done anything as wondrous for me. My brother is trying to barter me off with a dowry to the most eligible man. He has no concern for my happiness or whether or not those men are gentlemen who will give me a good life. Ford's only concern is his own reputation and that I not bruise it. I know I am being childish and selfish, but I was jealous of how much your sister loves you."

"Now I feel like an ass. I have been unappreciative of my family's love. But, Phoebe, that is just Ford. Miles adores you. He respects your decision to go to Everton's and make a life for yourself." He could keep her wrapped in his arms forever and wished he had the power to stop time.

Turning toward him, she pressed against him. "I did not wish to make you feel bad. I'm sure the music was very emotional for you. Emma would have loved that sonata. It was happy and sad and tragic."

"Phoebe, I do not want to talk about Emma right now." Every inch of him longed for her and her body fit his perfectly.

Wide golden eyes stared up at him. "No. What do you want to talk about?"

A war raged inside Markus and his good sense lost the battle. "Nothing. I want to make love to you and pretend the rest of the world does not exist."

"That would be completely inappropriate, Markus." She pressed closer to him.

"Then tell me to leave, Phoebe. Toss me from your room and I will go." It was a strain to hold back kissing her exposed neck and shoulder.

"I do not want to send you away. Soon I will be gone, back to my life. You will be here raising Elizabeth." A whimper escaped. "Is it so terrible to want one night to remember for the rest of my life?"

"Why must it be only one?" He was fully aroused and didn't know how much longer he could hold her like this without making love to her.

"You will be an earl and I will be an Everton lady, and that is just the way it is." She rose to her toes and kissed his chin. Her breasts pressed against him and ignited passion that would never be quelled. Taking her in his arms, he pressed his lips to hers and devoured her mouth before striding to the bed in two steps.

Completely trusting, she stared up at him with parted lips and flushed skin.

Markus stepped back, bolted the door, and tore off his cravat. Forcing himself to slow down and not ravage her like an animal, he reclined next to her and traced a path along the low neck of her shift. "Can I assume you are a virgin, Phoebe?"

Her breath came in short gasps. "I am."

"I have to ask you again. Are you certain this is what you want? I would hate it if you regretted this." Her scent intoxicated him, and he pulled the bow at her shoulder, exposing one perfect round breast.

"I will cherish this, Markus. Do not leave me now. That would be the only thing I could ever regret."

A low groan escaped him. No man could resist such sweetness or a gift so great and true.

Chapter 13

No. 26
The Society is here to support our ladies. Asking for
help is encouraged.
—The Everton Companion
Rules of Conduct

It wasn't so terrible to want one perfect night for herself. If Phoebe couldn't have Markus for her own, at least she could carry the memory of his lovemaking with her.

He undressed her with such care, kissing his way down her shoulder to her chest. When his mouth closed around her nipple, it was a lightning bolt to her sex. The Everton rules flew out the window with all the things she'd been taught a lady should be.

His velvet jacket brushed against her skin, soft and rough at once. Her flesh was sensitive to the lightest touch so that even the soft cotton shift flowing away made her arch and moan.

"Phoebe, you are so beautiful."

His words filled her with joy and the tenderness in his eyes warmed her heart. "You are overdressed."

Standing, he pulled off his jacket and tossed it aside. With each layer of clothing, he revealed strength and masculinity. Lean muscles covered his arms and shoulders.

"Do you do some sport, Markus?"

Head cocked, he smiled. "I used to work the fields with my tenants but lately I only ride. It seems riding for days without end kept me from getting too soft."

When his breeches hit the floor, Phoebe considered changing her mind for half a second.

He was beautiful and covered in a smattering of fair hair. Stepping out of his clothes brought him closer, and she reached out and touched the flesh covering his ribs. He shook at her touch, and she skimmed her fingers up to the pebbled nipples.

The firelight danced off his skin and glimmered in his eyes. "I do not think I have ever yearned for anyone the way I do for you. Even knowing I should go, I cannot leave you."

"I would be very vexed if you left now." She'd tried to lighten the mood, but it sounded more whine than joke.

Lying on the mattress next to her, he ran his fingers along her waist to her hip. "I am not going anywhere."

She shivered.

"Are you afraid, Phoebe?"

"I would be lying if I said I had no fear at all. I understand this will be painful for me." A knot formed in her throat and the last word squeaked out.

Him kissing the shell of her ear set her on fire. "I will do my best to make the one instant of pain worthwhile for you."

"An instant? Is that all it is?" Women rarely spoke of what happened between married people. Phoebe was raised on a farm, so she had some idea, and a few girls in Scotland had giggled about their experiences.

His kisses distracted her from her concerns. Soft, strong lips danced with hers as his tongue swept the inside of her mouth demanding she join as well. He gripped her bottom and pulled her tight to his shaft, yet she didn't fear him. Markus would never hurt her physically. And her broken heart was inevitable, so she pushed that fear aside.

Every touch set her trembling with desire and the moment he slid his fingers between her folds everything else fell away and there was only the pleasure and something tightening within her. Wantonly, she pressed against his hand, jerking and relishing his fingers sliding through her wetness.

Unsure but wanting more, she clung to his back. "Markus."

"Yes. Tell me, sweetheart." He pressed his shaft tight to her hip and slid his fingers inside.

There were no emotions designed to express the way his lips, hands, and fingers made her feel. It was the perfect moment of adoration, and

Phoebe soared above the world. Ecstasy crashed around her, forcing her to buck and she gasped. "Oh, God."

Markus wrapped his arms around her, holding her until the waves of pleasure eased. Brushing a wet strand of hair from her cheek, he leaned on his elbows and smiled at her. "You are a magnificent woman, Phoebe. You can have anything you want in this world. I hope you will come to know that."

"I have no idea what you mean."

He pressed his shaft to the juncture of her thighs, sliding between her lips. The intimacy was uncomfortable but good at the same time. He slid himself along her wet crease until she closed her eyes with the pleasure of it.

"Look at me, Phoebe."

The fire still glowed in his dilated eyes. Intensity shone through and she wanted all of him.

Thrusting forward, he tore her in half.

She bit her lip to keep from crying out.

"Just stay still for a moment and the pain will go away. I promise." He never took his gaze away from hers, and it was like he had some mystical hold on her.

True to his word, the pain that she was sure had killed her disappeared and only desire remained. She pressed her hips up and the pleasure increased.

"Sweetheart, you are making it very hard for me to remain still and give you time to adjust." His jaw ticked.

"Feels good now, Markus." She ran her hand along his cheek, his day's growth of beard rubbing the pads of her fingers.

With a growl more animal than man, he pulled back, leaving only his tip still inside before pressing fully into her. Markus set a rhythm that Phoebe could not resist joining. With every thrust, she lifted her hips to meet him. Each time her most sensitive bud would contact his body and her pleasure would escalate.

Greater than before, when the rapture came, a cry escaped her mouth.

Markus pressed his lips to hers and smothered her voice as he groaned.

Silence hung around them as he wrapped her in his arms and rolled until she lay next to him with her legs entwined with his. He kissed her forehead.

"That was wonderful, Markus."

"You are wonderful." He hugged her tighter, then eased from the bed. When he returned, he held a wet cloth and wiped her inner thighs and womanhood clean. "Can you trust Arwen with the sheets, sweetheart?"

A red smudge marred the white sheets. "I will take care of it. You should return to your own room before we are discovered."

Already her heart was breaking, but she knew it was the right thing. She could hold on to this wonderful memory for the rest of her life, and Markus would find someone suitable to fill Emma's role.

He knelt next to the bed and rested his forehead on her arm. "You want me to go and all I want is to hold you through the night."

Dear God, why did this have to be so difficult? "What we want does not matter. This is the way things are, and if we are discovered it would be a disaster for both of us."

Pain etched in his eyes and a deep crease formed around his mouth when he gazed up at her. With a nod, he returned the cloth to the basin on the table, pulled on his breeches, picked up his remaining clothes, and without ever taking his eyes from her left the room.

Despite how beautiful the night had been, she ached with longing to have Markus back in her arms. He might have wanted to stay, but he would come to regret that if they were found out. No one could ever know what they had shared. With that in mind, Phoebe got out of bed and began the process of cleaning up the evidence.

If she would never marry, then at least she would have this memory to cherish. She should feel ashamed, but when she thought about the way they had come together, joy shook her from head to toe and all the delicious places in between.

* * * *

Phoebe eased out of her chair in the breakfast room just as Mrs. Donnelly rushed in. A rest after the sleepless night was not to be.

"Miss Hallsmith, the nanny is here. Miss Cavot arrived a moment ago. I have asked her to wait in the small parlor."

"I did not expect her for another few days." Phoebe had not even spoken to Markus about Miss Cavot's credentials yet. She had hoped to not have to face him so soon. "Where is his lordship?"

"In his study with Mr. Blunt, Miss."

It took a force of will to stifle the groan building inside Phoebe. Not only Markus but Jared as well. She was being punished for being wanton and willful. It was the only explanation. "Very well. See if Miss Cavot needs tea or food and I will speak to his lordship. Please ask her to be patient, as she is early and we are not quite ready to receive her."

Mrs. Donnelly stood straight and folded her hands in front of her. "Of course. I will take care of her while you deal with the rest."

Phoebe walked down the hall and across the foyer. How she wished she were the kind of person to run from anything. As an Everton lady, she could not. She knocked.

"Come in," Markus called from inside.

With a deep breath, she pushed the door open and walked inside.

Both men froze looking at her from behind the desk. Jared stooped over Markus's left shoulder as the two had been examining some papers.

Markus stood.

Jared pulled a stern face.

Everton Ladies did not run. "My lord, the nanny is here. I apologize but I thought you might like to discuss her qualifications before I introduce her to Miss Elizabeth."

Jared straightened and frowned with his hands behind his back.

Markus nodded. "She is early. Blunt, please excuse us for a few minutes."

With a brief smile at Phoebe, Jared stomped out of the study.

Markus walked to the door and closed it before holding the chair near his desk. Fresh cut wood and spices that were distinctly Markus assaulted her senses. "Please sit, Phoebe. Are you all right?"

"Of course. Why do you ask?" She sat more slowly than she might normally, but hoped he hadn't noticed.

Once he rounded his desk, Markus sat. "I worried you might be sore after last night. Actually, I worried about many things with regard to your feelings this morning as well."

"Markus, can we just talk about Miss Cavot?" Her face burned, and she hated her inability to control her embarrassment. She should be flattered that he cared about her health, but she wished she could sink into the thick carpet and disappear.

Sighing, he ran his hands through his hair then rested them on the desk. "As you wish."

Sticking to business was the best way to get through the awkward moment. Phoebe gave a long account of the letters and references that preceded Miss Cavot by one day. "The agency must have sent her before we even had the mail in hand. I suppose they were confident that we could not disapprove."

"It sounds as if she is more than qualified. Shall we see if Elizabeth takes to her?" He stood.

She stood, forgetting about her aches and pains, but the quick movement reminded her.

Markus rushed around the desk. "You are in pain. I am so sorry, Phoebe. You must know I never meant to hurt you."

"I am only a little sore, as I imagine anyone would be. Please do not fret over me. These are strange circumstances, and we will have to endure each other's company for a few more days. If Miss Cavot is as wonderful as the agency says, I will be out of your hair very soon and we can resume our normal lives." Her voice was steady and she was proud of how calm and official she sounded.

His frown shot darts in her heart. "And that is what you wish, to return to London as soon as possible?"

"I am a Lady of the Everton Domestic Society. I have broken more rules than I care to enumerate. I would be most grateful if what happened between us was kept private, and since you are a gentleman, I have no doubt of that. My place is to return to the London office and await my next assignment."

"Is this because of Emma?" He tipped her chin up, but she pulled away.

"Of course not. There is no blame to be placed. You have your duty and I have mine. Our honor dictates how we go forward, my lord." She gripped the back of the chair and hoped he couldn't tell her fingers shook.

The muscle in his jaw ticked the way it had when he restrained himself the night before. "I am trying very hard to not become upset with you, Phoebe. There is no way I can pretend that I understand your decision, but there is no need to insult me or belie our friendship by calling me my lord."

If her heart tore from her chest, it would not have surprised her. Nothing could be more difficult, but she had no business with a viscount and certainly not with the earl he would become. She would do well to marry Mr. Blunt, but the thought repulsed her. No. Everton's was the perfect place for her. "I apologize. I do not wish to insult you or ruin our friendship, Markus. It is only that I have to leave, and it would be easier on both of us if we did not repeat what happened last night."

Impossibly, his frown deepened. "As you wish. Where is Miss Cavot?"

Swallowing the pain of his cool tone, she pulled her shoulders back. "In the small parlor."

He motioned for her to precede him out the door, every movement stiff and brisk as if he held back.

The situation was difficult, but she knew that in a few weeks he would be glad she had been the voice of reason. She couldn't bear another broken engagement, and surely that would have been the outcome of an entanglement with Markus.

"I will go and get Elizabeth and meet you in the parlor." He took the steps two at a time.

Phoebe stood outside the parlor door and calmed her breathing. Her emotions were a jumble of confusion, yet she was certain she was doing the right thing. Everton Ladies do their assignment, then they move on. One more deep breath and she pushed the door open.

A few years older than Phoebe, Miss Cavot had brown hair and blue eyes. She wore a brown dress with white trim and sat with her hands in her lap. She stood when Phoebe entered.

"I am Phoebe Hallsmith. I am acting as temporary assistant to the viscount."

"Winnifred Cavot. It is nice to meet you." She curtsied.

Phoebe did as well, then walked over, offering Miss Cavot her seat again. "We did not expect you for a few days, Miss Cavot. I only received the letter with your references yesterday."

Eyes wide, Miss Cavot blushed. "I am sorry. The agency said you were in need and sent me directly. If I had known you were not informed, I would have given you a few days to decline before setting out."

"Never mind that now. You are here, and if Miss Elizabeth approves, you will have the post. I must warn you, Elizabeth has had no mother and a difficult time of it. She does not speak, though I feel she is capable, just unwilling."

"Poor lamb. In some cases, the child can wait years to speak. I hope I will be able to help her." Miss Cavot smoothed her skirts and sorrow filled her eyes.

Sympathy was a good trait in a nanny. "Your last employer, Lord Guthry, said you had a way with children and they were sorry to let you go when their son went to school."

"John was a good boy. I miss him, but he and I write to keep in touch. May I ask you a question, Miss Hallsmith?" Miss Cavot leaned in.

"Of course."

"You said you were a temporary assistant. Do you mean housekeeper? I met Mrs. Donnelly who said she was the housekeeper. I am not quite sure I understand how this house works."

"I am from the Everton Domestic Society. This is my current assignment, and once you are settled in, I will go back to London. You should find the house in order. Watson and Mrs. Donnelly are capable of keeping up with the staff. You will be charged with caring for and educating Miss Elizabeth. All will be well." It was all true and should have made her happy. She had done her best and accomplished a tremendous amount in the short time she'd been at Rosefield. They did not need her anymore. A knot filled her chest like a lump of coal had replaced her heart.

"I have heard of the society, but you are the first Everton lady I have ever met. Do you like your work?" Miss Cavot's eager enthusiasm brightened the mood.

Phoebe forced a smile. "It is very satisfying to help a family in need. This has been a good assignment. The family is visiting. His lordship's mother, sister, and brother-in-law are here. They will stay a week or two, I believe."

"I see. Thank you for informing me." Miss Cavot rolled along with the change of subject and asked no more questions about Phoebe's work.

The door opened and Elizabeth ran in followed by Markus. She took one look at Miss Cavot and stopped short. With wide green eyes, she stared from Phoebe to Miss Cavot.

"It is all right, Elizabeth. This is Miss Cavot, and she is going to care for you. She is your new nanny." Phoebe forced calm into every word.

Miss Cavot stood and curtsied. "How do you do Miss Elizabeth."

Elizabeth dropped into an awkward and adorable curtsy, then stepped closer.

Phoebe said, "Miss Cavot, this is Markus Flammel, Viscount of Devonrose. Markus bowed and joined them.

Another curtsy from Miss Cavot and they all sat.

Question after question, Miss Cavot answered without flinching. She even managed to keep Elizabeth from breaking a vase while telling Markus about her former employment. By the time they left the small parlor, Markus, Elizabeth, and Miss Cavot were all satisfied with the situation.

Phoebe just wanted to go to her room and cry.

At the third step, Dorothea Wheel stopped her. "Miss Hallsmith, do you have a moment?"

Her tears would have to wait. Plastering a smile on her face, she turned. "What can I do for you, Mrs. Wheel?"

Dory threaded her hand around Phoebe's elbow. "I wonder if you would sit in the parlor and talk for a while. It has been years since I saw you last. I would like to get reacquainted with the woman who saved my brother and returned order to Rosefield in so short a time."

"I did not save him. He was ready to return to his life. I only pushed the issue and perhaps made him feel guilt over his behavior." Phoebe stifled her sigh and went to the larger parlor with Dory.

"I tried guilt when we came and he tossed us from the house. Markus can be quite stubborn." Dory called for tea.

Sitting, Phoebe smoothed her skirts. "As I said, Mrs. Wheel, he was ready to return."

"You should call me Dory. I know we have not seen each other in years, but I hope to count you among my friends, Phoebe."

"Thank you. Most of my friends disengaged with me years ago when I went to Scotland, and the rest abandoned ship when I joined the Everton Domestic Society a year ago. It would be nice to have a friend outside of my work." Phoebe fought off those emotions she usually kept tucked away. There was no sense feeling bad about the past.

"I think you have made a very brave and interesting choice. Are you happy with your work?" The tea arrived and they waited for Katy to leave before speaking.

"I am satisfied. I enjoy helping people and I am not forced to marry where I do not wish."

Dory rolled her eyes. "You were away when I proposed to Tom. Did you know he saved me from having to marry an old beast of an earl? We eloped."

Finally, someone who might understand. "I had no idea. I'm afraid very little news got to me in Scotland while my grandmother was ill. I heard only the news Mother sent. Usually she only wrote to tell me bad news or how disappointed she was in me."

A long sigh from Dory filled the room. "Mother and I have come to terms, but it was a difficult transition. I hope you and your mother will find a way to come back together."

That was doubtful but a nice notion. "I hear congratulations are in order. My maid told me you are going to have a baby."

A lovely blush bloomed across Dory's face. "We are thrilled. I hope it is a boy but Tom says he wants a girl. I thought all men wanted boys."

The vision of Markus telling the story of Jack the Giant Slayer to Elizabeth crowded Phoebe's mind. "Little girls have a way of warming their father's hearts."

"Not my father's." Dory's smile faded and sorrow filled her eyes.

"Markus dotes on Elizabeth." The moment it was out of her mouth, she knew she'd made a mistake. Calling him Markus and the dreamy quality in her voice surely didn't escape Dory's notice.

"You and my brother have grown close?" Her question held curiosity but no venom.

Phoebe lifted her tea and sipped it. "We are friends in the way that can happen when thrust together by circumstances."

Cocking her head made Dory's perfect blond curls slide to the side. "What was your father like?"

Thanking God for the change of subject, Phoebe said, "He was a kind and gentle man like Miles. He always made me feel like I was the light of his life, and I miss him every day."

"I have met your brother Miles. He is a friend of Tom's. He is a charming gentleman. It is strange he has not found a nice girl to marry."

Shrugging, Phoebe sipped the cooling tea. "As the third son, he has little to offer a girl of any breeding. He runs my oldest brother Ford's estates and does so very handily. I think he is happy."

"He has an allowance. Surely it is enough to keep a wife. Perhaps you can introduce him to a nice Everton lady. He should find someone smart and brave like his sister." Dory smiled over her cup.

"Men do not want women who have aged to the point where Everton's is their only hope." The lump of coal returned.

Dory laughed. "Men have no idea what they want until it is dropped into their laps, and even then, it can take some ranting to get them to see what is right before them."

Chapter 14

No. 1
*All assignments are to be satisfactorily completed before
an Everton lady is permitted to leave her post.*
—*The Everton Companion*
Rules of Conduct

She was leaving him, and there was nothing he could do about it. Markus had tried to talk to Phoebe, but she had sent him away. All day long the trunks were packed and things were made ready for her and Honoria to leave the next day. It might have been wrong, but he hoped the carriage would throw a wheel and keep her at Rosefield a few days longer.

Memories of one beautiful night ran wild in his mind as he stared at the ceiling above his bed. Phoebe's skin was silk and she responded to him as if they have been created for each other. Why couldn't she see that? Her strange sense of honor was keeping them apart, and he didn't know how to change her mind.

Markus tossed the blankets aside and pulled on his breeches and blouse before tromping down to the kitchen. The flickering candlelight stopped him on the servants' stairs. He eased down the remaining steps and peeked around the open doorway.

Head in her hand, she bit into a forkful of pie. Red hair cascaded over her arm and down her shoulders. Knowing its texture made him hard just at the thought of touching her. The candle glinted off a tear rolling down her cheek.

"Why are you crying?" He only whispered the question, but she jumped. Putting up both hands in surrender, he said, "I did not mean to frighten you."

"I thought you had come and gone." She took another bite of pie, but there was no joy in her face as she ate. Still, her skin gleamed in the flickering candlelight and she looked like a sad goddess of the night.

He sat next to her, took the fork from her, and leaned it on the edge of the plate. "You are sad because you are leaving yet I have asked you to stay."

Wiping her face, she sat up straight and pulled her shoulders back. "This is my third assignment and it is always emotional as they draw to an end."

Her words injured him but he was coming to understand this was her brave face. "Then you would tell me Rosefield has been no different from any other Everton posting?"

A deep breath brought her breasts to the edge of her shift as she leaned against him. "You know that is not true, Markus. No assignment will ever compare to being here with you and Elizabeth."

Joy burst inside him and he wrapped his arm around her. "Then stay, sweetheart. Stay here with us."

"I cannot. If you knew how much I wish things were different and how this is killing me, Markus, you would stop pursuing me." With another deep breath, she sat up away from him. "I have made my choice. I am an Everton lady. I come into a home and sort out the family's problems, then I leave and move on to the next assignment. It is a good life for a girl like me. When you remarry, is should be to a young girl from a substantial family. Someone who can add value to your home. I am on the shelf. This is no place for me."

He turned the chair to face her, grabbed the side edge of her chair, and pulled until the wooden seats met with a knock.

Phoebe gasped, wide-eyed, and stared at him.

"That is the most ridiculous thing I have ever heard. I do not care about your dowry and I certainly would not call you old."

She tried to pull away, but he held her shoulders. "You might not, but many would. People would say that I trapped you into marrying me. Eventually you would resent me. What happened between us is no reason to remain together. I will not marry you."

"I cannot pretend to understand your decision." He threaded his fingers through her hair and cupped the back of her head while pulling her into him with his other arm around her waist. "I see that what I want is not important. Your happiness is what is most concerning, and so out of respect for you, I will abide your wishes."

"Thank you." The words were a sad whisper with no force behind them.

Lowering his head, he kept his gaze locked with hers until their lips met.

She sighed into the kiss and he deepened it. Breath and body merged in a way he could compare to nothing else. Everything around him tightened to the one point where Phoebe was his. He made love to her lips the way he wished he could take her body. A lifetime of loving mashed into the few moments with Phoebe in his arms.

Every sigh and pant from her brought him joy and sorrow. She wrapped her arms around his shoulders and toyed with the hair at the back of his neck. Her touch set him on fire, branding him with her mark and tearing out his soul.

Sweet berry pie mixed with the warm taste of Phoebe overwhelmed his senses. His shaft tightened despite the knowledge he would get no relief. One last kiss was all it was.

Her tears mixed with salty remorse as he broke the contact. "I wish things were different. If you change your mind, I will honor my offer. Do not hesitate to contact me."

Lips parted and blinking at him so innocently, she was irresistible. "I shall not change my mind. You are a good man, Markus. Find a suitable wife and a mother for Elizabeth and be happy."

There was nothing left to say and his breaking heart held his tongue.

Phoebe slid off the opposite side of the chair and ran from the kitchen.

Head on his arm, he held his emotions in check. No good would come from mourning Phoebe, but this hurt almost as badly as losing Emma had. Every moment since she came into his life rolled around in his head. He searched for what he could have done differently to make her want to stay with him, but no epiphany came.

The sun peeked through the servants' door as Becca let the dairyman in with the milk and cheese. They stopped and stared at him. Becca said, "My lord, are you all right?"

Drawing a painful breath, he stood. "Fine."

"Can I get you something? I can have coffee for you in a few minutes." She rushed to the stove.

Markus walked to the door. "No. Nothing, Becca. I should go and start my day."

Instead of heading toward his bedroom, he crossed to the far end of the lower level and passed through a stone hallway to the wine cellar. Wine and brandy lined one wall in the perfectly temperate stone cellar. All he had to do was uncork a few and swallow away his pain. He ran his hand along the finest vintage and his mouth watered for a taste. Perhaps he could just have one glass to take the edge off. He might get through the day if he was just a little numb.

"It's early for a drink," Thomas said from the bottom step.

"Yes. I know." He swallowed and closed his eyes, hoping the need for drink would pass.

Thomas slapped his back. "Your very fine cook has some nice coffee brewing and food is in the works. Might be best if we went upstairs. I have taken the liberty of asking Blakely to have your bath drawn."

God, how he wanted a drink, but to have one would mean breaking his promise to Phoebe. Was her leaving reason enough to break his word? And what of his commitment to Elizabeth? "That was kind of you, Tom."

"Do you want to talk about whatever sent you into the cellar at dawn?" Thomas had always been the friend they could all tell their problems to. He was always there for his friends.

Markus had not been available to Thomas when he was in need. Another mistake he would have to make up for. "Miss Hallsmith is leaving."

"Do you still have need of her?" Thomas sat on the steps.

Markus clutched his elbows, hoping it would keep him from reaching for a bottle. "Not perhaps in the way you mean."

"Oh? Are you in love with Miss Hallsmith?"

Guilt and horror assaulted him. "I love Emma."

Cocking his head to one side, Thomas said, "Do you not think it is possible to love Emma and be in love with Phoebe?"

In the years he had loved Emma, another woman had never entered his mind in a romantic way. Not until Phoebe Hallsmith barged in and took over. Loving Emma was all consuming. "I do not know. I have loved Emma for so long."

With a nod, Thomas smiled. "You shall always love Emma. There is no reason you should stop, and I doubt Phoebe would ask that of you. As I understand it from your mother, Phoebe was a great friend of Emma's. If you love her, you might want to tell her."

"She is probably loading her carriage now. I asked her to stay and she refused. There is some silly code within the Everton Domestic Society that prohibits her from staying after her work is done."

Thomas shifted his feet. "Perhaps it is best to deal with one issue at a time. This cellar is cold and uncomfortable. Come upstairs and have a bath and break your fast. You can deal with your feelings for Miss Hallsmith later. She is only going to London. It is not as if she is leaving the country."

Hope edged into Markus's despair like an unwanted fiend. He turned back to the bottles. "Can you do something for me, Tom?"

"Anything." Thomas straightened his morning coat.

"Can you have all of this removed from Rosefield?" He gestured toward the wall of temptation.

A wide smile spread across Thomas's face. "It will be my pleasure, Markus. I have to say I am very proud of you."

"Thank you." Markus trudged up the steps forcing his desire for drink down. "I think that bath is just the thing, followed by a good meal."

Without commenting on the flurry of activity as Phoebe and Honoria made to leave, Markus went up the steps. He paused as he passed Honoria on the stairs. Her dark blue dress, cut with a nod to the Navy, she was more appropriately dressed than he'd ever seen her. "I wish you a safe journey, my lady."

"Thank you, my lord. I am sorry to see this assignment come to an end. I have enjoyed my time here at Rosefield. You have a lovely home. I hope you will spend more time here in the future." She made a pretty curtsy, considering they stood at the center of the steps.

"Your presence here has been a wonderful addition. You may consider yourself family and feel free to return any time. Elizabeth and I would be happy to see you again."

"That is most kind. I would enjoy seeing you both again. Now I must go and find Mr. Duck and say my goodbyes."

"Duck?" Markus was constantly surprised by the old groundskeeper.

She blushed. "He is quite good company and a fine friend."

Taking her hand, he bowed over it. "Best of luck to you."

"You will find Miss Hallsmith is finalizing her packing in her room."

"The lady has made it clear she does not wish to see me."

She patted his cheek. "You know nothing of women." With a giggle, she trotted down the steps and went toward the garden in search of Duck.

At the top of the stairs, he hesitated. Knowing he should ring for Blakely and not come out of his bath until Phoebe was long gone did not stop him from walking to her bedroom door. He stood outside, sad that soon this room would just be a guest room and not where his sweet Phoebe spent restless nights. He knocked.

"Yes, come in."

Opening the door bathed him in her clean fresh scent. She stood by the window staring out into the gardens while Arwen fussed over her trunk.

Arwen curtsied and excused herself.

A long sigh escaped Phoebe as she turned toward him. "We are ready to take our leave of you."

It was proper to keep the door open when visiting a lady without a chaperon, but Markus closed the door. He crossed to her and wrapped her in his arms.

She threaded her fingers through his hair and toyed with the curls at the back of his neck.

Kissing her cheek, her chin, then capturing her lips, he reveled in the moan that merged with his own. There was perfection in their kisses and the way their bodies fit together. Breaking the kiss, he breathed her in. "I wish you all the happiness you can stand, Phoebe. I want only good for you."

"And I for you, Markus. You and Elizabeth will be better now. I am confident you have turned a corner and will never go back."

If he lied, he could force her to stay. Tell her that he would slide back into his former drunkenness and she would feel compelled to remain. He tucked her silken hair behind her ear. "I will be the model father. You have nothing to worry about."

Lifting on her toes, she pressed her lips to his. Tears ran freely down her face but she smiled. "I will miss you."

"My offer still stands...."

Before he could renew the offer in words, she pressed her fingers to his lips. "No. I am an Everton lady and it is time to return to London. You have everything in order here."

Stepping out of his embrace, she patted her hair and brushed out her gray skirt. "Goodbye, my lord."

He watched as she stepped around him and walked to the door. "I have not changed my mind either, Phoebe. My offer still stands should you change your mind."

Back to him, she paused for a heartbeat. Shoulders straight, she opened the door and walked out of his life.

* * * *

Despite his need for Phoebe, Markus struggled with the idea of romantic love with anyone but Emma. After his bath, he went downstairs to break his fast.

Mother, Dory, Thomas, and Elizabeth all sat eating.

Miss Cavot fed Elizabeth, who played with as much food as she ate. The new nanny smiled and spoke in low tones as she coaxed more food into her.

Dory smiled. "I rather like this tradition of having Elizabeth at the table. Mother and I have decided breaking our fasts should be done here rather than in our rooms."

Markus sat and a footman brought his coffee. "I am surprised you approve, Mother. When we were young you always took your breakfast in your room."

"As Dorothea said, your tradition appeals to me. It is comforting to see one's family in the morning over a meal." Margaret sipped her coffee and watched him over the rim of the cup. "Miss Hallsmith did a remarkable job. I was sorry to see her go so early this morning."

"She will be starving by the time they reach London," Dory said.

Markus held his breath until the pain ebbed. "She did not break her fast?"

Dory shook her head. "Lady Chervil stopped in for a bite to eat, but Miss Hallsmith only said her goodbyes and out the door she went. Surely, she will have another assignment in short order. She really is magnificent at her job."

Jared Blunt entered the breakfast room and bowed. "Sir, I know you said I could not bother Miss Hallsmith, but I need to speak to her."

Fingers itching to strangle Blunt's skinny neck, Markus took the offered newspaper from Thomas. "You will have to go to London if you want to speak to her, Blunt. I no longer have command over who bothers Miss Hallsmith."

Wide-eyed and mouth agape, Jared Blunt stammered. "She is gone?"

"To London." Markus read the same sentence about some ninny who was engaged to an earl for the sixth time.

Blunt masked his features and stood straight. "I must request some time away, my lord."

It was within Markus's power to keep at least one suitor away from Phoebe, but if she wanted Blunt, she should have him. "Take what time you need. I can manage awhile without you."

With a bow, Blunt ran from the room.

Markus ate a bite of toast and drank his coffee before excusing himself to hide away in his study. The mountain of work forced on him by his father's negligence and his own was staggering and would keep his mind off Phoebe and her suitors.

He'd barely read a paragraph of a late notice from the magistrate when his mother walked in without knocking.

He stood. "Mother, is something wrong?"

It might have been the first time he'd ever seen his mother at a loss for what to say. She circled the room then stopped at the window and stared into the garden. A light snow blew snow flurries in all directions. "I am fond of Miss Hallsmith."

Unsure why his mother made the statement, Markus waited for more information. When none came, he said, "I am fond of her as well."

"Did you ruin her?" Here was the mother he knew. Direct and insulting but thoroughly observant.

"I do not believe that is an appropriate question. However, if I had, Mother, you can be sure I would have done the right thing and made the lady an offer of marriage." His heart beat as if he were back in front of the headmaster at Eton after hitting Wormwood with a bat.

Finally, she walked to the desk and sat facing him. "I thought she would be good for you and my granddaughter."

He eased into his chair, wary of where this conversation was going. "And you were right. Going to Everton to help me sort through things was an excellent idea. I appreciate what you have done, Mother."

"I chose Miss Phoebe Hallsmith specifically because she has always had a strong will. I never liked her mother much, but the girl always struck me as sensible and smart." Mother picked a piece of lint from her royal blue skirt.

"What are you getting at?"

"Why did she leave?"

"Her obligation here was fulfilled. Miss Cavot's arrival and success with Elizabeth was the last duty she felt necessary, and now she will take on some other chore with some other family." It hurt to say the words. Phoebe was more than an Everton lady. She'd ripped his heart from his chest and taken it to London with her.

"It pains me to say that I raised an idiot, but there it is. That girl was perfect for you. You clearly have feelings for her yet you let her get away and be courted by that secretary, and from what the servants tell me there is an old fiancé sniffing at her skirts as well."

"Mother, it is none of your business, but I asked her to stay. Miss Hallsmith declined. What would you have me do, chain her to the house? Lock her in a dungeon?"

Whatever Mother opened her mouth to say was stopped by a knock on the door and Elizabeth running in. Her pale yellow dress floated around her.

Miss Cavot stood at the threshold, red-faced. "I am sorry, my lord. She is due for a nap, but became hysterical and ran to your door."

Markus picked Elizabeth up and put her on his lap. "It is all right, Miss Cavot. You may leave her with me. I will take her up for her nap in a few minutes."

The door closed and Markus leaned down, taking in the sweet scent of her hair. Perhaps his heart was not dead after all. He certainly had room for Elizabeth. More than enough room, in fact. "What seems to be the trouble, Elizabeth?"

She turned her cherub face toward him. Eyebrows drawn down and nose scrunched up, she opened her mouth. "Papa, want Fee."

Though her words stung, the fact that she had said them forced joy into his heart until he thought he might drown in it. He wanted to dance around the house screaming about her having spoken, but he feared that might quiet her again. Pretending her speaking was normal would be best. "I am certain you miss Phoebe, as we all do, Elizabeth. She has gone back to her own life and we have much to do here at home."

Elizabeth stuck her thumb in her mouth and leaned her head on his chest. "Fee," she said around her thumb.

Daring to glance at Mother, he saw her raised eyebrows in that *I told you so* way she had. "I will be in the small parlor if you need me. I have several letters to write."

"I will see you at luncheon, Mother."

With a nod, she left the study and closed the door behind her.

"If the weather improves in the next day or two, I think you and I should go and visit your mother, Elizabeth. I have been negligent in visiting and you have never been. I have much to atone for." His mother was right. He was an idiot. So many things he should have done, but instead he drank, let his father run his inheritance into the ground, ignored his daughter, and let Phoebe Hallsmith walk away.

Holding Elizabeth with one arm, he jotted a note to James Hardwig asking if there was any progress finding Father. He addressed it to Bow Street and left it on the tray to be posted. "Time for your nap, Elizabeth."

"Papa." Her voice was scratchy but high and sweet.

It was the most beautiful sound he'd ever heard. "I am very pleased to hear you call me that. Do you like your new nanny?"

She nodded. "Nice, Winny."

Chuckling, he lifted her and headed toward the nursery.

Miss Cavot waited with a pleasant smile and the serenity that hovered around her. "Ready for a nap now, Miss?"

Elizabeth went to her willingly but mumbled something about Fee before Markus made his escape. Aching on the inside, he changed his clothes and went to the barn. A good long ride on a cool day would take one redhead off his mind. At least he hoped so. He waved to Duck, who put feed in the chicken coop.

A boy with pale skin and a shock of dark hair ran into the yard. "Mi'lord?"

"I need a horse saddled."

"Yes, Sir." He turned.

"What is your name, boy?" It was time he stopped thinking of everyone as the new stableboy or the new maid. This was his home, and he needed to know the people in it. He made a note to have the staff gathered for proper introductions and a short chat with each.

"Wyatt, mi'lord. I just come to work for you a week ago." His hair fell over his eyes and he brushed it back.

"Welcome to Rosefield, Wyatt. I am sure you will be a worthy addition to the staff."

Wyatt gave a toothy grin and ran into the barn.

Leaning on the fence that surrounded the stable yard, Markus shivered. Winter would be there any day. It had been teasing for some time. Emma's roses were cut back and nothing bloomed any longer. London would be quiet. What would Phoebe do for the long, cold months? Who would protect her from Durnst and Blunt?

Knowing she didn't need his protection didn't make him feel any less responsible. If only he could discover why she wouldn't stay. It could be that he was too much work and she had done all she could. Yet she was not without desire for him. Phoebe was not the type to share herself with a man she did not care for.

"Your horse, my lord." Wyatt handed him the reins.

Markus jumped into the saddle. "Thank you."

When Wyatt opened the gate, Markus trotted out and kept a slow pace for a mile or so before he kicked the horse into a gallop. The cold air whipped his cheeks and made his eyes tear. The panting horse forced Markus to slow at the far end of his property.

George Harper strode down the road toward him. "Good afternoon, my lord. Are you well? You look a bit…"

Leaving the sentence unfinished was a kindness. Wet streaks nearly froze on his face. Dismounting, he patted the horse and took the leather over her head, then wiped his face on the sleeve of his coat. "I am fine, George. Just a bit out of sorts."

They walked along together. "Anything I can help you with?"

"Unless you can explain women to me, I think not." Legs aching from the strenuous ride, Markus struggled to keep up with George.

Laughing, George slapped him on the back. "On one hand, it's good to hear you have such troubles, my lord. On the other, I feel for you. Women are too complicated to ever fathom."

"Do you think a man can truly love two women in his lifetime?" Markus wished he could take the question back but the thought that plagued him popped out before he could stop it. There was something kind and easy about George that made talking to him natural.

George stopped and kicked the dirt road. "I think the heart has an infinite ability to love. Is that what's troubling you?"

He had gone this far in embarrassing himself; he might as well take the next step. "If I love Phoebe, does that mean I did not truly love my Emma? Or if my love for Emma was pure, how can I love Phoebe the way she deserves?"

"Ah, I heard Miss Hallsmith left Rosefield today. She's a good girl, that one. I'm not sure I'm the best person to give advice on matters of the heart. Pearl had to practically bash me over the head to make me realize she was the woman for me."

"You both seem quite happy."

A wide smile spread across George's face. "I would say so. Pearl is the light of my life."

"Then you think there is only one love for a man in this world?" Heart aching, Markus struggled to draw breath.

Sticking his hands in his pockets, George stared at the ground and walked on down the road.

Markus tugged the reins and followed. The chill seeped through his jacket and he resigned himself that George would not answer because of course a man can only have one great love. Emma was his, and he would not tarnish that memory by pretending another woman could fill her place in his heart.

George cleared his throat. "I think there is room for more than one love in a man's heart."

Stopping, Markus had to replay the words in his head. It was the last thing he expected George to say. "You do?"

Nodding, he walked on with his eyes narrowed in thought. "I'm not saying a great love can be replaced. I don't think that is possible. Maybe you've been looking at this the wrong way, my lord."

"How so?" Markus leaned into the mare's warmth.

"You said that you worried if you loved Miss Hallsmith it means that you didn't truly love my lady, as if you would be replacing one with the other. Her ladyship is part of you and part of your family and always will be. You need not wipe her memory away to add another family member. A man with a big heart, like yourself, can make a new place for a great love. I don't think Miss Hallsmith would want to take her ladyship's place anyway. She is the kind of woman who makes a place for herself in the world. Just because they would share a title does not mean one must disappear to allow the other. You will always love her ladyship and she will keep her place in your heart and in your home. You have little Miss Elizabeth, and she is an extension of the love you shared. If you love Phoebe Hallsmith, then she has found a new place in your life like the pieces of a puzzle slide together. I cannot imagine the Lord would be so cruel as to limit your capacity for love. A man may have ten children and enough love to encompass them all." George said the last as if talking to himself.

"I should not have let her go." Markus's heart ached and his hands shook. He had made a monumental mistake.

George turned his head toward Markus for the first time since beginning his speech. "London is not so far away."

Hope tugged inside him. He slapped George on the back. "Thank you for your time, George. I had no idea farmers were quite so wise."

Laughing, George said, "Don't you go spreading it around. We'll have a line out the door if you tell folks all the good advice we farmers have to give."

They shook hands and Markus mounted his horse. At a slower pace, he headed back to Rosefield.

A light snow drifted down but he was warmer than before. He needed to find a way to convince Phoebe that he was the right man for her and the rest of her concerns were irrelevant.

Thomas stepped out of the house as Markus approached. "We have been looking for you."

Dismounting, he sensed Thomas's tension and his own tightened. "I went for a ride. What has happened? Is Elizabeth all right?"

Handing the horse over to a footman he said, "Thank you, Robert."

"My lord." Robert pulled his collar up and his hat down against the cold.

"Elizabeth is fine. I did not mean to alarm you. The earl has arrived." Thomas's usually easy manner was stiff and filled with rage.

"My father is here? How odd. If you would like to take Dory and leave, I completely understand. The man tried to kill you. There is no need to subject yourself to his antics, Tom." Markus climbed the steps and Watson opened the front door for them.

"At the moment, his lordship is unconscious in your parlor. I cannot say that I am thrilled with his presence but I will not leave you in your hour of need."

A change of clothes and a hot meal was what Markus needed. He stopped at the steps leading to the bedrooms. "I can deal with Father. You may either seclude yourself or head for home. I will not blame you for either course. I am certain Dory has no desire to see our father."

"What will you do?" Thomas asked.

"I was planning to go to London tomorrow, but I suppose that will have to wait." The ache in his chest returned. Damn, but he wanted to see Phoebe and find out if she loved him. He had things to tell her, but he could not leave with Father in the house. Lord only knew what havoc the man could cause if left on his own.

Chapter 15

London held none of the appeal it had in Phoebe's youth or even months before when she had fled her brother's estate to join the Everton Domestic Society. The rutted streets bounced her about like a ragdoll and even Honoria's light chatter did not brighten her mood.

"Phoebe, you made your decision, now stop pouting," Honoria said from the opposite seat in the closed carriage.

Swallowing down her sorrow, Phebe pulled her shoulders back. "You are right. I wish I knew I did the right thing."

Honoria made a face as if she'd eaten something horrible. "You already know my feelings on the subject, so I will not beat the matter to death."

Markus didn't love her. He felt obligated to her. Perhaps she could tolerate that from someone she didn't love, but not from Markus. It would break her into a million pieces to see him every day and know he could never love her. He was a good man, but his heart belonged to Emma, and she left no room for anyone else. Besides, Emma had been the daughter of an earl. Being disowned meant she was just Miss Hallsmith now. Men like Markus Flammel did not fall in love with girls like her. He cared for her, if his sweet lovemaking was any indication, but that too was not enough. She was an old maid and she would have to accept that and be happy with her decision.

The carriage stopped in front of Everton House. Lady Jane Everton waited on the top step. She clasped her hands in front of her gray skirt. The crisp white of her blouse stood out in relief against the dark stone and black door. Not one hair out of place, Lady Jane was the perfect example of what to be.

Phoebe's inadequacies glared in her presence. "Lady Jane, is something amiss?"

"Not at all, Miss Hallsmith. I heard the carriage approach and thought I would spend a moment with you before you go to your room for a rest. Lady Chervil, you look as stunning as ever."

Lady Chervil beamed and kissed Lady Jane's cheek. "It's good to be back, though Rosefield was our finest assignment yet. I do not know when I have seen an Everton lady make more of a difference in the lives of her clients. I imagine the Flammels will rave about the society after what Phoebe did for them."

"I have already had a letter from the countess declaring Miss Hallsmith a miracle. I believe they are all well pleased. Can you spare a few minutes, Miss Hallsmith?" Jane let the footman open the door.

"Of course." Phoebe followed Jane and Honoria inside.

Honoria went directly upstairs saying she needed to rest after the long trip. "I will see you both at supper."

Letting Arwen deal with her luggage, Phoebe followed Jane into the office. "I am glad Lady Castlereagh was pleased with the outcome of my employment."

Jane sat behind the desk. "She actually used the word *overjoyed.*" I did not even know the countess knew that word."

They laughed.

Tapping her fingers on the desk, Jane hesitated. "Something in her ladyship's letter troubled me though, Miss Hallsmith."

Phoebe's heart stopped. "Oh. What was that?"

"May I be blunt, Miss Hallsmith?"

"I suppose you had better call me Phoebe if you have something of this much concern to discuss, my lady."

Jane sighed. "She said his lordship's attachment was great and a friendship had developed between the two of you, which she had not expected. Is it merely a friendship, Phoebe?"

A large part of Phoebe wanted to burst into tears and confide in Jane, but that would not do for an Everton lady. "His lordship and I are friends.

I would not call that a mere thing, but our friendship grew out of the need for him to trust me as his recovery required."

Another long sigh pushed from Jane's lips. "You are in love with him."

Phoebe sat forward, afraid she was about to be put out on the street or worse, sent back to her brother. "My feelings are irrelevant, my lady. I did what I was hired to do. His lordship has stopped drinking, Rosefield is in order, and Miss Elizabeth is safe, with a father who loves her and a nanny who will see to her needs."

Jane raised a hand for peace. "Do not panic, Miss Hallsmith. I only worry for your happiness. No one is trying to force you out of the society. You will always have a home here, if you wish it."

All the air rushed back into Phoebe and she sat back against the hard chair. "I am more grateful than you can know."

"There is no need for gratitude, and you would be surprised how much I know about such things. Is there no hope that his lordship returns your feelings?" Surprising sadness marred Jane's usually stoic expression, and she placed her hands on the desk, fingers threaded together.

"It is an inappropriate match, my lady. No, there is no hope, but thank you for your concern. I will be fine. Knowing that I am safe here is more than a girl like me could ever hope for."

"Pish. Inappropriate by some standards perhaps, but if he loves you and you clearly love him, the rest can be overcome." Jane waved an all-encompassing hand.

"Even if he did love me, and he does not, that is not realistic. It does not happen in the real world, only in dreams."

Jane laughed and shook her head. "Did you know that I was the nanny to Lord Everton's son? I had no title and was of good but unimportant birth. My family had no money and my father was in trade."

Unable to believe her ears, she shook her head and closed her mouth. "I did not know that, my lady."

Standing, Jane smoothed her skirts and walked to the window. "Yes, well, I do not like to make such a thing public, as it might be damaging to the domestic society. Still, it is the truth. Rupert was a widower and his housekeeper hired me to care for his young son. I had barely been making ends meet on my own and my parents could scarcely afford to take care of themselves. When my mother and I failed to find me a husband who could take me off their hands, I made the decision to step out on my own. If not for the post as a nanny, I do not know what would have become of me. We fell in love over chess in the evenings and he asked me to marry him. Of course, I resisted, stating the inappropriateness of the match. I went as far as to resign my post, but Rupert was persistent in his pursuit and eventually I saw that neither of us would be happy alone."

Phoebe lost herself in the singsong tones of Jane's voice and the romantic tale. "He must love you very much."

Still looking out the window, Jane's shoulders rose and fell. "Yes. We have been quite happy and all of this happened many years ago. When I told Rupert of my struggles to live before I began working for him, he suggested there may be a way to help other women in similar positions. That is how the Everton Domestic Society came to be."

Phoebe's head spun. "I had no idea."

"I only tell you this so that you will be open minded should Lord Devonrose make an offer." Jane returned to the desk.

The angry hand that had been strangling her heart for days gripped tighter. "I do not think that will be the case, but thank you, my lady."

Jane cocked her head and shrugged. "One other thing, Miss Hallsmith. If you could stand a short assignment in two days, Miss Tara Winkle needs our support for the Davenport ball. It would only be for the preparation and the night of the ball. Her mother, Lady Tollfield, fears the girl will sit in a corner all night and never be married."

Exhaustion lay like a blanket over Phoebe. Still, there was work to do and she was committed to her career. Her inability to sleep must never interfere with her being the best Everton lady she could be. "Two days will be sufficient time to recover. I am sure I can help Miss Winkle for one night."

"Thank you, Miss Hallsmith. Go and get some rest now. I will see you at supper." Jane returned her expression to the pleasant, calm and reassuring face she generally wore.

Phoebe was privileged to have seen another side of her benefactor. She left the office and went to find the comfort of her own room for a few hours. Of course, sleep was impossible and all she could think of was Markus and having his arms wrapped around her.

It would not do. She pulled on her boots and coat and went to walk the gardens. Perhaps the cool air would blow away these feelings.

* * * *

Phoebe spent the afternoon overseeing Miss Winkle's dress and hair before they arrived at the Davenport ball. She had the carriage deliver them early in the evening as Phoebe felt the lighter crowd would be less intimidating for her young charge.

"Oh, Miss Hallsmith, I do not know how I will get through this. There are so many people," Tara whispered. Tara Winkle was a pretty girl of sixteen with brown hair and blue eyes, fair skin, and a shy disposition.

"It will be more crowded in an hour. That is when it is more fashionable to arrive." Phoebe scanned the room. The Davenports had one of the largest ballrooms in London. One wall was completely dedicated to several arched French doors that led to a patio. The walls were painted pale blue and trimmed in rich cream. Several mirrors reflected the light of four chandeliers. It was elegant, and when all the finely dressed ton swirled around the highly polished floor, it would be stunning.

Young John Stagemore had arrived early as well and stared from the other side of the ballroom. His crisp white cravat gave him an elegant air. More stylish than she would have thought, he wore a burgundy waistcoat with his fine black suit. Shy as he might be, he had a sense of fashion that was appealing without making him seem a peacock.

As his older brother was friendly with Phoebe's brother Miles, she had met him on several occasions. She nodded toward him.

With a wide grin, John approached. His charming blush exaggerated by his fair hair and stark blue eyes. "Miss Hallsmith, I feared I would not know a soul at this ball. It is good to see you."

"How do you do, Mr. Stagemore? May I introduce my friend, Miss Tara Winkle?"

John bowed. "A pleasure to meet you, Miss Winkle."

Dropping into a curtsy, Tara said, "How do you do, Mr. Stagemore?"

His blush deepened. "I am embarrassed to admit, I do not care for the crowds at these events. My mother insisted I come and I thought to arrive early and beat the crush."

Tara smiled and exhaled for the first time since they'd arrived. "I understand completely, Mr. Stagemore. It can be daunting to walk into the middle of so many of society's finest and not know anyone. Miss Hallsmith was kind enough to suggest we arrive early as well. I am not accustomed to large gatherings."

"Nor I." John's smile was enough to light the entire room without the benefit of the chandeliers. "Perhaps you would do me the honor of the first two dances, Miss Winkle? Surely that will ease the torment for us both."

Phoebe admired John's smooth request even if he did not know he'd been both savior and rogue at once. The boy had potential.

"I would be delighted, Mr. Stagemore."

"Until then." With a bow, John strode away far more confident than when he arrived.

"Well done, Miss Winkle. We are off to a fine start." It was good for Phoebe to be distracted by someone else's life and not mired in thoughts of her own.

Tara clapped, sending her reticule into a spin. "He seemed very nice."

"He is and he comes from a good family. No title, but a family your mother would most definitely approve." Phoebe scanned for more dance prospects, then groaned as Gavin crossed the threshold and made straight for her. "Please excuse what you are about to witness, Miss Winkle."

"I beg your pardon?" Tara asked.

Gavin stopped a foot from them and bowed, his pretty face marred by rage at not getting his way. "Miss Hallsmith, I do not appreciate having to trek across the country after you. You might have left word that you were leaving Rosefield."

He was so rude she didn't bother to introduce Tara. There was no need to subject the girl to more of Gavin.

Despite how loudly Gavin had spoken, Phoebe kept her voice soft so that the entire room did not hear. "I am not answerable to you, Mr. Durnst, and my assignment was over. I am sorry if you traveled out of your way, but I did not ask you to come after me. In fact, I am certain I forbid it."

"I am trying very hard not to become furious with you. As we are in public, I will hold my tongue, and we will speak during the first dance." He crossed his arms.

"And if I refuse to dance with you?" She already knew she was pushing him, but she didn't care.

"Then I will make a scene right here and now." His smirk was enough to make her want to kick him in the shin.

Tara stared, wide-eyed. Lady Tollfield frowned from across the room, then narrowed her eyes on Phoebe and patted her white wig.

A scene would not be welcome. Phoebe stifled a sigh. "I will dance with you, Mr. Durnst, but only one dance and only if you promise to not make a spectacle of yourself."

He bowed, smirked, and strode away.

Leaning in, Tara giggled. "Miss Hallsmith, you are turning out to be the most interesting person at this ball."

"Goodness, I hope not, Miss Winkle."

As if it were some tragic comedy in the theater, Jared walked in through the garden door and pardoned himself around the outside of the room toward them.

"Unfortunately, Miss Winkle, this is not my best night. Please excuse the next chapter of this farce."

"I beg your pardon?" Tara turned her head, looking for whatever was coming.

Jared stopped in front of them. "Good evening, Miss Hallsmith. You look lovely."

"Thank you, Mr. Blunt. It is surprising to see you here."

He bowed and glanced around as if he might be tossed out at any moment. "I had to call in a few favors to gain an invitation. Working people like you and I rarely are favored at such balls. However, it is early in the season, and I think Lady Davenport feared there would be a lack of men for dancing."

Since he was oblivious to his insult, Phoebe pretended she hadn't noticed. "May I introduce my friend, Miss Winkle?" Phoebe was attempting polite conversation. Perhaps she could distract him.

"How do you do, Miss Winkle?"

Tara curtsied and hid a giggle behind her gloved hand.

"You followed me to London, Mr. Blunt?" Phoebe failed to hide the annoyance in her voice.

Jared grinned as if he had no clue she was put out by his behavior. "Of course. You cannot be ignorant of my intentions, Miss Hallsmith. I could not let you run off and not pursue. Though I admit it would have been nice had I heard of your leaving Rosefield from you rather than his lordship."

"My assignment was finished. I did not need to report to you."

His lips twisted to that pert pucker he got when annoyed, then flashed to calm before he spoke. "May I dance with you tonight, Miss Hallsmith?"

"My second dance is free." She resigned herself to the ridiculous evening.

Grinning, he bowed to each of them and had a distinct bounce in his step as he walked away.

"Who are these men, Miss Hallsmith? Forgive me, it is none of my business. I like the second one better than the first. Though, the first was better looking." Tara fluffed her skirt and sat in one of the chairs lining the ballroom.

Suddenly very tired, Phoebe sat next to her. "They are vying for my hand and they are both the wrong man."

Tara leaned forward. "Is there a right man in this scenario?"

Clearly, Tara was brighter than Phoebe had originally given her credit for. "It is a long story and one we cannot discuss in the middle of a ball where it is my job to get you seen by the ton."

Pulling a face, Tara said, "I think I would rather hear your story."

Phoebe laughed. "Another time. The music is starting and you have a gentleman walking this way."

Unfortunately, it also meant that a gentleman was heading toward her, though Gavin's gentlemanly qualities were questionable. His blond curls bounced around his strong jaw as he bounded across the ballroom. He held his shoulders back and bowed with his hand out for her to join him in the minuet. Despite how good looking he was, Phoebe cringed.

Luckily the complex dance meant that they would not be in proximity for any length of time. She passed Tara, who grinned happily. At least someone was enjoying the ball.

When the music stopped, Gavin bowed and she curtsied. He escorted her back to the mantel side of the room where he had collected her. "I would like a few moments of your time, Miss Hallsmith."

Honoria glided over with a flower in one hand and a fan in the other. Where she had found a lily in the cold of London, Phoebe had no idea. Sparkling with too much jewelry and smiling, she settled next to Phoebe. "Miss Hallsmith, you look lovely."

"As do you, Lady Chervil."

Gavin cleared his throat. "Miss Hallsmith, may I have a few minutes of your time?"

"I really do not see why, but if you must, you may speak to me on Tuesday afternoon. For now, I have promised the next dance to Mr. Blunt." Phoebe curtsied, dismissing him.

Tara returned to her side, said something in Mr. Stagemore's ear, and he rushed off.

Face twisted with emotion, Gavin leaned close. "Your brother is very much in favor of our marrying."

"Then perhaps you should marry Ford." The temper she tried so hard to keep restrained simmered near the edge of her control. She was not setting a good example, but she would not be bullied by Gavin or Ford.

"He will hear of this."

Phoebe took a breath and stepped forward so that she was inches from Gavin's red face. "If you think that threatening me with the wrath of my brother is the way to win me over, you are sadly mistaken, Mr. Durnst. And if you continue to offend me you will not be welcome in Everton House on Tuesday afternoon to say whatever it is you mean to. I suggest you stop now and enjoy your evening. Perhaps there is another young woman here who would be pleased to dance with you."

"Is this a random day you have picked?"

He had a point, but she held her head high and pulled her shoulders back. "It is the first day I am available for visitors. You may feel free to decline."

Gavin held his breath and his eyes widened before he relaxed and stepped back. "Until Tuesday then, Miss Hallsmith."

Waving her fan in front of her face, Honoria placed the flower on the mantel. "Oh, you do entertain, Phoebe."

"I am so glad you are amused, Honoria." Phoebe needed air, but Jared was on his way over to claim his dance. "Miss Winkle, how did your first dance go?"

"Better than yours. Mr. Stagemore is a perfect gentleman. He is coming over with lemonade. However, now I wish I could just stay with you. Your life is far more interesting than anything else at this ball."

Phoebe turned and narrowed her gaze on Tara and Honoria. "I am so pleased to be an amusement for the both of you. Now if you will excuse me, I must dance with another man determined to give me what I do not want." Spinning on her heels landed her directly in front of the approaching Jared Blunt.

The moment they reached the dance floor, Jared said, "Tell me you will marry me, Miss Hallsmith."

It was like a cruel joke. For years, no one asked, and now everyone wanted to marry her but all for the wrong reasons. "I most certainly will not. I told you that in the country and I do not see why you would think asking me in public would make me respond differently." The dance carried her away for several phrases.

Jared clomped along through the steps until he returned to her side. "I had hoped some time would give you clarity on the subject. If you would prefer to speak of this in private, I understand. It is out of the ordinary to propose during a dance, but I am smitten and could not wait."

"You do not sound smitten." Another partner swept her away for a turn around the room. Once again in line, she took Jared's sweaty hand. "You sound desperate."

"I…you…that is not true. Though I must be completely honest, marrying the daughter of a viscount would be quite good for me. And as you will be my wife, it would be good for you as well. I can take ample care of you."

Silently she allowed herself to be promenaded while her mind raced and her rage grew. It had taken years of her life to keep the least provocation from erupting. However, this was not the least. No one should have to endure these idiotic men. The dance came back around to Jared. "I thank you for your honesty, Mr. Blunt. I can see how you have calculated everything. I'm sure you also have hope of my reconciliation with my family and perhaps a dowry at some point, Mr. Blunt."

"I will not discuss it here." His lips drew into a thin line.

The music drew to a close. "Very well, you may visit me at Everton House on Tuesday afternoon. You can also come up with a good reason for me to say yes to your request for my hand. Your adoration notwithstanding."

Phoebe turned and walked to the mantel where Honoria watched while chatting up the chubby Lord Countroy.

The ball could not end quickly enough for Phoebe. She made sure that Tara had several other dance partners all of whom were eligible to marry a woman of her standing. Late in the evening, Tara danced the last dance and her mother asked if they could drop Phoebe home. Thankfully Honoria was still skipping around the ball.

"I will manage with Lady Chervil, thank you. I hope you enjoyed the ball, Miss Winkle."

Clapping, Tara grinned. "It was wonderful. I could not have done it without you, Miss Hallsmith. Thank you. I hope you will allow me to call on you. I do so enjoy your company."

Lady Tollfield frowned.

Plastering a smile on her face, Phoebe said, "It is not proper for a young lady to pay a call to Everton House. It is a place of business. I do wish you all the best, Miss Winkle."

Tara gave her mother a look that said this was not the timid girl of a day ago. "Never mind, Miss Hallsmith, I am sure we shall meet again."

"I look forward to it." She made a curtsy and corralled Honoria before calling for the carriage.

Once inside, Honoria waved her fan around. "Do you think you will marry either of them?"

"No." Phoebe watched the city go by dark and shadowy with only the moon to light their way.

"That Mr. Durnst is very hansome."

"He is a snake."

Honoria smiled but quickly hid it behind her fan. "And what of Mr. Blunt?"

"He is a fool, and they both are only after me for titles and money."

Honoria put her fan in her lap and snapped it closed. "But Mr. Blunt liked you from the moment he met you."

It was true. Jared might make someone a good husband, but it would not be Phoebe. The notion made her groan. "I have given this matter far too much thought. Neither will suit. I will just deal with Ford's temper and then go back to being disowned at his convenience."

With a sharp laugh, Honoria said, "He does seem quite involved in your life for a man who disavowed his stewardship."

A long sigh spread through Phoebe and exhaustion seeped into her bones. "Indeed."

Chapter 16

No. 5
Everton ladies and staff are never to be a burden on the client.
—The Everton Companion
Rules of Conduct

Markus has seen his father in every state of drunkenness over the last fifteen years, but he was not prepared for the wretch standing in his study.

Geoffrey Flammel, the Earl of Castlereagh, teetered near the bookshelves. His skin was a yellow color and his eyes red slits. While he wore a fine suit, it hung on him as if it had been made for someone else. "Where is the damn brandy?"

"I gave it up." Markus sat behind his desk, hoping the enormous piece of furniture would distance him from the similarities in Father.

Father turned and stared at Markus, though his eyes never found focus. He waved a hand and collapsed onto the chair. "Wine will do."

"There is no wine either, Father. I have given up drink." Leaning back in his chair, he dreaded that he had ever appeared so weak and stupid to his sweet Elizabeth. If not for Phoebe, he might have found himself in this state.

"Gave up drink? What nonsense is this? A man does not give up what is rightfully his." His head lolled to one side and his eyes closed before he snapped back awake and gazed at Markus as if he not seen him before. "Ah, son. Go and get me a brandy, will you?"

Markus leaned forward placing his elbows on the desk. "Father, there are no spirits in this house. I have given up drinking in favor of taking care of my family."

Lips pulled back to expose his yellowed teeth, Father made a scoffing sound. "Do you think I'm blind and deaf? Do you think I don't know what everyone is saying? You have no family. A mute child and a dead wife is all you have, boy. Now go and fetch me a drink."

"You have no power over me, Father. I can see that you have ruined your health and I am sorry for that. I would suggest that you stop drinking or whatever vice you have fallen to, but I know my words would fall on deaf ears. I will tell you this: if you ever say an unkind thing about my daughter again, I will not wait for the drink to kill you." This was not the man who had played with him as a small boy or even the tyrant who had railed at him in his teen and adult years. A wretched stranger sat across from him and while he said he was unaffected, his heart broke.

Cocking his head, Father blinked several times. "No spirits? You really have stopped drinking?"

"Yes, Father." Markus pressed his hands to the wooden top and braced for whatever Father would say.

Running his hand through his graying hair, Geoffrey leaned forward, barely catching himself on his knees. "You are stronger than me, Markus. I let it all go to hell. I never hoped to be perfect, but there was a time when I had hoped to be a better father and husband."

"There was a time when you were better. A time before you let your vices rule your life."

"I tried to kill little Dory's husband. Did you know that?" His voice scraped like stone against stone.

Markus wanted to comfort him, but Phoebe's toughness had snapped him out of his stupidity. "I heard."

"She will never forgive me." His shoulder shook.

"No. I do not imagine she ever will. Certainly, not as you are." He clutched the desk pushing away his jumbled emotions. Caving in or breaking down would not help this man, and it would not make him feel any better. He had to stand strong and be the stable force in his family. It was his duty.

Tears streaked Father's cheeks when he lifted his face. "Is there any chance?"

It took his swallowing several times before he knew his voice would carry the strength necessary. "Stop drinking, pull yourself together, give up gambling, and stay away from the sort of people you have befriended in recent years. Show her that you have made changes."

"Then my girl will look at me as she did when she was little?"

Unable to lie, he said, "Probably not, but after a time, she might not look at you with disdain."

Geoffrey slumped farther into the chair and his eyes rolled back and closed.

Watching the rise and fall of his father's chest, Markus sat back and made a mental list of the things he needed to see to. The pieces of his father's estate that needed immediate attention, the repairs to the front of Rosefield and the fence in the north pasture. He wanted to meet with each of his tenant farmers before the spring planting to discuss George Harper's methods and increase production. Time ticked away on all his plans and most of all, Phoebe. He had to convince her to come home, to be his.

"Where is the damn brandy, boy?" Father sat up and looked around the office with unfocused eyes.

"Perhaps you might have a bite to eat, Father. I shall have Cook prepare you some nice soup." It was worth trying.

The green of Father's eyes glowed against the bloodshot whites when they widened then narrowed. "You want me to eat?"

"I believe you need to eat. Do you even remember the last time you had a meal?"

His pasty skin flushed red and he shot to his feet overturning the chair. "I ask for brandy and you offer me soup. I am your father, not some beggar off the street."

The hardest part was detaching his emotions from his voice. Markus stood as well. "You act more like that beggar you speak of."

"I will kill you." He gripped the other chair and smashed it against the wall and bookcase with more force than Markus would have imagined possible. Wobbling, he gripped the desk to remain standing.

The shelf cracked and a dozen or more books tumbled to the floor. A short time ago Markus had caused destruction in the room and the comparison was not at all pleasant. "I would be more concerned if you could stand up straight for more than a moment at a time. As it is, I have little issue with stopping you, and you may feel free to break all the furniture in the house if it pleases you."

Father pushed away from the desk and stepped toward the door forgetting about the overturned chair. His foot caught on the leg and he crashed down with a sickening thud.

Rushing around the table, Markus cursed himself for being so callous. No. It was not his fault. He pulled the cord for Watson. Gently, he turned Father face up and pulled his frail form into his lap. Leaning down, Markus checked if Geoffrey breathed but it was thready at best. The reek of brandy seeped from his skin sickening Markus. "Oh father, what have you done?"

Watson stepped inside. "My lord?"

"The earl has fallen. Prepare a room and call for the doctor. I will carry him upstairs."

Watson rushed from the office and barked orders in the foyer.

The door swung wide as Mother stepped across the threshold. "Is he dead?"

"No. Sick and weak. He may have ruined his health. I have sent for the doctor to look at him."

"I will get a footman to help you, Markus." Mother's eyes were clear and strong but there was a catch in her voice.

"No. I will carry him up. He barely weighs anything. I do not think he has eaten in some time."

Tom stepped into the room as Markus lifted Father into his arms. When they had been spies for the crown, they had learned to assess every situation and Tom scanned the room as if he were in a French outpost gathering intelligence. "Has the doctor been summoned?"

"Yes," Mother said.

"Did he fall or pass out?"

"A bit of each, I would say." Markus carried Father out of the office and up the steps.

Watson waited on the landing and led him to a room where several maids and Mrs. Donnelly where rushing around with sheets and wood for the grate. The final tuck was put on the bed as Markus placed his father in the center.

"Watson, have these clothes burned. They are tattered and rank."

"Yes, my lord. I will have his lordship cleaned up and dressed for bed."

Gripping Watson's arm before he ran off to do his bidding, Markus held his emotions just below the surface. "Be gentle with him, Watson. He is frail as a bird."

Watson met his gaze and his stoic resolve eased. "Of course, my lord."

* * * *

Geoffrey Flammel had never been a good father, but seeing him withered away and stinking like alcohol hurt Markus more than he'd prepared for.

Had he not come to his senses this could have been his fate. Phoebe had made him see that living in a drunken fog was not living at all. He hurt the people around him much like Father had hurt them.

Skin pasty and eyes sunken, Father wouldn't last long like this. Perhaps food would help. The doctor had been located but was several hours away dealing with a sick child. Stepping outside the guest room, Markus nearly bumped into Watson. "Good, you are here. I think we should see if you can get some soup into him. I do not think he has eaten. Lord only knows where he has been for more than a month. Clearly, he is in desperate condition, but perhaps it is not too late."

Dory stepped out of the shadows of the hallway. "Is he that bad, Markus?"

With a curt nod, Watson hurried down the hall to the servants' stairs.

Markus opened his arms and Dory stepped into his embrace. "He looks very bad, Dory. I have no idea if he will survive or if he even wants to. His coming here seems a good sign. We'll know more after the doctor arrives."

She rested her cheek on his chest. "Even though he has been a terrible father, I am sad that he has done this to himself. I hate to see him end this way."

Kissing the crown of her head, he sighed. "He is not dead and he may live on. Let's not be too hasty."

She stepped back and nodded. "Will you send for Adam?"

"I think I will send him a letter explaining the situation and let him decide for himself if he wishes to come. We each have had our troubles with Father. I do not want to bully Adam into coming."

"That is fair. I am not ready to see him yet. Maybe tomorrow." Dory had suffered the most at Father's hand. He had tried to marry her off to an old codger who he owed money to. To save herself, Dory had eloped with Thomas Wheel. Father had been so enraged he publicly challenged Thomas to a duel. Despite Father's drunken state, Thomas didn't fire and had been badly injured.

"I completely understand. You can help me write to Adam, then perhaps a walk outside. I want to take Elizabeth to Emma's grave this afternoon. Would you like to join us?"

Dory pushed a golden curl behind her ear. "I will help you with the letter, but you should go alone with Elizabeth. It will be good for both of you."

* * * *

Markus called for the carriage and a reluctant Miss Cavot handed Elizabeth over to him.

"Are you certain you would not like me to accompany you, my lord?" As if Markus might toss the child in the woods, she gripped one of Elizabeth's hands before finally relinquishing.

"I can care for her, Miss Cavot. She is my daughter and I am not an imbecile." Markus smiled hoping it would put her at ease.

Elizabeth chirped and giggled in his arms. Patting his cheek, she said, "Papa."

"Indeed." Joy filled Markus's heart. "Do not worry. We will be back in an hour or two if the weather holds. You should take some time off, Miss Cavot."

Ducking into the carriage and settling them in, Markus knocked on the roof. "Drive on, Patrick."

"I think we are making your Miss Cavot quite nervous, Elizabeth."

"Winnie," she shouted and clapped as best she could with the layers of clothes meant to keep her warm.

It was hard to become sad about their destination when Elizabeth brought such joy to his life. The horse chugged up the hill to where Markus had set aside property to be a family graveyard. The Flammels had long been buried at Castlereagh Manor, but he wanted Emma close and she had always loved the wildflowers that bloomed on the hill. They were gone until spring, but a few dandelions had still survived the cold.

Gray storm clouds and the chill in the air meant those remaining flowers would not last long.

The large stone came into view and Markus knocked for Patrick to stop. He stepped down and lifted Elizabeth out of the carriage. "We will walk from here, Patrick. I do not imagine we will be long."

"I will be here when you are ready, my lord." Patrick pulled his coat closed around his throat and leaned against the horse.

Markus put Elizabeth on her feet and took her hand as they walked toward the grave. As they neared the stone, Markus slowed then stopped still twenty feet away.

Elizabeth stared at him. "Go?" Her bright green eyes questioned him without censure.

"It is time, is it not? Let's go and see your momma." The first tear left a cold streak down his cheek. He brushed it away.

Elizabeth let go of his hand and approached the stone. She patted the flat front. "Momma."

Kneeling next to her, he ran his fingers over the carved stone.

Emma Elizabeth Flammel

Beloved Wife and Mother
Forever in our hearts

Elizabeth patted the stone as if it were Emma's cheek. Her little shoulders rose and fell with a deep breath and she sighed.

Markus settled back on his haunches and admired the beauty of the spot. From there, nearly half of his property was visible. Hills rolled down toward Rosefield. The fields lay at rest but in a few months the planting would begin again. Every season would bring new beauty to the spot and Emma would see it all. It was good and right that Emma rested up there where she could keep her eye on all of them.

Elizabeth toddled away and plucked dandelions as if they were roses and lilies.

"Forgive me Emma for not coming sooner. I am afraid I have not been at my best since you went away. I hope you were not watching as I tried to drink you out of my heart. A miserable failure, you will be happy to know. You are fixed in that spot, my love.

"Elizabeth has a good heart and has already forgiven all my transgressions. She is so much like you, Emma."

Brushing dust from the stone, Markus kept an eye on Elizabeth's progress with the last of the meager weeds. "Phoebe came and sorted us all out after I made a mess of Rosefield. I now see why you loved Phoebe so much. She is smart and kind, a very intriguing combination. The thing is, Emma, I have fallen in love with her. I never supposed it possible to love anyone but you in that way, but she opened my heart and I cannot remove her."

He rubbed the ache at the back of his neck and tugged a long bit of grass. "Frankly, I do not want to. Emma, you will always be here in my life, my mind, in the face of our daughter. I never want to lose that and I will tell Elizabeth all about you until she is sick of my stories of our life together. Still, I want Phoebe to be part of our family as well. I love her as much as it is possible for a man to love a woman and I think it is too great a gift to ignore. A man does not get a second chance at love so often he can afford to wait. I hope you approve. I think you would. That is, if I can convince her to return. I have made a mess of that as well. Without you, Emma, I am all thumbs in every aspect."

Elizabeth squealed as she ran over with her fistful of crushed blooms. She put them on the ground in front of the gravestone. "Momma."

"I am sure she is smiling down from heaven and thinking how beautiful those are, dearest." Taking Elizabeth in his arms, he stood. The first flakes of snow fluttered down as he walked back to the carriage. The tree on the hill left a shadow on the gray sky and the brown grass soon gleamed white. His footprints, left as evidence of his coming, would soon be filled white.

Glancing back at the snow that already covered the stone in heavy wet flakes, he smiled away his sorrow and dreamed of all that lay ahead.

In his arms, Elizabeth fell asleep on the ride home, and by the time they pulled in the drive, the snow was falling hard. Before long everything would be a stunning winter scene.

Miss Cavot rushed out the front door and down the steps to meet them, her cape flapping around her.

Markus restrained his laugh. "I will put her to bed. She has been asleep for ten minutes." He carried Elizabeth up to the nursery, pulled off the layers of warm clothes and put her to bed.

A smiling Miss Cavot curtsied as he left.

Markus walked down the hall to the room where his father lay. Entering, he found Mother sitting by the window and Doctor Johnston putting a bottle in his bag.

Mother glanced at him, then back out at the falling snow. The back of the chair stood high above her head. The window frames made a light pattern on the bed, dividing Father in parts. The sum was not greater than his parts as it turned out.

Wearing a powdered wig, Doctor Johnston bowed. "My lord, your father is very ill. I do not believe the small bump on his head from the fall is at fault. He has a fever and his lungs have taken on fluids. I would like to sit him up with some pillows, as that might help him breathe easier. You did well to feed him soup. I will instruct your cook to fix a light broth to be fed to him every few hours. I think he has starved himself, and it would be best to get him used to eating slowly."

"Will he live?" Markus was prepared for the worst, but after the trip to Emma's grave he didn't know if he could take more.

Dr. Johnston rubbed his round belly. "I do not know. If his lungs clear and he eats, his heart is strong enough and he should recover. Honestly, if he does not modify his life, it will not matter. He is ruining his health."

"I understand." His gut twisted. Once again, Father's selfishness affected the entire family and his own behavior had not been much better.

"I will leave my nurse with you, my lord. She will know what to do if his condition worsens, and I will return tomorrow to check on him. I do not believe his condition is critical for tonight."

"Thank you, Doctor."

After the doctor left, Markus stood near his mother and put his hand on her shoulder.

The nurse came in with a few of the maids toting pillows and they worked to prop Father up.

Geoffrey moaned and coughed but did not wake.

The nurse pressed her fingers to his wrist for a few moments, nodded, and left them alone.

Mother took Markus's hand. "I would not be very sorry to see you as earl. I know that is an unkind thing to say about my husband, but he has not been much of a father or husband."

Squeezing her hand, Markus sat on the window seat next to her chair. "Do you remember going to Bath when I was a boy, Mother?"

She smiled. "You were only six, and Dorothea was just a baby. I had grown sad after she was born and your father insisted that the waters would lift my spirits."

"We walked along the street and a parade of circus performers danced by. Father laughed and laughed." Markus let the memory warm him. It had been years since he'd remembered the holiday so long ago.

"Geoffrey loved fanciful things like the circus or an amusing theatrical. Back when he was young he wanted to join a circus as a high wire walker. Of course, it was more to drive his father's ire. He did love to laugh."

"You did too, Mother. I remember the two of you when you laughed quite a lot."

"That was a very long time ago." She brushed the moisture from the corner of her eye.

So much time had passed while his family was sad or angry. "Did the waters help?"

She stared out at the snowy afternoon. The hint of a smile lit her eyes. "After a month, I felt better and we went home. Geoffrey insisted it was the water and I did not dispute his claim."

"I am going to ask Miss Hallsmith to marry me." Markus had not intended to speak of his intentions to his mother, but suddenly he wanted her approval.

She turned away from the window and took his hand. "I am happy to hear that. I know she will make you happy. The way you looked at her it was clear that you had feelings for her."

"Was it?" He didn't realize his regard was so obvious. "I asked her to stay, but she was determined to return to London. I will go to London when Father's health recovers."

"And if he does not recover?"

"Mother, we shall all cross that bridge when we must and not a moment before. There is no preparing for these things. I am in no rush to become an earl."

She drew a deep breath. "As much of an ass as your father is, I am in no rush to become a widow. It is only that things would be easier if he were not always making them so hard."

It was the first time he had ever heard such language from his mother and he couldn't help laughing. He squeezed her hand. "We are a tough bunch, we Flammel men."

"You are not like him, Markus. You made some mistakes, but you are stronger than your father." She used a scolding tone, but that was Margaret's way.

The tone, more than the words, comforted him. He kissed her cheek. "Do not sit here too long, Mother. I will send the nurse in. You should rest. I know that I am exhausted from this very long day."

"A short nap might be just the thing. You go. I will have a word with your father, then go to my room."

It was the most relevant conversation he had ever had with Mother. "Thank you, Mother. You and I have had our differences, but you have been a very good mother."

She blinked through unshed tears and smiled.

He left Father's room and went to his own. Sitting on the edge of his bed he longed for a drink to ease his sorrow and blur his memory.

Chapter 17

No. 4
*When an Everton lady finds herself in a volatile situation,
she should keep her chin up, her shoulders back, and use
her wits to soften the scene.*
—The Everton Companion
Rules of Conduct

The snow continued to leave London deserted. At least it appeared so to Phoebe. No one braved the cold to walk the streets. The fire crackled in the hearth, keeping it cozy inside. She pulled her legs under her on the wine-colored damask settee. Staring out the window, she imagined how pretty Rosefield must look in the snow. Markus might take Elizabeth out to play in it or they might huddle by the fire sipping chocolate.

"This is not helping," Phoebe scolded herself.

"What is not helping?" Honoria breezed into the front parlor in a wispy gown and a flowered hat. She wore sapphires around her wrist and neck and each large stone was surrounded by a ring of diamonds, a stark contrast to the dark wood paneling and masculine decor.

Turning as she put her feet on the floor, Phoebe pulled her wrap tighter. "Never mind. I am just watching the snow pile up and feeling sorry for myself. Why are you dressed for April?"

Honoria's dress floated around her. "It makes me feel better than bundling up for winter. I ordered tea."

Everton House was the residence of mostly women, but the rooms were decorated for male sensibilities, with polished hard wood and dark furniture. Still, it was comfortable and unfussy, something Phoebe appreciated.

Phoebe relaxed back. "You will wish for bundling in a few minutes when the chill hits you. But the tea sounds lovely."

With a swish of her voluminous skirts, Honoria flounced into a cream, overstuffed chair facing Phoebe. "I dislike the city during a stormy winter. No one is about and there is nothing to do. I may go to my country estate for a few months as this weather will ruin the season. If you would like to join me, I would be happy for your company, Phoebe."

Maybe she could hide at Honoria's country estate. No one would find her if she just slipped out of town and told only Lady Jane of her intentions to get some peace. Inwardly, she groaned over her responsibilities. "I must stay here through Tuesday, as I have promised those gentlemen I would see them. If you are willing to wait that long, I would consider a time in the country. It is very kind of you to offer."

Honoria waved her hand. "Not at all. I enjoy your company, and we both deserve some time away from the demands of society. It is no bother to wait a few more days and I am curious to see what Mr. Blunt and Mr. Durnst have to offer themselves. Will one of them change your mind about marriage?"

Outside, a carriage pulled to a stop in front of the house with snow six inches up on the wheels and the familiar Thornbury crest emblazoned on the side. Phoebe sighed as Billy, the footman, jumped from the back and ran up the steps.

Without waiting for a response, which would have been that Miss Hallsmith was not taking callers, Ford, Miles, and her mother stepped onto the street. Mother pulled her hood tight against the driving snow and took Miles's arm to climb the steps.

Mrs. Grimsby opened the door and cleared her throat. "I couldn't stop them, Miss."

As tall as the doorway and broad in the shoulders, Ford pushed the stout housekeeper aside nearly toppling her. "Step aside. I have a right to see my sister."

Standing as the familiar angst associated with Ford rose from her gut in a pyre to her head, Phoebe forced her voice to a civil tone. "You may, but you do not have the right to push people around in Everton House, Ford. I will thank you to act the gentleman or I will ask you to leave."

Mrs. Grimsby clutched a chair near the door.

"It is all right, Mrs. Grimsby. You may go. I will see them." Phoebe put her fists on her hips. "Why are you here and why with so little civility?"

Miles left their mother next to Ford and crossed the room. He kissed Phoebe's cheek and whispered, "I thought you might need some moral support. He is in a mood."

The youngest of her three brothers, Miles had a way of easing every moment. She almost smiled over his amusement at the situation. Still, Ford glowered and Mother stood with arms crossed and snow melting on her cloak. They had not waited for Gray to take their outerwear. "Hello, Miles. It is always nice to see you."

"You had no right to turn down a perfectly good offer of marriage!" Ford stomped his huge, wet boots on the brown-and-red rug, dirtying the cream border.

"Did you come all the way from the country in a snowstorm to complain about my not wishing to marry a man who broke our engagement and embarrassed me in front of England and Scotland?" Phoebe liked the strength in her voice. It was good to stand up to Ford without the constant fury turning her into a banshee.

Mother huffed and tugged her gloves. Her golden eyes, so similar to Phoebe's, never wavered from their angry stare. Petite and her hair faded to a graying strawberry blond, Mother was still lovely when not wearing a hateful glare.

Gray rushed in. "I did not know you had company, Miss Hallsmith. May I take your guests' coats and hats?"

"Thank you, Gray."

He collected the wet items before leaving the parlor mumbling something about there never being surprise guests at Everton House.

Since Mother had not spoken to her in months, Phoebe hesitated to address her. Still, her upbringing demanded she acknowledge her. "How are you, Mother?"

Lucretia Hallsmith narrowed her gaze. "I am not speaking to you, Phoebe. You have seriously disappointed me with your willful behavior. Your father and I did not raise you to be—whatever it is you have become."

Phoebe returned to her place on the settee, wishing her mother would go back to silence.

Honoria winked and smiled. It was the quietest she had ever been as she watched the family drama unfold.

After flopping onto the seat next to her, Miles squeezed her hand.

At least not everyone was against her. "I am an Everton lady, Mother. I help people and I like it. I do not wish to be married to a fool or to marry out of desperation."

A loud, disgusted grunt pushed from Ford's lips. "You are in service and an embarrassment to this family. I will forgive you if you marry Durnst. All will be right again. However, I will make your life miserable if you do not give up this venture. It will be my goal to see you an outcast. Marry Durnst or you are finished, Phoebe. This stupid behavior has gone on long enough."

"If you think you can threaten me, Ford, you may as well leave now. I am happy as I am and have no need of your support. I live well enough and have friends."

"Friends..." Ford's mouth twisted in disgust and he might have said more, but Mother grabbed his arm.

"Phoebe, you are my only daughter. Why can you not do your duty by your family and marry a man of means? It is what you were raised to do." Mother sat in the chair near the door.

It was true. Phoebe had been raised to be a good girl and marry where she was told. Five years with her strong-willed grandmother had cured her of that notion. "Do you know that Grand never wore a corset and had six offers of marriage after grandfather died? She turned them all down because she did not love them nor need their support. She ran her farm and sold her crops all by herself without needing a man's guidance."

Lucretia sighed. "My mother was an odd sort. She was always more comfortable in a pair of breeches than a dress. That does not mean you have to follow in her footsteps. She was not liked by society. I could not bring her to England to meet my friends. She would have been laughed out of any ballroom."

That society was more important to Mother than Grand hurt Phoebe's heart. "Mother, even though you were ashamed of her, she loved you very much. I see now that I am more like her than like you. Though, we do have one thing in common. I too am ashamed of my mother."

Mother gasped.

Guilt seared through Phoebe and she wished she could take it back the instant she'd said it.

"Enough." Ford strode forward until he hovered over her. "You will marry Durnst. He has made a formal offer and I demand you marry him. He has a large piece of property adjacent to the one Grand left to Mother. Mother has generously agreed to turn the property over to you as a wedding gift. You and your new husband will live on the combined estate in Scotland, and that will be that."

"No wonder he is chasing after me like a starved cat to a bowl of cream. You are offering to double his farmland and make him a wealthy man. All this just to save face, Ford? You would sell me into a terrible marriage just so that my work as an Everton lady would no longer embarrass you? I have news for you, brother. No one cares. You are not that important and no one in the ton cares that I make a living helping others sort out one problem or the next. In fact, they like that I can help them."

Ford's fleshy cheeks turned bright red and his neck was blotchy with rage. "You are talked about in every parlor. They are all saying that Phoebe Hallsmith is disgraced. You might as well walk the streets. It is all the same."

Horrible man. How had she come from the same family as this monster?

"Enough!" Miles stood. "That is not true. You go too far, Ford. You cannot force her to marry where she does not wish. I am fairly certain that your current mode of convincing her will never work."

"I go too far? Look at your little sister, Miles. Look what she is costing this family."

Ford was mean and uncaring, but to call her a whore—was that what he really thought? Maybe it was true. She'd given herself to Markus. She was not a pure and good woman. In Scotland, they said she was cold and unfeeling, and she had proved that by leaving home and disobeying her mother.

Miles stepped between Phoebe and Ford. "You are supposed to protect her, not hurt her. She is doing what she thinks is necessary, as are you." Turning, he gazed earnestly at Phoebe. "We are staying in town for a few weeks. When the weather is better, Mother and Ford will return to the country. I hope you will come and see us before they leave. I assure you, Ford will be better behaved."

"You cannot make such an assurance, Miles, but I appreciate the effort." Phoebe folded her hands in her lap, pretending to be calm. Ranting at Ford would do no good. He was the most hardheaded person she had ever known.

Mother stepped forward. "Will you all excuse us for a few minutes? I would like to speak to Phoebe alone."

Grumbling, Ford stomped out of the room.

Miles squeezed her hand and followed him out.

Honoria stood. "I will be just outside the door should you need anything, Miss Hallsmith."

Heart in her throat, Phoebe forced a weak smile. "Thank you, my lady."

It had been years since she and her mother had been alone together. Suddenly, Phoebe had no idea what to say. "Would you like to sit, Mother?"

Lucretia took the seat that Honoria had vacated. Smoothing her gray skirt, she was out of place in the parlor with her pink blouse and lace around her neck. Her back pole-straight, she stared toward the fire. "I know what you think of me."

Guilt warred with standing strong inside Phoebe. "I owe you an apology, Mother. I should not have said that."

She turned, meeting Phoebe's gaze. "It was the truth. You are ashamed of me, and I was ashamed of my mother. It is ironic, actually."

"What is?"

Frowning down at the wet hem of her skirt, she sighed and flounced the fabric away from her legs. "The way things turned out. The way they have of coming around full circle. When I was a girl, my parents were very much in love. They met as children and married as soon as they could. They were wild and playful and always running here and there together. As a family, we laughed and enjoyed life in Scotland with its green hills and mad residents."

Phoebe tried to imagine her mother laughing with Grand, but she came up blank. "What changed?"

"When I was twelve, my cousin Meredith came from England for a visit. She was all of fourteen and very refined. She had attended finishing school and knew all the customs of England and London society. I was fascinated and all I wanted was to be like Meredith. Mother made me wait four entire years before she would allow me to travel to London, and I swore I would find a husband and never come back. You have to understand that my desire to conform to society's rules was as much an act of defiance to my parents as you wishing to be an unmarried Everton lady is to me." She smiled, but the expression didn't touch her sorrowful eyes.

"I am not trying to be defiant, Mother."

"No. Nor was I. I wanted a certain life and it was not the life my parents had planned for me. I met your father at my first ball and we were married less than a year later. I did not love him, but he was kind and good looking and after a time we came to care very deeply for each other."

"Do you regret your decision to come to England?"

"Not for a moment. I have enjoyed my life. My only regret was that my mother and I never sat and talked about my decision and that she believed, in the end, nothing had changed. I know now what she endured and I am sorry I did not tell her so." Mother pulled a handkerchief from her pocket and dabbed the corners of her eyes. "You will do as you please, just as I did. So you see, we are not so different, Phoebe."

A.S. Fenichel

It was irony that their being opposite made them the same. "Yes. I see. I hope you and I will remain cordial regardless of where my decisions take me."

Standing, Lucretia brushed out her skirt and took a deep breath. "Come and visit me before I go back to the country, Phoebe. We can have a nice cup of tea. And in the meantime, consider what your brother has said. Two eligible men have offered for you despite your age and situation. You could have a family of your own and you are smart enough to manage either of them quite nicely."

Manage a man so that he didn't drive her crazy. That is what her mother expected of her. Phoebe stood and rounded the table to stand in front of Mother. "I will give it some thought for your sake, Mother."

Her eyes brightened and she smiled. Kissing her cheek, she said, "Thank you."

Miles waited in the foyer, but Ford had already gone to the carriage. When they were gone, Phoebe wanted to go to her room and sleep for the rest of the day. Of course, she would only stare at the ceiling and find no rest. Still, hiding appealed to her.

"How did the talk with your mother go?" Honoria stood near the stairs like a barricade to self-pity.

Running her hand along the wood paneling, Phoebe longed for a day with no drama from her life or anyone else's. In her current occupation, that was unlikely, and wishing it wouldn't make it so. "Better than expected."

"Your brother Miles is delightful. So charming and amiable. He's nothing like you." Honoria swirled her skirts and returned to the parlor.

"Thank you very much."

Honoria laughed. "Not that you are not charming, my dear. You are direct, funny and highly intelligent."

"Miles runs all of Ford's businesses and estates. He is highly intelligent too." Either she was defending herself or Miles. Phoebe was not certain which.

Cocking her head, Honoria paused and stared out the window into the falling snow. She shrugged. "He hides it better than you. He is all things charming. He and I had a long talk about the weather and how it was cutting into the entertainment provided by London. What is your other brother like? The one who was not here today."

"Aaron is the smartest. He is the second son and is afforded a very nice sum each month. He must use it wisely as he never comes home and asks for more. In fact, he stays out of Ford's way entirely. He is not as easygoing as Miles, but he is well liked and as big as Ford." The last time Phoebe had seen all her brothers in one place had been at Father's funeral. Yes. Aaron was definitely the smartest of the bunch.

"Where does he reside?"

"He keeps a gentleman's apartment in town. He could use the townhouse, but then he would be obliged to see our brother when they are in London. I think he sees my mother, but only if he can avoid Ford."

Honoria huffed and folded her hands together as if straining to be calm. "I hate to say it. That eldest brother of yours is a menace. He stormed out of the parlor and paced for five minutes before demanding Gray fetch his coat and hat. Gray was all too happy to have him out of the house. Even his horses complained when he stepped outside. I apologize, Phoebe, but I just do not like him."

Sighing, Phoebe stood by the window. A draft pushed through forcing her to return to the settee and the dwindling heat from the fire. "Ford has always been thus. He wants his own way and will bully the rest until he has it. Sometimes I wonder if he even knows why he wants a thing. Like giving me Grand's property if I marry Durnst. What do Ford and Mother gain from such a deal?"

"I cannot see that they gain anything besides you would be married and out of the country. Perhaps he just likes things to be tidy." Honoria lifted her tea but when she tasted it she winced and put it back on the table.

The tea had long gone cold. Phoebe took a biscuit but it only made her think of Markus and their clandestine meetings. She put it back on the tray with a long sigh. "No. He is stupid and selfish and wants his way. He will not have it this time." Phoebe had decided on the spot that she would never again do anything just because Ford wished it. "If Miles did not play steward and man of business for Ford, he would have run us all to the poor house years ago. I cannot let his behavior determine the course of my life. I must stand firm and do what is best for me. Mother will understand and Miles will likely cheer me on."

"Good for you, Phoebe. I look forward to Tuesday more and more." Honoria pulled the cord for the kitchen staff to bring more tea.

Everything was going to be all right if Phoebe could stay the course. She would settle into a comfortable life at the society, Ford would act as if she didn't exist, she would see her mother on occasion, and Markus would eventually find a suitable wife to spend his life with. It was as it should be. Her heart tore to pieces.

Chapter 18

No. 23
*An Everton lady will do all in her power to avoid falling
in love with the client as it may lead to a broken heart.*
—*The Everton Companion*
Rules of Conduct

The words on the page blurred. It was Markus's third attempt at writing a letter to Phoebe. He tossed it in the wastebasket with the other two. What he needed to say he couldn't put on paper. Mostly because he didn't know what to say. Would an apology be enough to bring her back? No. He didn't think so. Besides, what was he apologizing for? He asked her to stay, to marry him. It had not been enough.

"Damn." He slammed the quill pen down on his desk. Ink marred the grain. Using parchment, he tried to clean up the ink, but it only made it worse.

His study door opened and Dory peeked in. "May I come in or are you busy?"

Standing, he pushed the ink well aside. "I've ruined the desk Emma bought me."

"It is only a stain. It adds character to the desk." She smiled.

Drawing breath, he let the idea sink in. Emma's desk and ink over his frustration with Phoebe. Perhaps it was character as Dory had said. "I was trying to write to Phoebe, but I do not know what to say."

"What do you want to say?" Cocking her head, she gazed at him in her *don't bother to lie because I know you* way.

Senseless to avoid the truth. "Come back to Rosefield and be my wife."

"You suspect that would not bring her back?"

"I asked her to stay and she said she preferred her life as an Everton lady."

"She said that?"

Every time he thought of her, which was all the time, his heart hurt more. "Perhaps not quite that, but she said no, nonetheless."

Dory sighed. "You will have to tell her what's in your heart, Markus, then see what happens. She does not feel worthy of you. If you want her, you will have to make her believe differently."

Changing another's opinion of themselves was no easy task. Perhaps he should have begged while she was still under his roof. He shook the idea away. "You came in for something. Is it Father?"

Dory patted her red hair into place and sighed. "No, his condition is unchanged. I just thought it would be nice to spend a few minutes together without Mother taking over the conversation."

Whenever Mother was in the room the focus was on her. Even if she didn't speak, her presence altered the conversation. He pointed toward the chairs. "Come sit."

"This letter for you was on the tray in the hall. I decided to bring it to you." She handed him the letter sealed with the blue crest of the Hallsmith family.

Markus's palms grew damp despite the fact that the address was clearly not in Phoebe's hand. Staring down at the envelope, he fought tearing it open or tossing it in the trash.

"Do you suspect bad news, Markus?" Leaning forward, she put her hand on his.

"I have no idea." He broke the seal and opened the letter. "It is from Miles Hallsmith."

"Is she all right?"

"He writes that both Mr. Durnst and Mr. Blunt are in London and Miles suspects they both will renew their wish to marry her in short order." His heart broke, and he struggled to draw breath.

"If you are in love with her, then go to London and tell her." Dory sounded as if it was just that simple.

"I asked her to stay and she said no. I said I would marry her, but she declared it ridiculous. I do not know how to change her mind." Every statement was a knife in his chest. He tossed the letter on his desk.

Dory took his hand. "You said you would marry her? Did you tell her that you love her in all of that?"

"Perhaps not in those words. But if she thinks marrying me is a ridiculous idea, she does not wish to hear about love from me. You do not know her as I do. She is a practical woman. Flowery talk will not win her."

"Markus, women, even practical ones, like to hear that the man proposing is in love with them and not marrying for some other reason. She has waited this long and found a way to support herself; she'll not marry for less than true love. Her honor will never allow it."

His hands shook. He pulled away, stood, and walked toward the window. Leaning against the cold glass, he watched the snow fall. "She would laugh at me."

"There is always a risk. But I doubt she will laugh. What were you going to write to her?"

Rounding the desk, he glimpsed the discarded letters in the waste bin. "I was planning to apologize and hope that was enough to bring her back to Rosefield."

"I realize that I am your younger sister, Markus, but listen to me. Doing the least amount to win back the woman you love is not the best plan. Women want you to make a fool of yourself for them. We want you to stand on the top of Parliament and declare your undying love. Pecking away at the least dangerous path will not win you the glory you desire." She stood. "When Father is better, go to London."

"And if she promises herself to someone else while I am trapped here by snow and the earl's ill health?"

Dory smiled. "You cannot know what she will do when you are not with her, but I suspect Miss Hallsmith will wait for true love or have no love at all."

"You might be wrong."

Shrugging, she stepped to the door. "Mother has asked me to play tonight. I agreed, though it is always difficult for me to play in front of her."

When his sister played the pianoforte, it was as if the heavens opened up and let the angels drop to earth. "I would love to hear more of what you played for the prince."

Looking back, she smiled. "For you, I will play a few pieces and risk Mother's critique."

"Was she unkind the first time?" He cringed knowing he was not there to support his sister. Too drunk to even remember he was supposed to be in London that day, he'd woken the next morning in the storage room of a pub in Shopshire with no idea how he'd gotten there.

She shook her head. "No. She seemed to approve. After all, if the prince was pleased, what more can Margaret Flammel want?"

"What more indeed? I wish I had been there, been sober enough to be there." Rounding the desk, he crossed the room to her and took her hands.

"Markus, you were grieving and ill. I do not blame you for being absent. I would have loved for you to have been there, but you can hear me play for many years to come if you wish. One concert, no matter who was in attendance, will not change that you are my older brother and I love you."

He kissed her cheek. "You are too good to me. When I deserve rancor, you offer sympathy."

"What you deserve is to be happy, Markus. We all deserve that." Smiling, she left him to watch the defiant snow blanket the ground, making the roads impassable. Between the weather and his father's health, everything was working against him. He should have chased her back to London right away. What a fool he was.

If Miles was in London, that meant that Ford was probably there as well and would be bullying Phoebe to marry that ingrate Durnst. Or maybe the family favored Mr. Blunt. He had a good living. If she married Blunt, she would stay in the county and he would see her from time to time. Torture.

Needing a distraction, he went to check on his father.

* * * *

Markus choked back emotion while Dory poured her soul out through the pianoforte. The music spoke to him, tore his heart and healed it in a single phrase.

He doubted Dory had written the piece with him in mind. She had her own life. Still, it was as if she had captured the past two years of his life and laid it out in music for everyone to hear. Her gift was to take the audience on a journey and Markus was embarrassed within his own emotions.

A cough sounded from the doorway.

Turning, Markus found his father standing in the doorway. He rushed over and wrapped an arm around his frail form, then guided Father into a chair. "Should you be out of bed?" Markus whispered.

"I could not resist a better position to hear her play." Father's color was more normal. Not quite pink and healthy, but not the sickly gray of a week earlier.

Happy to see Father had made it all the way down the steps to the music room, Markus still voiced his concern. "Dory may not be pleased to have you in her presence."

"I deserve her disgust. Still, I wanted to see her play as well as hear."

Markus let the lilt of every note roll over him. The sorrow and the joy. This was what life offered and Dory captured it perfectly in her music. Emma had died and left him to wallow in desperation. The music darkened. He had left Elizabeth and abandoned his responsibilities. A cascade of crashing notes vibrated the walls. His salvation was a petite, red-haired woman who shamed and revived him. Lighter notes flowed from Dory's fingers with joy and hope. The gambit of emotions jabbed his heart.

With her fingers barely touching the keys, Dory played the final notes.

Markus steeled his nerves and determination. "Father, I am going to London in the morning."

"Is this about that woman everyone is talking about?" Father leaned forward so that only Markus heard him.

"Phoebe Hallsmith. Yes, it is."

"I see. You should go then. The staff speaks of nothing else. She must be quite a girl." Gripping the back of the chair, he hauled himself to his feet and turned to the door.

"Hello, Father." Dory stepped away from the pianoforte.

Not looking back, he said, "You play more beautifully than I remember, Dorothea."

"Thank you, Father." Choked with tears, she kept her distance.

Nodding, Father shuffled from the room. Watson met him at the door and supported him down the hall.

Markus rushed to Dory and pulled her into his arms. "That was the most beautiful thing I have ever heard."

"I wrote part of it with you in mind. Your pain, my troubles. I wanted to believe we would both be better. The end is about Thomas and me."

Kissing her cheek, he laughed. "Perhaps it will one day reflect my life as well."

"You will go to London?" Her smile was as bright as the sun.

He nodded and turned to his mother. She stood a few feet away disapproving of the show of affection. "Mother, I will be leaving at dawn and do not know when I will return to Rosefield. I apologize for abandoning my own house party, but I have something important to take care of."

"If your father recovers and the weather permits, we will go back to Castlereagh. I do not know if we will be here when you return." Stoic as always, Margaret strode out of the room.

Thomas and Dory both laughed.

Markus shook his head. "She actually told me she believed Phoebe and I would suit. Yet from that response, it is impossible to tell if she approves or not."

Still chuckling, Thomas said, "If she truly did not wish for you to go, you would have gotten a long speech about propriety."

"I suppose that is true." Markus had a lot to think about. "Thank you, Dory. I am happy to have heard you play tonight. I hope I will not be long in London. I doubt Father will be well enough to move for several weeks. Should the weather clear and you wish to remove yourself from Father, I will understand you leaving."

"Perhaps it is time to forgive him." Thomas stared down at his feet and at the carpet. He would not meet his wife's gaze.

"I do not see how you can forgive him. He shot you, Tom!" She crossed her arms over her chest.

"Would you two excuse me? I have much to prepare." Markus bowed and left them to their disagreement. He had to find Blakely and have a bag packed.

* * * *

It was slow going to get to London with snow on the ground. Luckily warmer weather and sunshine helped them along. Once he'd cleaned up and changed clothes from traveling, he went directly to Everton House.

Stomach in knots, he beat on the door far more vigorously than was polite.

The door creaked open revealing an ancient butler barely able to execute a bow. "How may I help you?"

"Lord Devonrose to see Miss Hallsmith." Markus handed the butler his card.

"Please follow me, my lord."

Markus imagined for an instant he detected a smirk on the butler's dour face, but it was gone so quickly, he must have been mistaken. "Is the lady at home?"

"She is seeing callers in the small parlor, though it seems the larger one might have been more prudent."

"I beg your pardon?" Markus followed him to a doorway at the back of the house.

"Um, perhaps, you might prefer to announce yourself, my lord." The left side of his mouth definitely turned up.

It was highly unusual. "What is your name?"

"Gray, my lord."

"Is there something I should know before entering, Gray?" It was as if Markus was coming into the middle of a conversation and the other parties were quite far ahead.

"I believe you will see for yourself in a moment, my lord."

"Miss Hallsmith has other callers this afternoon?"

"Indeed, my lord."

Markus nodded. "I will announce myself. Thank you, Gray."

With a barely notable bow, Gray ambled down the hall and around a corner.

Turning his attention to the door and the room beyond, Markus steeled his emotions, gave a knock, and entered.

In the palest gray dress, Phoebe was like a dove seated in a highbacked chair near the hearth. Her eyes widened when he entered and the hint of a blush bloomed across her cheeks and down her neck, where it disappeared below the lace hiding a low neckline.

His pulse raced at the sight of her. It hadn't been that long, and yet he reveled at the way her hair gleamed like fire and the surprise in her gaze made her eyes sparkle. If they had been alone he would wrap her in his arms and dance with joy just because he adored the way her sweet lips pursed when she didn't know how to react.

"Lord Devonrose, is something amiss?" Jared Blunt stepped into his view, concern etched on his face.

Durnst watched from the window, his arms crossed and a scowl on his face.

The parlor was aptly named as the five people took up most of the space along with a small seating area centered around a table and the fireplace. He could have reached Phoebe in two steps, swept her in his arms, and carried her away. Acting like a jealous lover would not win the lady, so Markus bowed to Phoebe and Lady Honoria who grinned from the brown divan. "Nothing is wrong. I have come to see Miss Hallsmith. I did not realize you were otherwise engaged. Shall I come back at another time?"

Honoria popped up from her seat and rushed over. "Oh no, my lord. We are delighted to see you. How is little Elizabeth?"

He bowed over Honoria's hand, then watched Phoebe who had still not said a single word to indicate she was happy or unhappy to see him. "She is well. In fact, she is speaking."

Clapping, Honoria spun with joy. "How wonderful. I knew it would not be long. Phoebe said the sweet child could talk and she was right."

"Yes. Miss Hallsmith was correct about a great many things." Markus didn't take his gaze from Phoebe as her eyes brimmed and joy lifted her lips.

"What brings you to town, my lord?" Durnst asked a bitter twist to his voice.

Something about Gavin Durnst made Markus's skin crawl. The man could not be trusted. He would rather see Phoebe with Blunt and living a quiet life in Benton than with the snake who addressed him. "I had some personal business to attend to."

"Is there something I can help you with, my lord?" Blunt nudged Honoria out of his way to get closer to Markus.

Offering Honoria his arm, Markus escorted her the short distance to her seat. "Have I come at a bad time?"

Phoebe stood and curtsied as if she just realized the gesture was required. "Not at all, my lord. I have just ordered tea. I hope you will join us."

"Today is not about tea, Miss Hallsmith. You said to come on Tuesday and I am here. Why is it you have arranged a circus instead of a private meeting?" Durnst stomped dangerously close to Phoebe with his hands balled into fists.

Markus's emotions were in check, but he would let no harm come to her from anyone, especially not from Durnst, who had already injured her more than enough.

Taking a step back from the towering brute, Phoebe cocked her head. "You are overreacting, Mr. Durnst."

"I do not believe I am. You are making a mockery of me and my feelings for you. First you invite this secretary here at the same time as you are to hear my proposal and now his lordship. What is your game?" He advanced on Phoebe, hovering too close for Markus's comfort.

Phoebe sat and raised one brow. "I see no circus. I may have invited both you and Mr. Blunt here at the same time, but Lord Devonrose's visit is a surprise. And frankly, I can invite anyone I wish to call. I am not in your charge, Mr. Durnst."

"I have your brother's blessing and you will eventually have no choice but to acquiesce."

Blunt bumped Durnst's shoulder. "She will do no such thing. I am in love with her and she will have me. Her brother has relinquished his rights."

Phoebe let a rush of air out through closed teeth while Durnst and Blunt continued to state their cases one louder than the other.

Markus sat next to Honoria. Leaning down to her ear, he asked. "How long has this argument been going on?"

Frowning, she harrumphed. "These two dunderheads have been here an hour."

"And what is the lady's position?" His heart knotted in his throat.

Honoria let out a dramatic sigh and patted his hand. "She has barely said a word or had much expression at all. I think it is a good sign that she asked you to stay for tea."

"I think perhaps I have come at the wrong time." He sat back and watched Phoebe.

Her lips were set in a serene smile, but fire built in her eyes and her knuckles were white where she gripped her skirts in her lap. She couldn't hold on for much longer.

The idea of tossing both of the other men from Everton House made his palms itch, but he knew Phoebe would hate for him to handle her problems. She could deal with this herself, and it would only serve his own pride to interfere. He relaxed and waited. If it took all day and into the night, he would speak to her alone and know her feelings or at least state his own.

Durnst stomped his foot. "You are a man of business. Miss Hallsmith is too far above your station. Go back to your desk and figures and leave us alone."

"There is no shame in a hard day's work. Miss Hallsmith has not sent me away. She has been a lady throughout. If you were a gentleman, you would see that she favors me, and step away so that we can begin our life together." Blunt fisted his hands and propped them on his hips.

The door opened and an extremely rotund woman carried in a tray. Keys jingled at her waist, indicating this was the housekeeper. She surveyed the room, lips twitching in amusement, winked at Honoria, and placed the tray of tea, bread, meats, and biscuits on the table.

Phoebe's chest rose and fell in a long sigh. "Thank you, Mrs. Grimsby. I will pour the tea."

"As you wish, Miss Hallsmith." Chuckling, she left the parlor.

"Gentlemen, will you sit and have tea?" Moving to the edge of her seat so she could reach the table, Phoebe indicated two additional chairs placed close for enjoying an intimate conversation over tea in the parlor.

Markus began to see the humor in the situation and had to hide his amusement behind his hand and clearing his throat.

Chapter 19

No. 10
An Everton lady will behave like a lady at all times.
—The Everton Companion
Rules of Conduct

Was Markus laughing at her? For nearly an hour Phoebe had endured the two imbeciles bickering over who would be a more suitable husband for her. Neither one had taken a moment to ask her if she would like to marry them. It seemed an irrelevant point to them both.

To add to her mortification, Markus sat in the parlor amused by her troubles. A dozen questions bashed around in her head, but she couldn't ask any of them while Jared and Gavin were there. Neither one was inclined to leave before he'd said his piece.

She poured the tea and served each person. Happy for something to do other than examine her current situation. If not for the fact that she had promised her mother she'd consider these men, she would have tossed them from the house forty minutes earlier.

Gavin slouched into the chair next to hers, took a cup from her, and gulped it before rattling it down onto the table. Without taking a napkin, he grabbed three biscuits and shoved two in his mouth at one time. Crumbs spilled onto his jacket, and he ate the last biscuit while his mouth was still full. Brushing the crumbs onto the rug, he scowled and huffed.

If Phoebe had to listen to that crunching and gulping for the rest of her life, she'd lose her mind. Not that she had any intention of marrying Gavin.

He had kicked her at her lowest moment. She would never tie herself to such a thoughtless man. Far too much like Ford, Gavin was not the man for her.

Jared sipped his tea and smacked his lips, the pinkie finger of his right hand sticking out. He stared toward the fire as if looking for something, then shot a glance at Phoebe. "I would like your answer, Miss Hallsmith."

Looking over her teacup at him, she gave herself a moment to keep from laughing. "Was there a question posed, Mr. Blunt?"

Eyebrows drawn together, he frowned. "I would like to know if you will marry me."

Not exactly the romantic proposal a woman would like, but considering that she had set the stage, she couldn't blame poor Mr. Blunt.

Before she could develop a civil response, Gavin cut in. "I expect you will marry me, Miss Hallsmith. You and I will have an amiable life in Scotland where we both know you belong. London is no place for a girl like you. You will come back to Scotland, we will marry, and my farm will keep us in very good standing for a large family."

"You mean the farm that will be doubled in size because my mother will give you Grandmother's property for marrying her old-maid daughter." Phoebe's calm was quickly slipping. She stole a glance at Markus.

He raised one eyebrow and drank his tea, managing the feat without lip smacking, slurping, or gulping. His fingers, though large compared to the dainty teacup, did not poke out or look about to shatter the porcelain. Markus was at ease but watchful.

Gavin stuffed meat in his mouth and spoke around it. "That is of no consequence and it is inappropriate to mention in company."

"I will have your answer." Jared put his cup and saucer down without the slightest sound. Standing, he crossed his arms.

Phoebe stood. "Well, Mr. Blunt. If I may pose a question, why do you wish to marry me?"

Facing her, he stared wide-eyed then tugged on his jacket and adjusted his cravat. "I…I think we make a fine match. You are a lady of the highest order. I know we can get along together. You will give me children and make me happy."

"Is that all?" Phoebe rounded the table separating them.

"What more is there besides happiness and companionship?" His petulant tone grated on her nerves.

She bit the inside of her cheek to keep her temper at bay. "What more indeed. I thank you for your interest, but I must decline, Mr. Blunt."

"Decline? You would decline a perfectly good offer of marriage from an upstanding man to marry this Scotsman?" He turned a petulant gaze on Gavin, who smirked back.

"Mr. Durnst has nothing to do with my refusal to marry you."

"Then why have you refused me?"

It was incredible that she had to explain and humiliating that this was all happening in front of Markus. "I will not marry you because you do not love me and I do not love you. You mentioned your happiness and the children that I would give to you but made no mention of how you were going to make me happy."

"I will take you out of here and give you a home."

It was an effort to keep her shoulders back and remain standing. Everything about the afternoon exhausted her. "I am afraid that is not enough for me, Sir. I thank you for your attention, but I will not marry you."

Gavin jumped up. "Good, then we can get to planning our wedding."

"No. If you were the last man on earth, I would not marry you, Gavin Durnst. You certainly do not love me and you could not care less about anyone's happiness other than your own. I believe you would be a terrible father and husband, making you even less appealing than Mr. Blunt. Even if we had not had a history where you humiliated me, I would never accept you as my husband."

Face red, he stepped closer. "Ford will make you marry me."

"No. My brother has no control over my decisions. I do not need him or his protection. I do not need any man's protection. I have the Everton Domestic Society."

Honoria clapped.

Gavin's eyes narrowed. "You are an ungrateful old maid. You will never have anything if you do not marry me."

It was enough. Phoebe took a step back, picked up her teacup, and threw it at Gavin, hitting him in the head.

The pretty pale porcelain with its pink painted flowers crashed to the floor where it broke into several pieces.

Gavin held his forehead where it turned red. "How dare you assault me."

"Get out before I throw something heavier."

The door opened and Gray stood waiting with their coats in hand.

"I am going to see Ford right now. You will be my wife before the month is out; then you will wish you had been nicer to me." He trudged out barely escaping the figurine she flung at his back.

Jared looked at her then at the open door. "I would hate to be thought of in the same light as that gentleman, so I will say good day, Miss Hallsmith. I am sorry it did not work out between us and I wish you well."

Phoebe watched him take his coat and go. Struggling to catch her breath, she buried her fingernails in her palms. She could not bear to look at Markus. He must think her a madwoman.

"Perhaps this would be a good time to take my leave of you ladies. Thank you for the tea." Markus's calm warm voice did nothing to make her feel better. In fact, she was tempted to throw the entire pot at him as he bowed then took his coat from Gray.

After a moment, Honoria wrapped her arms around Phoebe. "You have done the right thing. It was very dramatic, but ultimately the right thing. Neither of them would have made you a good husband."

Her emotions boiled over and Phoebe cried on Honoria's shoulder. "I hate men."

"I know dear. However, Lord Devonrose did come to see you and he watched the entire scene with interest. Perhaps things will work out after all."

"I have ruined that too. Now that he has seen the full extent of my stupid temper, he will never come back. Why would he?" Despair ripped through her until she had to sit and let the wracking sobs claim her.

Honoria stayed with her until the tears abated. "I am going to arrange a bath for you, then you will go to bed and sleep this away. When you are rested, you will feel much better, I promise."

Following orders like a woman in a dream, she bathed and went to bed. Sleep claimed her but only nightmares followed.

* * * *

It was after ten when she could no longer stand her bed. Many residents of Everton House were talking and laughing in the grand parlor when Phoebe stole past in her nightgown and robe. She had tugged on her boots, grabbed a blanket, and headed for the garden and fresh air.

The winter chill helped clear her mind of the mortifying afternoon. Snow made the garden look like a fairy tale. The wall around the veranda showed several inches of it and the trees were painted white.

Phoebe breathed deep and watched her breath in the full moon's light.

When she stepped off the veranda onto the snow-covered path, someone else's footprints shocked her into stillness. "Is someone here?"

"Do not be afraid, Phoebe." Markus stepped out of the shadows and into the moonlight.

Heart pounding, she had to catch her breath. He was the last person she expected to see. After the mess at tea, she wondered if she would ever see him again. "What are you doing here?"

"Hoping you would have trouble sleeping and need some air." He eased closer.

"How could you know I would not go to the kitchen for a treat?" Wearing only her nightgown and robe, she tugged the blanket tighter both against his gaze and the cold.

"You do not eat when you are upset, and I expected after the events of this afternoon you would have lost your appetite. It was a risk, but I wanted to see you alone. I hope you will forgive my impertinence." The sleeve of his coat brushed her fingers.

He knew her habits, her moods. Not even her mother could have said such a thing, and he risked the freezing weather that it was true. Longing to reach out and touch him but terrified, she backed up a step. "I am sorry you saw all of that and left without saying why you had come. We are friends and I did not behave well."

Again, he closed the gap. "Under the circumstances, your behavior was exemplary. Durnst deserved a good thrashing and it was all I could do not to give it to him. Jared's behavior was marginally better and he finished well. At least I do not have to find a new secretary. That is, unless his presence will make you uncomfortable."

"Why did you not thrash Gavin?" A dozen questions rumbled through her mind, this was the safest.

He cocked his head and brushed her hair back from her face.

She shivered from the touch rather than the freezing temperatures.

"I did not interfere because I knew you could handle things yourself. You are a very capable woman and do not appreciate being coddled by a man."

So close now, she had to arch her neck to look at him. "I think sometimes it might be nice to have someone take care of me."

"Should I have beaten Durnst and tossed him from the house?" He smiled and it shone in his emerald eyes.

"No. I would have hated that. It is good to see you Markus. I was so happy to hear that Elizabeth is speaking."

He toyed with the ends of her hair between his fingers and his warm smile widened. "It was amazing. She speaks all the time now. It only took one word; then she was communicating all the time."

Hurt that she had missed that first word, Phoebe longed for the closeness she had shared with Markus and Elizabeth. She swallowed the lump in her throat. "What did she say? What was her first word?"

He leaned down and brushed his lips over the lock of hair he sifted between his fingers. "She said Fee."

Tears welled in Phoebe's eyes. Emotion shook her entire body.

"Are you cold?"

"No. Yes. No."

"When I came in through the gate in the alley, I saw a small wooden building."

"Potter's shed," she said.

Before she knew what was happening, he scooped her up in his arms and trudged through the snow toward the rear side garden. His arms were like coming home after a long journey. "Why are you carrying me?"

"You are hardly dressed for walking through the garden. Do you mind my carrying you?"

Unable to resist him, she buried her face in the crook of his neck. "I should mind, but I do not. Tell me about Elizabeth speaking."

"She came to find me in the study and wanted to know where you were. I did my best to act as if it were an everyday occurrence, but it was not easy. I wanted to jump for joy." He approached the shed and put her on her feet. Keeping her close with his arm around her waist, he opened the door.

It was as cold inside as out, but with no wind to chill her bones. Markus went to the table and struck tinder to light a candle.

Phoebe closed the door once the candle was lit. "I wish I had heard her."

"I wish you had too." He placed the candle on the stool, lifted Phoebe by the waist, and sat her on the high bench. In winter, the shed went unused and all the gardening items were neatly tucked away, leaving the bench clear.

Heart pounding, she had no choice but to speak of the afternoon's mess. "I am very sorry you had to witness the scene at tea today. I thought I could control my temper, but it got away from me."

He stared at her for a long moment. "Are you under the impression that I was put off by your behavior in the parlor today?"

"It was embarrassing to be so out of control. I could have handled the entire situation better. I assure you I can control myself." She was rambling but she couldn't stop herself. "Those men were just so aggravating and overbearing. I suppose Mr. Blunt did redeem himself as you said, but even so."

Placing his fingers over her lips, he stopped her. "You lasted far longer than I would have. No one should have to endure what those two idiots put you through, acting as if they were doing you some service by making an offer. They were rude and intolerable. Had I not known you would hate my interfering, I would have thrashed them both and tossed them from the house."

It was hard to think beyond his touch and the kind words.

He dropped his hand to the bench beside her thigh. "But I did not wish to become a part of your regrettable afternoon, at least not to the point where you wish to never see me again."

"I could never want that."

Placing his other hand on the bench so that she was trapped between his arms, he leaned into her. "Does that mean you are happy to see me tonight?"

"You surprised me." She ordered herself to say something intelligent, but nothing came to mind. "I did not expect you to come to London."

"I would have been here sooner if my father had not turned up at Rosefield. He is unwell and I could not leave."

"I am sorry to hear that. Will he recover?" Aching for him, she touched his upper arm. The muscle flexed beneath her fingers, and the memory of being wrapped in his strength washed over her leaving her dizzy.

With a shrug, he stood straight and rubbed the side of his head. "I think if he stops drinking, he will live on. However, I do not believe he will stop drinking."

Phoebe took his hand and held it against her heart. "You cannot expect to control the behavior of others, Markus. I have no doubt you have done your best for your father. The rest is up to him."

Leaning in again, he kissed her forehead. "Is that what you thought when you demanded I stop drinking?"

Heart pounding, there was no hiding her excitement. "Yes. All I could do was tell you the consequences of your actions. You had to be ready to find your life, or it would not have worked."

"And here I assumed you had worked a miracle." Grinning, he freed his hand from her grip and caressed along the opening in her robe to her throat.

"No. It was all you." So close, her senses filled with Markus.

He rested his cheek against her forehead and his Adam's apple bounced. "I could not have done it without you there to hold my hand. You have been a good friend to me, Phoebe. Do not minimize what you do."

Heart in her throat, she said, "Thank you. I assume your father is doing better, since you are here."

"I think he is out of danger for the moment. However, I did not come to London to discuss my father."

"No? Why did you come?" Her head spun.

He stepped back and she wished she hadn't asked. His touch was an addiction she never wanted to break.

He shifted his feet and turned his back to her. "I wanted to see you."

"You came all this way in the snow to see me?"

Facing her again, he shrugged. "Why do you think that strange?"

"Do you visit all the servants who have been in your employ?"

Closing the gap, he frowned. "You were not in my employ. You were hired by my mother. I came to see you because I missed you. Elizabeth misses you. Rosefield is empty without you."

Her heart sank. "Sometimes clients become attached. I am sorry, but I cannot stay at Rosefield. I have a responsibility to Everton and Lady Chervil is not available as a chaperon indefinitely. I would not have left if you were not ready to manage your home without me. You and Elizabeth will be fine."

"I am afraid I must disagree with you on that last point." He crowded her until his breath mingled with hers.

"You do?"

"Yes. We will not be fine without you, Phoebe." He feathered his lips across hers.

It was lightning to her heart. "Elizabeth will be happy with whoever you choose for a wife, Markus. I was just a temporary…"

His kiss stopped her but it ended far too soon. "You were not a temporary anything. You are the only woman I want, Phoebe Hallsmith. Elizabeth's need for a mother is not why I have come to London in the snow. I came because I want to marry you."

"Why would you want to marry me? My brother has not promised you land or dowry." The familiar fear of her family's manipulation of her life edged in to her joy at seeing Markus.

"I have not spoken to Ford. I decided it best to speak to you first. After all, it is your life not his."

She pushed his shoulders, but he did not move away nor did he force himself closer. "As I told those men this afternoon, I do not need a protector."

"Marry me, Phoebe?" He spoke against her cheek and the vibration of his words shook her soul.

"Why, Markus? Why are you doing this to me?" Tears flowed silently down her face.

Markus pulled back and gazed into her eyes. Cradling her face between his hands, he used his thumbs to wipe away her fear. "I love you. I need you. You are the woman who makes me happy. In your arms, I find peace and joy. If I can do the same for you, it would complete me. Maybe I am selfish and foolish to have come. I heard what you told Blunt and Durnst, but they wanted you for themselves alone. I want you for you. Not because I can gain land or children. I have all the property and finances I need. I want you to be my wife, my partner, lover and friend for as long as we live."

"You love me?" A heavy fog cluttered her mind. She must be asleep in her room and this was all a dream.

"I love you very much." He kissed her nose.

"But, you love Emma."

Moisture sparkled in his eyes, and he nodded. "I do love Emma and I always will. When you left, and I am stupid not to have learned this earlier, I discovered that there is room in my heart for Emma and you. She is part of me and Elizabeth, but you are flesh and blood. You are my future, if you will have me."

"Everton Ladies do not fall in love with their employers." She was numb. Everything she thought she knew rattled like glass on the teetering shelf.

He hung his head. "Are you telling me that you do not share my feelings? If that is the case, I will go and never trouble you again."

"I love you, Markus." It must be a dream. She would wake at any moment and her bedroom in Everton House would be all there was to comfort her.

Looking at her, joy replaced his sorrow. "Marry me. Not because we made love or because your family would approve. Marry me because we can make each other happy. Chances like this do not come along often, Phoebe. I was sure Emma would be the only woman I could ever love this way. Now I find there is room in my heart for a new love. Different from what Emma and I shared, but just as beautiful. Tell me you will be my wife and make me the happiest man in England."

Shaking, she didn't know what to say. In Markus's arms was the only place she had ever truly been content, but she had agreed to the Everton Domestic Society rules, which prohibited her from becoming attached to her clients. Her conversation with her employer ran through her head. "I will have to speak to Lady Jane."

"I do not wish to marry Lady Jane."

A mad little laugh bubbled up and she couldn't stop it. "No. I doubt Lord Rupert would allow that. I mean, I have an agreement with the Everton Domestic Society and I need to talk to them about not fulfilling it."

He leaned over her until she was forced back and had to catch herself on both palms. "Does that mean you will marry me or must we have some approval from Lady Jane first?"

Shifting her weight to one hand, she wrapped the other around his neck. "I cannot believe I am saying this, but I will marry you, Markus Flammel. I will be your wife, your friend, and your lover. I want to journey through life with the only person who comforts me, eases my worry, and brings me joy. I want you."

Either she lifted her head or he lowered his, perhaps both, but the kiss crashed around her more volatile than the worst tempest.

Markus thrust his tongue between her lips and she met his passion with equal measure. He ravaged her mouth and wrapped one arm around her back. With his other hand, he held her leg, easing her nightgown up and pressing his hips between her knees.

Edging forward on the bench, Phoebe wrapped her legs around his thighs and tightened until her bottom reached the table's limit and her center pressed to the front of his breeches. She ached with need for more of him. All of him. "Markus."

"Sweet Phoebe, I will never have enough of you." He slid his hand under her thigh and pushed her nightgown into a bunch around her waist.

The blanket fell behind her on the potting bench as she wrapped her arms around him and pressed her chest to his. The worn wood teased her bottom.

"I should leave you and go home before you regret this night." He kissed her throat and chest nudging her robe aside and kissing her through her gown.

"You should stay here and make love to me, Markus. I have no regrets now nor will I later. I want you and will be very vexed if you leave me in this state."

He suckled her nipple through the material.

The delight of his mouth sent her mind reeling. Her craving for more Markus pooled between her legs. Releasing his neck, she fumbled with the fall of his breeches until the buttons came free. Taking his shaft in her hand, she stroked him, forcing a moan from deep in his chest.

He slid his fingers to the apex of her thighs and toyed with her slick folds.

Although she tried to keep a rhythm, the pleasure of his fingers distracted her and she cried his name. Heart pounding, she had to clutch his shoulders to gain balance.

"My love, I cannot wait." He thrust forward, joining their bodies.

She stretched deliciously to accommodate him. Holding tight until the pressure eased and she had to move her hips for more. Why on earth would he wait? It was heaven to have him inside her, linked in the most intimate way. It was perfection and with every lift of her hips, more pleasure rolled over her. Tiny gasps filled the small shed, and she realized they came from her.

Following her cadence, Markus eased out, then thrust deep, cradling her in his arms. He slid one hand to cup her bottom and deepen the penetration.

Her womb tightened until she shattered and pure pleasure erupted inside her.

Markus pumped hard once, twice, then stilled on a grunt and filled her with his warmth.

Everything was bright white, clutching and undulating. She ached with strain as the ecstasy flowed over and around her then eased.

"Are you all right, my love?" Markus spoke against her ear still holding her tight.

"Perfect. Are you?" It was the most satisfied she had ever been. In the arms of the man she loved, the man who would be hers forever, and completely sated. The only thing that would be better would be to wake up in his arms when the sun rose tomorrow. It was a giddy notion that soon she would live that very dream.

"I could not be any better at this moment." Easing out of her, he took care to go slow. Once he righted his breeches, he closed the gap in Phoebe's robe. He picked up the blanket from the potter's bench and wrapped it around her shoulders.

She kissed his chin and nuzzled into the crook of his neck. "I suppose I must go back to the house."

"I will speak to your brother in the morning."

Pushing back, she hated the idea of bringing Ford and his ugliness into their future. "I wish you would not."

He cocked his head. "Do you fear he will disapprove of me?"

"No. But he will find a way to taint what is so perfect." She tugged the blanket tight. Just the mention of Ford stole all the warmth from her.

Tilting her chin up with his fingers, he kissed her nose. "He cannot bring any harm to what is between us, Phoebe. I love you and nothing with change that."

She forced her shoulders back and jumped to her feet. "I would like to go with you to see him."

He bowed. "I will pick you up at eleven. Will that give you time to speak with Lady Jane beforehand?"

"Yes. Thank you, Markus." The knot that formed in her gut eased its hold.

"You ask very little, my love. I do not know why you are surprised by my agreement."

"Because most men care little about the wishes of women. Most men think what a woman wants or needs is trivial compared to their own desires."

Markus wrapped his arms around her and pulled her into a warm hug. "You may be assured that your wants and needs are at the forefront of my agenda. I only want to make you happy. If you wish to face Ford on your own terms, then I will stand beside you as I expect you to stand beside me when I face my demons."

The knot in her stomach moved to her throat. Everything she had ever hoped for in a husband had been handed to her in this wonderful man. It was all too perfect to be real. She prayed nothing would destroy their happiness before they could arrange a wedding. Brushing her doubts aside, she sighed against his chest. "I shall always stand by you, Markus."

Chapter 20

No. 3
*Each Everton lady has been chosen for a particular
assignment because she is the best person suited to
complete the goals.*
—The Everton Companion
Rules of Conduct

Markus practically floated into Everton House the next morning.
Knowing Phoebe Hallsmith was going to be his wife was like a dream.
He had barely slept, but it had been excitement rather than grief that
had kept him up.

Gray opened the door. "It's nice to see you again, my lord. The house
has been abuzz with kind words about you this morning."

"Good morning, Gray. I resolved to arrive early to lend Miss Hallsmith
my support." He didn't know Lord and Lady Everton and worried they
would disapprove. He hoped their opinion would not change Phoebe's
resolve to marry him.

"Miss Hallsmith is in the office with his lordship and her ladyship."

"I will direct him, Gray." Honoria greeted him in the foyer.

Gray bowed. "As you wish, my lady."

"It is nice to see you again so soon, my lady." Markus bowed over her hand.

Taking his arm, she led him down a hall to the right of the stairs. "I
feel sure we shall see each other on many occasions, my lord."

"Can I assume Miss Hallsmith shared our news?"

"She was kind enough to inform me that she has agreed to marry you. I could not be happier. I was sorry to hear about your father's health, but it explains why you took so long in arriving." Honoria stopped in front of large double doors.

"Thank you. It was very difficult to stay away."

"All is well now. I wish you great joy." She patted his arm and drifted down the hall, leaving him to enter the office on his own.

Turning to the doors, he gave a brisk knock.

"Enter," came a deep masculine voice from within.

Markus opened the door. The Everton Domestic Society office was no different from any London townhouse. One wall was filled with books while windows faced the garden with snow on the sill. The smoke of a fine tobacco scented the air. Phoebe sat on a wooden chair with her back to the door, facing a seated woman with her dark hair pulled back in a bun. Her hands were stacked on top of the desk and she contemplated Markus with barely a change of her calm expression.

A man of middle years smoking a pipe stood at her shoulder. He rounded the desk, hand outstretched. "Lord Devonrose. Welcome to Everton House."

Phoebe turned toward him and her stunning smile lit her face.

Markus shook Everton's hand and bowed to the ladies. "Forgive my early arrival. I wanted to make sure all was well with Miss Hallsmith. I know she thinks the world of you both and I would hate for there to be any strife between you."

Lady Jane smiled. "We are very happy for Miss Hallsmith as long as marrying is what she wants rather than what she feels compelled to do. The ton has a way of manipulating members of the feminine sex, my lord. We are only concerned that Miss Hallsmith has fallen victim to undue pressure."

Biting his tongue was the only way to avoid a cutting response to Lady Jane's directness. Of course, she was right, but he hated the idea that Phoebe felt pressured to marry him for any other reason than love. "I see. And what have you discovered?"

"Phoebe assures us she wants to marry you. So, we support her decision." Lady Jane raised one brow.

Lord Rupert slapped Markus on the back. "My wife only worries about the ladies. They are very important to us, as we have made them family. We are very fond of Miss Hallsmith and hate the idea of her doing anything that will not lead to her ultimate happiness."

"That is all I wish for as well," Markus said.

Standing, Phoebe said, "I will accompany Lord Devonrose to see my brother now. I think we are done here."

Lady Jane stood. "I only wish to say that should you change your mind before or after your wedding, you will always have a home with us, Miss Hallsmith. There is no need to ever remain unhappy in your situation."

Did they think he was going to abuse her? Markus took a deep breath. "No harm shall ever come to Phoebe as long as I live. She and my daughter are all I care about in the world. My purpose in life will be to see to her happiness. You need not worry, my lady."

"Yes. I am sure you will be a fine husband, my lord. I only wish for her to know she has options should things ever be different. It is an option I give to all the Everton Ladies who leave our care." Jane rounded the desk and hugged Phoebe.

Rupert bowed over her hand. "Best of luck, my girl."

"Thank you both for everything. You saved me when my life was a disaster. I do not know what I would have done without you and the Everton Domestic Society. I am sorry to leave you with so much work to be done." A tear rolled down Phoebe's cheek, but she dashed it away.

Showing straight teeth, Jane grinned. "Do not fret about us, my dear. We will survive, and other young ladies will find their way to us."

They left Everton House and took the carriage to Mayfair where the viscount of Thornbury had long kept a townhouse.

Phoebe's silence in the carriage worried him. "Are you all right, Phoebe?"

Eyes like clear pools, her shoulders lifted and fell with a long sigh. "I am fine. It is only that I shall miss them."

"There is no reason you cannot visit. I already expect we shall have visits from Lady Chervil. Our marriage does not mean you must give up your friends. I would not stop you from continuing with the society if that is what will make you happy."

She leaned against his shoulder. "That is the nicest thing you could have said. But my spot will be filled by a lady who needs Everton to survive. It would be unfair for me to remain when I have a wonderful husband and step-daughter to fill my life."

Wrapping his arm around her shoulder, he loved that she was concerned for someone else and how her moving on would help another. He hugged her tight. "I see how it works now."

The carriage stopped and a moment later Patrick pulled the door open and lowered a step.

Markus took a deep breath and stepped down. He turned back and lifted Phoebe to the ground. "Are you nervous?"

Grinning up at him, she took his hand. "Not about Ford. It does not matter what he says. We are only here out of your sense of right and wrong.

My mother's opinions are more complicated. I would like her approval. Are you worried he will disapprove?"

It took all his will to keep his voice steady. "Ford has the power to make our getting married difficult."

She slipped her hand into his and squeezed.

All his doubts eased away. "We had better go in. It is likely we have been noticed loitering in the street by now."

"Indeed. Do not worry, Markus." Taking up her skirts meant that she released his hand to climb the steps to the front door.

Immediately, he missed the connection of her slim fingers tucked inside his palm. Pulling his shoulders back, he reminded himself that he was the viscount of Devonrose. It was time he acted like it.

The door opened before they reached the top step. A tall butler with dark brown hair swept to one side and sharp brown eyes stared down his hawk nose at them. "Lady Phoebe, how are you?"

"Hello, Bertram. I am well, but it is just Miss Hallsmith now." She tugged off her gloves and let Bertram take them and her coat. "This is Lord Devonrose. Is my brother at home?"

Giving a nod, Bertram took Markus's coat and hat. "How do you do, my lord?"

"I will tell his lordship that you are here and wish to see him. Please wait in the rose parlor, Miss." Bertram retreated down a hallway.

Phoebe straightened her back, lifted her chin, and walked to a door to the left of the entrance.

Following her inside, Markus admired her courage. "Do you know, I think you are the bravest woman I have ever met?"

She circled a grouping of rose damask chairs surrounding a dark wood table, then went to the window and stared out at the street. "Hardly, but thank you. It has been a while since I have been here. Since before I left to care for Grand. It feels quite strange."

If her family were not about to join them, he would take her in his arms and comfort her. "I am sorry. It seems I am more and more selfish with every moment. I did not even think about how difficult the memories of being here would be for you. There would be nothing wrong with you taking the carriage back to Everton House, Phoebe. I will return by hack and inform you of what has happened here."

Smiling, she turned toward him. "This was my idea, Markus. My discomfort is not your fault. As tempting as your offer sounds, I have never been one to stay and wait. I prefer to face my fate head on. Besides, most of my memories of London are from when my father was still alive and he and Mother were happy. I made my debut from this house, and even though it was not successful in the eyes of the ton, it was filled with excitement and delight."

Unable to stop himself, he went to her and took her hands. Kissing each one for longer than was proper, he breathed in her soft scent. "I cannot be unhappy that your time in the marriage mart was unsuccessful. If you had found love when you were younger, I would not have the good fortune of standing here with you today. Again, my selfish nature rears its head, but that is how I feel."

"Who knows why life takes its odd twists and turns, Markus. Perhaps all things happen so that we can stand together for as long as we can." She leaned in to his embrace.

Even in her brother's house, holding Phoebe made for a perfect moment.

They hastened to part as the door opened.

Ford filled the threshold. Eyes drawn together, hands fisted and breathing hard, he might have been a bull rather than a viscount. "What are you doing here?"

Phoebe faced him. "Ford, you know Lord Devonrose."

Barely sparing Markus a glance, Ford stomped in and hovered over her. "You refused Durnst after I commanded you to marry him. He came here in a rage yesterday."

Markus stepped between Phoebe and Ford. "I have come to ask for Phoebe's hand in marriage, Hallsmith."

Gaping, Ford stood like a statue. "Marry her? You cannot marry her. I have promised her to Durnst. I already signed over the property."

Phoebe gasped. "Why on earth would you do that? What exactly is this arrangement you have with Gavin Durnst, Ford? Why is it so crucial that I marry a man who dislikes me and broke our engagement?"

A low growl rumbled from deep inside Ford. "Have you ruined yourself with this, this drunk? I will kill you both."

What had been curiosity over Ford's urgency for Phoebe to marry an untitled landowner transformed to rage at his threat. Markus slipped into his old role as a spy for the crown. A sense of calm swept through him. "Think very carefully before you issue such a threat to me or those I care for. I am not a man to be called names or toyed with. I do not know what trouble you have gotten into and what Durnst has to do with it, but no harm will come to Miss Hallsmith. Do I make myself clear?"

Ford took several steps back and fear flashed in his eyes. He paled, and there were several heartbeats where he might have been thinking straight.

But it passed. "I will never allow you to marry my sister. She is mine and I will marry her to whomever I choose. And I have chosen Durnst."

"Why?" Phoebe asked.

"That is none of your concern." Ford propped his fists on his hips.

"If you intend to marry me off to an imbecile, the least you can do is tell me why." Gripping the back of a rose damask chair, her knuckles whitened.

"I am not required to explain myself to you." Ford crossed his arms and his jaw ticked.

"I will tell you." Phoebe's mother glided into the room, her blue-gray dress whooshing past the door and Ford.

"Mother?"

Lucretia Hallsmith sat and gestured for Phoebe to take one of the other seats. Once she complied, her mother sighed. "Your brother has made an ass of himself. He managed to go into debt to Mr. Durnst and refuses to discuss the matter with Miles. As such, he has taken it upon himself to resolve the issue by offering my lands as payment."

Phoebe blinked several times and fiddled with the lace at her wrists. "I see, and while it is reprehensible, what does that have to do with me?"

Shaking her head, Lucretia sighed. "Mr. Durnst ended your engagement because he was courting Lady Ann Forsyth. I suppose he had high hopes of marrying her and getting what he wanted, plus her substantial dowry. Of course, Lady Ann is the daughter of an earl, and when their tryst was discovered, her father put an end to it. By that time, Mr. Durnst had ended his engagement to you and you had returned home. Having nothing, he cleverly engaged your brother in a card game. It seems Mr. Durnst is quite skilled. That was when he managed to gamble your brother out of a tidy sum and made the deal to have not only the property but you as well. Marrying the daughter of a viscount, while not as advantageous as that of an earl, would still get him in most of the parlors in London. He is quite the social climber."

"Does Miles know of all this?" Phoebe's voice shook.

Mother shook her head. "Of course not. Miles would never have allowed it and would have told you about the scheme, ruining Ford's plans."

Miles stepped around the doorjam and into the room. "He knows about it now."

While Markus held his tongue and waited for the entire story to come out, his amazement at how low Ford Hallsmith would stoop escalated. Selling his own sister to pay a stupid debt rather than admit his idiocy to his brother.

Red-faced and bug-eyed, Ford might have been about to suffer apoplexy. They should be so lucky. "None of this matters." He pointed his fat finger at Phoebe. "You will marry Durnst because I command it."

Having enough, Markus stepped into the fray. "I beg to differ. You cannot force her to marry where she does not wish. If you will calm down, I might be willing to help you out of this mess for the sake of your mother and brothers. As for you, you are vile, and I have a mind to give you a sound thrashing."

"You, thrash me? You are nothing but a drunk about to lose his inheritance." Ford's face twisted and he spat on the rug.

Lucretia gasped. "Ford, please."

"You gave up any rights over me when you disowned me. I have been publicly disinherited. Why on earth would you think you can tell me what to do?"

Ford ignored her. A sickening smirk tugged at his lips. He stepped toward Markus with his hands fisted. Rearing back with his right hand...

Slowing down the attack, Markus shot his hand straight into Ford's throat. While Ford gripped his neck and struggled to draw breath, Markus swept his legs out from under him.

Ford went down like an old tree and lay still on the floor his face pressed into the thick Persian rug.

Screaming, Lucretia went to him.

Markus leaned over and checked to make sure the idiot was still breathing. "He's just unconscious. He will be up and ranting in a few minutes. He really should keep up on his gossip. Then he would have known that I have given up drink and with Phoebe's help, have saved my fortune and estate."

Taking his mother's shoulders, Miles lifted her from the carpet. "He is fine, Mother. And moreover, he deserved a far worse thrashing. I am sure we could have paid his debt in many ways. He was just manipulated by Durnst." He turned to Phoebe, who stared wide-eyed. "If I had known any of this plot, Phoebe, I would have put an end to it. I hope you know that I would never wish for anything other than your happiness."

"I do not know what I would have done if you were in on this scheme, Miles." She walked into his open arms. "I am going to marry Markus, and there is nothing any of you can do about it. That is, if he will still have me after Ford's ungentlemanly behavior."

Filled with pride and love, Markus admired her strength and the way she would defy anyone to be with him.

Miles met his gaze. "From the look on his face, I am certain he still wishes to marry you."

Late morning sun glinted off the window, illuminating Phoebe like an angel as she turned to face him. Her smile was more brilliant than the sun and Markus's heart expanded until his chest could barely contain it. "Shall we go and get a license then, Phoebe?"

Lucretia stepped forward. "Ford can still make it very difficult for you to marry. He will make protests with the church and the king. He is not beyond ruining you both."

"Mother is right." Miles rubbed his chin.

Taking Phoebe's hands, Markus drew her forward. The look of complete trust on her face nearly undid him. "I know this will cause a scandal, but might I suggest we run off to Scotland and get married?"

She blinked and her mouth dropped open. "You want to marry at Gretna Green?"

"Splendid idea," Miles said.

"Miles." Slapping her son's arm, Lucretia stepped in. "That is no way to begin a life together, sneaking away in the dead of night with your brother chasing after you."

A groan rose from Ford.

"Perhaps we should speak in the foyer, Phoebe." Markus tugged her hand and she followed him out of the parlor.

The high transom windows allowed shards of light to streak through the wood paneled entrance hall.

Miles and Lucretia followed and closed the door with the waking Ford yelling vulgarities inside.

It was a risk to ask her to run off and marry him before her brother could make them suffer. Markus took a deep breath. "You may already know that one of my closest friends has a rather large castle in Scotland."

"Kerburgh?" Miles asked.

"Exactly. Michael and Elinor have a chapel on their estate. Going there would put Ford off our trail."

Phoebe stared at her feet.

"I know it is not the grand wedding that every English woman dreams of. If it were my choice, I would shout our marriage to all of London in the biggest way. But at least, this way you would be my wife without delay, and all I want is to be your husband."

Tears shone in her eyes. "I would marry you in a shack in the woods, Markus. Going to a castle in Scotland sounds perfect. When do we leave?"

Ignoring that her mother and brother were only feet from them, he dragged her into his arms and held her tight. "We should leave today before Ford has time to take action against us."

"I am coming with you," Lucretia said. She held her shoulders and crossed her arms like a soldier who would not be denied.

"Mother?"

In a softer tone. "You are my only daughter. I will see you happily married. I am sorry I let this plot of Ford's go so far. I assumed that if you said yes to Mr. Durnst once, you must have had tender feelings for him. I can see now I was mistaken."

"We can take my carriage, Mother, and follow them." Miles grinned and clapped his hands.

"Are you eloping with us too, Hallsmith?" Markus asked.

Nodding, Miles slapped his back. "It seems it's to be a family elopement. We shall pack our things and meet you on the high road north. In fact, it is probably best if we stay here until Ford wakes and put him off your trail."

Taking Phoebe's hand, he nodded to Miles and bowed to Lucretia.

Phoebe hugged her mother. "I will see you soon, Mother. Thank you."

Markus and Phoebe rushed out to his carriage still waiting in the street. There was much to do and little time. Once inside, he leaned in and cupped Phoebe's cheeks. "Are you certain this is what you want? I can find another way for us to be married in London with all the frills you could want. I have friends in high places, and they can help me make that happen."

Lips parted as if to speak, she leaned forward and brushed her top lip over his bottom lip. She ran her tongue along the crease, then nipped his upper.

Love, desire, joy, and a thousand other emotions warred for position inside Markus as he wrapped her in his arms and devoured her mouth. "I just want you to be happy."

Fingers clutching his hair, she moaned his name. "I am happy. I do not care how or where we marry as long as I am yours and you are mine. I only need Arwen to pack me a few things and we can leave London within the hour."

The notion of Phoebe being his wife sent his pulse throbbing to the point of discomfort. It was wonderful.

Dobson poked his head in the window. "Sir, where to?"

"Back to Everton House."

With a nod, he jumped into the seat and snapped the horses into moving.

Markus folded Phoebe's hand into his. "I'll take you to Everton House, then go to my townhouse and gather my things."

Relaxing against the carriage bench, she sighed. "This will be an adventure. Imagine, Phoebe Hallsmith eloping to Scotland. No one would believe it."

"I don't see why not. You are by far the bravest woman I know."

* * * *

Phoebe ran up the main staircase at Everton House like a hoyden on a rampage. She found Arwen and quickly told her what was happening.

Arwen grabbed her in a hug. "I'm so happy for you, Miss. I knew it would all come out right."

"You may be the only one who thought so. Can you pack our things? I have to find Lady Chervil." She could not leave without a word to her friend.

Efficient as ever, Arwen shooed her out the door with one hand while opening the wardrobe with the other.

Phoebe caught her breath outside Honoria's bedroom door before she knocked.

"Come in." Honoria sang from inside.

Peeking her head around the door, Phoebe was suddenly nervous.

Honoria sat up on a chaise near the window. "Oh, my dear girl. How are you? Tell me all the details? When is the wedding to be? Did you get a special license? I'll bet that horrid brother of yours was shocked. But your mother must be pleased."

"My brother refused."

Jumping from the soft chaise, Honoria colored and her eyes bulged. "He refused. How dare he. You'll forgive me saying so, but Ford Hallsmith is an ass."

A bubble of laughter forced its way out of Phoebe despite Honoria's horror.

"I see nothing funny. What are we going to do?" She spread her arms wide.

"Markus and I are going to elope this very day."

Honoria plopped down on the chaise. "Gretna Green?"

"No. Kerburgh. But you mustn't tell anyone. Ford is enraged and we are determined to throw him off our trail. Mother and Miles are delaying him before they follow in Miles's carriage." It was like a storybook. Well, only if they had a happy ending.

"Kerburgh Castle." Honoria tossed off the lace wrapper covering her sensible day dress of blue and gray muslin. It was a rare sight for her to be so unremarkably dressed.

"I think this is the first time I have seen you in such a costume." Phoebe admired how respectable she looked.

"I had a feeling today would be the day for it and I was right." Honoria pulled the cord for her maid.

"What do you mean?"

"Well, of course I'm going with you, my dear girl. You cannot think after all this I'll not see you properly wed and sweet Markus too. The two of you deserve each other and will be very happy."

"You want to elope with us too?" The notion that her family and friends would support such an outrageous adventure brought tears to her eyes. She swallowed down the lump in her throat.

Honoria hugged her and kissed her cheek. "I wouldn't miss it for the world."

Chapter 21

No. 25
An Everton lady will not put herself in danger.
—The Everton Companion
Rules of Conduct

They drove as far as they could before stopping for the night at a small inn. Markus wished he could drive straight through and lessen the chances of Ford finding them, but he could not risk the women or the horses. Dobson found a rather homey inn, The Wastrel's Manor, where they found rooms enough for all of them.

He'd been wise to hire a second carriage for the luggage and servants. It was no surprise when Phoebe informed him Lady Chervil would join them on their journey. Other than his own desire to have time alone with Phoebe, he was overjoyed their friend had come along. He could wait a few more days to have Phoebe for the rest of his life.

The stairs creaked as he escorted the ladies to their rooms. "We will leave before dawn."

"I understand." Lady Chervil stopped at the door to her room. "Sleep well."

He bowed. "I apologize for the unsuitable accommodations, my lady."

Honoria smiled and patted his arm. "Not at all. This is the most fun I have had in years."

"I'm glad you're enjoying yourself. Good night." Markus opened the door for her and pulled it closed once she was inside. He and Phoebe waited until they heard her throw the latch before they continued down the hall.

Phoebe squeezed his arm. "You are worried we won't make it?"

They stopped in front of her room. He leaned down and kissed the crown of her head. "Is it that obvious?"

"I'm afraid so. Anyone can see that you are nervous. I took a guess hoping it isn't about marrying me." She tipped her chin down not meeting his gaze.

"Phoebe?" He waited until she looked at him. "I want to marry you more than I want anything in this world. It would be very inconvenient if I had to fight with your brother, but fight him I would."

"What is it you think Ford will do?" Worry creased her forehead.

"I don't know," he lied. He had a great many notions of what Ford might try to retrieve his sister. "You should get some rest. Dawn will come before you know it."

Rising to her tiptoes, she pressed her lips to his for a kiss that ended too quickly. "I would not mind if you came in for a while."

Temptation tugged at his resolve. "If I did that, neither of us would get any sleep. Besides, I'm sure Arwen waits for you within. Go to bed, my love. I'll wake you in the morning."

Her chest lifted with a great sigh. "I suppose you are right, but I still wish you would come in and hold me until I fall asleep."

Kissing her cheek, he yearned for more. "I wish I would too. Good night." He opened her door.

Arwen said, "Miss, I have put your things out for the morning."

Giving him one last smile, she stepped inside. "Good night, my lord."

He closed the door and again waited for the latch to sound before going to his own room.

* * * *

Markus instructed Dobson to waste no time and as a result they were being bounced around until his teeth gnashed mercilessly. Nearly noon and they had seen nothing but two farmers and the Post. He banged on the wall of the carriage. "I think you can go at a slower pace now, Dobson. At least until the road is better."

The carriage immediately eased and Honoria and Phoebe relaxed.

"Thank goodness." Honoria patted her hair back into place.

Phoebe bit her lip. "You do think Ford will do something drastic. What can he do?"

Sighing, he fisted his hand. "He might give chase or he might send a runner to track you down. My worst fear is that he will have gone to the prince regent and told him I kidnapped you."

Both women gasped.

"He wouldn't?" Honoria said.

Phoebe sighed. "I wish I could say it was beneath him, but I cannot."

Markus couldn't either. He would not feel easy until Phoebe was his. "If he's done that, then they will have sent troops to find us. I hope they will be headed to Gretna, but I cannot be certain."

They rode on at a reasonable pace. Honoria slept and Phoebe read a book while he worried.

Moving next to him, Phoebe left Honoria alone on the forward-facing bench. "You know, Markus, it would be a shame to waste all the trouble Lady Chervil is going to pretending to be asleep."

Markus examined the unmoving Honoria. "Is she pretending?"

"Of course. Who could sleep with all these ruts in the road?" She sat touching him along his arm.

"She is doing a fine job," he said, holding back a laugh.

"And what will you do about it, my lord?" The gold of Phoebe's eyes captured him.

"I suppose I must kiss you, Miss Hallsmith." He leaned in until his lips hovered just above hers. "Are you ready, Lady Chervil?"

Honoria stifled a giggle.

Markus pushed aside Honoria's presence the moment his lips touched Phoebe's. Soft, warm and always responsive. He let the kiss take on a life of its own. Softly, he nibbled her full bottom lip. She sighed giving him access to her warm mouth and tongue. His pulse pounded as he drew her tighter against him. Not even the rumble of the road could break them apart.

"Carriage!" Dobson yelled.

It was the last thing he wanted to do, but Markus released Phoebe and called up to the driver. "Who is it?"

"Not sure, but they're coming up fast. Shall I try to outrun them, Sir?"

Calm rationale was what he'd been known for when he was in service. His training kicked in. He put a knee on the bench next to Honoria, who was now fully awake. The small back window offered him only the confirmation that someone was indeed gaining on them. All the dust churning in the road left him without the ability to see who.

"Markus, we should try to get away. Ford will hurt you if he must and what if it's soldiers?" Panic rose in Phoebe's voice.

He looked again. He saw no red coats or men on horseback. "I don't think it's soldiers. There is no sense in getting ourselves killed." He went back to his seat. "Pull over, Dobson."

Despite his calm, he couldn't know what he'd do once the other carriage reached them. If they were lucky, it would just be someone in a hurry and they would pass. The waiting was always the hardest part. Tension emanating from Phoebe and Honoria was palatable. Phoebe's eyes filled with fear and fury. Lord, how he adored her temper. So much passion wrapped up in one woman. He couldn't wait to unleash every last bit of it.

In the meantime, the pursuing carriage drew closer and slowed. No such luck that it would pass them by. "Stay in the carriage, ladies. This could just be someone wanting to see who stopped. No need to panic."

Phoebe grabbed his coat sleeve. "Don't do anything ridiculous. I would never forgive myself if Ford hurt you."

He tucked a lock of ruby hair behind her ear. It had come loose while they kissed. "I can manage your brother. Be calm, sweetheart."

He took his pistol from its hiding place under the cushion. Stepping out in the road, Markus hoped he had not lied. A man was as dangerous as what he was willing to risk. He assumed Ford was not willing to risk much while Markus would risk everything for Phoebe.

He took a stance leaning against the side of the carriage and crossed his arms over his chest. As the carriage drew closer, he noted there was no Hallsmith crest on the side. He relaxed just enough to cross one leg over the other, and in case it was bandits he eased a pistol's hammer back.

The familiar halloo of Miles Hallsmith set his nerves to rest and he let the hammer ease back to safety and let out the breath he'd been holding. "You might have followed a bit slower, Hallsmith. We thought you were brigands."

"Or worse, Ford." Phoebe poked her head out the window and laughed.

"Ha! No, it's just Mother and me. We got a late start and have been riding like to devil to catch up to you." Miles stepped into the road.

Lucretia waved from the window. "That stupid son of mine was intent on following you with the militia. It was all Miles and Aaron could do to talk him out of it."

"Has Aaron gotten involved in this too?" Phoebe pulled her eyebrows together. "I hate that he is distressed."

Miles said, "He was happy to help. He even went with Ford to Gretna Green to retrieve you. They will be halfway there by now and by the time Ford realizes he's in the wrong place, it will be too late."

Markus could have hugged Miles. Instead he slapped him on the back. "Good work. Here I was planning how to out maneuver Ford and you have him chasing his own tail. Well done!"

Miles laughed. "We have a long way to go yet. I say we'd better get moving."

"Agreed." Markus climbed back into the carriage and stored his pistol. He hoped his soon-to-be bride didn't know how worried he'd been. There were still things that could go wrong.

The carriage pulled back into the road with Miles's carriage following behind. They kept a good pace, stopping only for necessary rest and to change horses.

* * * *

Phoebe stood at the small chapel's altar facing the rest of her life. Markus was still in his traveling clothes, but she had washed and changed into a light blue wisp of a dress.

The worry that had creased his brow throughout the long ride to Scotland remained. He might have changed his mind. She couldn't blame him if he had. All this trouble to wed a girl of no standing and no dowry. As beastly as Ford had been, Markus remained steadfast in his desire to marry her. He'd kissed her whenever Honoria faked a nap. While they had spent each night at inns separated by walls, Mother, and Honoria, she'd invited him to stay with her and desire had burned in his eyes.

She wanted to throw her arms around him, but doubted the clergy would approve.

Honoria sniffed from the front row.

"If any man can show just cause why they may not lawfully be joined together, let him now speak, or else hereafter forever hold his peace." The minister's words echoed in the stone chapel.

Every breath in the place held.

Phoebe nearly laughed at the silence and had to pinch her leg to keep from becoming hysterical from the building tension.

No one spoke, and everyone let out their breath as one sigh.

Markus promised to love her until death, and his gaze met hers. Joy sparkled behind his eyes.

The minister put the question to her. "Wilt thou have this man to thy wedded husband, to live together after God's ordinance in the holy estate of Matrimony? Wilt thou obey him, and serve him, love, honor, and keep him in sickness and in health, and, forsaking all others, keep thee only unto him, so long as ye both shall live?"

"I will." No one had ever been this happy. She was sure of it. Phoebe Hallsmith was in love with a man who would always love her in return. She felt she might jump out of her skin while the minister droned on.

The minister pronounced them man and wife and suddenly she was Lady Devonrose. Nothing could have prepared her for that idea. Throat clogged with love she clung to Markus's hand as he led her from the chapel.

Michael, Duke of Kerburgh, slapped Markus on the back. "I think all my friends should run away to Scotland and be married at my home."

"It does seem to have become a tradition." Markus laughed.

Phoebe tried to keep her elation in check.

Mother and Miles hugged and congratulated her. Everything sped by in a fog.

Honoria dabbed the corners of her eyes with a square of lace. "Oh my, that was the most beautiful ceremony." She pulled Phoebe into a hug. "I'm so happy for you. I knew it would all turn out right."

"You did, didn't you?" Phoebe said.

"I shall miss you at the Everton Domestic Society. You were always my favorite. But this is a fine start for your real life, sweet Phoebe. Time for you to be taken care of instead of you taking care of everyone else."

Phoebe looked at Markus.

His smile was all she would ever need.

"I will miss you too, Honoria. If you wanted to come and stay with us, we would be quite happy to have you." Phoebe grasped her hands.

"Oh, you are too kind. I shall come and visit, but I love traipsing around the country with Everton ladies. I shall not give it up. Not yet."

"I will hold you to your promise to visit," Phoebe said.

"You can keep a room made up for me." Honoria patted Phoebe's cheek and danced off to talk to Lucretia.

Markus took her hand. "She may change her mind and want to stay."

"Maybe." Phoebe shook off her disappointment. The days of travel were catching up with her and she stifled a yawn. "Shall we thank our hosts?"

Her Grace insisted on being called Elinor. She clapped and grinned. "I love these impromptu visits and weddings. All we need is an anvil and this could be the new Gretna. Shall we celebrate your marriage in the morning, Markus? It is very late, and your wife looks ready to drop."

Markus stared at Phoebe for a long moment before turning back to their hostess. "A wedding breakfast would be excellent, Elinor. Thank you."

With a nod, Elinor said, "All your rooms have been prepared while we were in the chapel. If you need anything at all, just ask."

Two maids rushed in to lead the newlyweds, Lucretia, Honoria, and Miles to rooms above stairs.

Once inside a lush bedchamber, Markus told Arwen that he would assist her lady and bolted the door. "Are you all right, Phoebe?"

Numb, she sat on the edge of the bed. "I suppose I am a bit overwhelmed."

Markus sat next to her and pulled her into his lap. "Most people get months to prepare for their wedding. I wish you could have had that and hope you are not regretting our haste."

"No. It's just…"

"What?" One word, but laced with worry as he tipped her chin up.

Here was a man who had put himself back together for the sake of his daughter. Somehow, he had fallen in love with her. It was all so improbable, she struggled to grasp it. "I was prepared to be an old maid. When I went to care for my grandmother I knew I was throwing away my best chance at marriage. Then Gavin Durnst courted me and I resolved that even though I did not and could not love him, at least I would have a home and family of my own. He embarrassed and hurt me when he broke the engagement, but it was also a relief. Everton became my home and my family. It was comfortable and perhaps safe. Never in a million years did I expect to fall in love or to be loved in return. Now I have a beautiful family of my own. Today is the happiest day of my life, but I am afraid I will wake up tomorrow and it will all be a dream."

He kissed the top of her head. "It is a dream. The most wonderful dream and we get to live it for many years to come. You, Elizabeth, and I will make a life in Rosefield and should you honor me with more children, they too will grow up happy and loved."

"And no one will force them to marry where they do not wish?" Phoebe's heart grew too big and her breath caught.

"Never."

"I truly love you Markus Flammel."

His eyes smiled before those beautiful lips tilted wickedly. "And I love you, Everton Lady."

Epilogue

"You realize this is ridiculous?" Phoebe's neck and shoulders ached from sitting still while Maestro Capelli dabbed his brush on the pallet, then the canvas. A large chair had been brought into the front parlor where the light was best. Her nose itched from the freshly stuffed pillows.

"Madam, please, do not move." His long black robe and white hair sticking straight up from his head was enough to make her laugh for the first thirty minutes, but three hours later, she'd had enough.

Markus laughed. "Sit still, Phoebe. It will be well worth it when it's done."

"To whom? I have no desire to see it." The itch was intolerable, and her lower back ached. The sun glinted off the windows and hit her directly in the eye. She squinted against the glare.

"Then do it for me. Is it so much to ask that your portrait hang beside mine in the gallery?" It was near to a whine.

"Emma hangs beside you, and your Uncle Ebert is on the other side. Is that not sufficient?" She stretched her neck, which gained a groan from Capelli.

Barely containing his mirth behind a cough, Markus said, "My dear uncle has been moved to the opposite wall near my parents, and you will occupy that space, my love."

"Mama Fee!" Elizabeth ran into the parlor with Miss Cavot trailing behind.

Maestro threw his hands up. "Impossible. The light has gone anyway. We shall continue tomorrow." He drew a cover over the painting and tossed the brush into the cup before quitting the room.

Everything she could ever want was inside the parlor. It was impossible that things had turned out so well, but here she was. Ecstatic to move,

Phoebe reached down and lifted Elizabeth into her arms. "How was your day, dearest?"

"Winny plays. Horsy, doggie." She whacked the overstuffed pillow with one chubby hand.

"I see. You went out to visit Mr. Duck?" Phoebe glanced at Miss Cavot for confirmation.

Nodding, Miss Cavot smiled. "He is very fond of Miss Elizabeth."

"And why not?" Markus plucked Elizabeth from Phoebe and offered her a hand up. "I think we shall take a walk in the garden. Her ladyship is in need of the exercise and it is a nice day. You may take a break from your duties, Miss Cavot."

"Oh, yes. A walk would be just the thing." Every muscle in her body ached.

He kept her hand cradled in his and they stepped into the hallway. "First let me show you the spot where your portrait will hang, Viscountess."

The entire notion of being painted was embarrassing. She was not the kind of woman men painted. She was just Phoebe Hallsmith. She shook her head and corrected herself. No. She was Phoebe Flammel, the viscountess of Devonrose, and she had been for nearly two months. It was time she started thinking like a viscountess and not an Everton lady. Though, perhaps there was some middle ground that could be found between the two.

Markus's long legs ate the floor and Phoebe had to run to keep up with him lest she be dragged down the hallway.

"Markus, for heaven's sake, slow down before you have to collect me off the carpet and carry me as you are Elizabeth."

Giggling, Elizabeth clapped, evidently liking the idea very much.

They shared a smile and Markus slowed to a walk that Phoebe could keep up with. Phoebe had only been in the gallery one time with Elizabeth when they were talking about Emma. It was important that she knew who her mother was and how wonderful and beautiful she was. The experience had been so emotional for Phoebe, she had not returned.

They climbed the stairs and the floor changed from scarred wood to white marble as they crossed the threshold into the gallery. Light poured in from high windows but no direct light made its way to the priceless art. A bronze bust of Markus's maternal grandfather stood proudly in the center of the room and around him several statues in the Greek and Roman style.

Still clinging to her hand, Markus led her to the west wall, where his portrait was the centerpiece. To his left, Emma smiled down on them. The space to the right was empty showing no trace of the uncle who had previously graced the location.

"I think once you see the portrait, you will prefer to put your uncle back in his spot."

Elizabeth pointed to the bare wall. "Mama Fee."

Kissing her cheek, Markus smiled. "Indeed. That is where Mama Fee will be placed. I think it is a fine and suitable placement for the viscountess."

"I think you shall both be disappointed when the Maestro informs us that he can do nothing to make me look presentable for a portrait." Phoebe tugged her hand away and walked to the other side of the room. She avoided the accusation gazing down from Markus's ancestors and stared at the reproduction of Venus in the corner.

Little footsteps pattered across the room, accompanied by Elizabeth's laughter.

Markus hugged Phoebe from behind. "Why do you say such things? You have every right to be on that wall and you are more beautiful than anyone else I know inside and out."

"I suppose I still feel like an interloper in Emma's life." Her voice caught. Despite the happiness she'd found, she was terrified it would all end the moment Markus realized he'd made a terrible mistake.

He spun her to face him and gripped her shoulders. "Phoebe, I love you. Nothing will change that. Not even death. Emma would be happy we found each other. She loved you very much and often said you were the smartest, kindest and bravest woman she knew. Do you not think she would want you to be happy?"

"Of course, she would. Emma wanted everyone to be happy all the time. She hated to see anyone suffering or sad." The memory of her friend crushed her heart.

Markus stared until she met his gaze. "Then is it that I do not make you happy?"

She launched against him and wrapped her arms around his waist. "Oh God, Markus. No. You have made me happier than I have ever been. You are the best and kindest husband."

He wrapped his arms around her and kissed the top of her head. "Then why are you uncomfortable with this portrait?"

"While I am thrilled to be Mrs. Flammel, I am not quite ready to be the viscountess of Devonrose. Being remembered for one moment in time when someone commissioned a portrait is not exactly what I had expected from my life."

"What then? You want me to send Maestro Capelli away?" His shoulders lifted and fell against her.

She was being silly. "No. I just want…"

"What?" He stepped away.

She immediately missed his embrace. "Maybe we could start a charity or I could go around to the farms with you and meet with the wives and see what they need."

Elizabeth ran around and around Grandfather's bust singing "Ring Around the Rosie."

The lack of response from Markus forced her to turn and see if he had left her standing alone with her ridiculous notions of what a viscountess might do.

Still standing in the same spot, he stared at her with wide eyes. "You are bored."

How could anyone be bored when they have what every debutante wanted? "Yes, horribly."

His laugh echoed off the marble and plaster.

"Papa!" Elizabeth ran to him and he lifted her up.

"For goodness' sake, Phoebe, why did you not say something? Here I thought you were sorry to have married me."

Closing the gap between them, she fell into the family hug. "I've never been happier, Markus, or more useless. I hate sitting and making lace for no purpose. I do not paint or play well, though I am not opposed to learning both. How do women exist with nothing to do?"

"The question is, what would you like to do? Run an agency like the Everton Domestic Society?" He took her hand and led her out of the gallery and down the back stairs before they pulled on coats and exited into the gardens.

Winter was not quite finished with them but a few plants peeked green, and the bitter cold had fled.

Phoebe breathed deep. "No. I will leave that to Lady Jane, but I would like to do some good."

"Then do so. I support whatever you wish to do. Look how wonderfully you have made Rosefield run."

"So well, I have left myself with nothing to do," she complained, but she loved the efficiency of the staff.

With the sun behind him, he shone like a Greek god. "Think it over and find what you are passionate about, Phoebe. If you want to talk it through with me, I would be happy to help or give input."

"You would not be ashamed of a wife with a career of some kind?" Her heart raced so fast she had trouble catching her breath.

"I think it's too cold for Elizabeth out here. Let's go back inside."

Miss Cavot met them at the garden door and took Elizabeth to the nursery.

Holding hands, they walked through the house to the office where Markus closed the door and led her to the settee. "Phoebe, my love, I married a woman with an occupation. It was stupid of me to think you could be happy doing what other wives do. Find what makes you happy and we will make it happen."

"I was thinking about your friends in Scotland." The Duke and Duchess of Kerburgh had adopted several children and also had some of their own. It was madness at the castle, but they were all so happy.

Markus's face turned white. "Please do not tell me you want to adopt a slew of children. I might be amenable to one, if you found a child you fell in love with…."

He really was the best man in the world. "I think it might be nice to find homes for orphaned children. There are so many. Just here in Benton, the vicarage is housing four who lost their parents to a carriage accident."

"Yes, the Wills children. I looked for relatives to take them in but the vicar and I both failed."

"Can we start a small orphanage and see how well we do finding good homes for them? The vicar and his wife are old and cannot care for four rambunctious children indefinitely. I would not want the children to end up in the type of place where children are abused or sold off as farm hands. I have heard some terrible stories." She held her breath.

"There's a small house at the edge of the property. It's quite close to George Harper's land. Mrs. Harper might be able to help you along. She's a fine cook. I can have someone out to see what needs repairing." He got up, went to his desk and made a note.

"Really?" If a person could die from happiness, Phoebe was about to meet her maker. The notion of a noblewoman working was so outrageous she was certain Markus would laugh at her and dismiss her idea.

Not once, in her daydreams about the project, had he offered to help.

"Of course, Phoebe. I am not some monster who wants to lock you up in the tower. I fell in love with all of you and that includes the part that takes control and fixes what is wrong. My only condition is that you let me help you with this orphanage and adoption agency. I wish I had thought to do it long ago."

She launched herself into his arms. "I love you, Markus. You are the strongest man I know. Together we are going to make families happy."

He claimed her lips in a kiss that shook her world, making love to her mouth until she moaned and wrapped her legs around his hips. It was the middle of the day and someone could walk in at any moment, not to mention she was in a ball gown for the portrait sitting. She didn't care. "I love you, Markus. Forgive me for ever doubting you."

"Keep kissing me like that, and I will forgive you any transgression." Gripping her bottom, he kissed her nose and placed her on the edge of the desk. Tugging at her skirts, he asked, "Now, is there any way of getting through all of this material and making love to my wife?"

Vibrating with happiness and desire she ran her hand down his chest. "Go and lock that door and I will show you the fastest route."

He pressed forward until his shaft nudged her through the material.

Gasping, she arched into him, then cried a protest when he stepped away.

Markus slid the bolt, turned, and smiled with mischief gleaming in his green eyes. "It might be more fun to take the slow way around."

Phoebe liked the sound of that. She propped her slippered foot on the desk and lifted her skirt until the top of her stocking was shockingly visible. "I do not mind a slow stroll, my lord."

In an instant, his hips were between her legs and his mouth on her throat. "My viscountess, my love, my Phoebe."

She arched her neck so he could access more of her. This was the man of her dreams and the man she never dreamed she could obtain. Nothing, not even death, would change that. "Yes. All yours."

Be sure not to miss the final book in A.S. Fenichel's Forever Bride series

DESPERATE BRIDE

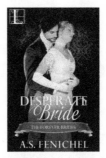

An unexpected promise . . . an everlasting passion.

An accomplished musician, Dorothea Flammel has refused more proposals than any London debutante; her only true love is her music. Dory's shimmering talent and beauty have long been adored from afar by Thomas Wheel, an untitled gentleman who can only dream of asking for the hand of a nobleman's daughter. But when her father, the insolvent Lord Flammel, arranges for Dory to marry a lecherous Earl in order to pay off a debt, she runs to Thomas—and proposes marriage to him.

Eloping to Scotland saves Dory from a disastrous fate, but what is for her a mere marriage of convenience proves more passionate—and more complex—than either imagined as rumors, scandal, and buried emotions come to light. And when a vengeful challenge from a drunken and embittered Lord Flammel puts Thomas's life on the line, will the fragile trust between husband and wife be enough to save them both?

A Lyrical Originals novel on sale September 2017!

Learn more about AS Fenichel at
http://www.kensingtonbooks.com/author.aspx/31620

Chapter 1

More than an hour reading the Westgrove Estate titles and entailments left Thomas Wheel with an aching neck. If he acquired the property, those two fields neighboring his family estate's two would be perfect for the Dutch four-crop rotation method. Increased productivity could mean putting the local children in a schoolroom rather than laboring for pennies to help feed their families. The little barn on the property could be converted into a schoolhouse.

Crowly cleared his throat. The butler was tall and wide and occupied the entire doorway. "Yes, what is it, Crowly?"

"Sir, I know you said you didn't wish to be disturbed, but you have a visitor." Many visitors found the unseemly size of the man intimidating. Crowly was quiet and efficient and that was good enough for a bachelor of Thomas's standing.

Thomas pulled the watch from his pocket. Nearly midnight, no decent person called so late. "At this late hour? Send whoever it is away. It is too late for callers."

The butler shuffled his feet but did not leave.

"Is there a problem, Crowly?"

"Well, sir, you see, the visitor is a young woman of apparent good breeding. She arrived in a hack and I am reluctant to put her back out on the street."

Thomas stood. "She is alone?"

"It would seem so, sir."

"Who is it?"

"The lady refused to provide a card and wishes to speak to you rather urgently."

After pulling his jacket from the back of his chair, he dressed himself. "I suppose you had better let the mystery lady in."

"Yes. Thank you, sir." Crowly's shoulders relaxed.

Within seconds, a woman draped in a black cape with a hood hiding her face entered the study.

Thomas stood behind his desk and waited for her to speak, but she fussed with the edge of her cape and shifted her feet. He suspected that she was contemplating running away. "How may I help you?"

Her head snapped up and her hood fell away. There, standing in his study, was Lady Dorothea Flammel. The amber in her blond hair came to life in the firelight and Thomas had to grip the back of his chair for balance. He did not know what he had been expecting, but in his wildest dreams he never thought to see Dory in his home. Well, maybe in his dreams, but never in reality.

Compared to the burly Crowly she looked lost in the doorway. She was petite and her green eyes ringed red as if she'd been crying.

His initial excitement overshadowed by her distress, his concern mounted. He crossed the room, stopping only when he realized that she backed away from him. "Lady Flammel, what is wrong? Is it Markus?"

Markus Flammel, Dory's older brother and one of Thomas's closest friends, lost his wife during childbirth a year before. The child had lived, but losing Emma had sent Markus into a desperate depression.

"No. It's not Markus. He is in the country as far as I know." She stared at her feet.

Thomas waited for her to say more, but she pressed her lips together while avoiding his gaze.

"Perhaps you would like to sit," he suggested.

When she looked up, he thought she might run, but then her expression softened and she nodded.

When he offered her the chair in front of his desk, she skirted away from him to reach the seat. Never had he seen her so out of sorts. He rounded the desk and sat in his office chair.

The silence in the room was palpable. Thomas cleared his throat and the sudden noise made her jump in her seat. Dory had always appeared so calm and in control, his interest piqued. "Lady Flammel?"

"Yes?" Snapping her head up, she revealed her wide eyes and pale skin.

He smiled. Most women found his smile engaging, but she looked at him with wide eyes and trembling lips, like he'd bared his teeth for the kill.

He leaned forward, resting his arms on the desk. "I can only assume that you have come to me for some reason. You risk quite a lot coming to a bachelor's home, in the middle of the night, in a hack and all alone. You must permit me my curiosity at such an unorthodox act. I have known you most of your life and this is the first time you have arrived on my doorstep. What can I do for you?"

She sighed. "Perhaps it was a mistake."

"Was it?" He asked.

She stared at him. He had watched her play the pianoforte dozens of times over the past few years. She was an artist of the highest order. Her emotion when she played was enthralling, but away from her instrument she always appeared so calm and controlled. Here in his study that seemed to have escaped her. She was near tears. He wanted to stand up and go to her but he did not wish to scare her. The last thing he wanted was to allow his height to intimidate her.

"I am in trouble," she said.

Anger seared through Thomas. "Who was it? I will cut out his innards." He pounded his fist on the desk.

She flinched then waved her hand in a dismissive motion. "Not that kind of trouble, Mr. Wheel."

His fury seeped away. Watching her from the shadows for years, her music had drawn him in but those full eyelashes and deep green eyes kept him mesmerized. For a long time, he had yearned to touch the soft skin of her cheek and kiss those delicate ears. It was impossible. She was the daughter of an earl. She would marry a man of her own station, not Mr. Wheel of Middlesex.

"Perhaps you should just tell me why you are here since you have made the trip. I will help you in any way I am able. I assure you that your presence here will remain our secret. My staff is very discreet."

She frowned. "I suppose as you are a bachelor, they would have to be." There was a bitter twist in her voice.

He did not comment, though her distaste rang through her statement and the twist of her lips.

She took a deep breath, making her full bosom rise.

Distracted for a moment, he then steeled himself and watched her eyes, which he found almost as intriguing.

She cleared her throat. "I am in need of a husband and I have decided that, if you would not mind, you and I would suit nicely."

It took a full count for her meaning to penetrate his mind. "Perhaps earlier you didn't understand my anger." Anger rose again in his gut. He didn't want to frighten her. "It would seem that I must be blunt. Are you with child?"

She picked up her chin. "I understood you, Mr. Wheel. I am not with child nor have I been ruined. It is only that I need to marry immediately."

He sat back in his chair and scratched his chin where the late hour had left him with a shadow of a beard. No one intrigued him as Dorothea Flammel did, but she was the unattainable. Now, here she was in his home offering herself to him. Saying yes and rushing off to Gretna Green rumbled through his mind, but doubt reared its head and he asked, "Why?"

Those beautiful eyes drew together. "I suppose you have a right to know." Staring at her shoes, her hair fell in loose curls around her neck and shoulders. She shook her head. Some inner turmoil etched on her face. "My parents will sign a betrothal agreement for me in the next week."

His stomach clenched. "To whom, if I may ask?"

"Lord Casper," she said through clenched teeth.

Thomas jumped from his chair. "Henry Casper is old enough to be your grandfather. What are your parents thinking?"

She flinched but did not cower. "That I will be a countess."

"There are other earls in the realm."

"I am afraid that I have refused quite a few offers of marriage."

It was almost legend the amount of offers that Lady Dorothea Flammel had turned down. A duke had even offered for her and reports indicated she had broken his heart. "There must be someone left other than a man who walks with a cane and can no longer hear a word spoken."

She stood and pulled her cloak back over her head. "I completely understand. You do not wish to marry or the idea of marrying me is repellent. Forgive me for taking up your time, Mr. Wheel."

She headed for the door.

He rushed over and took her arm turning her around to face him. "I am honored by your offer, Lady Dorothea, and wish I could help you, but I am only Mr. Wheel. I have no right to marry so far from my station."

Her face reddened. "I did not realize you were such a bigot, Mr. Wheel."

"Thomas."

"I beg your pardon."

"My name is Thomas."

His face was close to hers. Her warm sweet scent filled his head with nonsense, a mixture of flowers and herbs.

"I…" she stuttered. "Forgive me for the late intrusion. I am sorry."

He did not release her. "Tell me one more thing, Lady Dorothea?"

"Dory, my name is Dory," she said in a smoky voice, while looking up at him.

It took every ounce of his control to keep him from sweeping her up in his arms and taking her to his bed. To hell with society and rules. "Why me?"

"I beg your pardon."

He leaned in closer. "I am curious why you chose me for this honor. You could have gone to any number of men who would jump at the chance to have you. I would like to know what made you come here."

She pulled away from him. "You seemed the safest choice."

He laughed so hard that she flinched as the noise of it filled the room. "I do not mean to insult you."

"I am not insulted, Dory, just surprised that you would see me as a safe choice." He continued to laugh.

She was not laughing. Her eyes were again filling with tears.

The sight sobered him. "I am sorry to laugh but I see nothing safe about me being alone with you, my dear."

She dashed the tears away. "I only meant that you would not intentionally hurt me. You have a reputation for being kind to women and you like my music. I knew you would never stop me from playing or composing."

His gut twisted. "Why would you have to stop?"

"Mother has long told me that once I am married, my music must be put aside. I have resisted marriage for the last five seasons so I can continue to play."

"Dory, I will give you two insights into men of which you may not be aware. First is that we are not all tyrants and the second is that not all men are like your father."

Sorrow coursed through her eyes like the waves in the sea. "He lives to find ways to embarrass my mother in public. I will grant you she is no treat to be around, but I think she loved him once a long time ago. He is cruel beyond reason."

"Not all men are like that."

She shrugged. "I know. I do not think you are like that. For example, when you take a mistress you will be discrete. You would never cause me undue pain. That is why you would suit so well."

He crossed the room to where she stood with her arms wrapped around her middle. His hand moved of its own accord and reached out and touched the skin where her shoulder met her neck. It was like silk under his fingers. "What makes you think I would take a mistress?"

"All men do eventually. At least you would be kind about it." She pulled away from his touch.

"I must repeat myself, Dory. All men are not like your father."

She shrugged and waved off his comment. "Will you help me?"

How he wished he could. "What is your plan?"

Turning, she faced him. "I would like to leave for Gretna Green in the next day or two. It is best to not tell anyone. I have not even let on to Sophia and Elinor about my plans."

Sophia and Elinor had married two of his closest friends and were Dory's longtime confidants. It was incredible that she would not share something so monumental with her best friends.

"I know I can trust them, but I thought it best not to put them in an awkward position. It's not fair."

He sat on the chair near the fire. Too big for the delicate seat, he'd always hated it as it suited a lady better. He curled his long legs under, leaned his elbow on one knee and his chin on his fist. "Once we married how would we get along in this plan of yours?"

"What do you mean?"

"Would you share my bed?" He sat up and found her standing only a few feet away.

She flinched but did not run away. "It would seem the least I could do."

Laughing, he said, "Not exactly the romantic image I had hoped for."

She walked closer until she stood in front of him with only an inch separating them. "You may have me now if you wish." Her voice trembled.

His groin jumped in response to her offer, but he put his hands on her hips and leaned his head against her stomach.

She trembled, but stood her ground.

Incredible as it sounded, she would allow him to deflower her. "Oh, Dory, you do tempt me."

Tentatively, she touched his hair. "I think I heard a 'but' coming next."

He gazed at her perfect face. Her hand was still in his hair moving in tiny circles. It was an innocent touch but it felt erotic to him. Any touch from her would have had that effect he suspected.

Forcing a smile, he only wanted to ease her fear of him. "But it would be beneath both of us to make love here in my study without a marriage to make it legal."

"Are you saying you will marry me?" No joy bubbled in her voice at the notion. She sounded more like a death sentence had been averted and she would only suffer life in prison.

He took her hands out of his hair, kissed the back of one, and then the other, and stood. So she could sit in the chair he'd vacated, he pulled another from a few feet away. He sat so close, their knees almost touched.

"I hope you will forgive me, Dory, but my answer is no. I cannot believe I am saying it myself. If you truly wished to be my wife, it would make me unspeakably happy, but like this it is less than romantic. In fact, it borders on the morbid."

She frowned. "I could have come to you with lies and told you I was madly and rapturously in love with you and could not live without you another moment. Would that have altered your decision?"

"It might have."

A furrow appeared between her brows.

Thomas reached out and smoothed the wrinkle. "I am glad you did not attempt to mislead me, Dory. I wish I could help you. For the first time in my life I wish I was a lord or a knight so I would be worthy of your hand. However, my station is to be a gentleman and yours a countess. It would be selfish of me to lower your status in society."

She let out a long sigh. "I do not give a damn about titles. I am to be married to a lecherous old man who will keep me as a trophy and perhaps allow me to play pianoforte from time to time to entertain his friends. Everything I have ever wanted tossed aside. My mother will do as she has always threatened and burn all of my music." She leaned forward and touched his face. "Everything I am is about to be ripped from me. Can you understand, Thomas?"

He put his hand over hers and kissed her palm. "You are overwrought and have exaggerated the situation. I have never heard anything violent about Henry Casper. Though he is old for you he lives well and will provide for you in the fashion to which you have been raised."

"You are wealthy," she said.

He laughed. "I have ample funds, but I am not titled and I never shall be."

"You are a snob, Thomas. If I do not care about a title, then, why should you?"

"You should care, Dory. I will admit that my association with Marlton and now with Kerburghe has afforded me more invitations than most gentlemen of my station receive, but I fear you would find life as Mrs. Wheel very unappealing."

"Are you a man with a terrible temper?" she asked.

Surprised by the question, he sat up straighter. "I do not think so."

"Would you keep your wife from pursuing her own goals?"

"I don't believe so, as long as the goals did not put her in harm's way."

"So, if I wanted to join the fire brigade you would be opposed to that venture?" Her eyes narrowed but she did not smile.

He shook his head but answered. "The fire brigade would be quite a dangerous endeavor, and I would advise my wife against such foolishness."

"Yes," she said. "You do sound like a tyrant. I think it obvious we would not suit." Sarcasm dripped from her words. She squared her shoulders and stood.

"I do not believe you have thought this through." He stood with her.

She turned and raised her eyebrows. "You believe I am impulsive and rash?"

A small voice inside his head told him he should take care with his next statement, but he ignored it. "In this decision, you seem to have jumped before looking."

Pursing her lips, she nodded. "Do you know what it takes to play the pianoforte as I do?"

The question was so out of context, he fumbled for his answer. "I believe I do. I have tried to become more accomplished and my talent has limited me."

"Have you sat for hours at a piano to achieve perfection in one stanza?"

"I have," he admitted.

"I have not heard you play, Thomas, though I hear you are accomplished, and I have heard you say you are not. I suspect you play very well but are not gifted with that something which makes one musician stand out among the rest."

He hated that she was so accurate in her description of his skills.

"I do not mean to insult you. It is just fate that makes one person good and another great. A cruel joke, if you will. My curse is being a woman. If I were a man with the talent that god gave me, I would play to massive crowds and kings would sponsor me. Not that this is what I want really. I want to be allowed to play every day for the rest of my life. I am not the type who jumps in without looking and have been analyzing my options for weeks. I examined it as I would a new piece of music. You were not a whim of mine to get me out of trouble. I believe we could make a nice marriage."

"Nice," he repeated in the same monotone she gave her speech.

"There is nothing wrong with nice."

He closed the distance between them.

Her chest heaved.

"Nice is not good enough for me." His arm came around her waist and in spite of the twelve-inch difference in their heights his lips were on hers before she could protest. She was stiff in his arms, but she put her hands on his shoulders and did not push away. Patience kept him gentle while he wanted to thrust his tongue in her mouth and taste her sweetness. One sip at a time, he caressed her lips with his. He ran his hand up and down her side from her hip to the edge of her breast, longing to feel her flesh rather than the soft material of her gown. Not touching her anywhere too intimate strained his desires.

She softened in his arms.

A sigh escaped her lips and Thomas took the opportunity to sweep the inside of her lips with his tongue.

She gasped and he plunged inside. Her tongue was less forceful, but she joined him in the pleasure of the kiss.

Nipping at her lips, he watched her. "I will think about everything you have said tonight, My Lady. I am also cautious and like to give a large decision my full attention before jumping in."

He released her.

Dory straightened her dress. If he had wanted to put a name to the expression on her face, he would have said she appeared confused. He thought it was not a bad start.

"May I ask why you are so hesitant?"

"Shall I be completely honest?" he asked.

"I would prefer that you were always honest with me."

He nodded. "I am very fond of you, Dorothea, and have long thought you are one of the most beautiful and talented women in London. What you propose opens you up to a rather large scandal. Elopement is bad enough, but to run off with someone beneath you in station could be something you would not recover from."

"I am not concerned with my reputation," she protested.

"Well, I am. I think not being invited to the most fashionable homes in London would make you unhappy. I would not want my wife to be unhappy."

"That is very kind of you, but I am willing to risk censure to have a life that includes my music."

Wishing she would say something more heartfelt would not make it so. "I would like a wife who wanted me for something other than my love of music. I am also concerned by your apathy toward a romantic involvement."

"So idealistic, Thomas." She rolled her eyes.

His fingers itched to pull her back against him and take all she offered, but the damned voice of reason kept his hands at his sides. "I did not realize it myself, but I find the notion of a wife whose only interest in me is escaping a worse situation abhorrent." He held up his hand to stop her from further comment. "However, that kiss we shared was not apathetic nor were you uninterested. I wonder if helping you would not also suit my own desires."

Her eyes widened. "I already told you I would share your bed."

He touched her cheek. "Oh, Dory, I wish you could believe all men are not cut from the same cloth as your father."

She shrugged.

"Perhaps in time you will learn differently." He brushed a single tear away from her lashes.

Straightening, she stepped away from him. "My parents will announce my betrothal in less than a fortnight at mother's ball."

He dropped into a low bow. "You will have my answer before then."